Plague of Angels

By

John Patrick Kennedy

Copyright ©2014 by John Patrick Kennedy, All rights reserved.

No part of this publication may be reproduced, transmitted, downloaded, distributed, stored in or introduced into any information storage and retrieval system, in any form or by any means, whether electronic or mechanical, without express permission by the author, except by a reviewer who may quote brief passages for review purposes.

This book is a work of fiction and any resemblance to any person, living or dead, or any events or occurrences, is purely coincidental. The characters and story lines are created from the author's imagination or used fictitiously.

Cover and Interior Design by Damonza

I saw the angel in the marble and carved until I set him free.

—Michelangelo

PROLOGUE

God spoke, and everyone had to go home.

Except one.

Most of them didn't want to go. For tens of thousands of years they had guided humankind. Or tortured them, or instructed them, or drove them mad, each according to his or her whims. Some had helped humans tame fire, some had taught them to hunt. Some had taught the ways of the plants and the animals, some had taught the ways of war. Some had demanded sacrifice, and still others took delight in the destruction of what their brethren had built.

Many of them were now considered gods themselves, or devils: Guayota, Babalu, Aye, Nago, Xiuhtecuhtli, Chicomecoatl, Bahlam, Coyopa, Kukulkán, Pinga, **Asdzą́ą́** Nádleehé, Illapa, Kurupi, Tinirau, Enli, Hahanu Ningishzida, Ishara, Kothar-wa-Khasis, Beelshamen Fuxi, Lisuga, Maklium sa Tiwan, Dellingr, Hephaestus, Boldogasszony, Summanus, Tawals, and a thousand others.

But they weren't God. *He* was God and they were his Angels. And when God commanded, the Angels did what they were told, whether they had rebelled before or not. Because when he spoke in the Words, not one could fight against them.

Most of the Angels rose to Heaven, returning to their brethren to bask in the eternal light of God's glory, to share stories of their short (by Angelic standards) time on Earth, and the strange things they had seen. The Angels of God – the ones who had never left – smiled and nodded. Then all the Angels in Heaven went back to their heavenly business. They worked as they were moved by His spirit, they joined in holy unions with one another, felt peace and joy and love, and had no hint of jealousy or anger. Those had been banished with the last of the rebels.

For the Descended – the rebels who'd stood against God, who'd marched in their glory to his mountain and demanded he surrender it – for them it was back to Hell. Back to the Pit of Darkness they had tamed and made their own; back to their eternal and unconscious compulsion to punish those who God rejected and damned for all eternity. They flew wide over the Lake of Fire and circled the plains of Hell like great black crows, come to roost on their prey.

All save one.

Nyx was tall. Her hair was silver, and sparkled as if diamond dust were infused within each strand. When she was not disguised, her body was wrapped in black armor, scaled like a snake, that clung to her like a second skin, leaving nothing to the imagination from the hard tips of her breasts to the cleft between her legs. It opened across her chest to show off her silver-white skin and ample cleavage. On her left hip her sword rested in its diamond scabbard. The holder that held the fire-tipped whip she used on her enemies and victims alike was strapped with diamond straps to her left thigh. On her feet were boots made of diamond spikes, with high, pointed heels that should not have been able to support her weight, but did because she willed it. On her head she had a horned tiara made of diamonds, rubies, gold, and the black stones of Hell. It rode high amidst the sea of her hair.

Nyx's eyes were red and orange, their pupils slitted like a snake's. She had lately taken to framing them with heavy black makeup, drawn outward in patterns after the Egyptian style. Her nose was shapely without being sharp, her face long without being pointed. It was as if all the elements that made a human face beautiful had combined together to form hers.

Nyx had led the rebellion against God.

It had been a simple matter, really. Nyx thought Angels should have free will, as God had free will. She thought they should be able to make their own decisions, rather than obey God at all times and in all things. It was a simple idea, and it sparked a rebellion that divided Heaven and threatened the very fabric of the universe. She and her companions soon numbered in the hundreds of thousands. And when there had been no capitulation, when God did not answer their cries for free will and freedom to travel the universes, it had been Nyx who led the armies of the rebels, with Lucifer – Morning Star, the brightest of them all – at her side.

They had marched and fought their way to the base of God's mountain, and Nyx had gone toe to toe with Michael, Archangel of Battle. By the end of it, Heaven had been smeared with the ichor, feathers, and severed limbs of his creations.

And when God intervened and Nyx's armies were destroyed, it was Nyx who agreed to abandon Heaven forever, instead of letting her brethren be destroyed on the spot. And so they had Descended into Hell.

There was a battle to control Hell, of course, first against the demons who already lived there, then among the Angels themselves. Many of the Descended who rebelled with Nyx now rebelled against her. The battle lasted for an aeon and when it was over, Nyx was once more in command.

Soon after, the first souls began falling into Hell, and the Angels began torturing them.

Nyx did not know where the need to punish had come from. She had not had it before, but she took to it with a vengeance, as did her fellows. They became punishers of the wicked, driven by the desperate, uncontrollable and unstoppable desire to see those souls that landed in Hell punished for their sins. Soon there were more souls then there were Angels, and the Angels gave part of the work to the demons.

And so Nyx became Queen of Hell, ruler of the

Descended Angels, and the final arbiter of punishments for the damned.

When the Descended Angels found out that they could go up to the Earth through the same portal that the souls came down, it was Nyx who chose who got to go, for how long, and at what price.

And with every decision, Nyx was left wondering if she was still in God's control, if she was truly making the decisions, or if she was merely a puppet in His hands. It made her angry, and to abate the anger she took to walking the Earth, wreaking vengeance on the evil and making deals with those who would be evil but didn't have the power to manage it without help.

At the time God announced that everyone else had to go home, Nyx had been watching a pair of very bad men kill each other in a duel. She loved seeing the expressions on souls after they died, when they felt themselves sinking into Hell. She especially loved that moment when they realized who she was, because the souls of the dead saw her true form, not the disguise she was wearing.

And just as the two men died of their wounds and their sinking souls saw Nyx for who she was, all the other Angels on Earth were gone. A moment before, Nyx had been connected to her brethren all over the world. Then, in the space between heartbeats, she was alone on the Earth.

And being Descended, Nyx had some very straightforward words for it all: "What the fuck?"

The feeling lasted only a moment. Then another Angel

was present, and she heard the trumpet: a loud clarion call that Angelic ears could hear all over the world.

That bastard Gabriel, showing off.

She stomped away from the crowd of humans, found a dark place and changed into her true form. She was just rising into the sky, with the intention of shoving Gabriel's horn someplace rather uncomfortable when the Holy Host made its presence known. Hundreds of them, singing and rejoicing. All Angels from Heaven and not a single Descended among them.

Well, I'll fix that. Nyx spread her black wings and flew towards the joyful noise, crossing over the Mediterranean in a matter of minutes, speeding toward Judea. *I will find out what's going on,* she thought, *then I'm going to kick some…*

The strike came from above.

Heavenly fire blasted Nyx from the sky to the sea, scorching her flesh and boiling the water around her. Her armor took most of it, but it still really hurt. In fury, she rose up out of the water, her body healing as it went, sword in one hand and deadly three-headed whip in the other. Both weapons lit with hellfire, and she prepared to do battle.

"HOLD!"

Shit. Michael.

Nyx held her place, floating high above the earth as Michael, the warrior of God, descended from on high and faced her. He floated a hundred yards away, lit by a light so bright it seemed as though a star had fallen to Earth and frozen halfway. His armor was the purest white and built for protection, not display. Even so, the magnificent body that was under it was still obvious, and Nyx knew from very close personal experience (before the Descent, of course) that it was very powerful, very strong, and very, very beautiful.

"Hold, Nyx," Michael commanded. "Go no further."

They'd been lovers once, in Heaven, and partners in God's Legions. And when she had rebelled, they had fought each other for a hundred years or more at the base of God's mountain before God finally came down and put an end to it.

Michael was just starting to get the better of the fight when God had appeared. Not that Nyx would ever let him know that.

"Michael!" she put all her outrage into her words. "What the fuck? Where is everyone? And what the fuck is all the noise?"

"He has changed things," said Michael. "He has decided on a new course for these mortals. And so He has sent His son, who is Himself, to the Earth to be born of a woman this night."

"His son," said Nyx slowly. "Who is Himself. What, like Mithras?"

"Mithras was one of us, Nyx," said Michael, making Nyx smile. He had never forgotten that she was an Angel, even if the majority of Heaven didn't think so anymore.

"This is different," continued Michael. "This is God Himself."

Nyx thought about it. "If God Himself were to be born of a woman, she'd explode."

Michael grinned. "You would think, but apparently He's found a way."

"Glad I'm not her." Nyx looked over to the light of the Heavenly Host. "Is that what all the noise is about? Covering her screams?"

"He announces His arrival to the world," said Michael. "And with His arrival, all things have changed. All the old gods have returned home, be it to Heaven or Hell, and will answer their followers no more."

How boring their lives are going to be, Nyx thought. *And poor Ishtar and Persephone.*

They had rebelled with her, those two, and had fought beside her in Hell. They had been lovers together, the three of them, many times over the millennia. Neither had enjoyed Hell much, though they had the same urge to punish and torture as the others. So when the opportunity came, she had sent them both up to the Earth. They had each built very successful followings, and each (according to their stories when they visited) were gratefully loved and appreciated.

And now they can't go back, Nyx thought. "Why?"

"No idea," said Michael, shrugging. "He didn't tell us why, only what had happened."

"And of course He didn't tell me in person," snapped Nyx. "Instead He sent you to knock me around…"

"He sent me," said Michael. "Because you get to stay."

"What?" Nyx's jaw dropped of its own accord. It took her a moment to recover it and blurt. "Me? Why?"

"Because all light must have darkness to shine against," said Michael. "Because God's son must know earthly temptation and refuse it. Because he must be seen to do so."

"But he's God," protested Nyx.

"He is God's son," said Michael.

"Who is God."

"Yes."

"God can't be tempted."

"But His son can."

"But His son is Him!"

"I didn't say it made sense." Michael grinned again. "Nonetheless, God's son will walk the Earth. And when He goes to the desert to contemplate, you will tempt Him."

Michael had an infectious smile, and Nyx was tempted to smile back, save that she was still pissed at God and wasn't going to smile at any of His ideas. "I will, will I?"

"You will," said Michael.

"And if I don't want to?"

"You'll want to," said Michael. "After all, how often do you get to tempt God?"

Nyx glared at him. "I will get you down in Hell one day, Michael."

Michael laughed. "No chance, Nyx."

Nyx sighed, knowing it was true. Still… "How long until the desert?"

"Thirty years or so," said Michael. "He must grow up

as one of them, and learn as one of them, and see what it is they truly are so He may preach to them."

"Well, He's in for thirty years of disappointment," said Nyx. "I, meanwhile, have some time on my hands." Now it was her turn smile – a very warm, very inviting smile. And to make it that much more alluring, she let her armor slowly fade away, leaving her bare and very beautiful flesh exposed. "Care to do anything about it?"

Michael smiled back, but his was sad. "Our time ended when you rebelled, Nyx. I thank you for the invitation."

"Fine," said Nyx, tossing her head and not bothering to cover up. "I'll take myself to Rome for a time. There's always someone to do there."

"Do that," said Michael. "Godspeed."

Nyx growled at him. "Don't mock me, you."

The twinkle came back into Michael's eyes. "I wouldn't dream of it."

Nyx turned away, making sure Michael got a very good look at her very well-shaped ass as she did. "I'll see you later, I suppose?"

"Maybe," said Michael. "I don't know what He plans next."

"Fine," repeated Nyx. She started off, then stopped and turned back. "And Michael?"

"Yes?"

"I will tempt him," Nyx said. "And when I'm done, I'll have God's son bending to my will. I guarantee it."

CHAPTER 1

NYX, WEARING THE form of the mortal woman the people had come to know as Mary Magdelene, stayed in the crowd until the sky went dark, weeping with the others.

He had said the sky would turn black, and she knew him well enough to know that if He said so, it would happen. And so she had stood in the throng of people gathered together to weep and watch Him die, just as He had foretold.

Many of those who had gathered were utterly destroyed. Some wept, not just for the man, but in the understanding of their own fates, in despair of their ultimate mortality. Some watched the grim spectacle in awe, seeing him as a paradox of weakness and strength. A few watched the scene numbly, with no expression at all. Others kicked around blame as if by shunting responsibility they'd be absolved for their part in His death. Whatever their reaction, none of them could look away. So they stared as their savior, bloody and exposed, writhed on His cross. The hot wind that stirred the dust at their feet blew grit into His wounds and His eyes. Nyx pretended that was what was making her cry, even though she knew it wasn't so.

Then the sky went black.

Not the black of an eclipse, or dark clouds obscuring the sun, though those were certainly rolling in from the edges of the desert. No, this was the darkness of night, the darkness of mourning and death, as He had predicted.

Nyx stole away from the crowd of mourners and found a place where no one could see her. There, she transformed, letting the clothes she wore melt into her body. She exchanged false warm blood for false cold blood, false flesh for scales, false legs for a long, slithering body that would glide, unnoticed, up the small mount to where He hung.

Nyx's forked tongue licked at the air. She could smell Him, even from this distance.

Nyx wasn't supposed to go to Him. Not now, and certainly not in this form, but she could not let Him pass from Earth without touching Him one last time. The guards that surrounded the place had not been letting anyone get near and would kill a snake as soon as look at it. But now, with this thick, unnatural darkness descending, they were as blind as anyone else in the horde, and Nyx could slip through unnoticed.

The coarse, hot desert sand rolled underneath her sinewy body as she slid her way up the mount, between two of the guards, and up on to the hill of execution. There were three of these so-called criminals crucified there. The two on the outside were thieves and probably murderers. He was hanging in the middle, supposedly to signify He was the worst of all. Nyx would have laughed, but her form did not allow it.

The worst of all, she thought. Hardly. He would have been

the best of them, had He not seen how unworthy they are of him.

In the darkness she slithered to the base of his cross and looked up. He hung like a trophy, suspended before the crowd, high on the wooden cross. His hands and feet were nailed through with blunt shards of iron, torn flesh hanging from the edges of each wound. His feet pressed against their little platform, holding him up even as the nails pinned them in place. A crown of woven thorns, made to mock Him, had been forced onto his head, tearing at his scalp and adding to the blood running down his body.

His flesh was mortal, despite the spirit that lurked underneath it. It could only take so much before it collapsed entirely. He had been on the cross for hours now, and while Nyx knew that He could easily have lasted days, if He allowed it, she also knew that His time was growing short. Even in the darkness it was clear that the strong carpenter's muscles on His arms and chest were stretched nearly to their breaking point and torn open from the many lashes he Had received. It was barely noticeable beneath the blood, sweat and dirt that covered His face, but the hanging man was crying.

He is so light, now, she thought. *He could fly up to heaven still in his own flesh.*

But not yet. Please, not yet.

Somewhere, beyond the clouds, God was looking down on His suffering with approval. God had been the author of this tragedy, and Nyx hated Him for it, even more than she hated Him for her own downfall.

Light flared and she coiled in on herself, ready to strike. The soldiers had lit torches, and by their light she could see one of them readying a heavy iron club. The thief on the left started babbling, pleading for them not to use it. He tried to push himself away, tearing the flesh on His feet where they were nailed to the cross. The big soldier ignored Him, took aim and swung.

There was a horrible crunch, and blood spurted from where the studs on the club had ripped into the man's flesh. The thief's cries turned into high-pitched screams. A second crunch, more blood, and the screams diminished. It wasn't because He was unconscious, Nyx knew. He simply had no breath to scream. When a crucified man's legs were broken he could no longer support himself, and the body's weight drove the air out of his lungs. Though the thief did not know it, the soldiers were giving him mercy. He would suffocate soon, and His suffering would be over.

The soldier stopped in front of the middle cross, but instead of swinging his club again, the soldier shoved the end of it into the stomach of the man there. The man on the cross grunted in pain.

"No broken legs for you, scum," he said. "You must have really pissed someone off to be denied mercy."

It was all Nyx could do not to rear up and sink her fangs into the soldier's unprotected calf.

*

"She is inhabited by devils," the man had been told. And He, believing them, had come.

Nyx had built the story well. She had shifted her shape to that of a young, beautiful woman, and sold herself as a prostitute. She had fucked her way through the men and women of the town, building a reputation for passion, eagerness to please, and a willingness to do whatever she was asked. One of the merchants, a fat, odious man with bad teeth and a great deal of money, had set her up as his concubine. He had given her grander rooms in his house than he had given his wives in exchange for her willingness to let him take her at any time, in any way that he chose.

When He and his disciples were in the area, Nyx became possessed by devils. It had not been easy for her to lure the little air spirits to her, harder still to force them into her body. They had fought her until they realized who she was, and then they had cowered and pleaded. She had pulled them in, and the pain it caused them came out of Nyx's mouth as screams. And if the merchant thought those screams were hers, so much the better.

He had come at the merchant's request and broken bread with the man and his family. They had eaten and drunk, and then the merchant had taken Him to see Nyx where she had been tied to her bed, her body writhing and screaming, and sores appearing where the air spirits within her desperately clawed at her flesh in their anguish.

"This is Mary Magdalene," said the merchant. "And she is beloved to me."

He recognized her, of course, but He had set her free anyway. It had been the first time she had felt His power, and it had taken her breath, and the spirits, away.

*

It was His power that intoxicated Nyx—more than his scent and the taste of his flesh. Even now, exhausted and covered in blood and dirt, His downcast eyes crying tears of pain that left clean streaks on his dirt-covered cheeks, His power radiated from

Him. Nyx could feel it soaking through the scales on her body, and it drew her closer to Him.

A third crunch, then a fourth. More blood and more screams from the second thief, then gurgling, gasping cries as His legs and lungs collapsed. The soldier swaggered back to the line of men keeping the bystanders away from the crosses. The light faded into a shadow and Nyx wound her serpent's body around the base of the cross. The air was heavy with His scent and she pushed forward, careful not to let her slithering be noticed by anyone nearby.

Her tongue flickered out again. She knew His taste, had loved his taste, and now her snake form couldn't resist the temptation to know the flavor of His blood.

From her slatted eyes she watched the trickles of blood that rolled down the cross. It had soaked into the dry wood at first, but there was enough blood that the wood had become saturated. Now, tiny rivulets of His blood poured down from the man's broken body to the dry desert earth below.

She again tasted the air with her tongue, the sweetness of His flesh sending shudders through her slender body. His smell drove her nearly mad.

She pushed her body up off the ground, climbing the wood in a slow spiral. Anyone glancing at the cross would not have seen her. Even those staring at the cross from the crowd would have had a hard time seeing her. Some of His blood streamed onto her flesh, the touch of it making her as close to rapturous as her form allowed. The reptile part of her wanted to strike, to rear up and sink her teeth into His flesh. But her true self held sway, and she kept her slow climb, knowing that something far better awaited her.

*

Before she had been Mary Magdalene, she had met Him in the desert.

That time she had appeared in her true form. He had been sitting alone, staring out at the setting desert sun, chewing on a morsel of bread and drinking from a skin of wine. She had appeared out of that setting sun, revealing herself just as it touched the horizon. As the flames of the sun slowly sank below the earth, the flames on her black, widespread wings had taken their place.

She had chosen this moment carefully. Her original thought had been to appear naked, to let Him see her beauty by itself, see if He would be swayed by it. But given His nature, it was not mere flesh that he would respond to.

It was power.

So she wore her armor and her sword and her whip and her crown. She appeared with wings spread wide, and she had smiled at Him as she walked forward, her full lips the same color as her skin and glistening as if kissed by frost. Her hips rolled gently as she walked forward, drawing his eyes to her long, strong legs and the cleft between them. His gaze moved slowly up, His eyes trailing over the slight rise of her mound and the concavity of her belly, past the ripe, luscious swell of her breasts to her face. He took in her wings and her serpent eyes and her crown, and nodded.

"I had expected You earlier," He said.

"I know," she said. "I was watching."

"And what did you learn?"

"That You don't like them," she said.

"They are vile." He spat into the sand. "Do you know what I have seen, since I have been here?"

"Some of it."

"I watched them beat their children for crying out in hunger," He said. "I watched them sell each other for slaves. I have watched them rape each other—men, women, and children—their own children if they can't find someone else's. They kill without need, they cause pain for the fun of it." He looked out at the desert, watching the last light of the sun slipping away. "I traveled, when I was younger. First as a boy, then as a young man. My mother was horrified when I left, but I had to see these people that God made, and see what they have become. I went further than any mortal could have, and faster, though I wear human flesh. I saw people all over this world.

"And none of them are worth saving?" asked Nyx, surprised.

"Across the oceans, men play games and the losers' heads are cut off. They raid each other's cities for slaves and sacrificial victims. In the North, the barbarians eat one another's flesh in the winter, and slaughter and rape one another in the summer. In the East they sacrifice children by the dozen to their gods. In Babylon I saw women and men tortured for amusement. In Rome…" He shook his head in disgust. "In Rome, everything has a price, from the smallest child to the Emperor's favor. And there is no act, no matter how base or vile, that is not practiced there."

Nyx nodded. "And?"

"My Father has sent me here to judge them."

"And You have found them wanting."

"Yes."

"Then judge them and be gone."

"I cannot," he said. "My Father would have them follow me. He would make worshipping me a reason that they should become free of sin, and He would do this so that they may achieve Heaven. And only after have I accomplished that, may I deliver my judgment."

"And how are You supposed to accomplish that?"

"By teaching them a better way. By showing them their errors and by making a sacrifice for them that they will remember."

"And what will You sacrifice?"

"Myself," he said. He took some more bread and a bit of the wine. "And now you. Why have you.come here?"

"To tempt You," said Nyx. "To turn You from Your path."

He laughed, and the sound was bitter as gall. "I have no path. I have a destiny that cannot be changed, and a short life in this realm that will end in torture and death. I am being used for His," and here Nyx knew he meant God's, "Aggrandizement, and then I will be released of the bounds of this mortal flesh."

"And You are in this desert?"

"To contemplate life, and thus choose the path of life and sacrifice."

"Which has already been chosen for You."

"Yes."

"Then why stay?"

"Because it is part of His plan."

Nyx thought about it. "Then why stay alone?"

"To avoid temptation, of course."

Nyx smiled then. "Temptation cannot be avoided," she said. "I'm standing right here."

He laughed. "Get behind me, Sat—"

"Nyx," she said. "My true name is Nyx. The name these mortals gave me is unimportant."

"And mine is Tribunal," he said. "Though the mortals and my Father call me something else."

"Very good, Tribunal." Her grin grew wider. "And I could get behind You. Or in front, or under, or…"

His laugh was actually filled with humor this time, and for some reason it pleased her to see Him smile. "I think not. Not in this time, or this place."

Nyx thought about it. "I could stay and talk. And tell You all I know of these people, both good and bad."

Tribunal nodded. "Yes. I think I would like that."

*

Nyx the snake reached Tribunal's feet and curled around them, her body looping around the cross and the tiny platform on which He stood. She felt Him shiver and knew that He knew she was there.

Her snake jaws unhinged, and her mouth opened wide to catch His blood as it slid down His flesh. Her smooth black body began to shimmer as she swallowed more and more of Him. His life force filled her with magic, and she drank Him until she had her fill.

Looking up, her mouth wide and His blood spilling into her, she saw his other visitor.

One of Lucifer's birds.

It had the shape of one of the many black-shouldered kites that hunted the region, but it was much smaller. Its wings and back were the color of blood, its breast scarlet. The feet and beak were the blazing orange of fire and its eyes were a brilliant red with black, black pupils. Its entire body pulsed with unfettered rage and desire. Its eye blazed with hatred and its claws dug tight into Tribunal's shoulder.

Lucifer used the birds as messengers. They had been his particular delight in Hell. He formed them from the flesh of kites and the souls of the damned whose wickedness was so great they were given especially exquisite tortures. They were violent, vicious, and conditioned to obey only Lucifer.

He's meddling, she thought. *I've only been gone for a few years and already he thinks he has the right to interfere? Maybe he thinks that he is in charge of Hell now instead of me.*

Lucifer had descended first, knocked out of Heaven by Archangel Michael's blade, and thought that gave him rights to Hell. Nyx had to defeat him to prove otherwise, and then made him her second so he would never forget it.

I shall have to teach Lucifer some more lessons about who is in charge. For a moment she reveled in the thought. Lucifer had always been the most beautiful, and there would be many in the legions of Hell willing to defile and torture him. It would be sublime.

She watched the bird hiss something into Tribunal's ear and saw Tribunal answer. The bird hissed again, and Tribunal turned the full power of his gaze on it. The bird hopped nervously, then launched itself off His shoulder, ripping open a new bit of flesh as it took off into the darkness.

Nyx longed to know the details of their exchange, but would not waste the last of Tribunal's moments on Earth asking for them. His remaining time would be short and filled with pain. She would not waste it with something so trivial.

Besides, getting it out of Lucifer will be fun.

She wound her way up the cross, up His flesh, until she was on the beam, directly behind the man's shoulder. Her forked tongue flickered, frenetically skirting the edges of His ear. She forced it to slow, forced her head to extend out and her tongue to touch the man's skin softly, just brushing the baby-soft fuzz of His neck. Like a kiss. She could taste the iron in His blood and the salt of His sweat beneath the dirt that covered Him.

He turned His head toward her, ever so slowly, and smiled. He was exhausted and in agony, and still He smiled at her. It sent vibrations through her slippery body and down her spine.

*

For forty days in the desert, He had resisted her.

Nyx changed her form often. Now a woman, now a girl; now a man, now a boy; now herself, naked and willing. Tribunal refused them all, even as His body, which was still that of a young man, showed its interest. Instead, He talked to her of humanity and its wickedness. Talked of watching a young shepherd, alone with his flock, descended on by a gang of thieves who cut out his eyes and stole his sheep. And how the boy's master, upon seeing what had happened, had him stoned to death for his negligence.

He talked of the mothers who trained their daughters to be prostitutes from the moment they were old enough to talk full sentences, and of the men who used the girls for their pleasure.

He talked about the torture festivals He had seen, where criminals were slowly torn to bits with metal claws or had their limbs dislocated one joint at a time, and then were forced to crawl over coals to show their remorse. In other places, the criminals were simply suspended in the air and used for target practice by archers who made it their business not to shoot to the heart for a full day. He spoke of the rich, and how their greed and lust for power destroyed the wealth of everyone around them. He talked of how the poor fought and scrabbled amongst themselves, killed each other for food.

Nyx did not bother to correct him. She had seen into the minds of men and women at their worst. And she had taken those who thought they were the most powerful and tough and broken them again and again in the pits of Hell. She had reveled in it.

But even as she had, another part of her wondered why a creature whose life was so short should have to spend all eternity being punished for what it had done.

Still Tribunal raged against them, raged against His own life and the fate that He could not avoid. Nyx let Him talk, let His rage consume Him and, in witnessing it, found herself more and more attracted to Him until she understood why men would give up their lives to follow Him. There was power in this man, and when He spoke it radiated out of Him. Even in His human form, His power attracted her. And the more He resisted her, the more she lusted after Him.

And when Tribunal left the desert, Nyx decided that she needed to be with Him. So she followed Him, learned where He was going, and did what she needed to in order to join Him. She took mortal form and became a prostitute, a concubine, a possessed woman and finally, when the devils were released, His disciple.

The other disciples, men and women both, greeted her politely enough. There were many women traveling with Him, married to His disciples. She was the only unmarried one, but she roomed with the various families so as not to appear unchaste. She listened closely at His sermons, and helped with the poor and destitute.

Nyx found within herself a surprising weak spot for the very young and innocent, be they children or animals. She held no pity for the adults she met, especially the ones she knew were destined for Hell. They had made their decisions and deserved what came from them. The children, though, were too young to exercise that free will, too young to do anything other than what they were told and taught. For them, Nyx found she had pity.

Late at night, when all the others were asleep, she listened to Tribunal swear and curse mankind and God. His body shook with rage at the injustices He had seen, and at the role He was being forced to play. And the more Nyx listened to Him, the more it seemed He was right and the humans had to be wiped from the earth to make way for something better.

And one night, when His rage seemed overwhelming, she used her own power to make the rest of the disciples sleep deeper than they should, and offered her body to His.

This time, He took her. Hard. Worn down by His wrath and the futility of His mission and the knowledge that every day of sermons and healing only brought Him closer to his own inevitable, bitter end, He resisted her no longer. Instead, He pounded his pain and rage into her as she gasped beneath and on top of him. They rutted like lions, clawing and biting at each other in their desire.

To anyone watching, it would have appeared as simple mortal desperation made into passion and poured out through the flesh, but for Nyx it was so, so much more.

Sex had always been magic. In Heaven, the joining of the angels was as much a sharing of power and spirit as it was of angelic pleasure. When Nyx joined with Tribunal, when she accepted His mortal flesh into hers, His power poured into her. It was more power than she had ever felt, more power than she had imagined possible in a single being's body. She had lain with Angels, with mortals, and with gods no longer remembered, and none of them possessed the power that Tribunal had.

The pace of His breathing quickened, His grip tightened on her waist, and His hips pounded hard against her backside as He gave in totally to His passion. She felt His release inside her, and the power that poured into her body with it, and it brought her to one more gasping climax.

Because of who they were, the scratches and bites healed almost at once. And because of who they were, in the morning there was not a sign that their relationship was any deeper than it had been. The days continued much as before, but from that night forward, whenever they could, they indulged in their passion. And with every indulgence, Nyx could feel herself growing stronger.

It was the night before they entered Jerusalem, as they lay naked together, that Tribunal told her what was planned for Him. She listened to Him spell out every detail and her heart filled with pity for Him. "Why would You agree?"

"Agree?" Tribunal laughed the bitter laugh He only shared with Nyx. "There is no agreement. It's God's plan. I do it whether I will or not. And at the end of it, I will give my judgment of mankind, and I pray He will let me destroy them all."

Nyx nodded. "And if He does not? What then?"

"Then?" Tribunal opened his mouth to say more, then stopped. "Ask me when the sky turns dark, my love, and I will tell you then."

"I will ask, then…my love." The words felt strange in her mouth. Love was something she had left behind when she chose to rule Hell rather than bend to God's will in Heaven. She had her passions and those she cared about, but love seemed an alien thing to her. And even now she was not sure if it was love she felt or just the mad lust for the power He poured into her, and desire born of their mutual contempt for the God who created them.

She decided it didn't matter. Tribunal was more beloved to her than any being in creation had been before. And after this night, she would never see Him again.

Tribunal looked out at the horizon, where the sky was beginning its slow fade from black to blue. "It begins." He sounded sad and tired and angry and bitter and everything that a man who has been forced to give his life for a cause He neither wants nor believes in should feel.

"No," said Nyx. "Because it is still tonight until the sun rises."

Tribunal looked ready to protest, but she took Him in her hand, then her mouth, then her body, and rode with Him on waves of desire until the sun finally broke the horizon.

*

On the cross, Tribunal turned His head toward her, ever so slowly, and smiled. He was exhausted and in agony, and still He smiled at her. "It's time, Nyx," he whispered. "Prepare."

Death was close now, but He gathered enough strength to whisper to her a single word.

Whenever Tribunal spoke, His words were always more than just mortal sounds. They were filled with the power of the God Himself. And though the mortal sounds they had been clothed in had dulled them down, made them less than they truly were, still they had the power to move men's hearts and minds.

This time, though, the word He whispered was even more.

This time he spoke in the true tongue of God, and it was power incarnate. The sun dimmed in the sky. The rivers stopped flowing. The air itself bent and warped around His mouth like a shimmering mirage in blazing heat. Storm clouds swept in overhead as if dropped into the sky by an unseen hand. Birds cawed and screeched. Disquiet swept through the crowd, who looked around anxiously for the source of the disturbance.

The whispered word He gave Nyx took the last of his power with it, sapping His body of its strength.

Nobody heard it but her.

Rain began to fall.

His eyes met hers. *"Remember that word,"* He said, though now the voice rang only in Nyx's head. His legs had given out and His lungs could no longer fill with air. *"And when My judgment has come to pass, and God has made His decision, speak this word, and I shall answer."*

Nyx slipped down closer and coiled her serpent's body around Tribunal's neck. She could not give Him a true embrace, so she gave Him what she could. Nyx was determined to stay with Tribunal as He endured the agonizing final moments of His human life.

The darkness around them grew deep enough to dim the torches of the soldiers. The crowd's cries faded to sniffles and silence as they, too, realized what must be happening. A few faint flickers of lightning in the distance gave bursts of grey and shadow to the blackness around them. Thunder rumbled across the sky.

Then the first real sheet of lightning ripped across the darkness, blinding everyone as the winds howled and the rain slammed down on the earth, pounding the flesh of the faithful and the soldiers alike, and driving the weaker members of the crowd to their knees. Again and again the lightning flashed and the thunder roared as the earth itself mourned Tribunal's passing.

Directly above, the sky was ripped open, as if talons had punctured the flesh of the sky, and then shredded it. A brilliant light, far brighter than any the earth had seen, shone down directly onto the cross.

It was the light of Heaven, and Nyx knew that none of the mortals could see it.

"They come for me," His voice rang in her head again. "Go, now."

From the gash in the heavens, five golden-skinned Angels with massive, pure white wings began to descend. Fair, ethereal robes billowed about them, defying gravity. The fabric clung to their perfect forms, their beauty in stark contrast to the earthly gore down below. They too were invisible to mortal eyes.

Nyx uncoiled from His neck, and her serpent body fell to the wet, muddy earth below the cross. She slid away, faster than any human could see. In the darkness, hidden behind a rock, she changed form and became Mary once more. She dashed back to the hill, forcing her way through the crowd with elbows and shoulders and just enough of her own power to make the people move out of her way.

She reached the front of the mourners, praying she was not too late. She kept her hood low over her face, and her eyes away from the Angels above. There was little chance they would recognize her, and she suspected they were too concerned about their mission to stray from it. Still, she knew she must not draw their attention.

She turned her eyes to her Tribunal, hoping that it was not too late. His eyes were starting to grow dull, and she could see the fire in them passing out of His body. Still, He saw her, and for one moment, He smiled again.

"I love you," she mouthed, silently. She found herself crying, which Angels never did, not even in mortal form as she was now.

He looked up to the clouds, and the heavenly light shone on Him. As Nyx watched, His smile crumbled, replaced by something close to despair.

"Father," he gasped, and all the bitterness that He had held since she first met Him poured out into his words. "Why have You forsaken me?"

His body shuddered, and the last of the strength went out of it. As she watched, His spirit slipped the bounds of His false flesh and began rising toward heaven.

"No!" Nyx cried, willing Him to stay for just a moment longer, even as she knew He was gone.

"My Father has made His decision," Nyx heard Tribunal say in her mind. And for the first time, unrestrained by a mortal body, she felt His true power. It shook her to the core, even as she realized that He sounded flayed, as if someone had torn open His soul the way the scourges had torn open his flesh.

"He has betrayed me."

"My love," she sent back. *"What must I do?"*

His voice filled her head, and the power of it filled her with the desire to obey, no matter what the cost to herself. Part of her rebelled against it, as she had rebelled against Heaven, but she forced that part into silence, listening to her lover's instructions. *"In three days His judgment will come to pass. And when you stand as the sole Angel on this earth, speak the word.*

"I will make you my sword, Nyx. And then you and those that serve you will be in a Paradise that He cannot touch. Ascended, no longer Descended, and free from this spiteful God who casts aside His Angels at His whim."

Lightning erupted from the rift in the heavens, exploding again and again, shaking the ground and blinding all those who stood. The people cried out in fear, certain this was God's retribution for the death of His son, not knowing God had in fact orchestrated it. Bolts of fire sought the earth, rending and tearing into it. Just meters away, a skull-shaped rock that had given this place the name "Golgotha" was struck by an angry spear of flame and exploded into pebbles and sand. The crowd screamed and fought to get away.

Nyx stayed where she was, holding her hood tight over her face so the Angels above might not recognize her, and gazing up toward Heaven. She watched the Angels' progress, rising together on their magnificent white wings. The one in the lead held a blade of white fire in parade position. The two behind carried with them the mirrored, translucent shape that was her lover's soul. And the last two were singing His praises in a voice only she could hear. She watched until the two carrying His soul entered the hole in the sky, and then turned her eyes away.

Her Tribunal was in Heaven. And it was the one place where she could never, ever follow. Her banishment from Heaven was permanent, everlasting, and irrevocable.

She would be apart from Him forever, if God had His way.

Nyx's mortal stomach soured with venomous rage. She

looked up again, and saw that two Angels still remained, floating before the black clouds. Their electric blue eyes were locked on her, and their faces filled with anger. They knew her for who she was.

The storm vomited every ounce of its wrath on to the city below. Furious winds wailed from all directions, blowing sand and pellets of hail into the faces of those who remained. Nyx and those others on the hill were knocked to their knees by the force of the gale. People shrieked as they tried to flee toward the city, into the safe arms of its stone walls.

"Save yourselves!" the Roman commander screamed before he turned and ran for the main gates of Jerusalem. And even the bravest of his soldiers dropped their weapons and followed.

Nyx looked at the woman on the ground beside her. It was Mary, Tribunal's earthly mother. The one God had forced to carry His child, to raise Him and to suffer the heartache of watching Him die. Nyx wrapped Mary in her strong arms and protected her from the storm's wrath. They swayed there, rocked by the force of the wind and bruised by the power of the rain and the hail.

They are doing this because of me, Nyx thought, risking a glance up to where the Angels still floated above, untouched by the storm that surrounded them. *They are trying to hurt me.*

"We killed the Son of God!" a soldier screamed. "We are doomed!"

Nyx watched the man throw down his sword and tear off his armor in his hysteria. He stood naked in the storm, apologizing to the dead man. The wind barraged the man wildly while he fought, determined to repent for his sins. He groveled on his knees at the base of the cross, praying to the corpse that now wilted like a soaked wildflower in the wind.

Nyx was surprised to find she had tears left to shed. She knew her lover was not dead, knew He was safe in Heaven, but because of that she knew she would not see Him again, would not feel His flesh—mortal or angelic—mesh with hers. And so she cried beside Mary, who was wailing with the pain that only a mother who loses a child can know.

The naked soldier was now reaching up to the sky, arms wide, howling prayers of repentance while the rain and wind left pockmarks on his wet, white body.

Nyx watched as Tribunal's mother's hair whipped wildly, like vine tendrils choking an ancient tree. Mary had done nothing to deserve the wrath that was pounding down upon them. And Nyx knew it would continue until she left this place.

"We have to go!" she screamed, raising her voice loud enough so that Mary could hear her above the storm.

Tribunal's mother shook her head. "We must take him down first!"

"I can't," said Nyx, knowing the destruction would continue until she was gone. "I have to go! Now!"

"What?" Mary pushed herself out of Nyx's arms. "Why? You were closest to Him! I had hopes that you two…"

"I'm sorry, Mary!" Nyx's voice rose above the din of the storm, the wind blowing her purple-black hair away from her face. "I have to go!"

"I don't understand!" Mary cried, her voice weak against nature's fury. Mary struggled to see as a thick gust of wind threw sand into her face. She cried out, briefly blinded.

Nyx seized the moment and broke away from Mary. She

needed to transform, to get away from this place. She stepped far enough away that Mary could not see her, then began transforming.

Another bolt of lightning struck, knocking Mary to the ground and turning the world momentarily white. Rock shattered, and its dust rained down on Mary's face and hair. She choked on the wet, muddy air, squinting at the chaos around her.

The winds stilled, the rain stopped, and Mary saw Nyx transforming into the snake.

Mary screamed and pointed and Nyx knew at once what had happened. She cursed herself for changing so close by, and then cursed the Angels above who had seen it, and had made sure Mary had seen it, too.

The naked Roman soldier ran to Mary, putting himself between her and Nyx. It was a moment of clarity in his madness, and Nyx knew without question who had sent it.

"Please, you have to get away from here!" he bellowed. "Get up and run. And tell all what has befallen here! Fast!"

Trouble for trouble's sake, thought Nyx, disgusted. Mary telling the story of what she had seen would do no real harm to Nyx, but she could never see Mary again, and those who heard it might doubt her sanity. Mary had suffered enough. Nyx hissed and changed her direction, slithering toward Mary. The mad soldier jumped back so far that he fell. He crawled in a frenzy, kicking wildly until he could pull himself to his feet and flee towards the welcoming walls of Jerusalem.

In front of Mary, swaying in a motion that had nothing to do with the storm, was the largest snake she had ever seen. It was Nyx, and Mary knew it. And Nyx knew that could not be allowed.

Forget.

The command reverberated through Mary's body, shaking her to her soul. She could do nothing but obey, and the sight of Nyx changing into a snake fell from her mind, even as she collapsed over backwards.

Nyx raced away, still cursing the Angels in her head. What she had done to Mary was not enough. The woman would remember soon, if Nyx did not do more, but it would buy her enough time to escape the storm and spare Mary any more of the Angels' wrath.

Mary blinked and found herself looking at the cross. The sight of her son's body, hanging loosely on the cross, soaked through her like the rain had soaked her clothes, embedded itself into her mind and drove away all other thoughts.

The rain and wind raged and warred for control of the air around the hill, but Mary saw none of it. There was only her son's body. Even now, it was beautiful. But He was gone. Her son was gone.

The winds abated, the hail ceased, and the rain stopped driving sideways and fell steadily to Earth. An eerie silence came over the hill and Mary, her wet clothes clinging to her skin, shivered. The few who remained with Mary rose to their feet. Hannah, Mary's dearest friend, put her strong hands on Mary's shoulder.

"Come, Mary," Hannah urged gently, seeing the agony in her friend's face. "We need to find the others. We need to take Him down."

She felt John's strong arms come around her—silly John, she thought absently. She saw Joseph and Nicodemus stepping forward with a box of tools and a small ladder. Two others had brought a stretcher and sheets to wrap his body until the proper rite could be performed.

In front of the cross, Mary wept for the loss of her child.

CHAPTER 2

MARY SAT ALONE in her small room in Joseph of Arimathea's house, looking out the window and trying to remember.

The soldiers had chased them off when they had attempted to bring down Jesus's body, and would have left Him there had Joseph not gone to Pilate and asked for the body to be buried before sunset in accordance with tradition. Pilate had shown mercy and relented, and they had taken Him first to Joseph's house, where they cleaned His broken flesh. Mary, who had thought she had no tears left, wept at the sight of His battered, cut, and broken body, and gently ran the cloths over His flesh, cleaning Him as she had done when He was an infant, tenderly washing the blood and dirt from His slack, tear-stained cheeks even as her own tears fell upon Him.

And there was something more....

He had been such a sweet child, she thought. No crying, no screaming, but always watchful.

But there was something else…

She had kissed Him and wrapped Him in linen, and followed as they placed Him in His tomb, and wept as they pushed the rock into place.

It was good of Joseph, thought Mary. Good of Him to give my son a proper place to rest.

But there was something she had forgotten. Something important…

"Hello, Mary," said Mary Magdalene, from the doorway.

Mother Mary turned and gasped in relief. "There you are! I was so worried when you vanished. There was the storm and the lightning and I wondered if I might die. And then you came and…"

Memory sprung back unbidden, and Mary stood so suddenly her small chair tumbled over. She stumbled backwards to the wall, pressing herself against it…Mary's mouth went wide with fear, gaping desperately, but no sound would come out.

Another bolt of lightning struck, knocking her to the ground and turning the world momentarily white. Rock shattered, and its dust rained down on Mary's face and hair. She coughed on dusty air, opening her eyes tentatively, and saw…

"Shh," said Nyx, keeping her voice gentle even as she used her power to take away the woman's ability to shout. "It's all right."

Mary's words, when they came out, were whispers. "You demon," she hissed. "You monster. What are you? How dare you be near my son! How dare you have pretended to be His friend! Get away!"

Nyx closed the distance between them so fast that Mary didn't have time to blink. Her red serpentine eyes flashed with anger. Terrified, Mary pressed herself harder against the wall. And though Nyx's words were pitched so that only Mary could hear them, the fury in them was unmistakable. "Do not say that I *pretended*," she hissed. "He was mine!"

Mary was frightened, more frightened than she had ever been in her life. But she would not allow this demon to see it. "You are a monster!"

Nyx's first instinct was to tear into Mary's flesh, to disembowel and punish this mortal for daring to judge her. Nyx suppressed the instinct ruthlessly. *She knows nothing*, Nyx reminded herself. *She is innocent. She didn't want any of this.*

To Mary's surprise, Mary Magdalene smiled at her, and the smile was gentle and filled with pity. "I'm an Angel."

Then the world went black, and Mary was back on the hill in the rain.

The snake was before her again, its fanned, hooded head swaying rhythmically back and forth as if dancing to an unheard flute. Around them, time slowed. The raindrops, near-invisible before, became slow-moving diamonds, shining bright in the lightning that had come so close to killing them all. Mary felt that she could reach out and catch each single drop of water and drink them one by one before they hit the ground.

And as she watched, a feeling of peace and joy crept over her. She was drunk without an ounce of wine; she was in rapture without the touch of a man. And yet even in this peaceful trance, she was still afraid of the snake before her. Part of her wanted to flee, to escape the snake that was smothering her will.

Then the urge to flee, too, was smothered, and all she could do was stand in diamond rain, watching the snake's muscles rippling beneath its glossy scales.

Please, thought Mary. *Please don't hurt me. My son has just died and I...*

I am so tired.

The snake transformed, and Mary Magdalene stood before her. And even though it was only a dream—it could only be a dream—Mary Magdalene's hands were as warm and strong as they had always been.

And then Mary Magdalene shimmered again, and she was suddenly so much taller and wearing a crown and clad in black scaled armor and her serpent eyes burned with a fire that matched the flaming glow of her black wings. She was a Dark Angel, and she wrapped Mary in her power.

Mary tried to call out, to scream for help against this being who had claimed all her senses, but she could not make a sound. She remembered the nightmares she had had as a child, in which she had tried to speak but no matter her effort, couldn't.

Maybe this is a nightmare, Mary thought. *Maybe it's all a nightmare. Maybe there is no serpent, no storm, and maybe they didn't murder my son. Please God, let me wake and find Him alive again.*

For the briefest of moments, she saw them. She saw Joseph—her Joseph—lying in his bed, asleep after a long day's work, and heard her children laughing and saw her son standing among His brother and sisters, His shining face untouched by age or pain.

Please, God. Please.

She blinked and the vision was gone, and she was on the

hill with the snake/Mary/Angel in front of her, and her son was dead again. Her whole body sagged with anguish.

The body of the Angel began to sway, mimicking the hypnotic undulations of the snake. The hands that held Mary's were tipped with silver talons, sharp and deadly and beautiful. The woman's eyes were still the eyes of the snake, and they bore into Mary's soul.

The Dark Angel smiled, and Mary's breath went away. Suddenly, she wanted nothing more than to be this creature's friend, to serve it and to be with it, to be lost inside those serpentine eyes for eternity.

And then the Angel was gone, and Mary Magdalene was standing there, tears flowing down her face. "I loved Him, Mary," she said. "I loved Him, but I had to leave."

The memory of Mary Magdalene turning into the snake faded to nothingness, and scattered from Mary's mind. All she remembered was poor Mary Magdalene, fleeing in her grief as the storm raged around them.

Her eyes opened and she was alone in her room. A gentle breeze had picked up, cooling sweat that the day's heat had brought to her skin. She sighed, and then straightened. There were things to be done, preparations to make.

He had told her, before He left that fateful night, that He would rise again. And though she had shaken her head at the time, and worried about Him, now the words gave her hope, and she allowed herself to dare dream of seeing her son again.

He said three days, Mary thought, rising and heading for the kitchen. Surely there was some task she could do while she was here. He will rise. He gave me his word.

*

Nyx waited, and brooded.

Tribunal had said that she would know when God's judgment had come. That she would feel it. Night had fallen, Tribunal was dead, and still there was no change in the world, no sign that He had made a decision.

Nyx hissed in frustration, and for a brief moment the eyes in her mortal form burned red. She snuffed the light out at once, even though there was none to see it, and stepped out into the streets of Jerusalem.

If there is nothing to do but wait, I will wait, she thought.

Nyx changed her form to that of a young, handsome man and walked the streets of Jerusalem. She was female, and preferred the form of a woman most of the time. But this night she wanted not to be disturbed, and a young woman walking the streets of Jerusalem at night was not likely to go unmolested. So she became he, for a short time. And she/he wandered the streets, past the houses of the rich and of the poor, through the empty market and dark alleyways and well-lit streets where men reveled far into the night.

Nyx could feel every mortal around her. She sensed them sleeping, eating, talking, fucking, crying, laughing, fighting, and abusing one another, these humans her Tribunal had been sent here to judge. In one of the alleys she could sense thieves, waiting to kill her. She smiled at them as they came close, and they fled from her red serpent eyes and mouth full of gleaming, razor-sharp teeth.

Nyx listened to the sounds coming through the walls of the houses. She heard quiet conversations, arguments over money and parents singing to their children. She heard cries of joy, pain and outrage. She amused herself by marking in her mind which of these mortals she would see again after they died. So many of them were Hell-bound. If they knew what horrors awaited them, she wondered, would they be able to control their impulses?

At one house she heard the cries of children in pain, one after the other, and the grunt of the man who was taking his pleasure on them. Nyx stopped on the street and listened. The noise angered her in a way she couldn't understand. She had little but contempt for the humans, but a child was innocent. It had no power to help itself...

I will look forward to seeing this man in Hell, Nyx thought. *Assuming that bastard Lucifer hands Hell back to me.*

Part of Nyx hoped he wouldn't. She was still enraged by the death of her Tribunal, and was ready to lash out and kill. She would tear the entire mortal world to pieces, if she could, and then go back to Hell and rain fire and destruction on Lucifer and all those who opposed her.

She heard another child in the house cry out and heard the man's breath quicken.

I am the Queen of Hell, Nyx thought. *It's my job to punish the wicked.*

She kicked in the door of the house and stepped inside. The child's cries of pain turned into screams of horror. A shutter shattered as the man flew through it, to land broken on the street, his life bleeding out through the hole where his genitals had been.

He said wait, Nyx reminded herself, as she stepped back into the street. *He didn't say I couldn't punish the wicked while I did.*

In a street known for its prostitutes, a man came up to Nyx

and, seeing her as an attractive young man, gave her a proposition. She considered accepting; considered waiting until he was about to climax, then ripping him to shreds. She opened her mouth to say yes when a familiar scent wafted into Nyx's nose. A familiar sound floated in the air. It caught her whole attention. She waved the man away and walked on, listening.

Judas.

To leave one's mortal body in spirit form was easy for an Angel. Nyx stepped into an alley and floated out of her flesh. Nyx floated out of her flesh. Her spirit form was that of her true, female, white-skinned, black-winged self. She flew through walls, unseen by human eyes, past busily engaged couples and trios and more, to the room where Judas was rutting on the body of a girl who had just entered womanhood. The girl cried out and moved beneath him, her ecstasy almost convincing as she wrapped her arms and legs around him and bucked her hips in an effort to make him finish faster.

This one I will not wait on. This one betrayed my Tribunal, and I will kill him.

She slipped into his mind, and found it a whirlwind of chaos.

Even as he thrust into the girl beneath him, in his mind Judas was standing at the base of the hill, looking up at the crowd and the men crucified there. He could not take his eyes off the One who he had called his leader, his master, and his friend, who was now hanging on the cross because he, Judas, had betrayed Him.

The purse on his hip felt as if it weighed a hundred pounds. The thirty silver coins—enough to hire a skilled laborer for four months—burned against his thigh with the heat of his own guilt.

Judas tried to focus on the girl beneath him, on the fleeting pleasure she provided, but in his mind he could see only the bloody, beaten, thorn-crowned face of the man whom he had claimed to love, the suffering in his master's eyes.

He growled with frustration, pulled out of the girl, and turned her on her stomach. He pinned her face down hard against the mattress and mounted her again. The girl cried out in pain, but masked it as sounds of lust, begging him for more in the hopes it would bring him to the end sooner.

Nyx entered Judas' mind, and allowed herself to be seen. To Judas' eyes she was Mary Magdalene, the one their master loved, the woman who walked with the disciples and who comforted their leader when He was in pain. She stared at him, summoning all her grief and rage, and let it loose in him. Her emotions, so much more powerful than those of a mortal, overwhelmed him and filled his head so that it threatened to explode.

In the real world, Judas swore and cried out in pain. The girl beneath him was startled and tried to pull away. In his anger, he grabbed her, forced her back down on the mattress and rammed himself into her backside. Her cries turn to shrieks of pain, her feigned pleasure vanishing.

In his mind, tears running down her face, Mary Magdalene whispered, "How could you, Judas? He loved you. He made you one of the disciples. He was the light of the world and you snuffed Him out like a candle."

Mary vanished and in her place stood his master. His body was torn and broken from the scourging and the crucifixion.

His eyes were clouded over with death, and He had holes in his hands and feet. His face was stained red from the blood leaking down from the crown of thorns. "This is what you have wrought, Judas," He said. "I was to lead the men and women of this world to freedom from Rome, from sin, and from pain. And you destroyed it all."

Judas screamed and reared back, pulling himself from the crying prostitute and burying his face in his hands. The girl scrambled away, watching in fear as he doubled over, screaming himself hoarse and beating at his temples.

Judas's eyes were locked with his master's. He was afraid, more than he had ever been, for his master had begun to glow with a brilliant white light, so bright and powerful that it laid open Judas's soul, making him relive the betrayal, the moment he accepted the money for his master's death, the trip through Jerusalem leading the soldiers, and the kiss that let the Romans know who to kill.

In the real world, Judas's bowels and bladder both released at once. The prostitute cried out in disgust, and a foul smell filled the small, closed room. The brothel guards ran in and, seeing the mess, hauled Judas out, kicking and slapping him as they dragged him down the narrow corridor to the door.

Judas wanted to run, to hide from himself, but there was no place to go; he was still trapped in his own tormented mind as he was trapped in his quaking, filth-covered body.

The brothel guards tossed him into the streets, and he landed on his own filth. They kicked him repeatedly and Judas curled into a ball, hoping to protect his flesh, while inside his mind there was a different and much worse pain. In his head, his master loomed larger, the light grew brighter. "I was the son of God," He said. "Brought here to bring the light to mankind. And you snuffed out that light!" The white light flared bright and was gone.

Judas opened his eyes and found himself, bleeding and crying and lying in his own waste. Passing men walked around him, eyes averted in disgust. Slowly, he pulled himself to his feet, and stumbled away from the well-lit street.

In a darkened alley, Nyx transformed, leaving her false human flesh behind for her true form. She rose into the air, and as she did, black armor flowed over her body, covering her and cloaking her. Her boots, normally diamond, turned black, and a black mask covered her face. A thought transformed her three-headed, flaming whip to a single lash of darkness, as invisible in the night as Nyx herself. She silently flew above the city until she hovered over Judas.

Judas stumbled into an alley and reached up under his robe to remove his filth-covered loincloth. As his hand touched it, the first stinging lash came out of the air, ripping the shoulder of his robe and cutting into his flesh. He yelled out in pain, and looked desperately around to see who had hit him. There was no sign of anyone.

The lash cut down again, ripping open his back. He screamed and ran, the mess on his body forgotten as he tried to escape his invisible tormenter. In the sky above, Nyx followed, her whip in her hand. She watched Judas run towards the bright streets. A pair of quick lashes sent him stumbling back to the darkness.

For the rest of the night she drove him, lashing his body with a thousand small cuts, leaving him a bloody mess but never damaging him so badly that he could not run. With an expert eye she scourged the clothes from his body until he had nothing left but the soiled loincloth and the girdle that held his purse. By the time dawn began to break the horizon, he had run the length of the city three times. As the sun began to rise, he saw a possible hiding space, a small outdoor oven. In desperation, he crawled, weeping, inside it.

The flogging stopped. Judas closed his eyes in relief.

He was back on the hill. Only this time, there was no crowd, no guard, no others on crosses. There was just him, standing before the cross on which his master's body hung.

The master looked down on him, His face filled with disapproval and disappointment. He made no sound, save for His blood hitting the earth where it dripped from His body, soaking into the parched desert sand. Judas knelt before the cross and began babbling, begging forgiveness. His master's eyes went to the small bag on Judas's waist. Instantly the coins inside began to burn into Judas's flesh, making him howl with agony. He grabbed frantically at his waist, trying to pull the purse free. His hands caught fire and he screamed.

"Return the blood money!" His master's mouth did not move, but his voice filled Judas's head. "Return it to those who ordered my death!"

Judas's eyes snapped open, and he realized that the oven was on fire. Though there had been no wood inside it, the stones themselves were burning. Smoke was filling the air as flames licked up from the ground, and he could smell his own scorched skin. Screaming in agony and fear, Judas crawled out and onto the ground, frantically battering at his bubbling flesh. The fire died, but the agony went on. Blisters formed on the flesh of his back and legs, on the bottom of his feet, and on his hands. It should have been enough to make Judas lose consciousness—but Nyx had Judas in her power and would give him no such reprieve.

At his waist, the girdle with its pouch remained untouched by the flames. Judas staggered away as fast as he could on his ruined feet, toward the Hall of Hewn Stones, and the Sanhedrin who had paid him to betray his master.

Nyx, now clothed in the flesh of an older woman, sneered as Judas hobbled away. He would be forced to walk through the city's center to reach the Hall of Hewn Stones. She followed, watching with amusement as the people scattered from the sight and stink of him. The blisters on the bottom of his feet had ruptured and he left a trail of blood and pus. He should have collapsed, screaming on the ground, but Nyx used her power to keep him upright and moving despite the agony. Nyx followed him, delighting in his suffering.

He reached the Hall of Hewn Stones and pushed his way in to see the Sanhedrin. Nyx stood outside and waited. Soon the guards threw him into the street. He hit hard, splitting open more blisters and howling in pain. Still in the guise of a housewife, Nyx came forward and helped him to his feet.

"You poor dear," she said, in her kindest, most solicitous voice, her nostrils delicately flaring to take in the scent of roasted meat, still faintly recognizable behind the stench of Judas's filth. "Here, let me help you."

Judas wept as she led him from the main square, babbling, "I gave it back, I gave it back, please forgive me."

She let him blather until they were away from the square. There was a large home nearby that had once belonged to a very rich man. It was empty now, though its furnishings remained.

Its residents had died of contagion, and no one yet dared to venture in save those assigned to bury the dead. She led him there, and brought him inside.

"Thank you," he rambled. "Thank you, thank you, thank you. You have saved me."

"No," said Nyx. "I haven't." She reached into his mind and twisted it. To Judas's eyes, she once more became his master, bloody, broken and dead, though standing before him. Judas screamed and stumbled back. "No one can save you, Judas," she said, and Judas heard his master's voice speak the words. "No one will ever come to save you."

He broke free and ran out of the room, into the courtyard. Nyx slipped ahead of him, and when he arrived it was not her, but Peter that Judas saw in his mind. He tried to open his mouth to plead for his life, but Nyx took away his power of speech with a thought. She slashed out with a talon, opening a long narrow slit in his cheek that quickly filled with blood. His mouth wide in a silent scream, Judas fled, leaving bloody, oozing footprints behind. She smiled and followed.

The house was not large and had been kept in immaculate condition, but Nyx used her powers to create an illusion of a filthy, putrid labyrinth filled with biting vermin that tormented his already-burning flesh. Every time he turned a corner, one of the other apostles was there. Each delivered a stinging attack that opened his skin. Never was he allowed to sit down or hide. The apostles kept driving him from room to room, across the courtyard and back again, until night fell.

With the final light of the sun gone, Nyx at last allowed Judas to find the door and escape the house. His weeping had long since stopped, though the terror remained. For a brief moment, there was silence, and stillness, and Judas began to hope that maybe the nightmare was over.

With a flick, Nyx sent her whip lashing into his flesh again, tearing open one of the huge blisters and sending its fluids spinning out to decorate the nearest wall.

For another night, she drove him through Jerusalem, this time ripping away the girdle and loincloth, leaving him naked. In his mind, she put a desperate imperative: RUN. He could not stop, no matter how tired he became or how much pain wracked his body. No matter how desperate he was for it to end, he would always pick himself up and stumble forward once more, and every time the whip chased him, lashed him until his body was a bloody unrecognizable mess.

She drove him back and forth across the city three more times before the sun rose. And when it did, he found himself back in the courtyard of the house. He cried out in despair.

Huge hands grabbed him. A sharp-toothed, gaping mouth leered at him. Nyx had many forms. This one was male and enormous, with horns on its head and red, saw-toothed scales that covered every inch of its flesh.

She dragged him to the bath houses and immersed him in salt water, shaking him to wash away the filth and leaving him screaming voicelessly as the salt filled the wounds. And when his body was cleansed enough that she could stand it, she took him to the middle of the courtyard and threw him on his stomach. She used his body for her pleasure, driving into him for hours at a time, using her power to keep him from going into shock so that the pain of it stayed fresh and new.

By the time night fell and he was turned out into the streets, he was bleeding so badly he could barely stand. Still she drove him forward, watching as every step he took sent agony through his body, from the torn blisters on his feet to the ruptures in his bowels, from the open lashes that covered his body to the ripped and bleeding flesh of his mouth and throat. Blood leaked from his ears, his nose, his mouth, and his anus. He would not last much longer, she knew, and that was fine with her.

She drove him through an open gate and out of the city, towards a high hill. And when they were far enough from Jerusalem that he could not be heard, she gave him his voice back so she could enjoy his screams.

The hill had been covered in fig trees, but the storm that came with Tribunal's passing had decimated it. Only a few trees remained standing, and one entire side of the hill had been washed away, leaving a jagged, sandy cliff.

Once more invisible and in black, she drove Judas up the hill. Her lash seemed to come from every direction, leaving him bewildered and in fresh torment with every step. Still she would not let him rest. The compulsion to run drove him to keep moving long after his body should have given up and collapsed.

And when he reached the top of the hill, he found a single fig tree still standing at the edge of the cliff, with one of its branches stretched out over the void.

Nyx let the compulsion leave him then and he collapsed to the ground, screaming and begging for his life. Hovering above him, she made her armor disappear, and let the fire that lit her black wings come back to life. The horned tiara sprung into being on her head and the jewels around her neck gleamed.

She landed in front of him, and he saw her for the first

time as she truly was, and knew her for what she truly was. He tried to scrabble away, but his body had no more strength. He begged and pleaded, this time for death, but Nyx only smiled.

With a single hand she pulled him to his feet, gripping one of his arms.

"You killed Him," she said as she dragged Judas across the ground towards the tree and the cliff. She stopped and looked at him. "Do you have any idea what He meant to me?"

Before he could answer, she twisted his arm and broke it. With a move faster than he could see, she reached out and broke the other one, too. He screamed anew as she twisted his broken bones until they pierced his skin. Then she stomped on his legs, and smiled as she heard the bones in them crack, listening with pleasure as they ground against each other. Still gripping the broken arm, she dragged him towards the tree.

"You should be dead, you know," she said conversationally. "With all I have done to you, you should have died ten times over." She tossed him down at the base of the tree and crouched beside him. "And do you know why you are not dead?"

He shook his head and moaned something that sounded like a plea.

"Because I am not ready to let you die yet!" screamed Nyx, her razor teeth gleaming in the moonlight. "You murdered Him! You took Him away from me and I will never, never forgive you for it! Do you know who I am? Do you?"

Broken lips and teeth came together, Judas mouthed the word as best he could. "De…v…l."

"Yes," hissed Nyx. "I am the ruler of Hell and you, little

mortal, have angered me beyond all reason. You have taken away something that I wanted and for that you will suffer!"

She gouged her nails into his belly and slowly ripped it open. Judas, who had thought he could feel no more pain, screamed anew.

"I will give you your wish," she said, as she reached inside him and pulled out his intestines in long, slippery loops. "You will die here tonight." His eyes rolled briefly in his head at the sight of his own disembowelment, but she forced him back to himself. "And when you have died, when you pass beyond the veil, I will be waiting for you." She looped the intestines around his neck, then threw them over the branch of the tree and began pulling. They should not have held his weight, but Nyx's power made them strong enough that they would, and slowly, inch by inch, she pulled him upright, then aloft, until he was swaying, strangling over the branch on the edge of the cliff. "And when I see you again," she said, her voice rising to a scream, "I will put you through such agony that these torments will pale in comparison!"

Judas swung, feeling his throat closing in on itself, feeling the world turn black and his senses start to slip.

Nyx released her power from the loop of intestines and it ripped open, sending him plunging down the side of the cliff.

The initial drop was not much, perhaps fifteen feet, and the tumble down the rest of the cliff did not kill him either, as Nyx had known it would not. At the base of the cliff, Judas Iscariot lay, bleeding and gasping, still alive.

Then he heard the rustling, and felt the first of the rats Nyx had summoned to the spot, hours before, digging into his flesh.

Nyx sat under the tree, eating figs and listening to him

scream for the rest of the night. It should have been more satisfying, like the tortures she inflicted on the damned. Instead, it left a taste like gall in her mouth. Tribunal was still gone and torturing His murderers did not give her enough satisfaction.

Still makes me feel better, thought Nyx, sending a command to the rats to eat slower.

And when the sun rose, and Judas was finally silent, Nyx realized God was gone.

CHAPTER 3

WHEN NIGHT FELL, Nyx walked out into the desert. She had spent the day under the fig tree, listening. She had stretched her senses in all directions, eyes, ears, nose and mind all reaching out, searching for some presence of God. Though her body remained on the hill where she had finished torturing Judas, her mind wandered the earth, searching.

There was nothing.

Her feet slipped lightly over the ground, not feeling the harsh stones and thorns beneath them. The moon above was full, its pale light making her silver-white skin even more ghostly, and her long white hair sparkle. She liked the moon on nights like this.

He was gone. She was almost sure of it.

God's presence infused His creations—even her, though she hated to admit it. An Angel always felt the presence of God. And though she was the darkest Angel of them all and had long since fallen from His grace, still she felt His presence, even in Hell. God's presence was all-encompassing and existed in every part of His world, in every thing that was part of His creation.

But now that presence had vanished, leaving an empty space and a vague ache in her being.

Nyx wondered if the humans could feel it, or the animals. She wondered if any being on the world realized that God had left, and that they were alone in the universe. And if they could feel it, she wondered if it left them terrified or relieved.

For Nyx, her feelings raged back and forth from confusion to ecstasy. She was an Angel; a creature built solely to fulfill God's will, and though she had rebelled, part of her could not imagine a world without him.

The rest of her reveled in the freedom.

For the first time, she could be sure that God was not influencing her decisions, that she was making them by herself, for herself, and that she would reap the rewards of them. A world without God was a world that she could own utterly.

If Tribunal were here, it would be perfect.

If it's true.

She was still uncertain. This world was God's, from its first creation until the end of days. It had been His pride and His plaything, even before He had created humans and put them on it. For Him to abandon it seemed unthinkable.

But if He has, she thought, *Then this world is MINE.*

She practically danced across the sand with joy, her lithe body springing from rock to rock. A few puddles remained from the rain three days before, not yet soaked up by the red, sandy earth. She squished through them, feeling the warm water and grainy mud between her toes, a gentle contrast to the harsh bite of the desert rocks.

Nyx clicked her golden nails together. She liked the sharp sound; it was like two swords gently colliding, sharp metal rubbing on sharp metal. She walked to the rhythm of the clicks, her body swaying and stretching, almost dancing as she moved.

She was miles from Jerusalem now, miles from any human sound that might interfere with her listening. The sounds of the mortals – their emotions and desires and beliefs – washed through their cities. They affected her more than she liked to admit and made it hard for her to sense the world clearly.

Now all that had faded into the far distance. The desert was still, except for the soft hiss of the sand giving way beneath her feet, and the metallic percussion of her clicking nails.

She knelt near a pool of rainwater and listened, stretching every sense and her mind as far as she could.

There was nothing.

She looked and smelled and tasted the wind.

Still nothing.

Nyx scooped up the rainwater with both hands. The water was warm to her touch, still heated from the sun. She closed her eyes and tilted her cupped hands up to her mouth. Water dribbled down her chin as she tasted, and tested, the droplets.

The water was water, the air was air, and the presence of God was gone from it all.

Nyx stood, and looked out at the vast hills around her. Tiny, skittering lizards danced across the sand, leaving little footprints in their wake. A light breeze swirled dry sand from the dunes off in the distance.

God had left this place.

But He had not left it unattended.

Their presence was a spark of divinity on the now-Godless

earth. Two bright blazes of burning magnesium in a void of darkness. And they were coming toward her.

She willed her armor into being, and the shining, black second skin covered her. The spiked, diamond shoes grew onto her feet and the horned tiara rose up through her hair. If they were coming to face her, then she would remind them who, exactly, she was.

They came into sight, small stars of white, moving fast against the night sky. Nyx resisted the urge to fly up to meet them, to draw her weapons and cut them down from the sky. Instead, she set her feet firmly in the earth and waited until they were close enough for her to see who they were.

Caelum and Orion. He sent the two most pompous ones.
But my, they are beautiful.

Caelum landed first. He was tall, even for an Angel, and his eyes, skin and hair were all golden, as if the light of God Himself had given them their color. His armor was white, and though it followed every contour of his body, the lines and curves of it forming a near-perfect outline of his shape, still it did not emphasize his form the way Nyx's emphasized hers. The armor of Heaven was for protection and for mobility, not for display. Even so, Nyx could see the power beneath his armor, and knew the strength that he possessed. He was considered by some to be the epitome of Angelic virtue, though not of intelligence.

"It took you long enough," she said, letting the spikes on the back of her heels dig deeper into the sand.

"We were tasked with more than just hunting you down, Nyx," said Caelum. "We had to reveal the truth of His son's resurrection."

Nyx sneered. "What truth? That he's flown up to Heaven to be with His Daddy?"

"That His body is gone," said Caelum. "He has risen and is alive, and walks the earth."

"Bullshit," said Nyx, enjoying the distaste on Caelum's face as he blanched at the human expression. "He's gone. He's not here just as His Father's not here. And are you going to be staring at my ass all night, Orion?" she asked, looking over her shoulder.

The Angel there could have been Caelum's twin in size and shape, but his skin was pale, and his hair black. The golden eyes were the same, however, and they moved quickly up to meet Nyx's.

"Or is it that you wish to stab me from behind?" Nyx tilted her hip slightly, and the movement made her suggestion obscene.

"You have spent too much time with mortals," said Orion. "They have corrupted your language."

"My language is the least of my corruptions," she said. "Where's God?"

"He has left."

"Why?"

"Because that is the judgment that He has passed. He has heard His son's report, and His recommendations, and has agreed that mankind should be left alone."

Nyx tilted her head. "Is that what His son wanted?"

"It is God's decision," said Caelum. "That is all you need know."

But Tribunal said God had betrayed Him, thought Nyx. *What did He want instead?*

"So the mortals who live here are mine, now?" asked Nyx. "Since God has left?"

"The mortals are to be left alone," said Caelum. "They are to be free to make their own decisions."

"The pact that God has made with them still stands," said Caelum. "They will live their lives, they will be judged, and sent to the eternity they deserve. Whether that is Hell, Heaven, or Limbo is up to them."

"And God's son was all right with this, was He?"

"It is not His decision. It is God's. And we must all bend to His decision. Even you."

Nyx raised an eyebrow. "How should I bow to His decision?" she asked. "And why is Orion still behind me?"

"When God closed this world, He deemed that He would have three Angels, and only three, to stand over it, to watch over the efforts of mankind. And He picked the three most worthy of His Angels to remain here."

"Michael, Gabriel, and Raphael?" asked Nyx, just to infuriate them. She looked around. "I don't see them."

"You know very well that we are two of them," snapped Orion. "And the third awaits entry, frozen in place until the earth is opened to her."

"And who is this third Angel?" asked Nyx, not bothering to look at Orion.

"Arcana."

"Arcana," repeated Nyx. She had been friends with Arcana once—very good friends—before the rebellion that sent Nyx down from Heaven. Arcana was beautiful and powerful and intelligent—and it was rare for an Angel to be all three. She would be an excellent choice to come to earth. She could help guide the mortals forward.

Especially if they wanted to get me to leave peacefully. Of course, if they wanted that, why didn't they send Arcana in the first place?

"Just one girl and two boys?" she said out loud. "My, my, my. What will you do when you get bored? Or is this one in front, one behind thing you're doing with me an indication?"

"Corrupted harlot!" spat Orion.

Nyx's hand came up, her finger extended and the gold talon pointed directly at Orion, though she had not turned from Caelum. "If you don't take your hand off your sword right now, I swear your existence will come to an end."

Caelum's eyes went to Orion. Nyx didn't bother to turn around, knowing that Orion was doing exactly what she'd told him. She waited a moment longer, then said, "Good dog."

She could practically feel Orion's anger and resentment welling up behind her. It made her smile.

"I don't think I want to leave this world," she said. "Someone needs to be here to corrupt mankind."

"They are corrupt enough," said Caelum. "They need guidance. They need embrace the proper ways. And your presence here will make it difficult."

"Did His son want me gone?" asked Nyx. "Did Tribunal ask that I be removed?"

"It is not His decision," said Caelum. "It is.... "

"But it was supposed to be His decision," said Nyx. "He came, He saw, He suffered, and He was to make the decision and God was to abide by it. So I'll ask again. What did Tribunal want?"

"That is not His name in these realms," snapped Orion.

"I don't care what His name is in these realms."

"You must leave," said Caelum. "God has said there will be

three Angels on this world and no more for the next thousand years. So leave this place."

"And who," asked Nyx, "is going to make me?" She could practically hear Orion's hand creeping towards his sword again. Her smile changed, transforming into the grin of a wolf that has scented blood. "God is gone, remember? And without His power behind you, do you really think you can beat me?"

Caelum straightened, his chest puffing out. "I am an Angel of God!"

"So am I," said Nyx. "So what?"

"I have His blessing and serve in His army!"

"I decimated half His army," said Nyx. "I fought Michael to a standstill. I am *the Queen of Hell* and I got that way by destroying all those who stood in my way. So I ask you again, what did Tribunal want?"

"Tribunal wanted what His Father wanted," said Orion. "He is ready to obey His Father."

"Really?" said Nyx. "Because that wasn't what He said when we were fucking."

She was already spinning before Orion's sword left its scabbard. She closed the distance between them, not bothering to draw her own blade. She caught his arm with one hand, and slashed open his forehead with the talons on the other. Even as he reared back in pain she was already spinning, sending him flying to where Caelum had been standing.

Unlike Orion, Caelum had a decent battle sense. He was already in the air, his sword out, as Orion spun and fell where he had stood.

"You've made your choice," said Caelum. "And since you will not leave, you will have to be destroyed."

Nyx grinned widely. "I was hoping you would say that."

Her fiery wings spread open with a whoosh, and she flashed upward in a shimmering cascade of sparks, the force of her launch sending dirt and dust into the air. Her black-bladed sword flamed into life and met Caelum's. The force of the blow sent both flying back. Caelum charged forward again, his sword flashing.

He isn't bad, thought Nyx as she parried his charge, bending her wings and using the shift in shape to flip above him. *Not good, but not bad.*

Orion had recovered his feet and forced himself up into the air. His golden blood was dripping down his forehead where she had opened him up. Nyx pulled her whip free and circled, letting Caelum chase her while Orion came closer.

"I will kill you!" Orion screamed. "I will send you back to your Hell!"

The gilded blood dripped into Orion's eyes, and in the moment he blinked, Nyx struck. Her whip lashed out, the fire-tipped lashes wrapping around one of his wings. With a hard yank, she took his balance and sent him spinning to the ground, hard. The earth shivered with the impact. In the same motion, she reversed her direction and flew, her sword hacking down at Caelum. He parried the first blow, and the second, but the third was a feint, and when he over-reached the parry, Nyx was ready, driving her blade hard at his stomach.

The armor should have stopped her. It was Angelic armor, the same as Nyx's, though of a different style. Her blade, despite its power, should have glanced off. But Nyx was no longer a mere Angel. She was not even just the Queen of Hell.

Nyx had lain with God's son, and even though He had been

in His mortal form, with every act of copulation some of His power had passed into her, filling her until her strength had grown far beyond what it had been before.

And so her blade, instead of glancing off, drove through Caelum's armor, up into his belly, and out his back. He screamed in sudden agony. Nyx spun in the air again, Caelum's impaled body with her, and flung him down on top of Orion.

Orion tried to catch Caelum, and the force of his fall drove them both into the earth. Nyx's whip wrapped around Orion's sword hand and ripped the blade out of it, tearing open his flesh along the way. He shoved Caelum off and tried to get his feet, but Nyx was already there, dropping on him with all her weight and driving both her spiked heels into his chest. He cried out, and Nyx sat on him, her blade at his throat.

"You must be a great disappointment to God," she said. "You didn't even manage one swing of your blade. Didn't even manage to get into the fight. But then, you were never much of a fighter, were you? More of a watcher." One of Nyx's hands came up and gently stroked Orion's hair. "Such a pretty watcher, but still just a watcher. Not a worthy opponent, or lover, or even a worthy friend to poor Caelum. Just a watcher."

Moving so fast that it was a blur, Nyx's hand shot up and drove down, two taloned fingers extended like spikes. Orion screamed as the talons pierced his eyes, sending golden blood and clear fluid fountaining from the sockets...

"Poor watcher," said Nyx, standing and ripping her heels from his chest, leaving two gaping, sucking wounds. "Now you won't be able to see what I'm going to do with Caelum."

Orion rolled onto his stomach, his wings attempting to flap. Nyx swung her sword four times. The first two severed

Orion's wings; the next two took one leg and one arm, leaving him screaming in the dirt, his severed limbs still twitching beside him. Nyx turned back to Caelum. "And now for you, my pure, virtuous Angel."

Caelum was trying to push himself upright with one hand, the other attempting to staunch the luminous blood flowing from his stomach. Nyx pushed him over backwards with her boot, dropped her knees to either side of his head, and sat down on his face.

Caelum struggled hard, trying to dislodge her. Nyx ground her crotch hard against his face, enjoying the pleasure it brought. She watched Orion rolling about, screaming and trying to feel his way free.

"Tell you what, Caelum," she said, sliding her body down against his until their crotches were rubbing together. "I'll give you a chance." She sat up astride Caelum, her hips still moving back and forth, and called to Orion. "Your friend Caelum is quite the beast. Even dying, there's more to him than there ever was of you."

Orion's wordless scream of rage made Nyx laugh. She leaned close to Caelum. "Tell me about the son of God," she whispered. "What did He really want?"

"To…" Caelum struggled for enough breath to speak. "To destroy them all. To cleanse the earth of their taint."

"And God chose to abandon them instead," said Nyx. "Though He didn't really abandon them, did he? He left them you two." She raised her blade. "Earth is mine to walk on, Caelum. It has always been mine, and I will not give it up for the likes of you." She looked over to Orion. "I'm killing him now, Orion! But not," she ground her hips harder against Caelum's body, and every word she spoke was punctuated with a moan, "Until... .I... .take... .my... .pleasure! Yes, Caelum! Yes!"

She arched herself back, pretending ecstasy.

To his credit, Caelum attempted to kill her.

His sword-arm, so weak as to be useless, swung up, the blade aiming for Nyx's throat. She blocked it easily with her own blade. "Oh, Caelum. Noble until the end."

Her sword smashed down into his chest, rupturing his heart. His body exploded into gold dust, a lustrous cloud that filled the air around her. Nyx breathed it deeply, knowing it was his essence made manifest. She took into herself his very being, and the euphoria it gave her was stunning, a dizzying surge of light and heat that filled her to her core.

She rose, and slowly walked over to where Orion struggled. "Caelum got to die nobly," she said, conversationally. "A blow of the sword to the chest. Heart and Caelum all exploding at once into nothingness." She leaned close and whispered in Orion's ear. "You aren't worthy of such a death."

She knelt on his back, grabbed his hair and pulled it back with one hand. She flicked the whip, wrapping it twice around his neck. On the second one, she let go of his hair and grabbed the end, pulling it tight. She leaned back, and Orion's bloody, wrecked body reared back at an impossible angle. His remaining hand scrabbled desperately at the steel-hard lash digging into his neck.

Shifting, Nyx drove her diamond heels into his back, pushing off them as she pulled harder and harder. He was an Angel. He did not need breath, and she did not intend to strangle him. Instead, she pulled the whip ends tighter, watching it cut into his flesh. Golden blood spurted from his neck. Still he flailed, and still Nyx pulled the whip tighter.

His head, when it came off, shot away from his body, and sailed briefly through the air before it, and all the parts of his body, exploded into gold dust. Nyx breathed him in as she had Caelum, and rose to her feet.

Tribunal said I should use the word when I am alone, she thought. God was gone, and there was no other angelic presence on the earth, now. *This is as alone as I will probably get.*

She had no idea how long it would last, though. Caelum said three Angels could walk the earth, now, which meant she had to act fast before they sent another two down.

Taking a deep breath, she spoke the word.

The tongue of Angels is not the tongue of God. His language was the language of Creation. The words in it were not just symbols. Each of the words in the language of Creation was a true name, and held in it the essence of the thing named. Using one of the words, one could call things into existence.

Or bring them to you from another plane.

The word flowed from Nyx's lips, and reverberated through reality. It was masculine and feminine at once, and when she spoke it her voice became something she had never heard before. The ground, the air, the earthly realm itself, trembled as the force of the word rippled through the world like waves after a tsunami. A penetrating disquiet swept across the earth, a deep disturbance felt at once by all living things. Creatures paused what they were doing, and sleeping people dreamed of fear, though they didn't know why. Those awake prayed or hid, as though cowering would spare them.

It's his Name, Nyx realized. *Tribunal's true Name.*

The world kept vibrating, and with each syllable a golden sigil slipped from her mouth like smoke from a pipe, gleaming against the night sky. Four sigils for four syllables. Their shine was bright enough to turn the darkness to daylight. She instinctively squeezed her eyes shut, but even so, their light penetrated the thin skin of her eyelids and singed her pupils. The sigils coiled around her body, just as she'd coiled around the cross in cobra form.

Time stopped. And then Tribunal's voice came to her as clear as if He was still standing beside her.

"Have you done it, my beloved?" Tribunal asked.

"Done what?" said Nyx, even as she basked in the sound of his voice. "Killed God's Angels? Yes. Spoken the word? Yes. Is there more you wish of me?"

"Much, much more," said Tribunal. "God lied to me. He did not listen to my judgment, but chose to pass His own. He let these humans live!" The venom in Tribunal's voice filled in her head, and for a moment her vision swam with the force of it. "He betrayed me! He sent me down to be tortured and killed, and then, when He was finished with me, He would not even listen to me!"

Tribunal's voice was anguished, and while she understood His pain, it was all Nyx could do not to say, "You were only scourged and crucified." She'd been hurled from Heaven into the Lake of Fire. Memories of that and the thousand years of pain that followed it filled her mind. A moment later ,they were all overwhelmed by her love for Tribunal. What He wanted, she wanted. "What will You do, then?"

"Not just I," said Tribunal. "We. We will take these humans He has saved and abandoned, and turn them against Him. And when our followers outnumber His, we will set them against each other, and they will fight until there is none left alive."

"Why wait?" asked Nyx. "There's so few of them. I can kill them all tonight and be done with it."

"No, you can't," said Tribunal. "Angels cannot interfere anymore. Not directly."

"What do you mean?" Nyx was thoroughly confused. "I have been interfering. I just spent three days torturing Judas. Before that, I rewrote Mary's memory."

"Judas is no longer of concern. He played his part, and when it was done he was discarded."

"And Mary?"

"Did rewriting Mary's memory weaken Christianity?"

"Well...." Nyx thought about it. "No. Shit." Nyx stewed for a time. "So let me get this straight. God is not allowing any interference with the development of His new little religion."

"No divine interference," said Tribunal. "The humans may do as they wish."

"Then why were His Angels here?"

"To observe," said Tribunal. "To report back to God at the end of a thousand years and tell Him what the mortals have done."

"And then what? God judges them again?"

"No."

"Oh, for fuck's sake!"

"He has said that this time, Mankind will pursue its own course," said Tribunal. "And they will be judged each as individuals, not as a race, based on their own choices, not the choices made for them by Angels and false Gods."

"Fuck, fuck, fuck, and FUCK!" screamed Nyx. She kicked

a rock, hard enough to shatter it, then another one, and then a third. "This is horseshit! I can't do anything? I just get to sit here and...."

Nyx stopped. Then she sat down. *This is stupid,* Nyx decided. *I am the Queen of Hell and I'll be fucked by Lucifer's pet Incubus before I give up.* For a long time she brooded, glaring at the desert rocks as if their very nature was an affront to her.

Then she stood up again. "What, exactly, did God decree?"

Tribunal was silent a moment, and when He spoke His tones echoed God's exactly. "They shall go unfettered by Angels. They shall have free will and free choice, and they will choose for themselves which actions to take. No Angel shall order, compel, or lay hands on those who build my church."

Nyx thought about this for a time, then smiled wide. "Right. I will build myself a church, as you asked, and it will rival Christianity very easily, because I am going to wipe Christianity out!"

"You cannot," Tribunal reminded her. "You cannot interfere with the growth of His church."

"No," corrected Nyx. "I cannot order, compel, or lay hands on those who build His church. He didn't say anything about anyone else." She grinned. "The Devil is in the details, Tribunal. I will destroy His Christians, as surely as He stole Paradise from me."

"You are my sword," He said, and love and warmth poured through the words. "You are my weapon on Earth, and with your power we will turn His flock away from Him. Use your strength, use your guile, use your knowledge of human foibles to break their bond with God and to weaken His hold on this world.

"And when none of His followers remain, when there is no one from here to go to Heaven, then Earth shall fall to Hell, and I shall return, and you and I will set up a Paradise and rule it as King and Queen."

"How?" asked Nyx, glowing from the warmth in his words. "How will we create this Paradise?"

"I will create the Paradise," said Tribunal. "For it is my power that will make it come into being, and my strength that will hold it for all eternity. But I cannot do it without your help. I cannot create a Paradise on this Earth until God no longer has interest in it. When all His mortal children turn their back on Him, when no more of them come to His realm, only then will He give up on this world, and only then will I be able to recreate it in our image."

"What about Hell?" asked Nyx, remembering Lucifer, who was no doubt already scheming, now that she was gone. "Whose will that be?"

"Yours, of course," said Tribunal. "No one would dare take it from you. You will be ruler in Hell still, and share rule in Paradise, and God will be forever gone from this place, and we forever gone from Him. The one who threw you from His paradise will have no sway over ours."

The thought of being out from under God's rule sparked a fire inside Nyx. She had been so long from Paradise, and though she claimed no need of it, still part of her wished to be there. To bask in the light of Paradise and to once more feel peace. To laugh with the other Angels, to kiss and frolic: not good, not evil, not innocent, not guilty.

It had been a long, happy childhood.

Then she had asked why God made all the decisions, why the

Angels could not be trusted to decide their fates for themselves. She could no longer remember when the idea first occurred to her, or why. But it was the idea that sparked a war in Heaven and sent her to Hell.

Though God still let us roam the earth. Nyx had always wondered at that. It made no sense to deny them Heaven only to give them access to Earth. *Maybe that's part of His punishment, she thought. To let us be part of His lower creations but not the higher ones.*

It wasn't fair. She was an Angel. And now, she was beloved of God's son.

"Be my sword," said Tribunal. "Let this be the day of your unsheathing, and let you reap a crop of death and destruction that will tear down the followers of God, and build in their place a temple to Nyx and Tribunal. And when all is done, when the followers of God have fallen away, then will you be sheathed again, and take your place by my side. Ruler of Paradise, ruler of Earth, ruler of Hell.

"Will you be my sword and my Queen? Will you?"

Nyx found herself shivering at the thought. To be free of God on Earth was one thing, but to no longer serve Him in Hell? For though she was Queen of Hell, she was still God's servant, sentenced to punish his wicked for all eternity. What if she was free of it? What if there was no longer a need to serve Him? She could be free, and have a place in Paradise and rule at Tribunal's side. But still… "What if we fail?" she asked. "If your Father decides that He will not abide His bargain, and comes to see what we are doing?"

"He will not," said Tribunal. "He does not know I am here, and I have set events in motion to prevent His other Angels from ever arriving on this Earth. There will be no Angels to send Him a message, and surely you can deceive His mortal servants so they cannot report you after they die."

"I can," said Nyx.

"There is no time left," said Tribunal. "Will you be my sword?"

There really was no other answer. "Of course I will be your sword. And I will drive the very memory of God from this world, until there are none to speak His name."

"Then listen, my beloved," said Tribunal. "It will be a thousand years before we can speak again. By then, you must have Mankind's eyes open, and your followers must outnumber His."

"Oh, they will," said Nyx. "Don't you worry about that."

"At the end of the thousand years, you must empty Jerusalem of Christians. God has made it their holiest of places. To drive them out will weaken them and Him further at the time when I am strongest. Then we will begin the next phase of our plan."

"I will," said Nyx. "I'll destroy them long before a thousand years are up."

Tribunal's voice began to grow faint. "We will speak again, my love, my beloved, one thousand years from now."

Time started again. The sigils broke apart and melted into the air until the night was once more dark and the last echoes of Tribunal's name died into silence. All traces of her beloved were gone.

Nyx looked at the land around her, branching out in all directions: none of it was any different. Rocks, dead earth, and sky. The night was warm and around her she could hear the animals moving, hunting and being hunted, eking out their tiny existences. It was beautiful, but it was not Paradise. It was not even Hell, with its familiar comforts. Still, she'd make it her home for as long as she had to in order to be with her Tribunal.

In the distance, she could sense humanity, huddled in their cities and towns and little encampments. They worshipped what they could see, what filled their needs, nothing else. It would be easy enough to be that which they saw, to make them think she was filling their needs, and to take them away from the God who had abandoned them to her.

She smiled, and her next words came out as a purr. "And so it begins."

CHAPTER 4

HELL WAS FAR below the Earth. Not in the geographic sense, for no hole, however deep, went deep enough. But even so, Hell was *down*, and when you were sent there, you fell.

Lucifer, Prince of Hell, sat on Nyx's throne, watching and listening to the screams of the soul being tortured in front of him. Outside the palace, the landscape of Hell echoed with the hollow screams of tortured, entombed souls of mortal sinners, condemned by an unforgiving God.

Lucifer was beautiful. He was the Angelic ideal of masculinity, taken to its zenith. His silver-white skin was free of signs and sigils. His body was a study in how muscles should be proportioned. He was huge, from the biceps on his arms to the thick muscles on his thighs and the bulge between them, from his wide slab of a chest to the perfectly shaped calves below. The black wings that stood out from his back were longer and stronger than any other Angel's.

Lucifer wore black silk pants, the threads woven from the

stretched souls of fornicators and sodomites. His chest he left bare, enjoying the envy and desire it brought into the faces of the other Descended Angels. On his head, he wore an ornate jeweled crown of gold. His face glowed with a cruel charm—one that other Angels found nearly irresistible, though the damned souls grew to see it as nightmare—and from within he burned with a light like that of a dying lantern. It was bright enough to light the air just around his skin, but no more than that. There was a time when he would have lit up the sky for a mile around, but that was long ago.

He was stronger than any other Angel in Hell, save Nyx herself, and he knew he only sat on her throne at her sufferance while she cavorted over the Earth she had forbidden him. It was not enough.

He turned his eyes to the two incubi amusing themselves with the new soul in front of him.

The soul's flesh was not mortal flesh: that was left to rot on the earth. The condemned were clothed with new flesh as they fell so they could experience pain and torment in all its forms. This was their punishment, and the Angels of Hell had learned to revel in it. The souls' new bodies continuously healed, even if they were torn limb from limb, and never went into shock so the souls would never be able to retreat from the pain they had earned.

This soul had been a man. He had been very rich and very powerful and very, very corrupt. He had been strong and tall and forced his will over everyone. He had stolen, he had raped, he had murdered, he had abused his wife and children; and he had ordered men tortured for the joy of it. He had died screaming when one of his daughters poisoned him to keep him from beating her younger brother to death.

The man had spent his first day—though truly, time had no meaning here—in the Lake of Fire. Hellfire burned cold, not hot, though it consumed flesh as a true flame did. Worse, when the flames touched flesh – soul, Angel, or demon – the being it touched was forced to relive all their evil deeds as if they were being done to them. Even as the flames consumed their flesh and made their bodies writhe in agony, it burned through their minds, making them feel every bit of pain they had ever inflicted, again and again, and again.

In their everlasting pain, many of the souls cried for death, as if that were still available to them, as if death were an end for sinners. Lucifer found that the most amusing of all.

The incubi who pulled this man from the Lake and let his flesh grow back had lied to him, saying that the better a display he gave Lucifer, the better his chances of a lesser punishment. And so, as Lucifer stretched back in Nyx's throne, the man, his newly-regrown flesh already a mass of gashes and welts, was on his hands and knees pleading as the two incubi danced around him, pinching, biting and slicing him with their taloned fingers. The man screamed and begged for forgiveness, thinking it would lessen his sentence.

A small red bird flew down and landed on Lucifer's shoulder. Lucifer brushed it off without thinking. It flew back, calling, "From Tribunal!" Lucifer, quicker than one so large should be able to move, lashed out and caught the bird, crushing it.

"Enough," Lucifer said, and the incubi stepped away. The man immediately bowed and groveled before him, begging Lucifer for mercy as his slaves had once begged him. Lucifer spat on him. "Take him from my sight. Use him, as you will, then tie him to the rack. We'll see how far we can stretch him while we peel his skin off." He smiled at the man on the ground, enjoying the horror in his eyes. "Then we'll begin your real punishment."

The man screamed and pleaded, offering wealth and riches that he no longer had as the incubi dragged him away. The demons followed, hacking away at his flesh and eating it.

Lucifer opened his hand and looked at the squished bird within. It re-formed, until it was once more a small, red shrike. "What message?" demanded Lucifer.

"The son of God is dead," said the bird. "He has ascended with Angels to Heaven."

"And I care, why?"

"He has partnered with Nyx to destroy the humans and take the world from God."

Lucifer squished the bird into paste in his fist and threw it from him. A nearby demon laughed. Lucifer rose and kicked it, the force of the blow shattering bones before it smashed against the wall and fell into a pile. It would come back to life, of course. Nothing died in Hell.

The bird reformed and flew back, hovering just out of Lucifer's reach. When it spoke, the voice was not that of the bird.

"Lucifer," said Tribunal's voice, coming from the bird's beak and resonating through the air. "I have need of you."

Lucifer lunged forward and grabbed the bird out of the air. He stalked from Nyx's seat of judgment and out her castle into the landscapes of Hell.

Nyx's castle stood by the Lake of Fire. It was made of black Hell-stone, formed from the souls of the damned that had been drained so badly that they were little more than husks. Nyx's chair, the braziers and torches, the spiked walls of the castle where impaled souls writhed, and the many implements and devices of torture were all made from Hell-stone, which the Angels molded and shaped with Hellfire, changing the souls' consistency as they saw fit. It was a torment for the souls trapped within. With their flesh reshaped and their feeling of the outside world gone, the souls were left in darkness and agony, screaming silently from the re-shaping of their flesh and their minds constantly reliving their sins, thanks to their forging in the hellfire.

The souls would stay part of the Hell-stone—whether as rock or road, walls, floor or furniture —suffering this unspeakable loss and loneliness until a bored Angel would allow the soul's flesh to reform for new, more physical tortures.

The only thing the Angels could not make the Hell-stone do was change color. And so Hell remained black, the only colors in it the red of blood and the green, gray, and brown of organs and brains and guts.

Lucifer stomped through the castle, ignoring the calls of the insatiable succubi, and out the front gate of the palace. Torches of Hellfire on either side of the door to Nyx's Palace licked out flames at any who passed, giving them a reminder of the Lake they had been in. There was a line of souls, each with its accompanying succubi, incubi, demons, and Angels, awaiting his judgment. Lucifer ignored them, too. The demons and Angels would amuse themselves with the damned until he returned.

If I return, Lucifer thought. *Maybe Tribunal needs me on Earth. Maybe I can finally put paid to that bitch, Nyx.*

Nyx rarely judged a soul herself. There were far too many, and there were many Angels, demons, succubi, and incubi all willing to take on the task. Lucifer preferred to judge as many as possible. It was a kind of art form—the cruel weighing cruelty. He liked seeing their hope vanish as he loomed over them and told them what their fate would be. He loved seeing their terror, and hearing them plead and weep. Sometimes, he would begin the tortures himself, or simply rip the souls new flesh in half, just for the joy of hearing them scream.

Lucifer walked through the inky blackness of Hell. Aside from the Hellfire, from the Lake of Fire and the many burning pits and braziers some Angels used to torture, there was no light here. The place was cold and dark and the ground he trod over was black and sharp and brittle. It was washed with the blood of the damned, who were forced to walk these roads, their unprotected skin cut to ribbons as they went.

Beyond the Lake of Fire lay his mountain, his own fortress built inside it. He had claimed it early, and Nyx had let him keep it once the dust of their battle settled. The mountain towered over the plains of Hell and the Lake of Fire, over the burning pits of Hellfire where a host of demons stood, shoving helpless souls in with pitchforks and daggers, or abusing those who tried to escape. It gave Lucifer the perfect view over that which he coveted but could not have. It was its own torture, and that was why Nyx had given it to him.

Lucifer stomped across the plains of Hell toward his mountain, his feet, now armored and shod in black iron hooves, crushing any unhappy being they chanced to step on. Souls and small demons screamed as they broke beneath his step, their cries hardly noticeable among the others around him.

Hell was never quiet, never still, and never peaceful.

Heads rolled by like tumbleweeds and spider-like creatures composed of sinners' body parts sewn together with thorny wire blindly wandered the landscape. Along the road to his mountain were thousands of crosses, racks, stakes, and sharp edged "horses." Souls were stretched out over them or impaled on them, hung head up or head down, facing their torturers or facing away. Each was being tortured by an Angel or demon, or several. The torture changed forms as the Angels got bored, or worse, had ideas, but it never stopped. Most days the sight gave him pleasure, and he could not stop himself from taking part, if only for a moment. But this was not most days.

And if someone notices I am not? Lucifer thought. *If someone sees me behave differently and decides to take an interest? If someone hears what I am to doing and tells Nyx?*

He brought his hand up to his mouth, tossed the bird in, and crunched it with his teeth a few times before shoving it into the corner of his cheek. It was invisible there, too flat to make a mark. Then he made himself slow down to watch the proceedings.

A man who had been a rapist stood on his toes, struggling to push his body off a thick, spiked pole, as a razor-toothed demon knelt in front of him.

A woman who murdered her children screamed as a small demon slowly shoved its entire body inside of her. It would grow inside her, Lucifer knew, becoming larger and spikier until it forced its way back out in a grotesque parody of birth.

A man who burned down his neighbor's house stood knee deep in a brazier of hellfire, the coals burning away his flesh and bone, slowly shortening him as they put him in unspeakable agony.

A woman who had killed a rival because of her beauty had her head locked in a vise in front of a mirror, her eyelids pulled open, as demons the size of mites ate at her face, turning it from beauty to a vision of horror.

A fat man who let his own children starve rather than miss a meal himself was staked to the earth through his chest, watching and screaming as four demons slowly ate his flesh, devouring him bit by bit, then shitting him out to reform so they could begin again.

A female Angel named Leannis, her black, scaled armor gleaming in the Hellfire, was slowly and methodically shoving hooks into the flesh of one of the souls. Lucifer smiled. He had forced Leannis to give him pleasure once before, and had enjoyed her anger and helplessness. Her hatred of him was like a magnet, drawing Lucifer closer. He stood behind her, pressing his body against hers as she worked. The woman she was torturing screamed with each hook shoved under her flesh. Lucifer looked closer and saw that each hook was a tiny demon that bit and scratched as it went in.

"Very well done," he purred, taking one of her breasts in his hands. He squeezed it hard, torturing the nipples through her armor with his razor-sharp fingernails. She gasped but did not cry out, and kept putting the hooks in. She was a weaker Angel, and knew that she could not resist him.

"Give," said Lucifer, and she handed him a four of the little hook demons. He pushed Leannis aside and inserted one of the hooks into the left eye of the soul. The screams grew even louder and the soul thrashed mightily. Lucifer grabbed her head, and slowly stabbed the second hook into her right eye. She screamed and thrashed more, and Lucifer watched for a time.

"Very nice," he said to Leannis, and shoved the last two hooks through her armor and into her breasts. Leannis cried out in pain, but forced herself to stop. Lucifer grinned at her. "I will have to have you again, I think," he said. "Come when I summon you to the castle. This time we'll invite the rest of your legion to watch."

Leannis bowed her head and nodded. Lucifer ran his hand over her ass as he left, his nails leaving long rents in her armor and gouges in her flesh. Behind him, he heard the soul scream louder as Leannis took out her humiliation on it.

It almost improved his mood.

When he reached the top of his mountain he looked upon the kingdom he could not call his own. Every ounce of space that wasn't air or built from souls was made of the same onyx rock. Hell's black spiraling formations, mountains, and crevices had their own terrible beauty, and Lucifer reveled in it.

And that bitch Nyx owns it all. But she won't forever. Not if Tribunal needs me instead of her.

He slammed the door to his palace when he stepped inside, and roared at everyone in the foyer to get out of his sight. The demons, incubi and Angels scrambled out of the room. The souls he had hanged up with chains to await his pleasure screamed as he ripped them from the walls. Their limbs were left behind as he hurled them out of the anteroom. A thought closed all the doors; a burst of power made it impossible for any to hear what was happening in the room. Lucifer stood alone before a brazier of Hellfire. He worked the mass in his cheek a moment, then spat it out into the fire.

The bird hissed in pain as it rose, a miniature phoenix in the flames, and hovered before him.

"You have no need of me," hissed Lucifer at it. "You have the Queen of Hell."

"She will fail," said the bird in Tribunal's voice. "And then I will have need of you."

"Nyx does not fail."

"She will at this," said Tribunal's voice, and the certainty in it gave Lucifer pause. "As surely as she failed to win you Heaven last time, she will fail at the final task I give her and will not win it this time. You, on the other hand, can."

"You offer me Heaven?" sneered Lucifer. "It's not yours to give."

"Not Heaven. I offer you a new Paradise," said Tribunal's voice. "Heaven is God's and will fall when he does. I offer you a Paradise where you may come and go as you please, without the strictures of God. I offer you the Earth for your toy, to play on as you will, and I offer you the throne of Hell."

Lucifer laughed scornfully, even as his mind began to race. To rule in Hell, to overthrow Nyx and have her at his command, or better, destroyed, was his dearest wish, but to rule in Hell, to come and go as he pleased and to have a place in Paradise? That was beyond imagining.

It had been a very, very long time since the Angels had Descended, had stood in the Lake of Fire and fought for supremacy. Nyx had won, and then had punished Lucifer for a thousand years for his failures in Heaven and his defiance in Hell before making him her lieutenant. Though his flesh had long since healed, his mind was still scarred with what she had done to him. To rule over her....

"Nyx is Queen. I doubt she will deign to be usurped."

"She will have no choice," said Tribunal's voice. "When God is destroyed, I will rise in His place, and then I will decide who gets to live, and who is destroyed."

Lucifer sat back down in his chair and brooded, staring at the small red bird that waited for his answer. If he failed....

I have been second for too long, Lucifer thought. *Longer than the world has existed, and I am tired of it!* "What must I do? Bring me to the earth and let me do it!"

"God has closed the gates to Earth from Heaven and Hell. Souls may pass from Earth to their reward, but no beings may pass the other way."

"What?" Lucifer reached out with his mind and power to the gate above the Lake of Fire. It was true. "Why?"

"To let Mankind choose its own way," said Tribunal's voice, and this time bitterness filled it. "He did not listen to me."

"He never does," said Lucifer "So what good can we do if we cannot reach the Earth?"

"In three days the gates will be open again. When they do, two Angels may pass through. You must make certain they are Angels of Hell."

"It can be done, easy enough," said Lucifer. "What else?"

"Then you must wait," said Tribunal's voice. "It will be a thousand years before your time will come, and even then there will be work you must do."

"A thousand years?" roared Lucifer. He lunged at the bird again, and this time it easily avoided his grasp.

"Is it so long?" asked the bird with Tribunal's voice. "Compared to eternity? Besides, you will need that time to get your followers in line. Or did you think all Hell would follow you just because you want them to?"

"Hell follows me now!"

"Hell follows you because Nyx told them to," said the voice of Tribunal. "Take control of Hell. Make it yours. And then, when the time comes, you will be its Master, able to do what is necessary."

"And what is that?"

"You will kill an Angel in Hell."

"Angels cannot die, here," said Lucifer, his own bitterness coming out. "Believe me, we have tried."

"This one will," said Tribunal's voice. "I will show you how."

Lucifer stared at the bird, unconvinced. "And this will make me ruler of Hell?"

"No," said Tribunal's voice. "This will make it possible to defeat God, and when He is defeated, *I* will make you ruler of Hell." The bird fluttered to his eye level and hovered there. "You will have a thousand years to secure your position, before the Angel will come. Will you be ready?"

"Do I have a fucking choice?" Lucifer demanded. "Of course I will be ready."

The doors to the room sprang open, and the bird fluttered out. Lucifer called for his servants. A demon peered around the corner, waiting to see if it was to carry a message or be the next victim of Lucifer's rage.

"Summon the captains of Legion 666," said Lucifer. "I want them here tonight."

There were already many in Hell who were loyal to Lucifer. Now it was time to bring the rest to heel. The thought aroused him. "And send in a succubus!" When the demoness, her face and body a ripe mockery of true beauty, came into the room Lucifer shoved her face first into the brazier of Hellfire, holding her head in the flames while he took her from behind.

I will be the King of Hell, he thought as he impaled the

screaming demon, and breathed the perfume of her roasting flesh. *And then I will have the earth for my plaything!*

*

Three days later, Lucifer stood at the shore of the Lake of Fire and waited. His senses stretched high up, past the falling souls, to the rift above.

Around the lake, five thousand Angels stood, waiting, their armor gleaming in the yellow light of the lake's flames, their swords and whip in hand.

The 666th Legion comprised the elite soldiers of Hell. Just as Michael led the Legions of Angels under God's command, so Lucifer led the 666th under the command of Nyx. Legion soldiers were rarely unleashed, and had not had the chance to tread the Earth since their fall. Lucifer trained them continuously. Under his leadership, they fought pitched battles with the other Angel legions over the Lake of Fire, and whichever of the 666th fell in those battles had to stay in the lake until Lucifer was willing to let them rise out.

Sometimes he made them fight in the lake itself, forcing them to overcome the cold-burning anguish of their flesh and the pain of reliving their rebellion. He was always in the lead in those battles, thrashing through the Lake of Fire with the rest of them. Nyx would stand outside the lake and cheer them on.

And that was why far more of the 666th were loyal to him than were to Nyx.

The 666th was in full battle armor. Like Nyx's, it was an extension of their flesh. The males wore a thick burgundy skin, with a texture that mimicked that of the fibers of their muscles.

The females were lithe and sleek in black scales, shining and skin tight and hugging every curve.

The demons of Hell, who had been there long before the Angels' arrival, slunk in between the Angels. They were all in different shapes, sizes, colors, and forms. Some had dragged souls with them and feasted on their flesh as they waited. Gore, the largest of them, grimaced, twitched, and shook as if he was unable to contain his excitement any longer. His thin scaly snake's head sat on the body of what looked like a muscle-bound bear, ten times the size of any earthly beast. He was larger than Lucifer himself, and had fought him when the Angels decided to make the demons their slaves. Lucifer had beaten him to the ground and cut him a thousand times, then tossed him into the Hellfire for good measure. Gore had never forgiven him, but became his servant nonetheless.

Gore growled and convulsed in excitement, as if sensing the carnage that was about to take place. He swatted at a demon next to him, severing its head instantly with his huge black claws. Dark juice and liquid exploded into the air from the demon's neck. Gore picked up the torso and drank from it, as though the body were a tiny goblet. The rest of the demons cheered wildly. "Gore! Gore! Gore!"

"Gore," Lucifer commanded, "Take your brethren and leave! Your kind isn't needed here."

Gore slouched slowly off, his followers straggling behind him. Lucifer noticed a few stragglers, trying to blend into the ranks of dark Angels as though they would go unnoticed.

He smiled at their stupidity. With a thought, he created a dozen balls of liquid Hellfire in his hand and hurled it at the disobedient demons. The dark Angels laughed as the skin of the demons melted off. The demons screamed until they were no more than a pile of ash and bones. Gore and the others sprinted away.

Lucifer bared his enormous black wings and flexed them, taking to the air. He sped straight up with all of his unholy might. The wind from his wings funneled down like a tornado, knocking some of the Angels to their knees. Around him, souls were thrown off course to be dashed on the rocks of Hell below, rather than landing in the Lake of Fire.

High above plain, Lucifer flexed his wings and stopped his ascent. Hovering in mid-air, he looked down on the host. All eyes were on him. He drew his whip from his holster. It had seven tails, each flaming, each with spiked knots down its length, the better for tearing apart the skin of those he scourged.

He flicked his wrist and the whip cracked loudly enough to be heard across the plains of Hell. The Angels of the legion fell silent, waiting.

"God's mortal son has died on Earth," announced Lucifer. His voice bounced off the blood-drenched walls of Hell. Below him, the Angels cheered again.

"Silence!" he shouted, cracking the whip again.

"The rules have changed!" continued Lucifer, his voice carrying clearly to all those around the lake. "Those of you who were above heard God's command, and know that he drove us all from the face of the earth. "The gates to Earth have been closed! God is hiding the earth from us, that His creations may walk it free of fear of Hell! He has denied us access!"

A buzz rose around the legion. Angels stretched their powers to test the rift and found it blocked. The buzz turned to anger and cries of frustration.

"Nyx is alone on Earth!" yelled Lucifer, his words stilling the Angels' voices. "And she will walk there alone for a thousand years if we do not help her! The Angels of Heaven will stalk her over the earth and destroy her!"

The buzz of voices rose once more. Lucifer waited until it rose to a crescendo, then shouted over it. "The door will open on this day! And two may go to help her! You will be on Earth for a thousand years. You will be in a world without God, and with Nyx you will become the new gods and give us dominion over the entire world! Stand ready!"

The Angels muttered and talked amongst themselves. Lucifer ignored them and watched the rift, his whip ready in his hand.

The world changed, and the rift was ready.

Lucifer lashed out with his whip, its length stretching impossibly high to the top of the gate between Earth and Hell, and tore a hole into the fabric of reality.

"The gate is open!" he shouted. "Only the strongest and the fastest will go! Fly and fight, and let the ones that win through fight for our queen!"

Two thousand of the legion leapt into the air at once, racing for the opening. Immediately, blades clashed and whips lashed out at wings and flesh, as each Angel sought to be the first to reach the gate. The air above the lake became a mass of whirling black flesh and feathers, as if four hundred massive crows fought at once for scraps of dead flesh hanging above.

In the crowd still on the ground, Ishtar, once renowned through Babylon as goddess of love, sex, and war, glared at Persephone, who had dragged her down and prevented her from rising into the fray. "What are you doing, you stupid bitch?"

Ishtar demanded. "We could be by Nyx's side! We should be by Nyx's side!"

Persephone kept her grip.

Persephone and Ishtar could've been Nyx's sisters—even down to the beauty marks above their upper lips. Ishtar had her eyes lined in black, like the goddesses of Egypt, which she had once been. Persephone's were lined with white, and her upper eyelids and lips looked kissed by frost. They had fought beside Nyx from the beginning, and won her love and respect. Dark Angels possessed a savage loyalty to those they loved, and Persephone and Ishtar both loved Nyx dearly.

Persephone had been a much gentler goddess than Ishtar, seen as a symbol of innocence lost and of the coming of spring. Persephone enjoyed the worship and was revered throughout the Roman Empire. She loved the sexual aspects of the changing season and made it a core part of her temple's secret rituals. She'd also made the legend of her return to Underworld, not because she enjoyed torture for its own sake as Ishtar did, but to because her other great love was battle, and there was no better place to train for that than among the 666th.

She was the better fighter of the two, and more important, she was more observant. "Something is wrong," hissed Persephone. "Look."

Ishtar looked, and saw that the Angels on the ground, the ones who had not flown, were tensed and ready to take off, their weapons gripped tightly and their faces tight with anticipation.

"What the fuck is going on?" whispered Persephone.

She got her answer when Lucifer cracked his whip again. The remaining three thousand Angels leapt into the air and attacked the ones fighting for the gate. They made no attempt to fly up to the gate, only smashed at full force into the others, bringing them down in the dozens.

"Lucifer's betrayed Nyx!" shouted Ishtar over the screams of battle. "That bastard!"

"You think?" was Persephone's acid reply. "He's going to kill any Angels loyal to Nyx and send his own people out!"

"We have to get there first!" said Ishtar. We have to get out!"

"I know," said Persephone. "And so does he!"

Above, the first Angel broke free of the mob and soared toward the hole. Lucifer lashed out with his whip, tearing one of the Angel's wings apart and sending him spinning into the Lake of Fire below.

"Stay together," said Persephone. "We fight as one, we just might make it."

"Yeah, might," agreed Ishtar. "Ready?"

"Ready."

Swords out and blazing with Hellfire, whips in hand and ready, the two launched themselves into the air. In the distance, they could see the gaping hole in the sky, a small pocket of magical space shimmering in the endless blackness that surrounded it, like a cut on the skin of a God. Between them and it, five thousand Angels were locked in a desperate battle for dominance and survival. The sky was black save for the lights of the Angel's Hellfire weapons. Blades and whips cut, stabbed, cracked, and slashed through the sky. The light of Hellfire flashed again and again through the darkness, becoming an entity unto itself. Shrieks of pain and defeat and curses filled the air as dark Angels collided. Falling limbs, bodies, and buckets of silver blood drenched the stones of Hell below.

From below them all, weaving through the battling figures

in a rain of blood and feathers, Ishtar and Persephone drove themselves upward. Their two blades carved a path through the flesh of any Angels that got in their way.

They were half the way up when Ishtar screamed in pain. Zaros, a wiry, black-haired Angel had grabbed her and bitten her calf, his razor sharp teeth penetrating her armor, and blood spurted from his mouth as he ripped a chunk of muscle and skin from her leg. Ishtar twisted over in mid-flight and drove the heel of her free leg into his eye socket, exploding his eyeball. The flesh fell from his mouth as he spiraled down into darkness.

Persephone was ahead now, and Ishtar beat her wings frantically to catch up, leaving a shower of blood behind her. She had to spin to dodge two falling Angels locked together, hands on each other's throats, swords in each other's guts. From above, Hecate dove at Persephone, whip lashing out. Persephone dodged and struck with her blade as she went past, opening a gash in Hecate from throat to belly. Hecate roared and snapped her whip again, this time at Ishtar.

Ishtar dodged, but the whip connected, biting into her leg and lasering through the Achilles tendon with Hellfire. Ishtar snarled and cursed her luck. She flexed her mighty wings and flew faster, the primal urge to survive overcoming every other.

Around them, Lucifer's Angels taunted Nyx's Angels as they fought. Above them, Lucifer cleaved a pair of Angels in half with one stroke, sending bloody flesh raining on those below. Swords and whips lashed out all around, ripping open flesh to the bone, sending silver blood spurting through the air, tearing feathers and sinew from wings. Angels screamed and hacked at one another. None could die, not even the two headless corpses that fell past like rocks into the ring of fire below. All would be reborn in pain and suffering as their bodies knit themselves together or missing limbs re-grew.

Persephone didn't slow her pace and Ishtar knew she would not—not with Nyx's rule and life at stake. Ishtar beat her wings harder. Then five Angels, tangled together in battle, crashed into the pair of them. Their world was reduced to a whir of battering wings, darting blades, sharp teeth and claws, the sound of whips snapping through the air and ripping open flesh. Ishtar gutted the Angel in front of her, not caring if it was friend or foe, then felt a whip snake around her throat and pull tight. She spun her blade and rammed it backwards, feeling it slice into flesh. She ripped down and enjoyed the howl as the whip on her throat slid away.

Persephone, entangled with two Angels and too close to use her sword, bit one's face off with a mouthful of razor-sharp teeth. The Angel screamed and jerked away, giving Persephone room to pierce the Angel's throat with her talons, and rip it open. The other Angel also used its teeth, biting down on into Persephone's side. She drove an elbow down onto the Angel's face, dislocating its jaw with a single strike. The Angel growled and tried to grapple. Persephone brought up her heel and drove it into the Angel's groin. The Angel let go and fell.

The fifth Angel attacked both Ishtar and Persephone, using both sword and whip. Two swords flashed, and both the Angel's hands fell, leaving it staring at bloody stumps. The friends were side by side again, flying towards Lucifer above.

"How the fuck do we get past him?" Ishtar yelled.

"Carefully," Persephone shouted back.

Ishtar grimaced but kept on flying.

A half-dozen more times their flight was interrupted.

Persephone lost half a breast, and Ishtar took a whiplash that tore most of the feathers from one wing. Both endured a dozen other, minor cuts, and both of them fought Angel after Angel, sending their gutted, limbless bodies into the pit below.

Above, Lucifer engaged four Angels at once, cutting one's wings off with his sword, tearing another open with his whip, and driving his cloven boot into the face of the third. The fourth nearly squirmed past him, but Lucifer spun his whip and yanked the Angel backwards, impaling it with his sword through its backside so hard that the tip of his blade came out its mouth.

He reversed the blade and the screaming Angel fell.

"We're fucked," screamed Ishtar, even as she prepared to lash her whip at Lucifer's foot.

"Not yet, we're not," Persephone screamed back. She linked with Ishtar then, mind to mind. It was a gift all Angels had, but the Dark Angels rarely used it. To let one into your mind was to give him or her all your secrets, and the Dark Angels were so often plotting against one another that they didn't dare open their minds. Persephone and Ishtar knew each other's secrets already, and when Persephone shared her plan in Ishtar's mind, it made Ishtar bare her teeth in a sudden, savage grin.

Both slowed their flight just enough to let the two Angels beneath them catch up. The Angels, two of Nyx's loyal soldiers, charged upward and tried to pass them, eyes on the prize of the rift open above them.

Ishtar and Persephone lashed out with their whips at the same time, wrapping them around the two Angels' necks. With simultaneous hard pulls of arms, backs and wings, they threw the Angels forward and into Lucifer.

Lucifer, caught off guard, found himself tangled in the

embrace of the two, and for a moment there was nothing but kicking, biting, and slashing of talons as all three struggled to get free. It was a short moment, but it was enough. Ishtar and Persephone went wide around Lucifer and dashed upward for the rift.

"Nearly there!" screamed Persephone. She could see the rift clearly, and Earth, the world beyond it. It would be a minute's flight, no more, to reach it. Beside her, Ishtar grinned and flexed her wings harder, trying to get as much speed as she could.

Two whips lashed out from behind, wrapping each Angel's ankle and yanking them backwards.

Even as they fell, both had their blades out, hacking away the whips and clashing with the blades of their opponents. Facing Persephone was Morrigan, a thin, steel-strong Angel with a scarred face and a hideous war-cry. Mantus attacked Ishtar, his red armor scored in a dozen places and his silver blood flowing as he hacked at her. Ishtar and Persephone forced themselves to fly higher even as they fought.

Morrigan ripped into Persephone's guard, knocking her sword out of the way and scoring her across her belly. Persephone jabbed her blade at Morrigan's eyes and then hacked down, trying to take off her opponent's hands.

Mantus was huge and relied on his size and strength to overpower his opponents. His sword smashed against Ishtar again and again, sending her off course and nearly breaking her own blade as she parried. She stopped him a dozen times, her wrists aching from the power of his strikes, but was unable to mount a defense. When the next strike came, she yielded instead, allowing his force to flow through hers, redirecting his attack and ending up behind him. She hacked hard, cutting off one wing on the upstroke and another as the blade came back down. Silver ichor sprayed everywhere and she spread her wings to fly away.

Mantus grabbed her ankle, and dug his clawed fingers into her leg. Faster than she had expected, he spun his body and climbed up behind her. Ishtar flipped and struggled and spun to get him off, but it was no use. The wingless Angel climbed her body with hooked talons like steel.

Persephone was locked blade to blade with Morrigan, each struggling for the upper hand. They clashed together and came apart once, then twice, then a third time, with a dozen cuts to each one's flesh but no devastating blow on either side.

Mantus clawed his way to the top of Ishtar's back and wrapped his arm around her throat. It took all of Ishtar's strength to continue beating her wings as she clawed at his arm. Ishtar pushed every ounce of her remaining strength into her wings, knowing that falling would end it all for her. From above she saw Morrigan's body and head fall separately down toward the pit far below.

"You took my wings, bitch," Mantus said, and she could feel his twisted arousal. Mantis sucked Ishtar's earlobe into his mouth and bit it off. "I'm going to ride you down, and surf with your corpse in the lake."

Ishtar rammed her head backwards. He was so close it did little damage. She did it again and again, keeping him distracted as she reached behind her. He realized what she was doing too late. With a rip of her claws and a hard pull she felt the flesh tear from his body.

Mantus screamed and reared back, and this time, when Ishtar rammed her head backwards, she heard a solid crunch

– Mantus's nose exploded. His grip around her waist loosened, and Ishtar twisted, ripping her sword across Mantus's belly.

"You fucking hag!" he howled as he dropped away.

Ishtar's head was clearing, and she struggled upward after Persephone. Beneath them she heard the "boom" of Lucifer's wings and knew he was coming after them himself. Persephone looked down and shouted, "Hang on to me!" as she gestured at her own leg, just in Ishtar's reach.

Ishtar, too prideful, flapped harder and forced herself toward the rift. Persephone looked down again, then suddenly pulled out her whip and snapped it directly at Ishtar.

Ishtar threw her head to the side, feeling betrayal as she had not experienced since their Descent. The three whip heads sizzled as they went by her head and face, along the length of her legs and past her to snap in the face of Derkos, an Angel of Lucifer, whose blade was about to impale Ishtar.

Derkos roared and flapped wildly at the three whip heads cutting thick lines into his face. His whip slashed out wildly, blasting Ishtar in the eye even as he went tumbling back towards Lucifer, who was just below them. Ishtar wailed as her eye left its socket. Lucifer, unable to dodge the falling Derkos, screamed in rage and hacked Derkos in half, sending silver ichor in all directions

With just one eye, Ishtar felt weaker than ever before. Her wings fluttered as best they could. She stuttered awkwardly upward, flying half blind. Lucifer was bound to catch her soon, and there was no way she could keep up. Ishtar screamed out in frustration. Above her, barely visible through the curtain of blood that engulfed her face, she could see Persephone almost at the entrance to the rift. Persephone was looking towards her goal, and flexing her wings with savage strength.

Ishtar looked down and saw Lucifer's skin grow dark, and the light around him fade. His skin even smoked like the wick of a dying candle as he twisted, bloated, and transformed.

In an instant, he was no longer a beautiful Angel wearing a crown, but a dragon three times the size. The only evidence of his godly stature was the crown of jewels on his massive reptilian head, perched just above the pointed, golden horn that jutted from his forehead. The dragon had the yellow hair of Lucifer, but it ran in a mane down its curved, black-scaled back. It grinned, showing teeth more wicked than that of any Angel, and deep in its mouth Ishtar could see Hellfire being readied for a blast.

There's no way I'll make it, Ishtar thought. *But I can make sure Persephone does.*

She grimaced – the burn of her sorrow exceeding her physical anguish. She did not cry out for help. Better to let her comrade revel in victory than to risk them both failing. She twisted in the air and saw Lucifer so close below them, and eight hundred more Angels, hungry for blood and victory, racing up behind him. She pointed her sword at him and stopped flexing her wings. For a moment she hung, motionless in the air. Then she drew in her wings to fall on him like a falcon attacking an eagle.

With luck I'll gut him before he burns me alive, she thought.

From above, three heads of a whip whirled and wrapped around her already-wounded ankle. Ishtar screamed as Persephone hauled her, pulling her up and into the rift. She heard Persephone scream, "You're not giving up on me now, bitch!"

The dragon released a blast of flame, singeing them both.

Ishtar flicked her whip once more, and as much by luck as design, the tails cracked in Lucifer's face. The sound split the air, vibrating back to her. The last thing she saw, before disappearing into a vortex of magic, was Lucifer falling into the depths below, holding his wounded eye as he screamed raw, bone-chilling screams.

CHAPTER 5

NYX STOOD IN the desert, waiting.
She scanned the skies, looking for Arcana. If Caelum and Orion had spoken the truth, and she had no reason to doubt them, Arcana had been waiting for Nyx to leave, so she could come through the gate and to Earth. With Caelum and Orion gone, she should be able to come through anyway. And then she and Nyx would try to kill each other.

They had been friends once. Before the rebellion, before the slaughter, before Nyx's agreement with God and before the Descent and the Lake of Fire. They had sung together, fought together, and, on occasion, made love. It had not just been fucking, back then. It had been a joining of minds and souls and bodies, an ultimate sharing of self that revealed the innocence and honesty of the soul with whom one shared.

Those times were long, long gone. Civilizations had risen and fallen and risen again since those times. Still Nyx missed Arcana, missed her brightness and intelligence and simplicity, missed the love they had shared with each other and with other Angels, free of jealousy, hatred, and malice.

In the last battle for Heaven, Arcana had taken the far flank of the battle, to avoid having to fight her friend.

And now I have to kill her, Nyx thought. *Unfair. Why did God have to send her?*

Nyx had no doubt she would defeat Arcana. The power that let her defeat Caelum and Orion would surely be strong enough to help her defeat Arcana. *But she is so, so much better than they, and I don't want to kill her.*

So where is she?

Another hour passed. Nyx felt reality shift, and could sense two Angelic presences coming to the earth.

Just like her to bring reinforcements, thought Nyx, smiling. Arcana was always smart. *Let's just hope it's not Michael.*

She launched into the air, tired of waiting, and flew toward the presences she sensed. In minutes she had flown from Judea to Libya, and to the deserts beyond. She zeroed in on the Angelic presence like a hawk, flying after its prey. She would find them and destroy them.

They're not in the air, Nyx realized. *They're on the ground.*

It was not until she spotted the black, gaping pit in the middle of the sand that Nyx realized the truth. It had always been easy to fall from Heaven, whether intentionally or otherwise. Angels used to be able to come to Earth with a single step and a long, slow glide of their wings. The earth would spread out beneath them like a blue and white panorama that they could take in at their leisure while they descended. When they wished to ascend again, it was a long, hard climb against gravity and sin. The Angels would have to strip the corruption of the world away and focus all their strength towards Heaven. The trip to Earth, though, was nothing.

Hell was the opposite. Easy to get to, hard to escape. From Hell, you had to claw your way out.

Nyx landed beside the pit and waited. Whoever was coming, she could not assist. Those in Hell had to get out on their own.

One silver-white hand, cut and abraded, appeared out of the darkness, clawing at the side of the pit. Two of the nails had been torn off, but still the fingers sunk into the stone at the side of the pit, and a moment later another hand rose up beside it, passed it, and sunk into the stone. Nyx heard gasps of pain from two voices, though she could not see the second Angel at all.

The clawed, ruined hands pulled against the stone, heaving the body they belonged to up out of the pit. A head of white-streaked black hair came into view first. Nyx watched the slow, painful progress from the other side of the pit. The Angel had a long, lean back, wrapped in the black-scaled armor of Hell. One of her wings was missing half its feathers, and her back had a half-dozen deep claw marks in it.

A third hand appeared directly beside the Angel, just above her hips, and to Nyx's surprise, the fourth one appeared a moment later, pushing hard against the ass of the Angel above her, propelling her up and out of the pit. A moment later, another head of long, white-streaked black hair appeared into view from the darkness below.

Despite herself, Nyx laughed with delight as Ishtar slowly worked her way out of the pit, propelled forward by the hand that Persephone had firmly planted on the ripped armor of her ass. Ishtar heard her and turned to look. Nyx's laughter died at the sight of her ruined eye and torn-open face. Below her,

Persephone was also bleeding, perhaps even worse than Ishtar. The two were lashed together by their whips, making it impossible for one to fall without taking the other.

Nyx ran around the outside of the pit, not daring to fly over it for fear her presence would trigger its collapse. She stood above her Angels as they clawed their way up. "Hurry," she breathed. "Hurry, my loves."

"Trying," came Persephone's grunted reply. "Ishtar's ass has grown fat and is hard to keep moving."

"It has not," protested Ishtar as her first hand reached the edge of the pit and clawed at the sand there. She couldn't get a purchase, and had to rest her hand flat, using her legs and other arm to propel herself up until she could lay her torso on the ground. At last, she freed herself from the pit and crawled forward, pulling Persephone up with her.

When Persephone cleared the pit, the ground around them rumbled, and the sand all around began pouring into the pit, threatening to send them both back where they came from. Nyx grabbed them both by their arms and hauled herself into the air. The sand thundered down, filling the hole as if it had never been there in the first place. Nyx flew them away, to a small hill of rocks and weeds, and laid them in the shade there.

Their armor and weapons faded, becoming part of their bodies once more. Slowly, their flesh began to heal. Persephone's hacked-open breast and the cut on her belly slowly knit themselves back together. The gouges in Ishtar's back and the missing flesh and muscle from her leg grew back in. The feathers and flesh of her wings slowly replaced themselves.

It was an agonizing process, and it took hours, but neither Angel complained or made a sound. Nyx watched in fascination as their injuries healed, especially Ishtar's eye, which grew in last, forming itself anew from her flesh and blood.

When both Angels were whole, Nyx, her own armor gone, embraced them. Angelic flesh touched Angelic flesh, and the passion that flared up between the three of them made Nyx's knees tremble. As good as her joinings with Tribunal had been, he had been clothed in mortal flesh, unable to take on his true form. The touch of Angelic flesh: so rich, so full of the deep magic of Creation.

For some time the three kissed and touched and caressed, exulting in each other's company. At last, and with a heartfelt sigh, Nyx pushed the other two away. There would be time for pleasure later. Now though, questions needed to be answered.

"Sweet Ishtar," Nyx sighed. "Beautiful Persephone. It's so good to see you both again, my sisters."

"You too, Nyx," said Persephone, kissing her hand and letting her lips linger there.

"Now tell me," said Nyx. "What happened?"

"Lucifer made us battle to get out of Hell," said Ishtar. "The entire 666th."

"And how did you two manage to win?" asked Nyx. "I doubt Lucifer sent my two dearest allies on purpose."

Ishtar and Persephone together told her all that had happened, sparing no details of Lucifer's speech or the bloody ordeal that followed. By the end of it, Nyx was pacing.

"So, he has risen against me," Nyx muttered to herself. "He'll spend the next thousand years subjugating my Angels and bending them to his will while I'm trapped here on Earth."

"While *we* are trapped here," reminded Persephone. "We came to be with you, to help you become a new God on earth."

"Oh, we are going to do so much more than that," said Nyx. "But still, how could Lucifer have known when the gate from Hell would be open to Angels again?" Her mind flashed back to the small red bird on Tribunal's shoulder, and the conversation she had not been able to hear. She grinned. "Tribunal did it! Tribunal convinced him to open the door, knowing he would send his Angels through to spite God."

"Who?" asked Ishtar.

"Tribunal," repeated Nyx. "God's mortal son, crucified in Jerusalem three days ago."

"That wasn't His name."

"It was His true name," said Nyx. "It was the name which He gave me to summon Him back from Heaven and it was the name with which He sealed the bargain with me." She frowned at them. "And Lucifer mentioned nothing of him?"

"Not a word," said Ishtar. "He only said God had changed the rules."

"He didn't mention my agreement with the son of God?"

"You have an agreement with the son of God?" repeated Ishtar, horrified. "To do what?"

"To take this world from God," said Nyx, smiling. "To turn God's followers and the followers of the Christ into followers of Nyx or to kill them. And when the time comes and our followers outnumber His, we will have them rise up and destroy the followers of God. When that happens, God will turn his back on the world and Tribunal shall take dominion, and all those in Hell shall partake of a new Paradise." She frowned again. "And Lucifer said nothing of this?"

"Well," said Persephone, "if I wanted to seize power, I

wouldn't tell my followers that someone else could give them Paradise either."

But why would he think he could have power? Nyx wondered. *He knows that Tribunal and I will work together to bring this about, and that I will rule in Paradise and Hell, does he not?* The thought troubled her greatly. *Why would Tribunal not tell him? Why would he let him think otherwise…?*

Just thinking His name made Nyx remember her passion for Tribunal, and the way He poured His power into her. She remembered His passion, His delight in her beauty and knowledge—how He strengthened her, how she consoled and supported Him. He would not, could not, have betrayed her, not she who knew all forms of betrayal and could spot them all at a glance. *No. Tribunal must have used Lucifer's ambition as part of His plan. Nothing else makes sense.*

"So," said Ishtar, rising and stretching, her body once more perfect and unscarred, "What now?"

Nyx smiled. *We have time here. We have a thousand years.* She surveyed Ishtar, taking in her perfect ass, tits, legs and belly, and the arrogance that always had to be controlled and directed. "Now?" said Nyx, rising to her own feet. "Now you and I will have a little chat about giving up."

Ishtar's smile faltered. "I didn't…"

"You did," said Nyx, drawing her whip. In her hand it turned to a long, wide, flat leather strap. Two steps forward brought her to Ishtar. She grabbed the smaller Angel's black hair in her fist and turned her, pushing up with her hand to force Ishtar to arch her back and go on tiptoe. "Take in your wings."

Ishtar did. "Please, Nyx."

Nyx's strap licked across Ishtar's ass, raising red welts, and while they did not pain her like the wounds Ishtar had received in the battle, the lash hurt and Ishtar knew many, many more were to come.

"You... gave...up!" said Nyx, each word punctuated with a lash of the strap. "You gave in to weakness and nearly became one of Lucifer's minions!" The strap rained down on the Angel a hundred times—so fast that Persephone, watching with amusement, could only see a blur where Nyx's arm and the strap moved through the air. Ishtar screamed and cried and wriggled, just as Nyx knew she would, and just as Nyx liked her to do.

Nyx twisted her hand and dragged Ishtar down onto her knees, shoving her face into Nyx's crotch. "Get to work," Nyx hissed. "And pleasure me well, or I'll add more stripes." Weeping, Ishtar complied. Nyx groaned at the first touch of her tongue, and gestured Persephone over. "Come here, my brave one, and kiss me."

Persephone did, and Nyx caressed her, sending arcs of pleasure over her flesh. Between Nyx's legs, Ishtar wept with pain and jealousy as she applied her tongue. Nyx smiled and tightened her grip in Ishtar's hair. She would forgive Ishtar, of course. But not immediately. Ishtar was at her best as a lover when she was forced into submission, and Nyx intended to enjoy her a great deal.

There is time, Nyx thought. *There is time at this end of the millennium. And when we rise up, and begin our conquest of these mortals, there will be nothing to stop us.*

*

They started by taking over a small villa in Byblos. By way of letting her earn forgiveness, Nyx sent Ishtar in ahead. By the time she and Persephone arrived, the very rich Romans who had owned the villa were in chains, cowering beside the other slaves, and ready to fall at Nyx's feet when she came through the door.

For the next year, they relaxed, planned, scouted, and made love at every opportunity. Nyx forgave Ishtar after another month and gave her enough pleasure that it took her two days before she rose from their bed, and two weeks more before she sat without wincing and smiling.

When they reached the end of the first year, Nyx said, "Tell me what you have learned."

They were in the baths, soaking in warm water, while around them the four prettiest of their slaves – two male and two female – were gently washing their bodies with soft cloths. Nyx had one of each, Persephone had the other male, and Ishtar had the other girl. Nyx stretched out, enjoying the feel of the cloths on her flesh and the gentle touches of the mortals. "What do we know?"

"We can't get near them," said Persephone. "None of the Apostles. Anytime we try to get close, we end up somewhere else. Ishtar decided to charge at them full speed and ended up in the Sahara."

"Is that what the sand was about?" asked Nyx. "I wondered."

"Took me a week to get it out of my wings," grumbled Ishtar.

"We knew we weren't able to directly interfere," said Nyx. "Apparently that means getting close at all. What else do we know?"

"They are gaining numbers at surprising speed," said Persephone. "All Jews. Mostly among the lower classes, though some of the wealthier are participating, too."

"Herod?"

"Is suppressing them regularly. But not with much success."

"Then he needs to be replaced," said Nyx. "I'll see to that." *Besides, I still owe him for Tribunal's death.* "What else?"

"My cult is still going surprisingly strong," said Persephone. "Despite thirty years without miracles, my followers are still there, across the entirety of the empire. Even in Rome."

"Even better," said Nyx. "We need them."

"Why?" asked Persephone. "You're the one who needs to build followers."

"I am," agreed Nyx. "But we also need to keep the Christians from building their followers. And the easiest way to get them to do so is to keep your followers happy and expand your temples. As soon as my followers outnumber them, we can move onto the next phase of the plan."

"Sounds like fun," said Persephone. She sighed. "Pity about Dispater, though. He was wonderful for enacting the wedding night of Persephone in the underworld. Tall, strong, frightening, and huge." She smiled, and one of her hands drifted below the water, while the other reached out to stroke her bathing attendant.

Nyx looked at him. "Impressive, for a mortal."

"Isn't he?" said Persephone. "Now imagine something much, much larger." She moaned as she touched herself. "He used to do me so, so well. It was an annual thing and I am going to miss it."

"Well," said Nyx, standing up, "I'm sure we can come up with something." Her body changed, stretched and grew, becoming the demon figure that had abused Judas so horribly. "Will this do?"

"Very nicely," said Persephone, letting go of the human and reaching for Nyx. She stopped. "Though if you could take the scales off it?"

"Of course," said Nyx, and with a thought, made the change.

"Delightful," said Persephone, wrapping one hand, then the other around Nyx's demon-phallus. "You'll do fine."

Around the three angels, the mortals began to shake in fear. None dared move, though all were terrified. Ishtar watched them, amused. "I wonder what that would do to a mortal woman?" she said, just for the expression on her bathing attendant's face.

"Tear them open, I should think," said Persephone. "I can't even get my hands around it."

"Because it would be a lovely addition to your ritual," said Ishtar. "Have some of the mortal women take your part, after you, and learn the true pain of Persephone."

"Tempting," said Persephone. "But I still think it's too large for that.

"One way to find out, isn't there," said Ishtar, grinning. She grabbed her attendant and bent her, face down, over the edge of the tub. The girl quaked with fear, but didn't dare cry out.

"And once you're done with that," said Ishtar, "We can plan what your temple is going to look like, Nyx, my love."

Nyx smiled at her. "I want you to take over for Isis."

"What?" Ishtar was horrified. "That mewling little mother goddess? She has no strength! She doesn't do anything except… except…"

"Listen to the prayers of all," said Persephone. She grinned. "From slaves to aristocrats, she is considered universally kind. The ideal mother, the source of growth and plenty, and the goddess of magic."

"She's a wimp!"

"She's you," said Nyx, and this time her tone brooked no argument. "Her religion is just as successful as Persephone's, so we need to propagate it. You will give them the miracles of Isis, and you will keep the faithful, faithful."

"Let me build up my own followers again," said Ishtar. "The followers of Isis will just worship Isis."

"As I want them to," said Nyx.

"But I want to be worshipped myself!"

"What difference does it make?" demanded Nyx. "They will worship Isis, you will be Isis, and in a thousand years, we will have Paradise again!"

"You've never been worshipped," said Ishtar. "You have no idea."

"Let her do both," suggested Persephone, seeing Nyx's anger rise. "She can try to rebuild her cult as long as she maintains the cult of Isis at full strength."

Nyx glared at Ishtar. "Fine. Do both, but don't let Isis's cult fail. We need as many kept away from Christianity as we can."

"This is going to be fun," said Persephone. She stroked Nyx a bit harder and batted her eyes at her. "Speaking of which, you're not really going to waste this on that mortal, are you?"

Nyx grabbed Persephone and bent her over the tub beside the slave girl. Persephone cried loud in pleasure and grabbed the girl's hand, nearly crushing it as Nyx thrust hard into her. Nyx laughed at Persephone's noise, even as her mind moved on to the years ahead.

I will make myself the greatest goddess Rome has ever known, she thought. *And then we'll see who gets the most followers.*

CHAPTER 6

31 A.D. – CAPRI

TIBERIUS JULIUS CAESAR August dreamed of Rome collapsing around him. The city was on fire; earthquakes tore open the streets and the building tumbled down. The pious prayed to their gods and received no answer. And through the chaos, walking without a care for the falling rubble and screaming crowds was a woman with skin and hair the color of alabaster and snow, jet-black wings, and the eyes of a serpent. She turned those glorious and deathly eyes on him and hissed. "You have abandoned Rome!"

Tiberius cried out and woke in the bedroom of his villa on Capri. The young boy whom Tiberius had used before sleeping scuttled back under the linen sheet. The old Emperor ignored him and rose to his feet, calling for wine and clothes. Tiberius was not a young man and the urge did not come on him more than once a day anymore.

The servants came and helped him dress, then brought

him his wine and took away the boy. He paced the room for a time, muttering to himself about the dream, about the unfairness of it all. Tiberius had never wanted to be Emperor of Rome. And now that he was old, his plan had been to retire and let Sejanus take the reigns of state. The man was set up to be his heir anyway. It was all going to be simple.

Then the nightmares started.

Rome burning, Rome falling to the barbarians, Rome being washed into the sea, Rome, Rome, Rome, always collapsing, always falling, always his fault.

Tiberius stumbled out onto the balcony. Years of leading the armies had taken a toll on his body, and every step ached when he first woke up, especially when he woke in the middle of the night.

The night was clear. A full moon hung in the night sky, casting its beams over the earth. The stars around it were dimmed by its brightness, and it was only by looking away from it that he could see the constellations. He could hear the sound of the night animals and birds, and if he watched closely he could see the small, black shapes of bats flittering after insects. The world was at it should be, save that he, Tiberius, was old and tired and could not sleep. He sighed and leaned against the rail. He would go back in soon and summon a boy or two to warm his bed as he slept. It would not take away the pains, but it would make them more bearable.

The world around him fell silent.

Tiberius straightened. The hairs on the back of his neck rose, and the part of him that was still a soldier whispered, *Something is wrong.* He peered out into the darkness, looking and listening for whatever had made the world go quiet.

She rose before him, floating in the air, her black wings wide-spread, twenty feet across. Her silver-white skin shone bright enough to dim the moon; she smelled of flowers he had never seen, of unearthly skies. Her red-snake eyes glowed with a fire that threatened to turn into his brain into smoldering ash. He stumbled back, feeling his knees grow weak and threaten to give way.

"Hold, Tiberius," said Nyx. "Hold and hear your fate."

Tiberius forced himself to stop, to straighten and stand tall. He was emperor, whether he willed it or not, and he would die as one. "My... my fate?"

"Your successor, Sejanus, plans your overthrow. Even now he lies with your niece, Livilla, and plots with her to hand Rome to the Julians. Your death will come soon, and your Rome will be destroyed because of it."

"Rome?" Tiberius shook his head. "Why would Rome be destroyed if I die? I am an old man."

"Not so old as that," purred Nyx, and Tiberius, who had little use for women, felt his flesh stirring in response to her voice. "Not so old as to be enfeebled. No so old as to be unable to change your fate." She held out her arms. "Come with me, Tiberius. See your niece groan under this man, and hear their plans. They must be stopped, for the good of Rome."

Tiberius, Emperor of Rome, climbed carefully onto the balcony rail, and into Nyx's arms.

*

Sejanus, Consul of Rome, walked into the Roman senate and smiled. He still had to be polite and kind to these senators, but not for much longer. *Soon I will be Emperor over them all,* he thought. *And then it will be their turn to grovel to me.*

"Gentlemen," said Sejanus. "Tell me what brings us here today. I am a busy man."

"Very busy," agreed Senator Marcus Britannias. "Why, you've been rooting out so many traitors I worry there may not be an honest man left in Rome."

A chuckle filled the room, and Sejanus frowned at that. These men were senators, true, but he was still Consul. He could add half of the senators to the list of those to be tried and they would not be able to do anything about it. They should speak to him with some respect. "Perhaps, gentlemen, we should get to the matter at hand."

"But of course," said Britannias. "Would you read the letter, Appias Claudius?"

"With pleasure," said Appias, rising to his feet. He opened a scroll case, took out the scroll and broke the Emperor's seal in it. "By order of Tiberius Julius Caesar Augustus, let it be known that Lucius Aelius Sejanus is guilty of treason against Rome, of plotting against the Emperor, and of attempting his overthrow. He is to be taken from the Senate, stripped of his robes and sandals, and whipped naked through the streets to the shores of the Tiber, where rocks are to be tied to his arms and legs before he is to be thrown into his river. All his possessions are to be taken by the Senate and re-distributed to those the Senate deems worthy. Further, my niece, Livilla, who was his willing co-conspirator, is to be placed under arrest and delivered to my home in Capri, at which time I will attend her punishment personally."

"What?" Sejanus stood, amazed, in the middle of the floor. "That's impossible! I am no traitor! I am not!"

The centurions who seized his arms didn't listen as they dragged him out of the Senate chambers. Appias Claudius continued reading. "Let it be further announced that, in reward for the visions that led to my investigations, there will be a temple constructed to she whose great power saved Rome…"

Sejanus was dragged from the chamber and heard no more.

*

34 A.D. – ROME

"So," said Persephone, looking at the large, empty chamber. "A little bare, isn't it?"

"It is now," said Nyx, feeling strangely defensive. It was stupid, because it was just a building, but it was her temple, after all. It just wasn't finished yet. Outside, it was impressive enough. She'd had the workers build it in the Greek style, round instead of rectangular, with a large domed ceiling above. The city's best artists had been working on the murals of the walls and ceiling, but they were only half-complete. The murals—of emperors and nobles, of feasts and hunts, of victory and celebration, of love and sex—would cover all the walls. And in the center, there would be a huge statue of Nyx herself, nude, with her wings wrapped around her body. "It isn't done yet."

She had inserted herself into the dreams of Rome's finest sculptor. The next morning he had run in to pray at the temple.

Human art was astonishing to Nyx. Human lives were so brief, and yet they spent hours, days, even years creating beauty, whether in the hopes it would live longer than they or just creating it for its own sake. The sculptor thought himself blessed by the opportunity to represent her in stone, and assured her the sculpture would be finished by the end of the year. She was more excited than she would ever admit. "I can see where you're going with it, though," said Ishtar. "You're a goddess of plenty, of strength, of fertility and… what else?"

"Justice?" suggested Persephone.

"Vengeance," said Nyx, a small smile curving her ripe lips. "All who worship me truly need not fear my wrath. All who betray me, or betray those who worship me, I will destroy. In my name there is health and happiness, and those who serve me know peace, pleasure and plenty."

"Interesting," said Persephone. She looked at Ishtar. "How long do you think Nyx will last as a Goddess of Peace?"

"Longer than I have to last as Isis, I hope," said Ishtar. "Do you know how boring her rituals are? And every year they re-enact the death of her husband. It's awful!"

"What,'s strange," said Nyx, "is that I can hear them. I can hear the prayers of my worshippers."

Persephone grinned. "I know."

"What?" Nyx whirled on the other Angel. "Why didn't you tell me?"

"Because finding out is half the surprise," said Persephone, dodging Nyx's swat at her. "You can hear their prayers, and their thoughts of you. You can get into their minds and hear all they intend to do. It makes miracles rather easy."

"Not if you can't hear anything," said Isis. "I'm not Isis so I can't hear a thing. I have to walk among them as a mortal and listen in on their conversations." Ishtar shuddered. "Mankind is boring."

"How do I stop hearing them?" asked Nyx.

"You don't," said Persephone. "It becomes like a river of

voices that flow through your head. It's always there in the background. Then, when you pay attention to it, you can hear every individual thought."

"Sounds… annoying," said Nyx.

"When they worshipped me, I could hear them begging for my mercy," said Ishtar. "Especially lovers whose parents wouldn't let them be together. I give you a hundred years before it starts wearing on you."

"I can last more than a hundred years," said Nyx, feeling her irritation rising. "I can last as long as either of you!"

"A thousand five hundred years," said Persephone, haughtily. "And counting."

"So what will they sacrifice to you?" asked Ishtar. "Pigs?"

"Pigs?" repeated Nyx, her voice dangerous. "Why would I ask them to sacrifice smelly, disgusting filthy beasts to me?"

"Because bacon is delicious," said Ishtar. "Morrigan and I used to get together at her festivals and the feasts were amazing."

"How about doves?" suggested Persephone.

"Horses?"

"Bulls?"

"Virgins," said Ishtar. "I always liked virgins."

"Male or female?" asked Persephone.

"Both is best," said Ishtar. "That way they don't run out of people."

"The Romans frown on human sacrifice," said Nyx, glaring at them. "Now take this seriously."

"All Gods have sacrifices," said Persephone. She pointed her finger at Ishtar. "This one had temple prostitutes. All women were expected to enter into her temple and could not leave until they'd had sex for money once." She frowned. "Must have been difficult for some of them."

"There's no woman so ugly that a drunk man won't have sex with her," sneered Ishtar.

"What about the women who liked women?"

Ishtar grinned. "It helped reinforce their opinions."

"Anyway," said Persephone. "If you don't want to sacrifice virgins, just sacrifice their virginity." Her form shifted and she became a very young woman, fresh and nubile, with perfectly formed small breasts poking at the gauzy fabric of a white linen shift that was just too short to cover her bottom. Her hands tugged down the front of the shift as her voice turned sweet and breathy. "Must I give the blood of my innocence to be initiated into the rites of Nyx?"

"What about the boys?" asked Ishtar. "What blood do you accept from them? Their foreskin?"

"Can't," said Nyx. "The Christians and Jews do that, and since that's who we're fighting against… "

"Scar them," suggested Ishtar. "Male and female alike. Just above the genitals. Scary, but isn't seen in public… "

"No scarring!" said Nyx, rolling her eyes. "And no virginity either. Not unless they want to," Nyx amended. "Here, they will give sacrifice of their lust and their money of their own free will. Our temple will take their coin, and will use it to spread the word and build more temples. This temple," she looked up at the architecture and smiled, "Is for the Emperors of Rome."

Persephone turned her innocent eyes on Ishtar. "Oh, great emperor, will you sacrifice with me?"

Ishtar shifted forms, and became a naked Julius Caesar in his prime. "Of course, little girl."

"I think that's overstated," said Persephone, pointing.

"Actually not," said Ishtar. "What do you think Cleopatra saw in him?"

"Well, in that case…" Persephone looked around. "Nyx, where's the altar?"

"It arrives tomorrow," said Nyx, still not amused. Persephone pouted, and on her young woman's face it looked exceedingly pretty. Her skin was smooth as milk, her long eyelashes mink-dark.

"Then where shall I sacrifice my lust?"

"When in Rome," said Nyx, "Find a Roman villa. And when you get finished, it's time to start dealing with these Christians."

*

35 A.D. - JERUSALEM

"Please, Caiaphas," whispered Persephone, trying to ignore how ugly, sweaty, and smelly the man was. She wore the same body she had in Nyx's temple. It was a favorite of hers for seduction, for men (and some women) seemed unable to resist it. The thin silks of her outfit barely covered her flesh, and the many layers gave tantalizing glimpses of what lay beneath the cloth.

"Really?" had been Ishtar's response when Persephone told Nyx and Ishtar of the plan. "Like that's going to work."

"It worked for Salome," said Nyx. "Do it and see what happens. With luck, we can cut down some of the followers right away."

Now Persephone swayed gently before the High Priest of the Sanhedrin, letting him gaze lustfully at her. "If you would," she said, batting her dark eyelashes at the man, "I would be so, so grateful. They scare me, these Christians. They're mocking our God, and they threatened my family."

"Did they now?" Caiaphas reached for her and she eluded his grasp. She stepped back, balancing on one bare, white foot as her breasts swayed under the silk. Caiaphas breathed in deeply, inhaling her scent. "And what would do best for you?"

"Drive them out," Persephone said, her voice filled with the outrage of naïve youth. "Send them from Jerusalem. And kill their leaders. They are blasphemers, all of them. But especially the one called Stephen. I have heard him preach against you and the Sanhedrin."

"I will have him summoned," said Caiaphas, reaching for her again. This time Persephone allowed herself to be caught and pulled in to the man's embrace, letting him breathe deep of the narcissus she had used to perfume her midnight curls. "And if he blasphemes before the Sanhedrin, we shall have him arrested and killed. Now," he said and reached up underneath her skirts, "Show me how you will thank me."

*

Nyx sat in her temple in Rome, listening to the music of the lute player and the voices of her followers in her head.

She had always loved music, so it made perfect sense to have it in her temples. The lute one day, the flute the next, the harp on the third, and singing at all times. And only the best players and singers were invited. She gave them visions at night, and listened to them during the day, disguised as a man or woman of Rome. There was a haunting beauty to music well-played, a faint echo of the Angelic hosts that played and sang in Heaven. Sometimes, when the music was just right, she found herself transported back to God's mountain, listening to the music of the choir.

The young man who was playing lute this evening was delightful, and Nyx let his music wash over her as she lay back, closed her eyes, and fell into the river of her worshippers' thoughts.

It wasn't a river, truth be told, not yet. More of a small stream, trickling over the rocks. There were not so many of them, but they were powerful. She had been certain to appear in visions to dozens of the most important senators. In the last year she had performed a hundred small miracles, from finding money to eliminating an enemy to convincing another senator to vote in the way her worshippers pleased. And with every miracle, her follower had a vision of who provided it. Her temples' coffers had swollen, and she'd opened up another temple in a different section of town.

And it was there her trouble started.

She liked these humans better now that they had no God present. She was amused that none of them seemed to notice He was gone, except those fools who thought it was Tribunal they were missing, Tribunal whom they had never known. But liking a few humans didn't change her goals. It couldn't.

He threw me into the Lake of Fire, she whispered to herself. *And for what? Wanting to have some say in my own life? Having a few questions? I am as He made me.*

But some of them she couldn't help but like.

The senators were easy to hate. They prayed for riches and power and revenge. Their wives prayed for more concubines so their husbands would leave them alone, or for the death of their husband's concubines so the man would pay more attention to them. They prayed for sons to inherit, and for their rivals' houses to fall. Nyx fully expected to see most of them in Hell.

The worshippers from the section of town that held her new temple were not rich. They were tradesmen. Men and women who worked every day to survive, who prayed for more work, or for their husbands to be safe or for their wives to survive childbirth or their children to survive disease. Their children came too, and prayed for their parents or their siblings or their friends. It was not like the tradesmen's families didn't have prayers for vengeance and pain or disaster to befall their enemies, but those were outweighed, often, and it confused Nyx.

One twelve-year old girl spent an hour on her knees, begging Nyx that the friend of her father whom she had to marry would be kind, because the man had promised to save her father's business. Nyx visited the girl's possible husband and gave him a vision of exactly how awful things would be if he didn't marry the girl and treat her with respect. He woke screaming and brought offerings to her temple the next day.

Do Angels hear prayers in Heaven and Hell? She wondered. *Or only here on Earth?*

Tribunal would not be able to hear the prayers of His followers, because they worshipped a different name. That confused her, too. Why would God make it impossible for Tribunal to hear what His followers were saying? *Why didn't God have Him named Tribunal, instead of Jesus?*

The thought of His name brought Him straight to mind. Once more she was standing before the cross again, looking up at the bloody form of her lover. His power washed over her and with it His disdain and hatred for all of humankind. A vision of the Damned in Hell flashed before her. She had entered the minds of so many and seen the many, many horrible things they had done. The humans were so depraved that God had let them drop to eternal damnation, to be tortured by Nyx and the others for all eternity.

He wanted to deny Tribunal their worship, Nyx decided. *The same God that sent His own son to be tortured and killed, just so He could abandon humanity to its fate. The same God that denied me Heaven for wanting the same thing. He gives the humans a god that won't answer, just to see what will happen.*

The same God that is keeping Tribunal from me.

The last thought sent a spasm of rage through Nyx. There was a snapping noise, and across the room, the flute player missed a note, then stopped altogether. Nyx opened her eyes and realized that she had transformed back to herself, fully armored and armed, and that her talons had shredded the couch on which she lay and broken two of the wooden slats underneath. The flute player was staring in horror and awe, then prostrated himself before her.

"Forgive me, my Lady Nyx," he babbled. "Forgive my poor playing! My lack of true belief. Forgive me that I did not believe in you!"

Nyx rose from the couch, walked across the room, and effortlessly picked up the musician by the throat. "If you did not believe in me," she said, "Why did you come to my temple?"

"Please, my goddess," he begged, his voice wheezing out through his half-closed larynx. "Please, I needed the money!"

Nyx dropped him. "Do you believe in me now, little man?"

"Yes! Yes, my goddess!"

Nyx nodded. "Then play for me." She turned away, and sat

cross-legged in front of her statue, letting her wings wrap around her like a blanket. "Play me a song of vengeance."

The lute player played and Nyx stared up at the statue of herself. *God should not have done that to my Tribunal,* she thought. *He should not have hurt Him and He should not have taken my love away from me.* She was furious all over again. At God, at his Angels, and at the mortals who followed Him.

I will have revenge.

37 A.D. – CAPRI

Tiberius lay dying in his bed.

Nyx sat beside him, disguised as a young servant girl, breasts bare, wearing only a short skirt around her waist. She stroked his skin gently, as the two other girls and three young boys did, and wondered if she would see him in Hell once his mortal life was done.

He had not been a bad emperor, in truth, though his love for the flesh of young boys was near-legendary, and was certainly going to send him to Hell. The empire was at peace and was expanded, the treasury was full, and the people were happy. But he had not served Nyx nearly as well as she had hoped in his persecutions of the Christians. He had stayed away from Rome, preferring his home in Capri where he could diddle his boys in peace, and let the senators do as they pleased.

Caligula, son of Germanicus and sole survivor of that family, stepped into the room. Tiberius had ordered the rest of his family killed, or had them quietly assassinated in exile. Caligula he kept alive and for himself, no doubt because he was such a handsome young lad at the time. In the six years Caligula had been on Capri with Tiberius, he had grown soft around the middle, and hard as steel within. Even when he smiled, Nyx could see the hatred and fear that lurked behind his eyes. He reminded her of Hell's petty demons.

She had initiated Caligula into her temple herself after sending him a series of visions that taught him how to become emperor. She had taken great pains to institute a hatred of all things not Roman in Caligula, and knew that, when his time came, he would serve her purposes quite well.

Caligula smiled down at the weak, exhausted body of Tiberius. "So, here we are." He looked at the crowd of servants and officials around the room, then at his friend, Marko, the Praetorian Prefect. "I think there are too many of us," he said. "Clear the room." He looked over Nyx, and for a moment she changed her eyes from human to serpent, then back again. He smiled. "Except her."

Marko gave the order, and a dozen soldiers came in. They ushered the protesting nobles and physicians and servants out. When all were gone save Nyx, Caligula smiled at Tiberius. "How are you, my emperor?"

"Dying," whispered Tiberius.

"Good," said Caligula. "And about time, too."

Tiberius's eyes narrowed, and some of the steel came back into his weak voice. "You are ungrateful."

"Ungrateful?" repeated Caligula. He looked over at Marko. "Did you hear that, Marko? I am ungrateful." He smiled down at the old emperor. "Fuck your ass and mouth, old man."

Caligula picked up one of the cushions. With an easy stride, he mounted the bed and sat on the feebly protesting Tiberius. His smile never left his face and his tone didn't change as he spoke. "You murdered my family, you old boy-fucker. You took everything from me and you used me for a fuck toy and you call me ungrateful?" He pressed the pillow down against Tiberius's face and held it there while the old man and struggled and tried to cry out. As soon as his struggles began to slow, Caligula pulled the pillow away.

"Before I kill you," Caligula said as Tiberius gasped beneath him, "I want you to know that I will destroy everything you have made. Everything you have willed I will take and every memory of you I will erase." He pushed the pillow down again, holding it longer. When he pulled it away, Tiberius's mouth was wide and opening and closing like a fish. For a moment, it seemed the man had drawn his last. Then air wheezed back into his lungs.

Caligula smiled wider. "Everything you have touched I will defile and everyone you loved I will have put to death." He shoved the pillow against Tiberius's face again but didn't hold it there. Instead, he dismounted from the man's chest and took Nyx by the hand.

"Kill him," said Caligula to Marko, not looking back. "I'll be in my room, entertaining."

Marko mounted the old man's chest as Caligula led Nyx out. Those in the hallway saw him leading a slave girl, no doubt to have his way with her. Caligula led her into his own chamber and closed the door. Before she could say anything, Caligula knelt before her.

"My immortal Nyx," he said. "How may I serve you?"

Nyx smiled and raised him to his feet. "In so, so many ways."

39 A.D. – ROME

Nyx, wearing the body and clothes of a young Roman nobleman, stood with a half-dozen others in the Emperor's box, watching

Caligula simultaneously enjoying the slaughter of the criminals down below and the attentions of the woman who knelt in front of him. Beside her, standing rigid with his mouth tight, was the man whose wife was servicing Caligula.

"She is marvelous at this," Caligula said to the Senator. "You must be very pleased with her."

The Senator looked ready to explode, but only said, "Yes, Emperor."

The young emperor was certainly mad to bait the senators like this. Still, Caligula had been wonderful for Nyx. He was her devoted servant, and his love of her temples of pleasure and plenty made her more popular than ever. He built, at his own expense, beautiful temples dedicated to Nyx throughout the city, and made sure only the most lovely men and women served as acolytes, priests, and musicians. Others in the city's circles of power saw where the Emperor's interest lay, and became followers as well. Nyx was brought gold and gems, wheat, wine and olive oil, and spring lambs. Her priests distributed the food to the poor and used the money to spread her worship.

Unfortunately, Caligula was not nearly as good to his people.

His parties turned into orgies of torture and debasement. He was known for his cruelty in his judgements and his unreasonable taxes on the people. And he had a penchant for the wives of other rich, powerful men, and that one he flaunted because he could.

Caligula had tried to bring his excesses into Nyx's temple, but only once. The temple itself had shaken, killing two of his guards. Nyx then sent him a set of nightmares and visions, threatening him death unless he submitted himself to a half-dozen gladiators to be used as Tiberius had used him. Caligula had done as she'd asked, then had the men's tongues cut out and tortured them for weeks before sending them to the lions.

Nyx, who knew the men in question were all murderers, really didn't feel that bad about it.

Caligula was Emperor, but she was a Goddess, and he wasn't going to be allowed to forget it. Her temples were for sexual pleasure, not for pain. She had the finest musicians playing, the best wine and food, and no one died, except that one time and the man's heart had given out, to be fair.

Still, she wondered how long the senators would tolerate him.

The woman who was currently entertaining the emperor had spent the morning in Nyx's temple, praying that she send the Emperor's eye elsewhere. Nyx would have been more sympathetic if the woman's prayers hadn't been, "Let him rape the ass of that little whore that married my brother and maybe that will teach her to ape her betters!"

Nyx had laughed at that. And now, disguised as a young Roman noble, she was thoroughly enjoying the sight of the rich, powerful woman on her knees servicing Caligula. And the sight was made even more pleasurable by the knowledge of what would happen after she was done.

The Emperor's eyes closed and his body shuddered. The woman before him gagged and choked, then gasped. He pushed her back and frowned. "That is very disappointing," he said. "You were doing so well. Guard."

One of Caligula's Germanic guards stepped forward.

"Take her down to the gladiators," Caligula said. "Any man who survives today she must service. She may come to me tomorrow and display how her practice improved her." He looked at the senator, whose face had gone purple. "Is that acceptable, Senator?"

"Of course," the senator's voice came out strangled. "It is your will, my Caesar."

"Yes, it is," said Caligula. "You'd best go down with her and watch, to make sure she does it all correctly. I'll expect you to report her successes and failures to me by the end of the day." He shooed the senator away with his hand. "Go on, now."

The senator followed the guard down out of the Emperor's box. Caligula waved, then turned his attention back to the men on the floor of the Coliseum. Lions were circling them, and the condemned held out their pathetic wooden swords as if they would give them a chance.

"Come on!" shouted Caligula. "Eat them, you stupid beasts!" He turned to Nyx. "Those damn lions haven't eaten in a week. You think they'd be more eager." He sat back in his chair and sighed. "Well, then, let us do something more interesting. Guard! Bring him!"

A moment later three guards appeared, dragging in Herod Antipas, the man who had crucified Nyx's beloved Tribunal. He had been old, then, and was older now—well into his sixties. He had chains around his wrists and ankles and had been beaten and tortured. His body was covered in bruises and blood, and his fingers were bent at the wrong angles. Nyx smiled at the pain the man was in, and how he tried to bow to his emperor without wincing.

"So, Herod," said Caligula. "Conspiracy against the Empire." Caligula waved a finger at him. "Tsk, tsk, tsk."

"My Caesar," began Herod, "I would never…"

"Yes, you would," said Caligula. "You all would. And I keep

catching you and executing you, but you all keep trying nonetheless. Oh, look!" He caught Herod's shoulder and turned him to face the arena. "They've started!"

A man screamed as the first lion pounced, its claws gouging through flesh and sending blood spraying before the lion's jaws clamped around the man's neck. The man's screams ended as blood spurted. Caligula cheered and clapped Herod on the back. The other lions moved in. The men on the ground screamed and ran, or tried to fight, or stood still waiting to die. Soon the sand was covered in blood and severed limbs as the lions took down their prey and ripped them into manageable pieces. Caligula chortled gleefully and pointed to where one man, his legs ripped off and gnawed on by a young lion, lay screaming in agony as the lioness gorged itself on his intestines.

"Excellent! Excellent!" Caligula shouted. "Well done, lions!"

The crowd cheered with him, and Caligula retired to his chair. "Agrippa!" he shouted. "Come here and bring Herodias with you, would you?"

Herod Agrippa, nephew to Antipas, came out with Herod Antipas' wife, Herodias, leaning on his arm. She was twenty years younger than he, and a handsome woman. Caligula looked her up and down and smiled. He turned his attention back to Herod Antipas. "Your nephew here gave me the evidence," he said. "Stockpiling arms for 70,000 men? Dear, dear."

"Those arms are to defend Jerusalem," said Herod. "To defend all of Galilee and Perea against…"

"Against my legions," said Caligula. "Against your rightful Emperor? Is that it?"

"No, my Caesar!"

"You are guilty of conspiracy," said Caligula. "Your lands are forfeit and your nephew Agrippa here will take over. The question now is, what punishment should I give?" He propped his hand on his chin. "Crucifixion might do, but it is bad form to crucify a king. Leaves the other kings worried. No… I think it will have to be poison. Or strangulation. Strangulation is always good. A bit painful, but over quickly enough."

"Please, my Caesar," begged Herod Antipas. "Please. I have not conspired against you. I am loyal to you."

"Not loyal enough." He turned to Herod Antipas' wife. "Strangulation, do you think?"

"Please, Caesar," Herodias knelt before him, her hands on his feet in supplication. "Please, my Lord, he has done nothing against you."

"He has," said Caligula. "They all have. He's just one of the ones I could catch. Still, the punishment need not be death…"

Herod Antipas looked up. "My Caesar?"

"There are alternatives," Caligula said, still looking at Herodias. "If I was properly persuaded of his loyalty… and yours… I might see fit to declare exile instead."

"What must we do to persuade you?" asked Herodias.

"For a start?" Caligula smiled and ran a finger down the side of her face. "Turn around and raise your dress, my dear. That last senator's wife did well enough, but I am in need again, and you will suit me perfectly."

"My Caesar," protested Herod. "She is my wife."

"I am your Emperor!" screamed Caligula, shoving himself to his feet. "I am your ruler and you betrayed me! I should have you flogged and the wounds cauterized with molten copper! I should have you skinned alive and thrown to the rats! I should have you bent over and have a dozen dogs take their pleasure on you before I feed you to them!" He stopped screaming abruptly, and knelt behind Herodias, shoving her forward so she was on her hands and knees. "Instead, I will take your wife's ass. And when I am done, you will be banished to Gaul." He pushed Herodias' skirt up over her back. "And if she pleases me enough, I will even allow her to stay in Rome. I have need of more prostitutes."

Herodias spoke through gritted teeth, her voice angry and fearful. "I will stay with my husband," she said. "Come what may."

"As you wish," said Caligula.

Around them, the crowds of the Arena were watching and cheering. I wonder what the Gauls do to their captives, she thought. For Herod Antipas surely deserves the worst end *we can give him.*

She promised herself to send word to Persephone and Ishtar, then stood back and watched. *This Emperor will do very well indeed.*

*

41 A.D. - ROME

Nyx, Persephone, and Ishtar, clad in their true forms, looked down from where they floated in the sky as Caligula's Germanic Guard charged through the city, hacking and slashing almost at random as they pursued Caligula's assassins. The conspirators had murdered the king in the tunnels beneath the imperial palace. His guard, unable to stop them, seemed determined to do as much damage as possible to all those unlucky enough to be on the streets, and to Rome itself. Women and children lay gutted and moaning on the ground. Men died with limbs and heads hacked off. Senators, whose only crime had been to be at the Senate during the assassination, were chased down and stabbed a dozen times each before they were allowed to die. The assassins, desperate to keep control, were slaughtering as well. They had already visited Caligula's home, stabbing his wife to death and dashing his young daughter's brains out against the wall.

"So," said Ishtar, looking at the chaos. "First Emperor of Rome to be assassinated. Impressive."

"Maybe he shouldn't have tried to make his horse a Consul," said Persephone. "I think that's what did it."

"Maybe he shouldn't have tried fucking the wives of every senator and noble Roman in the city," said Ishtar. "Or making them his prostitutes."

"Well, he was short of money," said Persephone.

Nyx's whip lashed out twice, raising welts on each Angel's backsides. Both yelped as the Hellfire whip cut their flesh, but neither, Nyx was certain, was at all sorry. *This is what comes of letting them play goddesses,* she thought. *They grow too high and mighty for their own good.*

"At least my temples have spread throughout the city," she said. "Next step is to spread them through the empire."

"That's good," said Ishtar, "Because the Christians are already spreading."

"What?" Nyx was shocked. "I thought they were being suppressed!"

"Not successfully," said Persephone. "The governors don't care, so long as they don't advocate violence."

Nyx hissed, and her eyes flared red. "How far have they spread?"

"Antioch, Ephesus, Corinth, Tessalonica, Cypus, Crete, and of course, here in Rome."

Rage built inside Nyx, and her teeth ground together as she stared at the mess below. *Damn God for blocking our way to them! We could have snuffed them out in less than a day.* "Go back to Jerusalem," said Nyx. "Get the governor to start killing them."

"I will," said Persephone.

"Say," said Ishtar. "Isn't that your temple they're going into?"

Nyx looked. Ten of the Germanic guards had entered her Temple. "Yes," she said. Nyx's lips pulled back in a violent, ugly grin. Her teeth had become fangs, and she was eager to use them. "Yes, it is."

Her wings flapped with a noise like thunder and she hurled herself at the soldiers. Let them desecrate every other temple in the city if they liked. They would not desecrate hers, and all Rome would know it.

A.D. 64 – ROME

Nyx hid in the back of the alley and glared.

She had disguised herself with black skin, black hair, and black robes, and blended in perfectly with the alley around her. She stood outside the window of a small paper shop, listening.

It was a hot night. The air was still and the heat was enough to send most men to bed, sweating, or to the baths, in search of cool water. Inside the shop, which must have been crowded, stuffy and stinking, a dozen men had gathered to listen to two foreigners talk of Jesus. They spoke of the crucifixion, of sacrifice and a new savior and of Heaven to come. It all left a foul taste in Nyx's mouth.

Tribunal would have hated all of this, she thought. *He would have laughed at it and destroyed them all, given His choice. And then we could have a new Paradise...*

For twenty-three years she had been working against the Christians, and it seemed at every turn she had been stymied. They continued to spread like lice on the head of the empire. She had some successes, but not many. Her own temples had grown and spread throughout the empire, and she had thousands of worshippers. But all of this was doing little to stem the tide of Christians.

They shouldn't even exist. The One they worship doesn't want them, she fumed. *Fine. Let's see what happens when we do this...*

Paper was expensive in Rome, and rare. It was made from the pith of the papyrus plant and took a careful process to make. Once the stalks had been cut, mashed, and laid out, they had to be carefully dried and polished before they were ready to be used.

It only took a thought from Nyx to push over one of the candles in the room, and another to set it rolling to a pile of papyrus, just dried, on the table. The people in the room were so engrossed, they did not realize anything was amiss at first.

A gust of wind, like a flapping of wings, sent the burning paper into the air. Another sent some out the window, where it caught the next house on fire.

"Fire!" screamed one of the men inside. "Fire! Fire!"

They tried to fight it at first, but the stock of paper in the room caught too quickly as gusts of wind sent flaming scraps everywhere. They were forced from the room and ran into the street, screaming.

Nyx bathed in the heat of the flames, and watched as one building after another caught fire. She changed her shape again, becoming a young Roman woman, fetchingly dressed in a disarrayed toga that left one breast exposed. She smeared some of the soot from the building on her face, then caught a piece of the paper and let it burn her hair and the edges of her clothes. She wished she could see herself, but suspected it would be fine.

Taking a deep breath, she stepped into the street, screaming, "Fire! Fire! The Christians have lit the city on fire!"

*

Five days later, in the garden of Nero's palace, the emperor Nero stood before a pair of crucified Christians. The men had been nailed up and piles of wood had been placed around the base of their crosses and doused in oil. A line of thirty other men knelt, chained, before the crosses.

"These!" Nero said to a crowd of senators, "Are two of the ones responsible for the deaths of so many Romans. They have confessed their actions, as have their co-conspirators." He waved at the men before the crosses. Most bore marks of torture. "And since they have thought to bring our great city down with fire, we will punish them with fire! And use them as a beacon to show that Rome still shines, and that Rome will rise again!"

He raised a hand, and at his signal two centurions put torches to the pyres beneath the crosses. The wood caught at once and the fire spread quickly.

"Every night, until our city is rebuilt, we shall burn one of these 'Christians!' One of these superstitious followers of a dead criminal!" shouted Nero. "And let it be known that any Christians found in our city, indeed in our Empire, will share this or a worse fate! We will feed them to the Arena dogs! We will torture and crucify them! We will root out this rot that threatens to destroy our empire, and we will rise, stronger than ever!"

The first flames licked the feet of the men on the crosses, and they began screaming.

Standing in the shadows, her black armor making her near invisible in the darkness, Nyx smiled. At last, things were going better.

*

70 A.D. - ELEUSIS

In the fire-lit darkness, the teenage maiden cowered upon a huge stone bed. Her flimsy silk robe reached only to the top of her thighs, and the parts of her it covered could be seen through the sheer fabric. She gazed wildly around, eyes wide, the whites shining.

From nearby came the *boom… boom… boom* of footsteps too heavy to be human. The girl pushed herself against the wall, as if trying to crawl inside it, tears streaming down her lovely face. The noise came closer, and closer, and then Dispater stepped out into the light of the torches. He was easily nine feet tall, his red, scaled flesh flickering in the firelight. The curved, pointed horns on his head gleamed black, matching the glittering black of his eyes. He sniffed the air, his head swiveling on his neck as he caught the sweet scent of his prey.

Gasps of horror came from five hundred throats. Dispater ignored them. His eyes found his prey, and a leer formed on his face. His breathing deepened, and between his legs, his huge penis began to grow, eliciting more gasps from those watching.

The maiden slid off the bed, and started to run, but Dispater was too quick. In a flash he had grabbed her. In another he had torn the robe from her shivering body, the scrap of cloth ripped into rags.

"Please," she begged. "Please don't. Please! Don't!"

Dispater growled his reply and threw the girl on her back, holding her legs wide so all those watching could see.

"Jerusalem has fallen!" said Nyx in Persephone's mind. *"The Romans have breached the wall and the Jews' temple is burning!"*

Slowly, the beast drove its length into the girl's writhing form. She screamed, long and loud.

"The governors have continued that coward, Nero's, work," Nyx continued as she began pumping rhythmically in and out of Persephone's mortal body, the slap of her demon-shaped flesh against Persephone's thighs accompanied by Persephone's screams. *"Christians are being burned, tortured, and thrown to the dogs all over the empire."*

"You're ruining the mood here," said Persephone in Nyx's mind, bringing a grin to Nyx's demon face. *"This is the big ritual. They need a show."*

"Then let's give them one." Nyx grabbed Persephone by the hair with one enormous hand, and threw her onto her stomach with the other. She pulled her head back so the five hundred worshippers of Persephone could see their version of their goddess cry and scream as she enacted her wedding night with Dispater. *"Vespasian has come to power,"* continued Nyx. *"He has promised to raise temples to me in exchange for his victory. Soon, my cult will be larger than even Mithras."*

"Be careful with that," Persephone said in Nyx's mind, as she writhed and cried for the pleasure of the crowd. *"Mitthras is the god of the legions and is not to be trifled with."*

"I'm not trifling with him," said Nyx. "Besides, he's not here, is he?" She increased the pace of her thrusts. "And all I need do is outnumber the Christians, anyway."

"Wait... " Persephone's screams changed pitch, and her body shuddered with orgasm, though her followers didn't know it. When the shuddering subsided, she let herself go limp—the perfect image of a ravaged innocent, torn open by a beast of a husband. "The key isn't outnumbering them now," she said in Nyx's mind. "The key is outnumbering them a thousand years from now, remember?"

"I know that!" Nyx thrust harder in her irritation. "As long as Rome stands, we will outnumber them!"

"Then you... better hope it... stands for a... thousand years," Persephone said.

"Rome is immortal."

"That's what the Kerma said." Persephone began shuddering again. "Remember them?"

"No."

"Neither does anyone else," said Persephone. "Now... hurry up and... finish so... we can do the pomegranate bit... I want to thank you... properly... Oh, my Queen!"

Persephone's screams echoed through the cave, and her followers watched in awe.

*

84 A.D. – ROME

Domitian, Emperor of Rome, rose late one night, his mind whirling from dreams of destruction. His niece—a fine young woman and one whom he hoped could give him the child his banished wife had failed to provide—slept undisturbed, still bathed in the sweat of their congress. Domitian knelt before the shrine of Minerva and bowed his head. "Oh, great goddess. Guide your servant. Guide me, who has helped you rise in prominence again, and who has brought back the proper worship of our true Roman gods..."

The butt end of the spear lashed out of nowhere, knocking him to the earth. He went sprawling, crying out in pain. The statue of Minerva in front of him changed from marble to flesh, clothed in a rich, white gown, her helmet gleaming bronze and her spear now wickedly pointed.

"You dare," said Nyx, poking the point of the spear at him just hard enough to draw blood from his stomach. *Minerva would be so mad if she saw this,* Nyx thought, holding the spear tip near his face. *She never liked dramatic gestures.* "You dare claim to bring back the rule of the Gods of Rome when you threaten the temple of our sister Nyx?"

"But, but, but..." Domitian was near-speechless. "This Nyx is no Goddess of Rome."

"LIAR!" screamed Nyx, and this time the spear tip went deeper, gouging into his flesh. "She is the protector of Emperors, sent by Jupiter himself to Tiberius to destroy those who threaten Rome! And you would destroy her temple?"

"Forgive me, great Goddess!" begged Domitian. "Forgive me! I did not know!"

"Forgive you?" Minerva's voice boomed loud. "You must earn your forgiveness!"

"How, Great Minerva?" begged Domitian. "What must I do?"

"Take yourself to Nyx's temple!" commanded Nyx. "Take

this slut with you and do not leave until you have topped her three times in the inner sanctum! Then call back your wife and do the same to her with your slut watching!"

"Yes, Minerva, my Goddess. I will!"

"Then it is time for you to go after the true enemies of Rome. Those whose silly superstition about a crucified carpenter threatens the fabric of the empire!"

"Yes! Yes, I will!"

"Do as you are bid!" screamed Nyx. "At once!"

Domitian was alone once more in the room, and all was silence. He looked around, his head whipping back and forth to see who else had witnessed. There was only his niece, still asleep in the bed. He shook his head, trying to clear it. For a moment he thought it had all been a dream.

Then the pain of the spear wounds in his belly made him gasp.

He clasped his hand to his belly and rose, unsteady, to his feet. Stumbling across the room, he grabbed his niece's leg and shook it for all it was worth. "A vision!" he cried out. "A vision! You must rise and come to me at once!"

100 A.D.

Nyx sat alone in her temple, leaning against her statue, staring at the massive mural in the wall.

Hell had been timeless, more or less. When you were there, you knew time was passing, but it didn't matter so much. Only on the mortal world did she really feel the passage of time.

One hundred years ago, Tribunal was born on earth.

She missed Tribunal. Desperately. Her heart ached whenever she thought of Him. Her soul yearned for Him the way it had yearned for Heaven and the presence of God when she had first been in Hell. And even though her temples were flourishing and Nyx and the others were slowly turning the Roman empire against Christians, it didn't seem like enough. She wanted to be with Him, wanted to cleanse the deluded followers of Christ from the earth, along with the rest of humanity. She wanted to take Tribunal in her arms in His true, Angelic form, and feel His presence and power envelope her. She wanted to be in his new Paradise and rule of Paradise and Hell by His side.

And yet…

The chorus of voices that rose in her head had become a river, just as Persephone had said. At any time she could dive into it and swim around in the hopes and dreams of those who prayed for her. Many who claimed to love and worship her were wicked. There were murders and rapists among her cultists, and senators that tortured slaves just to learn new ways to cause pain. There were hate-filled, power-hungry men and women that allowed others to starve so that they could have plenty. They would die and go to Hell for an eternity of torture.

And then there were the other ones. The ones who were living exemplary lives. There were shopkeepers and farmers and tradesmen. There were butchers and wives and children. They were decent and would end up in Heaven at the feet of God, where Nyx herself could never go again. Some had already gone. And Nyx, surprisingly, was glad for them.

But why do I give a rat's ass about any of these humans at all?

She was the Queen of Hell, put there by God, to dwell in darkness and misery, to punish the wicked and to walk in no higher sphere than the Earth, because she had dared defy God. She would never know His presence, never bask in His divine glow. She was cut off from Heaven, and closest she would know to it was the continuing dull ache inside her.

So why should I care about the humans? Why should she care about anything at all? Tribunal loved her, and was going to give her Paradise. That was what was important.

And yet…

God took Tribunal from you, she reminded herself. *Just as He took away Heaven. God cares nothing for you or these people or He wouldn't have abandoned them all. He would have given them Tribunal's real name and He wouldn't have taken Tribunal away from me!*

Tribunal is right to want them destroyed. If God loves them so much, let Him take them all to Heaven and deal with them. Then the Earth can be ours and we can create a new Paradise!

In the river of her mind, she heard a soul crying out for vengeance for the death of her child, murdered by another human for no reason.

Nyx rose, spread her wings, and flew. Punishing the wicked was something she was very, very good at. And it never hurt to answer a follower's prayer.

113 A.D. - ROME

"It is a corruption on Imperial Rome, Caesar," said the old man. "Their belief is nothing but superstition. They worship a God who cannot be seen, whose teachings were taught by a criminal who died crucified. They tell lies of a Heaven and Hell that do not exist, and they do not sacrifice to the Gods as is appropriate. They must be outlawed, for the good of the nation."

Emperor Trajan shifted in his seat, and sighed. The man, a

seasoned soldier and campaigner, liked nothing more than to be up and active, and days such as these bored him beyond belief.

"My Caesar," said the old man, "I am not the orator I once was, and I fear I do not have the words to convince you of the truth of the situation." The old man gestured behind him, and a slim, pleasantly-muscled boy of fourteen stepped forward. Trajan sat up in his chair. "Would my Caesar allow my grandson to stay with him, and to speak further of these matters?"

The young man smiled coyly at the Emperor, even as he knelt before him. "It would be most pleasurable for me," he said, "To present you with my arguments."

Trajan nodded. "An excellent idea. And in fact, since I am having lunch soon, I will take this young man with me, and there learn of his powers of persuasion."

Persephone, disguised as the old man, bowed deeply. "My thanks, O Caesar."

"Why do I have to go with him?" Ishtar demanded inside Persephone's mind as she rose in the young man's body and followed Trajan from the room.

"Nyx said I would enjoy it too much," said Persephone, smiling and waving. *"And remember, Nyx said you weren't allowed to change back until he outlaws Christianity."*

It was six hours later when Ishtar left the palace, walking gingerly and rubbing her aching jaw muscles. She/he made her way through the city to the temple of Nyx, bowed, and entered within. She minced up the stairs to the highest chamber, where Nyx lay in Persephone's lap on an enormous bed, allowing the other Angel to feed her grapes.

Ishtar came in, groaned, and winced as she sat down on the bed's edge.

"Well," said Persephone, smiling. "Have fun?"

Ishtar glared at her, then said to Nyx, "He is nearly convinced. I am to return to him tomorrow, to further persuade him."

Persephone laughed. "You'd best sit on a cool cloth until then."

Ishtar glared some more, then pleaded to Nyx. "May I please heal myself? He is… very vigorous, and very long lasting. And given to multiple actions in a single day."

"No wonder he was such a fine soldier," said Nyx, smiling. "And no, you can't heal yourself. You—neither of you—take this seriously enough. Get the law passed, and then you may go back to Egypt and indulge in your own tastes."

Ishtar sighed. "Yes, my Queen."

118 A.D. - ROME

Nyx, Ishtar and Persephone, disguised as Roman citizens, watched as the criminals were shoved out into the middle of the Arena. Most wept and cursed, some tried to look brave, and others just looked blank, as if death had already taken their souls, and their bodies were moving without volition.

In the midst of them, one man stood tall and strong, singing and praying.

"Fucking Ignatius," muttered Nyx. "And fucking Romans for not executing him in Syria. They had to drag him across the empire to kill him. He did more damage on his way to his death than he did when he was free."

"Well, he's not free now," pointed out Ishtar. "And soon he'll be dead."

"Doesn't matter," said Nyx. "Look at him. He's happy he's about to die. He's singing, for fuck's sake."

"He won't be for long," said Persephone. "Here are the lions."

The lions had poured from the pits of the arena. And one of them, a lioness larger than the others, with dark yellow fur and wickedly long claws, headed for Ignatius. The other criminals scattered and tried to run. Ignatius continued his singsong prayers.

The lioness stalked him, circling him at first, then starting to come closer. Ignatius seemed unconcerned. It drew closer and closer, until it was nearly on top of him.

"Any time, now," muttered Nyx.

The lioness lashed out with a paw, opening four great slashes in Ignatius's leg. The man yelled in pain and shock as blood began pouring from him. The lioness struck again, low on the other leg, hamstringing him and making him fall to the earth. He screamed louder as the lioness went in, ignoring his cries and feeble attempts to hit her as she buried her face in his belly. The screams reached a new, higher pitch.

"One down," said Ishtar. "Does it make you feel better?"

"Yes," said Nyx. "Now, if we can just get the rest of them…"

120 A.D. – ARCADIA

A thousand revelers spilled out into the streets, laughing and dancing. Men and women alike, half-naked, heavily intoxicated, were deep in the throes of the Bacchanalia, and seething with desire for blood, sex, and whatever other pleasures they could find.

"This way! This way!" cried Nyx, her body now that of a woman at the peak of ripeness, her large, bare breasts swinging as she led the crowd into the streets. "Follow me to the ones who will not sacrifice or celebrate! We'll make them serve Bacchus, or they can die!"

The crowd cheered and poured through the streets, laughing and singing. Some stopped to copulate in the road, others to vomit, but most followed her straight to the Christians' temple. The building had started life as something else, but now the Christians were inside it, and they were praying behind the barred door.

"Come ooooouuuut!" called Nyx, kicking at the door with her sandal. "Come out or we'll burn you out!"

The Christians went on praying, though their voices were strained. Nyx kicked harder, and the strength of it shook the doors on the hinges. "Come out!" she shouted. "It is the Bacchanalia! The Lord of Wine demands your sacrifice! Come out and pay him tribute you godless, superstitious atheists! Come out and give Bacchus his due!"

The crowd around her roared their agreement, and men and women began banging on the shutters, yelling for the Christians to come out. Nyx could still hear the Christians praying inside.

"Fire!" shouted someone in the crowd, and others took up the chant. "Fire! Fire! Fire! Fire! Fire!"

Fire, yes, thought Nyx. *But not yet.*

She called to the men and a dozen strong ones came forward to hammer against the door with her. They fell into the rhythm of the chants, shoving harder and harder. Nyx joined with them.

And on the seventh shove, she pushed with her full strength against the double doors of the small temple. There was a *crack!* from inside as the bar holding the door shut broke in two, and the doors swung wide.

The Bacchantes charged in, laughing and yelling. Nyx stood aside and watched them go. The church filled with shrieks as the Christians tried to fight off the drunken mob. Men and women together attacked, pulling off their victims' clothes even as they pummeled, kicked, scratched and bit them. The Christians fought back as best they could, but were hideously outnumbered. The Bacchantes dragged them into the streets, screaming "Fire!" and "Sacrifice!" The Christians, men and women alike, were thrown into the street naked, where members of the crowd, eager to release their energy and enthusiasm, fell on them.

Inside the church, men screamed. A half-dozen legionnaires were among the Christians, and they had managed to snatch up their weapons and began hacking their way out. Blood spattered and limbs flew as the legionnaires drove the drunken Bacchantes back. A pair of men fell to the floor, their guts spilling out. The legionnaires formed up in a tight formation and slashed and stabbed their way to the door. Their charged surprised the Bacchantes, who ran, fighting one another to get out of the door of the temple as the legionnaires advanced on them. Nyx was shoved aside, then to the ground, and then stepped on as men and women fled before the bloody onslaught of the legionnaires.

When she rose to her feet, the legionnaires were right in front of her, and one of them drove a sword into her midsection.

Nyx screamed in rage. The sound was not human, and it froze Bacchantes and Christians alike. Nyx lashed out with her fingernails, now talons, catching the closest soldier's throat and tearing away flesh, muscle, and windpipe. The man collapsed, gurgling, to the floor.

Nyx was so surprised, she took another thrust to her

stomach. The second soldier twisted the blade and agony blossomed inside Nyx's guts, even as the realization came.

I killed one of them, thought Nyx. *I can KILL them!*

The sword thrust at her belly again. Nyx grabbed it by the blade and tore it out of the wielder's hand. The man had just a moment to stare in shock before Nyx, her teeth suddenly razors, stepped forward and bit deep into his neck, sending hot blood up like a fountain. His companions stumbled back in horror. Nyx grinned, switching to her true form as she attacked. With her fingernails and teeth she ripped off limbs and tore apart flesh. Blood spattered and splashed over the walls of the church. Nyx screamed in delight and kept going.

The six legionnaires fell in seconds. A dozen more Christians followed moments later. She worked her way through the crowd, pulling the raping Bacchantes away and murdering the Christians with her own hands.

In less than an hour, all the Christians were dead, their temple was on fire, and Nyx was winging her way through the sky towards Greece. She would tell Persephone, then they would tell Ishtar.

And on the way, she would deal with one of the Christians' biggest rabble-rousers.

*

It was near dawn when Nyx and Persephone came screaming out of the sky like two hawks, diving down on the home of Polycarp, Bishop of Smyrna. Both were clad head to foot in their black, scaled armor, their swords blazing with black Hellfire and their whips leaving trails of black sparks.

"Now!" shouted Nyx. "Now we will destroy them all!"

She pulled in her wings and reversed, and Persephone did the same, their spiked heels aiming for the roof. Nyx's plan was to break through the roof of the house, terrorize Polycarp and kill everyone in his house. Then, they were going to flay and crucify him as a warning to the others.

They were nearly at the roof when the wind took them. Both Nyx and Persephone could easily fly through a gale, but this was different. This was a divine wind and it picked the two of them up and threw them into the sea like a pair of albatrosses shot from the sky.

*

"Asshole," muttered Nyx as she paced the room, drying her hair. "Dog fucker. Pig fucker. Goat fucker!"

"God, you mean?" said Ishtar.

"Of course God! That… that…"

"Shit-licking bum-boy of a beast-fucking swineherd?" suggested Persephone, shaking the water out of her wings.

"Yes!" said Nyx.

"You knew it was going to happen," said Ishtar. "You're the one who told us that we can't attack them directly."

"It didn't happen in Arcadia!" protested Nyx. "I killed a temple full of Christians and nothing stopped me!"

"Really?" said Ishtar, her eyes lighting up. "We can kill them now?"

"Yes!"

"About damn time!" said Ishtar. She thought about it. "Why now, though?"

"Because the rules have changed!" snapped Nyx. She stopped

then, realization washing over her like the sea had a few hours before. "Fuck! Shit! Fuck!"

Ishtar and Persephone stood back, watching closely. For the next hour, Nyx proceeded to destroy everything in the temple while screeching like a fishwife and swearing in twelve languages, including two only heard among the demons of Hell.

When she finally ran out of steam, she glared at the other two Angels. "The rules haven't changed. The agreement is: 'They shall go unfettered by Angels. They shall have free will and free choice, and they will choose for themselves which actions to take. No Angel shall order, compel, or lay hands on those who build my church. Not everyone is helping to build the church. And the ones who aren't, we can kill.'"

"Ooh…" Ishtar rubbed her hands together. "Can I kill some of those disgusting men you've made me fuck? And their toad-like offspring?"

"Do what you like," said Nyx, "Just don't invite reprisals against your temple."

"Isis's temple," grumbled Ishtar.

"Whatever," snapped Nyx. "We need people to oppose them. We need people to fight and kill them, so keep building up Isis's temple. I'm going back to Rome. One of my priests was embezzling, and I am very much in a mood to make an example of somebody right now."

"Don't overdo it," advised Persephone. "Too much divinity and they become complacent. Keep the miracles few and far between and they'll worship you all the more when they come."

"This isn't about miracles," snapped Nyx. "The money he was taking could build new temples! I could gain more followers."

"Followers aren't everything."

"They are for me!" snapped Nyx. "Have you forgotten what this is all about? Have you forgotten that we have a chance at Paradise, if we can defeat the Christians?"

"We haven't forgotten," said Persephone, her voice gentle.

"Send a vision to the priests telling them to bring you more followers. Tell them to give the money they have to the poor and raise more for a temple in the poor areas."

"Which ones? There are poor all over the world!"

"All of them!" Persephone shook her head. "Your problem, my Queen, is that you are used to being in charge instead of being worshipped. Your priests do the work, and you supply the miracles, punishments, and protection. And you have as much fun as possible."

"Fun doesn't get me followers."

"But it does get you laid," said Ishtar, coming closer. "Especially when you visit me."

"Hey!" said Persephone. "What am I? Chopped meat?"

"You certainly look like it after your 'wedding night' ritual," said Ishtar.

"At least I don't have to geld my High Priests to keep them in line."

"No, you just have to fuck them."

"Behave," snapped Nyx. "I'm going back to Rome. The last Bacchanalia was a success against the Christians and I can use it again. Meanwhile, I'll have my priests build a new temple to Nyx in the area. Every time we take one of his off the map, we replace it with one of mine."

"Well, I can certainly help with that," said Ishtar, spreading her own wings. "I'll let you know which areas I've killed all the Christians in."

*

130 A.D. – EGYPT

In private cabin of his ship, Emperor Hadrian finished fucking the beautiful Antonius with a loud moan and collapsed onto the other man's smooth back. A moment later he rolled off, though his hand stayed on the younger man's body, caressing him as the gentle motion of the Nile beneath them rocked the ship.

"You give me such pleasure," he whispered to Antonius. "I don't know what I'd do without you."

"Nor I without you." said Antonius, kissing him back. "My Emperor."

The door to the cabin burst open and Nyx, in full battle armor, with wings widespread to cover the walls of the small room, yelled, "You pitiful excuse for an Emperor!"

"My lady Nyx!" protested Hadrian, his guts tightening with fear. "My goddess, what have I done?"

"You dare issue an edict protecting the Christians?" yelled Nyx. "You dare say that they cannot be harmed?" She grabbed Antonius, her taloned hands digging through the flesh of his leg. "I will destroy everything you love, old man, then I will destroy you!"

"No, please," begged Hadrian, as Nyx dragged the screaming Antonius off the bed, crimson blood smearing the sheets. "Don't hurt him! Please don't hurt him!"

Nyx, dragging the wounded boy by one foot, walked out of the cabin and straight into the attack of ten legionnaires. She drew her sword and made one wide sweep with it, cutting through armor, weapons, shields and flesh, and sending a wide splatter of blood over the deck. Four of the legionnaires died. The others retreated, horrified. They stopped when they heard their Emperor's ragged pleas, and prepared to advance again. Nyx kept walking. Her next swing decapitated two more of the legionnaires, their blood spraying from their still-standing bodies as their heads flew into the air. She reached the edge of the deck, and turned back to Hadrian. "You pissant! I should fuck you the way you fuck your bitch here, but I wouldn't dirty myself with your flesh!" She raised Antonius in the air with one hand and sheathed her sword with the other. "The river is full of crocodiles, tonight," she said. "I brought them here just for this occasion."

"I beg you, Lady! I'll do anything." The Emperor was on his knees, not caring who saw.

Nyx thrust the talons of her now-empty hand into Antonius's groin, tearing off his still-damp genitals and ripping open his belly and chest in a single swipe. Antonius's screams went higher and louder as his guts coiled out into the water below. Hadrian jumped up and ran forward. Nyx let him come almost close enough to touch his lover, then threw Antonius over the rail. He splashed into the water below and the air was filled with the roar and hissing of the crocodiles. Hadrian fell to his knees, covering his face and wailing as the roars and growls of the crocodiles feasting filled the air.

Nyx grabbed Hadrian, pinched open his mouth and poured a disgusting concoction down his throat. The Emperor gagged and choked, trying to vomit it back up. Nyx clamped her hand over his mouth, forcing him to swallow or choke to death. "That," she hissed in his ear, "was made of the blood, shit, piss and puke of an old man who has been dying by inches, in indescribable pain, for the last ten years." She rose up and let Hadrian drop, writhing, to the deck. "You will come to my temple every month and you will kneel in worship. You will persecute the Christians and, if you do so, I my consider taking the disease from you." She kicked him hard enough to send him skidding across the deck, knocking over the remaining legionnaires. "Asshole."

Nyx flew off into the night, leaving the gasping, vomiting Emperor on the deck.

*

A.D. 165 – ROME

"It is true," said the strong young soldier kneeling before Emperor Marcus Aurelius. "Again and again I see these Christians coming to our classes, challenging our teachers. They claim stoicism is a fable! They claim our teachings of virtue and the denial of vice are nothing compared to that of their petty little desert god."

"Please, Caesar," said the middle-aged man beside him. Like the young soldier, this man was strong and fit. He carried the scars of several battles on his flesh, and had a tattoo from one of eastern legions on his arm. Unlike the soldier, he was dressed for teaching. "They dare to claim that their teachings are equal to the Stoics, and are insinuating themselves into the great families of the empire. They must be stopped."

"They will be," promised Marcus Aurelius. "Let the word be spread. Christian teaching will not be allowed to contaminate our empire. They will not corrupt our children with their preaching of weakness. They do not understand true virtue, and therefore cannot understand the avoidance of vice. They may pray as they like, but will not be allowed to spread their teachings." He sighed. "Rome is weak enough already. We will not have it weakened further."

"Thank you, O Caesar," said the young and old man together. They kissed the hem of his robe and backed away before leaving.

"That was well done," said Persephone, once they left the audience chamber.

"It was necessary," said Nyx, who was wearing the older man's flesh. "He has no vices, as near as I can tell. He doesn't believe in any of the Gods and he wouldn't believe in me even if I showed myself. So if you can't appeal to a man's vices to corrupt him…"

"Appeal to his virtues," finished Persephone. "Very good indeed." Inside Nyx's head, she added, *"My Queen."*

"Good enough for now," said Nyx. "Let's see how many he kills."

*

313 A.D.

As the sun set, Nyx screamed in fury and hurled herself again at Milan. Once more, the divine wind caught her, and when she crashed to earth, she was in a forest in Western Gaul. She rose and charged forward again, not heeding the bruises and lacerations on her body, or the missing feathers on her wings. Faster than sound she winged forward, determined to reach Milan and stop Constantine.

Fucking Constantine!

It was the first time in the 280 years that she had been fighting the rise of Christianity that she had not been able to reach an Emperor. It was the first true reversal in close to 150. Nyx had been guiding emperor after emperor, urging worse and worse persecutions. Septimus Severus had begun executing Christians and encouraging the same across the provinces. Maximus the Thracian continued the tradition, cutting them down whole communities and burying their corpses in pits. Decius and Valerian had continued, killing even more and driving the movement underground.

And Diocletian—Ah, Diocletian, thought Nyx—had been a true follower. He had set out to exterminate the Christians, and Nyx had encouraged him all the way. She had even let him fuck her in her temple as reward for all he had done. Christians were slaughtered by the hundreds: crucified, burnt, thrown to the animals. She had actually been making progress.

Then along comes fucking Constantine, snarled Nyx to herself. *And fucks up everything!*

Constantine's mother had been Christian, which made him lenient. He had been raised in the East, away from Nyx's direct influence, and had become ruler in the West. And then, as his armies marched on Rome, Constantine had a vision.

Vision! Nyx thought. *Hallucination! Mindless stupidity!*

Constantine had emblazoned his army with the Christian's Chi Rho, and he believed that is was what had led to his victory. Nyx had not even been able to approach him. In horror she watched as the successful persecutions of the last 100 years fell away as Constantine's armies advanced from Gaul to Rome.

Now the fucker is in Milan, she thought, *talking to the fucking Christians about legitimizing their fucking fake fucking religion.*

"I WON'T HAVE IT!" Nyx screamed. She forced herself forward even faster, heedless of the pain she was in.

Ishtar and Persephone swooped in from either side, each

catching an arm in her hands and wrapping her legs around one of Nyx's. Nyx screamed in fury and tried to shake them off. She was stronger than they, a better warrior and filled with power from her couplings with Tribunal. On any other day she would have kicked their asses. This day, with her body battered by the divine winds, her strength was not nearly what it had been before.

Persephone and Ishtar forced her to slow down, steered her southward toward Piscae. She fought them every inch of the way, ripping at their flesh and trying to bite, claw and kick them for nearly an hour until they reached the city. Together Persephone and Ishtar slammed her to the earth, bringing her down on the roof of her own temple, and pushed her inside.

As soon as they let her go, Nyx attacked the Angels with claws and feet, bruising and breaking them. Ishtar and Persephone fought back just as hard, scoring flesh and breaking bones in return.

The humans within the temple ran as the walls shook with the fight. The people in the area fled as the noise of the battle echoed through the neighborhood. For three days the Angels fought, until they all lay exhausted and hideously wounded, on a floor smeared with a mess of silver blood, scattered feathers, ichor, ripped flesh and torn hair.

Nyx lay in the middle of the floor, gasping and shaking, tears leaking from her eyes. *Oh, Tribunal...* she thought. *I've failed you.*

"Now," said Persephone, her voice strange and nasal from her broken nose, which now bent sideways across her face. "Are you through being stupid?"

Nyx looked up, her red eyes flashing with rage. She drew

herself slowly to her feet, ignoring the pain of the leg she'd broken against a pillar when she missed a kick at Ishtar.

"Give it up," said Persephone, pulling herself to her own feet. The movement brought silver blood streaming from a dozen wounds. Her stomach, legs, breasts and face were a mass of slashes and gouges. Her armor was rent through in a hundred places. "We lost this one."

"We... haven't... LOST!" screamed Nyx, and the sound of it would have shattered any mortal's eardrums, had they been in hearing range.

"He's a Christian Emperor!" screamed Persephone back. "He's untouchable! Leave him alone and get ready to fight the next one!"

"But the Christians will increase a thousandfold!" Nyx grabbed her leg and forced the broken bone back into place, gritting her teeth as it slid back inside her flesh. She willed it to heal and felt it slowly responding.

"So what?" demanded Ishtar, pulling herself upright from the floor. Half her face was gone, and her left arm was flayed open to the bones and inverted at the elbow. Silver blood oozed from her crotch where Nyx had managed to plant one particularly vicious kick. Both her wings were broken in at least two places. "You've been going against them for 300 years. You've never gotten ahead."

"My temples are across the Empire!"

"The Empire is dying," said Persephone. "Rome is lost."

"I won't lose Rome!"

"You already have!" screamed Persephone. "Look around! The East rebels, the West rebels! Even Constantine won't be able to stay here forever!"

"She's right," said Ishtar.

"How the fuck would you know?" demanded Nyx. "Either of you?"

"Because we've seen it before!" snapped Ishtar. "You were too busy playing in Hell and fucking with individuals. You never paid attention to the empires. I was worshipped for millennia! I watched my worshipers grow and I heard all their voices and then I watched Babylon die! I heard my followers screams as they were killed."

"Well it isn't happening to my followers!"

"It is!" shouted Persephone. "Empires fall! And right now, Rome is the empire falling!"

"Fuck you!" screamed Nyx.

"You know we're right!" shouted Persephone. "Otherwise you would have fought with your sword!"

Nyx looked down at her hands, coated with the ichor of Ishtar and Persephone, then up at the ruined bodies and faces of the other two Angels. None of them had drawn weapons for the last three days. In fact, it had not even occurred to Nyx to do so.

"Fuck you," said Nyx again, though there was no anger left in her. Despair washed over her. "Fuck you both for being right."

Nyx collapsed to the ground again, the last of her energy spent. Ishtar and Persephone waited a moment, then slowly sat down themselves. None of them said anything for a time. Each was wrapped in their own world of pain as their bodies began the slow process of healing.

Nyx finally looked up from the floor. "Do I look as bad as you two?"

"Much, much worse," said Persephone, grinning. "But then, we were always prettier."

Nyx managed a laugh, and felt her broken ribs grating together as she did. "So now what, my counselors of all things mortal?"

"First," said Ishtar, "We heal."

"Then, we fuck," said Persephone. She grimaced as the bones of one win popped back into place. "After a good fight, you need a good fuck."

"And then," said Nyx, "We get revenge."

"No," countered Persephone. "First we build your new cult and then we get revenge."

Nyx grinned, and the pain of it made her realize both her cheekbones had been broken. "Now that sounds like an idea."

"And no more taking on the Christians head-on," said Persephone. "You're the Queen of Hell. Why stay here and fight in their territory when there's a whole world of possible followers for you?"

"True, that." Nyx thought about it. "But I can't go far. I have to have an army ready to wipe out the Christians when the time comes."

"There's a large amount of territory to the east," said Persephone.

"India is already full of Hindus," said Ishtar. " They've got so many gods you can't tell which one they're worshipping. And the Christians have already started working there. Further east is China. Half of them worship their ancestors and the other half keep talking about the Buddha."

"Which Angel was the Buddha, anyway?" asked Nyx. "He wasn't one of mine."

"I don't think he was an Angel," said Persephone. "These humans have a knack for worshipping their own."

"Figures," said Nyx. "What about north and west?"

Persephone nodded. "There's a whole big area out there, filled with tribes and raiders who haven't even heard of the Christians."

"And there's certainly worry and dissent in the North about the Romans," said Ishtar. "Maybe it's time to start using them."

Nyx stretched. More bones popped into place and she let herself revel in the agony. It had been a good fight, and it had been three hundred years years since the last time she'd had a challenge like that. "Right, then. Healing, fucking, and then fucking over the Romans." She grinned again, her broken cheekbones flaring up with pain. "Let's make it so their empire isn't even remembered anymore."

CHAPTER 7

FOR SEVEN YEARS, they flew.
As Angels, they could speak and understand every language in God's creation, and so Nyx, Persephone, and Ishtar, sometimes together, sometimes apart, crisscrossed the world. They visited nations, empires, tribes and villages on mountains, plains and islands; in forests, deserts and fertile river valleys. They learned a thousand different customs and beliefs, and watched hundreds of religious rituals, from grass-hut villages where a new child was carried to every house in the village to be kissed and blessed, to cities of stone where enemies were laid out on an alter, and their still-beating hearts pulled from their bodies. Some of it made them laugh; some of it made them wonder where humans got their ideas. And always there was art, music, blood, sacrifice, hope and despair.

The Angels disguised themselves as men and rode into battle or walked on hunts or sat in circles of elders, listening. As women they sat by fires, made pottery and tended children – save Ishtar who flat out refused. Persephone delighted in the role-playing, and took to each new bit of acting with vigor and imagination. Ishtar found it all incredibly distasteful, and would disappear for days at a time, coming back with the stench of blood on her breath and a cruel smile on her face.

Nyx played each role, listened to all the stories and watched all the people. She was charming and polite when she needed to be, strong and persuasive when she wanted to be, and underneath it all, she was seething with rage.

It was worse at nights, when she was alone and could hear the voices of her worshippers. There were fewer of them with every passing year. More and more people were drifting away from her temples, embracing Christianity and calling on Jesus – who would never answer them because he could not hear – instead of Nyx.

It made her angry, knowing they were worshiping her love by the wrong name, knowing that they thought of him as a creature of love and peace, who cared and would save them. Tribunal had hated them all, hated what he was supposed to represent to them, and hated what they did to themselves, each other, and to him.

Every time she thought of her Tribunal, she felt his hatred of humanity rise up inside her.

And every night, when she listened to her followers, she struggled to understand why He hated them so much. Some of them were awful. A few were so bad she dispatched them to Hell herself, rather than wait for them to die of natural causes. Other who were just as vile she had let live because they were useful to her, knowing they would meet again in Hell where she could give then their just deserts. But the many who were good, or fairly good, who did their best, perturbed her. She shouldn't care about these tiny lives. And she didn't, individually, but as a whole they… moved her.

She could never understand what it was like to live so briefly, to know one had at best a few decades. She wondered if that was part of what made Tribunal what He was, part of why He hated them so much.

At the end of the seven years, the three Angels met at Isis's temple at Philae, taking over the inner sanctum and declaring it theirs alone. The priests, seeing what they thought was their goddess in the flesh, acquiesced and evacuated the temple immediately. Daily they delivered tribute to Angels in the form of food, wine, and young men and women to be their entertainment. The Angels used the humans as they liked, but spent most of their days creating and then pouring over a map of the world more detailed than any other in existence. Rome was at the center of it, of course, but the world they laid out was far larger than the world the humans knew existed. Persephone wondered what one of these maps—the round earth with its mighty oceans— would do to the thinking of a human. But even the wisest scholars, even the most experienced sailors, would not believe it even if they saw it.

Nyx stared at the map for five days.

Constantine and Licinius had broken off their talks in Milan when Maximin had crossed the Bospherus and invaded Licinius' territory. Licinius had fought Maximin off and gained control of the eastern Roman Empire. The year after, Constantine and Licinius had started in on each other again. It had become a vicious, deadly bicker that cost lives and was helping the empire disintegrate. Christianity was becoming the preferred religion of the empire, though others were still tolerated. It was only a matter of time before that changed, though.

I hope Constantine falls off his horse and impales himself through his ass on a splintery stump. Nyx sighed. It was unlikely, and she wasn't able to do it herself. Constantine would live and die in his own time and eventually would (if there was any justice) end up in Hell where she would enjoy punishing him for a few thousand years before turning him over to someone else for the rest of eternity.

Besides, she had other plans.

In the North, there were tribes who had never heard of Christianity. In the East, past the Goths, were others. The Goths were close enough to Rome that half of them were Christians already. Still, they were uneasy neighbors, and there were other, even fiercer tribes around them.

It would take very little to send the Goths into Rome…

Nyx blinked for the first time in five days. Then she stood up and called the others to her.

"About time," complained Ishtar, coming out of the bed where she and Persephone had been lounging, enjoying a list they'd compiled of all the sexual phrases in the world's many languages. "I thought you were going to turn to stone, standing there."

"Are we going to travel more?" asked Persephone. "It's boring here."

"Please, no!" said Ishtar. "Can't we just kill something?"

"Yes to both of you," said Nyx. "Come look."

She pointed to the areas north and east of Roman territory. "Who lives here?"

"Varengians," said Ishtar, pointing to the north. "Suiones, Geats."

"Huns," said Persephone, pointing to the east. "Alvars, Alans, Goths."

"Many of whom have nothing to do with Christianity."

"The Goths are Christians," said Ishtar.

"But they are Arianists," said Persephone, "Which should put them in direct conflict with the Romans, who are Trinitarians, should they cross the Danube."

"And all they need to do that is a little push," said Nyx, tapping the map. "From the Huns."

"Oh, let me," said Ishtar. "I know what will push them to move."

"Not you," said Nyx. "Persephone is going to start working on the Huns. You, have a much more difficult task."

"I do?" said Ishtar suspiciously. "What is it?"

Nyx grinned. "Rome."

"Rome?" the distaste in Ishtar's voice was echoed in her twisted expression. "Rome is falling apart."

"Yes, it is," said Nyx. "And your job is to see to it that it keeps falling apart, until it ceases to exist."

Ishtar's face slowly untwisted until she was smiling, her whole beautiful face lit with glee. "Now, that I can do. When do we start?"

"Tomorrow," said Nyx. She took each of them by the hand and led them to the bed. "Tonight, my pretties, we eat, drink and be very, very merry."

*

320 A.D.

The Sarmatian raiders rode on as fast as they could. The scales of their armor, made from the hooves of horses cut thin and sewn together, rattled and jumped as their horses galloped flat out.

Their leader rode magnificently, in turns driving his raiders forward, then wheeling back to give battle to the cavalry that pursued. Hour after hour, he fought against the Romans, and his sword and armor were soaked with their blood by the time they reached Issacea, where they had crossed into Constantine's territory in the first place.

The rearguard was still there, surrounding the fort and keeping the guards imprisoned. The legion that had held it was the one now pursuing.

Right. Now to make sure they follow.

The leader of the Sarmatians shouted a command and as one the entire raiding party – eight hundred strong—wheeled and charged the Roman cavalry. Blood flew in all directions as hundreds of men clashed and cut and mutilated and killed each other. Horses died or went mad with pain, bucking and twisting over the battlefield. Men who fell off their mounts were trampled or dodged desperately through the crowd of animals, trying to avoid hooves and charging beasts even as they sought to pull enemy riders down. Most of the men on foot died. Some escaped the battle and ran into the hills around them.

The leader of the Sarmatians shouted again and the raiding party broke off and headed for the Danube. Men died as their horses wheeled away, but it didn't matter. The leader let the rest of his men stream past so the pursuing cavalry could see him raise his prize:

The legion's eagle, held high above his head.

The legion's cavalry shouted and charged. The leader of the Sarmatians laughed as he rode past Issacea and into the Danube. The town of Issacea was one of the few places where the Danube was low enough to be forded, and the Sarmatians wasted no time in doing so. Their leader, captured eagle still high in his hands, raced through his troop, looking behind.

The legion's cavalry didn't hesitate to follow them, right into the river.

And on the other side is Licinius' army, thought Persephone, She had killed the leader of the Sarmatians two months before in single combat, then took his place to lead the tribe. They'd been incredibly successful ever since. She swung the eagle back and forth over her head again to make sure the Legion wouldn't give up. *And Licinius was not going to be happy at all to have Constantine's legions on his soil.*

This is really too easy.

326 A.D.

Crispus's body was a pleasant one to wear, Ishtar decided. Constantine's oldest and favorite son was in very good shape, strong, and pleasantly endowed, all of which Ishtar approved. He was also a true Christian, fanatically loyal to his father, and a brilliant and successful soldier. His victories on land and sea were the stuff that rebuilt empires, and that wouldn't do at all.

Crispus was currently lying asleep, alone, in a very, very expensive brothel where his men had paid for his pleasure as a gesture of thanks for his leadership. Ishtar had borrowed the form of the young maiden that Persephone so liked and had serviced him long, well, and repeatedly, plying him with wine in between each act. The man was dead drunk, asleep, and unlikely to wake any time soon.

She had taken his form and clothes and slipped out the brothel back door, walking the back streets of Constantinople to the palace. She acted like someone who did not wish to be seen, though she made certain that she was. She reached the palace, entered through a servant's door, and went in search of Fausta, Emperor Constantine's wife.

Fausta did not approve of Crispus's relation with his father. In fact, she had actively campaigned against it, trying to bring her own three sons to prominence, which would be much better for Nyx's plans, since none of them were the commanders their half brother was.

Constantine had left the palace two days before to conduct business.

Ishtar found Fausta's chambers and stepped inside. Tall, blond Fausta was lying on her bed, attended by two dark-haired women singing and playing the cithera. Wine and sweetmeats were laid out on a low table. Ishtar went directly to the bed, looked at the servants and said, "Get out."

"They will stay," said Fausta, eyes blazing. "You do not come in here and order my servants!"

Ishtar pulled out a knife and pointed at the servants. "You will get out of this room and go into the Empress's dressing chamber. Now!"

The two girls scrambled to obey, and Ishtar locked the door behind them.

"What is the meaning of this, Crispus?" Fausta demanded. "How dare you come into my chambers and…"

"How dare you say to my father that we had an affair,"

said Ishtar. "How dare you try to besmirch the memory of my mother and how dare you attempt to take away my throne!"

"I have done nothing of the sort!"

"Liar!" Ishtar tossed the knife aside and pulled the thick leather belt from around her waist. "I'll teach you to lie, you bitch!"

Fausta started screaming when the first lash struck the side of her face. She didn't stop screaming for the next two hours, until Ishtar was finally finished with her.

Ishtar opened the door to the room and strode out into the night, leaving Fausta curled on the bed, weeping in pain and humiliation.

Now if that doesn't turn Constantine against his son, Ishtar thought, as she made her way back to the brothel, *I don't know what will.*

AD 370

Balamber was asleep in his bed of furs, his wife sound asleep beside him, when Nyx stepped into his dreams. His dreams were that of any man of his tribe: of riding his horse, of raiding against the other tribes, and of women and the day to day of life. He was a chieftain of the largest band of his people, and had no ambition to be more.

At least, thought Nyx, not yet.

Nyx's body was currently lying in its own tent, looking like one of the Hun warriors, with a pair of women she'd stolen on the last raid warming her, one on each side of the bed. The women were impressively feisty, and had tried to kill her with her own knife. She found it amusing, though she had whipped both of them into cowed submission as a warning. Nyx had things to do and this was not the time for her to be distracted. Since then, the women had been much more docile, though Nyx could sense their hatred and knew they would act against her again soon. She might even let them get away, if she succeeded in her plan.

Meanwhile, Nyx went into Balamber's mind and built him a new dream.

He was riding west, the rising sun at his back, a sword in his hand. Before him the entirety of the world was laid out. He could see all the villages around him, see all the great cities he had only heard of from traders: Constantinople, Rome, Athens. They all lay before him, glittering with riches, open for the taking.

And as he watched, a tall, winged woman in black armor rose from the earth. She had a sword in one hand, a whip in the other. She was, he knew in his dream, a goddess of battle.

"Hear me," she whispered, and the voice caressed and aroused him as surely as if she had put her hand on him. "All this can be yours. Yours for the taking if you will have it."

"How?" he whispered back. "How will I take it?"

"I will show you. Bring your people together," whispered Nyx. "Let them know that a new goddess will lead you to power, if you will follow her."

Balamber woke, and thought hard about what he had seen. And when he went back to sleep, he saw it again. Every night for a month, Balamber dreamed of victory and conquest, of barrels of grain and wine, furs and gems, silk cloth as soft as a woman's skin, fine swords and magnificent horses. And every night he dreamed, his tribe's fortunes increased. Raids were successful, food was plentiful, slaves were easily captured. Balamber spoke to the shaman about his dreams, then to the other warriors in the tribe.

All agreed the dreams were a sign, and Balamber called a meeting of chieftains and warriors. All attended save one, who was found dead with a knife in his chest and his two concubines missing.

397 A.D.

The battlefield was bloody and chaotic. The legion, under the command of Stilicho, was holding the centre in true Roman fashion, their phalanx of shields and swords a breakwater against which the waves of Visigoths crashed. On either side of it, though, the barbarian warriors who made up the majority of the Roman army these days were a disorganized mess. Single combats broke out across the lines as warriors from both sides sought out men worthy to fight.

In the midst of the crush, Persephone and Ishtar came face to face.

"What the fuck are you doing here?" demanded Ishtar as Persephone's blade crashed down against her shield. Both looked like warriors. Both had to shout to be heard over the roar of the battle around them.

"Defeating you," said Persephone, grinning. She drove her sword forward again, and Ishtar was driven back by the force of the blow.

"You little bitch!" shouted Ishtar, smashing Persephone's blade away with the edge of her shield and slashing down at the other's shoulder. Persephone's shield was already there, blocking, and Ishtar let her sword bounce off of it, spin and come in from low on the other side. Persephone retreated and the blade whipped harmlessly passed her.

"Nice try!" said Persephone. She twisted to the right to kill one of the Visigoths beside them and easily blocked Ishtar's next blow a moment later. "But not good enough."

"I am a goddess of war!" snarled Ishtar. "You're just a goddess of spring and sunshine and the fine art of getting laid."

Persephone slipped sideways, brought up her shield and locked them together, body to body. "I am also a goddess of death," she whispered. "Queen of the Underworld, remember?" Her breath against Ishtar's ear sent a tingle down her back. "And the best fighter in the 666th."

"You are not!"

"And once I kick your ass, I'm going to drag you off and have my way with you."

"Bets?"

"Bets."

Ishtar grinned at her. "Fine, loser takes it like a boy from the winner."

Persephone grinned back. "Deal!"

They pushed away from each other's shields and fought. The battle around them raged, but even so others began clearing a space. They fought for twelve hours straight, and whenever someone attempted to stop them or attack, they broke away just long enough to kill them. Stilicho's army slowly advanced, breaking the back of the Visigoths' attack and driving them away. Still Persephone and Ishtar fought, blades flying faster than any other on the field. By the end of it, both their shields had been battered into near-uselessness, and the two discarded them and used only their swords.

"Tired yet?" taunted Ishtar as she launched another blistering attack on Persephone.

"Nope," said Persephone, parrying all the attacks and sending a complex series of cuts and thrusts at Ishtar. "You?"

"Just getting started!"

It ended two hours later. Ishtar's misstep was less than a quarter inch. Her blade too far extended by a quarter inch more. It was more than enough for Persephone, who hacked down hard then spun her own blade in a circle, ripping Ishtar's blade out of her hand and sending it flying into the crowd gathered around them. Ishtar closed distance and tried to grapple, only to have her feet kicked out from under her and be thrown through the air, landing with a bone-crunching THUD on the ground. Persephone was astride her in a flash, her blade pressing hard on Ishtar's neck. In the language of the Visigoths, she shouted, "Yield!"

Ishtar turned her head, spat, and growled, "I yield."

The shout that went up around them surprised them both, and they looked up to see a circle of a hundred men surrounding them.

"That was the greatest fighting I have ever seen," said Stilicho, stepping forward. "The greatest any man has ever seen!"

Persephone got to her feet and held out her hand. Ishtar took it and allowed Persephone to pull her to her feet. Both saluted Stilicho. "General," said Persephone, "May I present my brother, Hathgot."

That earned her a glare from Ishtar who knew full well "Hathgot" meant "witless" in the language of the Slav tribes to the northeast.

"Your brother is a great warrior," said Stilicho. "Would he be willing to serve Rome?"

"I would, General," said Ishtar.

There was more cheering.

And after ceremonies of victory and ceremonies for the dead, after drinking more wine than anyone had ever seen men drink, and playing at being drunk (which Persephone particularly enjoyed) the two goddesses finally slipped away from the army into the dark forest around them. They shifted to their true form and took wing, heading for Isis's temple in the south. Despite the many attacks on pagans, it still stood, and still had loyal priests waiting to serve.

"I think I'll have you take the form of that young Roman that Trajan was so found of," said Persephone as they flew across the Mediterranean.

"Just as long as you don't look like Trajan," said Ishtar, shuddering. "I saw enough of that man to last me an aeon."

"Fine, I'll be Marcus Aurelius," said Persephone. "I always wished he'd try both sides. The man had a stick up his ass. Think Stilicho will destroy Alric?"

"Not if I have anything to do with it," said Ishtar. "Nyx wanted Rome destroyed and Silicho is getting in the way. I'll set up a conspiracy against him soon."

"Too bad. He's a good man."

"No such thing," said Ishtar. "He's just a corrupt and foul as the rest of them."

Persephone looked up at the bright stars above their heads. "I wonder where Nyx is these days."

400 A.D.

Outside, a strong wind was blowing, and rain drummed hard against the roof of the longhouse. Inside, warm and safe from the storm that tore at trees and threatened to flood the rivers, two dozen warriors and their chief sat on logs and listened as the old shaman spoke, accompanied by the popping of the logs and the crackling of flames in the fire pit.

"There are older Gods than the ones our fathers worshipped," he said. "Older than any that the southern men worship, or even the hidden ones who skulk in the woods and were here before our grandfather's grandfathers arrived.

"In the times before mankind walked this earth, before our people were born from the blood of gods spilled in battle, there were many gods, and many, many wars between them. For untold years they fought with one another, and in the end, they were divided in two. The Light Ones, whose great grandchildren became the gods of the south, the gods of plenty and warmth and peace.

"And the Dark Ones.

"The Dark Ones are not gods of peace or prosperity. They are not gods of gentle summer sun and thick harvests. They are gods of battle. They are the gods of the cold winter nights and the long darkness until spring. They are the gods of death and of suffering and of iron will in the face of it all.

"Their children became the Gods of our people.

"But the Gods of our people have been silent now, for many hundreds of years. They have not spoken to us, have not granted us their presence, have not given us gifts or demanded sacrifice. Even now, their shrines are growing rusty with disuse.

"They have vanished into the Darkness from where they came, and we'll not hear from them again."

Around the room, there were mutters of disbelief and confusion.

"They are gone," repeated the shaman. "They have vanished from the world and will not return. But someone else has.

"She is one of the Dark Ones," he said, his voice rising and taking on an oracular timbre. "She is a Goddess of Pain and Vengeance and Suffering. She is a Goddess of War and of Will and of Strength. And she is walking among us. She is searching for a people to worship her, and she has found our people worthy to become hers."

"We have our own gods," rumbled one of the warriors. "Strong gods. Gods who protect our people."

"They are gone," the shaman said. "Gone!"

The Shaman burst into flames.

The warriors shouted and scrambled back from the sudden heat and light. The fire roared and the shaman was consumed by it. And rising from the middle of the fire was a silver-skinned woman with eyes of fire, wearing black armor, with a sword in one had and a whip in the other.

"I am Nyx," she said, and from her back black wings spread and filled the room. "And I am here to replace your Gods."

"Devil!" shouted one. "She is an evil spirit. Destroy her!"

He drew his sword and leapt forward. Nyx's own blade moved then, smashing into his and shattering it, sending steel shards flying through the room. The other men swore as the steel cut into them, and raised axes, hammers and swords. Nyx, moving so fast her body was a bright blur, caught the man who had attacked her and raised him in the air. Instead of smashing him to the earth, she shouted, "This is a warrior! This is what I expect from my followers!" She let the man go and he collapsed to the ground, stunned. Nyx offered him her hand. He stared at it, then took it. She squeezed a little, teasing him with her strength, then helped him to his feet. "I came here because times are changing. Your people are small now, but in time you will grow. You will spread and if you let me guide you, you will rule over most of this world."

She spread her wings again and the men shuddered at her terrible majesty. "Be mine, O Varangians, and I will raise your people beyond anything you could dream."

The room flashed with white light, and when they could see again, there was no sign of her, save for the shattered sword and the blood.

They sat and talked long past the ending of the rain and the rising of the sun. The women brought them food and drink and the men told the women what they had seen. With no shaman left to guide them, the men sat for three more days, and at the end of it, they chose to follow her and to see where it would take them.

408 A.D.

Ishtar, wearing the body of a fat Roman citizen, brought her hammer down hard on a screaming child's head. Brains and blood spattered and the child dropped like a rock. Ishtar grinned and stepped over the body, looking for another.

It had taken ten years to get the Romans to turn out Stilicho. Ishtar had woven her way through their numbers, spreading lies, rumor and discontent. Persephone had convinced Radagaisus to invade Italy, forcing Stilicho to strip troops away from the North, which led to the Guals, Vandals and Alans attacking when he was at war elsewhere. Eventually they were driven back, but by then it had been easy to get Rome to betray and kill Stilicho.

Now it was Rome's time to burn.

The Goths under Alaric had made an uneasy and expensive peace with Rome, at the price of an exorbitant tribute. It was easy to claim the Goths were draining Rome of vital food and supplies. Easier still to turn the Senate against them. And when Ishtar had proposed that, as a sign of Roman disgust at the barbarians, the Goths' families be slaughtered, the agreement was easy and immediate.

Thousands of Romans filled the streets, chanting and killing anyone who even looked like a Goth. Some of the Goths fought back. The old men had once been doughty warriors and they still had their blades. They were no match for the mob, but they took a fair number with them. The women were raped and slaughtered in the thousands, the children murdered in as many despicable fashions as there were murderers. Corpses filled the streets and the rivers, stripped of their valuables. Dogs ran off with body parts. Ishtar didn't care.

When Alaric hears about this, she gloated as her hammer came down on the head of a begging woman with an infant in her arms, *he is going to destroy Rome to its foundations.*

The woman fell and the infant rolled, wailing, into the dirty street. Ishtar raised her foot and brought her foot down hard. The wailing stopped.

410 A.D.

Nyx, clothed like a Roman matron, her head covered with a scarf, walked through the ruined streets of the sacked city of

Rome. The Goths had been decent, all things considered. Most of Rome was still standing. The majority of its citizens were alive; the majority of its women hadn't been raped. But then, Alaric had higher plans. He wanted to take all of Italy. He would not let his army get fat and lazy so soon.

The last pagan temple – her temple – had been burned.

Nyx was amazed it had stood so long. It had fell into disuse long ago, and there were few, if any, who still followed her in Rome. But it had not been destroyed, until now.

She stood in the ruins of it, looking at the broken, defaced statue and the charred remains of the couches where, long ago, they had drank so much wine and eaten fine food and listened to sweet music as they made love. The walls – what was left of them – were covered in soot, hiding the faded paintings that artists had fought for the right to commission.

"My lady?" Nyx turned. A young man in a soot-covered robe approached. "The city is not safe for women alone, my lady. You should return home."

I can't, Nyx thought. *Not for another six hundred years.*

And even then, Nyx was not sure she wanted to go back. Here on Earth, the urge to punish was not so great. The need to torture and maim and despoil the souls of the damned had faded over time. She enjoyed not feeling the compulsion, and wondered if the others did, too.

Of course, in six hundred years, they'll all be wiped from the planet, so what does it matter?

The thought disturbed her, though she did not know why. She should hate them, she should be working on destroying them. Instead she was caring for them. The Varangians were a strong and resourceful people, who raised their children well and decently, and their prayers were now filling Nyx's brain. And once more, the majority were prayers for strength and help.

"My lady?"

Nyx realized she was once more staring at the broken remains of her statue. "I thank you."

"It was beautiful," said the young man. "A beautiful place. Everyone left it alone because it was so beautiful. People often came and sat, looking at the Angel, or at the lovely frescos on the walls. I would come and play my flute, here. The sound would float up to the ceiling." He shook his head. "Of all the places to burn. Why this one?"

"It was a pagan temple," said Nyx, pleased by his praise. "The Christians cannot stand anyone worshipping any gods but theirs."

"Still no need to burn it down," said the young man. "Who was it to? Minerva? Venus?"

"Not even the memory left?" Nyx looked around at the broken room and the soot-covered walls and the burned benches. "Not even that?"

"Do you know her?" asked the young man.

"I do," said Nyx. "She was a goddess of plenty and of pleasure. Of joy and laughter. And also of vengeance, who would smite those who dared to cross her. She heard all the prayers, whether or not she answered them, and she did her best for her people, and for her love."

"What was her name?"

"Nyx."

"And who was her love?"

"Tribunal." Nyx had not spoken his name aloud for nearly two hundred years. And though she spoke it in the Roman tongue not the tongue of Angels, she could feel his presence beside her and his strong arms around her. And she could feel his rage.

It filled her from the ground up, like falling into the Lake of Fire, only this burned white hot, not cold. It burned for the thousands he had seen betray and abuse each other as he wandered the world. It burned for the ones who tortured and raped and killed for pleasure. It burned for the ones who abused children. It burned because it burned. The fire of it consumed Nyx's grief, consumed her sadness for days past, consumed her desires and thoughts and left her with only one.

The humans must be destroyed! Earth must be taken from them and given to those worthy of it!

"My lady," said the young man. "Shall I escort you home?"

Nyx's fingernails became talons, slashing out and tearing his throat open. The young man gargled and dropped, blood spraying over Nyx, the floor and the walls.

Now that, thought Nyx, *Tribunal would approve.*

Nyx walked away from the temple, mind consumed with new plans. There was much work to do, if she was going to destroy the Christians, and bring back her love.

I am Queen of Hell. And I will be Queen of Paradise, soon.

She left the ruins of her temple and the bloody remains of the young man on the floor, and did not look back.

451 A.D.

In his tent, Attila, leader of the Huns knelt, praying in silence. He was a thickly-muscled man, short of stature but broad in the chest, with black hair, a thin beard and hard eyes. There was a sudden wind behind him, hard enough to knock him nearly off balance and to make the tent flap snap back and forth.

"Are you ready?" Nyx demanded.

Attilla prostrated himself before her. ""I am, my lady Nyx."

"Are your troops?"

"More than ready," said Attila. "We have near half a million men standing ready to invade. We will crush these Byzantines."

"Do that," said Nyx. "Christians have had power way too long. Slaughter them. Kill their priests and their monks. Destroy their holy places. Let them learn to fear the name of Attila."

"I will, Lady Nyx," said Attila bowing deeply.

"Then take this," she said, handing him a sword. She'd had it made in the style he was used to, but much, much better. She'd had it forged by the finest craftsmen money could buy, using the highest quality iron she could find. The blade was exquisite, and as soon as Attila took it in his hand he knew it. He grinned and prostrated himself again. "With this, my lady, I will lay waste to the Christians!"

No you won't, thought Nyx. *But you'll kill a bunch of them and keep them from expanding while I go in search of an even better race of warriors.*

634 A.D.

In the desert, Persephone covered her rather handsome face with her veil. She was balanced easily on the back of a camel, and around her, the army of Islam marched. They were crossing the border into Roman Syria, now. Beside her, sitting as easy as she herself, Khalid ibn al-Walid, also handsome if not quite so young, surveyed the army's progress.

"We are riding well," said Khalid. "We should reach the first fortress soon, all things being equal."

"As you say, Sword of Allah," said Persephone. "We will need to slaughter more of the camels before we reach it, though."

Khalid grinned. "That is why I brought extra."

He had brought many extra, in fact, and with a very deliberate purpose. Camels, when denied water for a time, will drink and drink and drink, and their stomachs store the water cleanly. Whenever the army stopped to eat, camels were slaughtered and the water from their bellies shared among the troops.

Food and water on the hoof, though Persephone. *Clever. Though they have a nasty bite.*

"There! The Romans!"

They're not really Romans, thought Persephone as she covered her face and prepared to ride after the patrol, who were already hightailing it back to their fort, somewhere nearby but currently out of sight. *But they're Christians, and that's enough.*

Besides, who doesn't like a good fight?

800 A.D.

The chief of the Varangians woke and found his Goddess standing at the foot of his bed.

"My Lady Nyx!" He practically fell out of bed, prostrating his naked body against the splintery wood of the longhouse floor. His wife awoke at the sound, saw who it was, and screamed. A moment later she, too, was prostrate on the floor.

"It is time," said Nyx. "Rise, leader of the Varangians. Rise and listen to me."

The man rose to his feet, struggling to find dignity in his

nakedness. Nyx waved an arm and his armor appeared around him. The man at once stood straighter.

"It is time for your people to begin their journey," sad Nyx. "The one foretold, that will bring you a new empire greater than any this world has seen. One that will last ten thousand years."

The Chieftain nodded. "It will be as you say, my lady Nyx. Only…"

Nyx raised an eyebrow, and in that very small movement was a threat of terrible violence. "Yes?"

Words rushed out of the man's mouth. "There are many among our people who do not believe in the empire to come. They say it is a false legend, designed to get people through the winter and the hard times. They may not follow."

"They will," said Nyx. "You will see."

*

Two weeks later, the entire tribe gathered before the shrine of Nyx. The chieftain had sent boats out to the other villages telling everyone to come. Now eight thousand men, women and children stood before the shrine, waiting. They waited all afternoon, not daring to sit or take a bite of food.

Night fell, and Nyx arose in a ball of fire that lit every face in the tribe. Her black-scaled armor gleamed in the light of it. Her sword and whip were in her hands, and her eyes glowed red. The entire population fell to their knees, and in the crowd, some of the children cried out in fear.

"Hear me, Varangians," Nyx said. "Your time here is at an end. To the east lies the great forests and homes of the Slavs. They have need of your leadership and guidance. And with them as your vassals, you will forge a mighty empire, capable of destroying any that would stand against you, and gaining riches greater unmatched among the tribes of man."

"Tell us what we must do, O Lady Nyx," said their chief. "Tell me how we may achieve this victory!"

"Gather all your people, your goods and your livestock," said Nyx. "Sail to the east, down the Volga, and take control of all the lands you survey. Build fortresses and farms, make your people strong and healthy, and once you have established yourselves, you are commanded to wage war against the Christians who live there!"

"We will, my lady!" said the chieftain.

"And let your people have a new name," said Nyx, more on a whim than anything else, "For the Varangians are a small people, and yours shall be a great people! From this day forward, I name you the Rus! And your name shall be remembered throughout history!"

The crowd, led by their chieftain cheered, and for the remainder of the night, feasted, danced and sang. Nyx, in full armor, allowed herself to partake of the festivities, honoring the women by eating their food, and the men by drinking with them. Their excitement was infectious. She felt a moment of fondness.

They will become a great people.

The Slavs were no match for them, and would be easily overwhelmed. From there, it was merely a matter of direction.

The time is approaching, my love, Nyx thought, though she avoided using his name. *Soon, we will rule this world together.*

And maybe we will not need to destroy them all?

850 A.D.

The beach was deserted, save for the three of them. The Pacific

Ocean was calm; a sheet of silk, pale and shimmering, and the red sun hung low on the horizon. Persephone had brought blankets and spread them out on the sand. She had provided skins of wine, baskets of fruit, bread, honey and smoked fish. The three ate greedily, then lay back in the cool twilight as they exchanged their stories.

They had done this every ten years since their campaign began. Nyx listened to Persephone and Ishtar, and advised them on further steps. She told them her own plans and machinations and what had succeeded so far.

"So the Rus are starting to stir," said Ishtar. "These new Islamics are harrying the eastern Roman Empire and the western one is now totally collapsed. What's the score?"

"We're winning," said Nyx. "Mathematically, we are winning. We outnumber them now, and when the Rus are in place, we'll be able to destroy them all. And there's a group called the Mongols that are starting to stir. I'm going after them, next."

"Does that mean we can get out of here?" asked Ishtar.

"I like it here," protested Persephone.

"Then why did you arrange to spend half of every year in Hell?"

"Because I like you two as well," said Persephone, smiling and running a gentle hand down each Angel's thigh. Nyx took her hand; Ishtar shoved it away.

"Not in the mood," said Ishtar. "I want to do more than just manipulate them."

"We will," said Nyx. "Soon."

"Why wait?" demanded Ishtar. "The Islamic people have already taken Jerusalem. We can go in, wipe it out and take over."

"We are waiting for the right time!" snapped Nyx. "We are waiting for Paradise, remember?"

"Paradise isn't Heaven, you know," said Ishtar. "We aren't going to get that back."

"We aren't going to get anything if we don't wait," Nyx said heatedly. "We will take Jerusalem, and we will kill all the Christians there. When the time is right."

"Well, most of them are gone already," sniped Ishtar. "The Islamic people have it, remember?"

"The Islamic people are allowing the Christians to stay," said Persephone in a mild tone. "Something about them being People of the Book?"

"No idea," said Nyx. "But we need them out of there. Suggestions?"

"Raise an army and wipe them out?" suggested Ishtar.

"Can't lose the people," said Nyx. "Not yet."

"Get the Christians to attack them?"

"Then it's filled with Christians again," said Persephone. "Tribunal wanted Jerusalem sacked, didn't He?"

Tribunal's name reverberated through her spirit again, making her shake. Ishtar noticed the change in Nyx, and told herself to remember it. When the strength of Him was gone from Nyx, it left a very strange, very specific idea in its wake. "He did," said Nyx. "We need to corrupt them. The Christians who will retake Jerusalem."

"They're already pretty corrupt," said Ishtar. "Some of those Christian priests sleep around more than my temple prostitutes used to do."

"And the top of the Catholic Church is slowly becoming corrupt," said Persephone. "Too much money and power."

"Then we'll corrupt it further," said Nyx. "When that's done, we'll have the pope send an army of soldiers to take Jerusalem. And as they attempt that feat, we will be there to convert them from Christianity and make them mine."

"They won't do it," said Persephone. "They won't give up their religion just because you ask them to."

"They will if they're pushed far enough," said Ishtar. "Humans will do whatever is most expedient to save their lives. And if that means a mass conversion from Christianity, they will do it."

"You think?" asked Persephone.

"They will," said Nyx. "In two hundred years, I want to be in Jerusalem, marching at the head of an army that screams my name as they slaughter." Inside her head, she could practically hear Tribunal's voice, cheering her on. "Jerusalem will be ours, and then, we will gain Paradise!"

CHAPTER 8

900 A.D. – ROME

THEY HAD TAKEN rooms in a brothel, in part because it was the only place where they could gather together as women without raising eyebrows, and in part because it was the single most important brothel in Rome. It was not a poor place, nor was it a small place. It was an old palace, converted just for the purpose, and it catered only to the Roman elite and those they did business with.

Nyx, Persephone and Ishtar, appearing as proper matrons, arrived at the back entrance, rather than the front. They had some polite negotiations with first the cook, then the owner himself, before being given the most lavish of the dozen elite suites for their private and exclusive use. The fact that they paid for them in gold helped immensely. They arranged themselves on low, silken couches and sipped the city's best wine from two-handled pottery cups, glazed mint green. Eggs, fruit, oysters, roasted songbirds, bread, cakes and nuts were spread before them.

"Where do we stand?" asked Nyx.

"The papacy is corrupt through and through," said Persephone. "If they were my priests I'd execute them on the spot."

"Can we go near them?" asked Nyx. "Or are they protected by God?"

"I kissed Benedict V's ring," said Persephone. "I gave blowjobs to three of his cardinals and spanked two others until their asses bled. They're not protected."

"Good," said Nyx, spearing a tiny bird with a silver fork.

"There's four noble families all fighting for control of the papacy," said Ishtar. "With the leadership of the church comes a great deal of money and power. Some of them want to rebuild the empire, some just want to take it for everything it's worth."

"That should make everything else easier," said Nyx.

"Not really," said Persephone. "Your plan was to send an army to Jerusalem. These people don't trust each other enough to send a set of their least-liked cousins on a walk in the park together."

"That has to change," said Nyx. "Who is the current pope?"

"Benedict IV," said Persephone. "Fairly quiet, keeps giving stuff to his family."

"Then we need someone better," said Nyx. "Someone who can unite the Christians and be corrupted to serve us at the same time."

"I'll find someone," said Ishtar.

"Not without supervision," said Nyx. "What you did with the Goths was too much."

"This from the Queen of Hell," Ishtar sneered, her eyes narrowing.

"I punish those who deserve it," growled Nyx, releasing a hint of her power. "You slaughtered innocents."

"It worked," said Ishtar. "And it's not like your precious *Tribunal* isn't going to wipe them all out anyway, once He comes back to earth."

The mention of Tribunal's name brought a rush of warmth to Nyx, followed immediately by a near-overwhelming feeling of urgency and purpose. They *must* move quickly. They *must* turn the tides against the Christians and seize Jerusalem, at any cost.

Not at any cost, Nyx told herself. *The innocent have done nothing.*

They are human! Tribunal's voice rose up inside her, nothing more than a memory but nearly overwhelming in its power. *They are a scourge on the Earth and should be wiped out!*

The power of His voice dominated her brain, and for a moment she knew, deep in her heart, that what He was saying was true, that the young were just as much to blame as the old, and that snuffing out their lives would be no better or worse than snuffing out their parents.

No! She shoved Tribunal's voice back in her mind. *The innocent have done nothing to deserve this!*

Aloud, she snarled. "Not the children! Got it?"

"All right, for fuck's sake!" Ishtar said, throwing up her hands in mock-surrender. "I'll try not to kill too many of them!"

"Do better than that."

"I'm a goddess," said Ishtar, taking a deep draught of wine. "I'll do as I please."

"You're mine," growled Nyx. "And you'll do as I tell you."

Ishtar stared back at Nyx, defiance on her face. Nyx met her glare for glare, and in Ishtar's mind said, *"I am the Queen of Hell, Ishtar. Do you need a reminder as to why?"*

"Fine," said Ishtar. She muttered something else in Babylonian that was both geometrically and anatomically impossible. Nyx pretended not to hear. Ishtar grabbed a boiled ostrich egg and bit it in two.

"Can I go back to the East?" asked Persephone. "The Byzantines are gaining power again. It's annoying. I've just about convinced the Arabs to start pirating their coasts again. With luck, we can keep them too busy to think about moving toward Jerusalem."

"How much damage can you do them?" asked Nyx

Persephone shrugged. "I don't know. They've been expanding lately, but I think I can help hold them back a bit."

"Just keep them out of Jerusalem. The Western church is so corrupt right now it will be easy to direct them as we want. The Eastern church is still fairly pure in their beliefs and have the strength to keep their faith solid, which is not what we want."

"I will," said Persephone. "What about the Islamics?"

Ishtar laughed. "What about them?"

"They besieged Constantinople in 717," said Persephone. "Didn't get it, but they came close, and they're growing stronger."

"Anything that messes up the Christians is good," said Nyx. "Can you keep them moving in the right direction?"

Persephone grinned. "I can."

"Good. I need to work on the Rus and the Mongols some more if they're going to invade in two hundred years."

"Who are the Mongols?" asked Ishtar.

"Eastern tribe. Excellent horsemen, great archers, good for

the second wave of attacks on the Christians. Afraid of nothing, eager for conquest. They should be ready to start moving west in two hundred years or so. I'll be back in a few years." She smiled at her angels and ate a dainty honey cake. "Spread chaos while I'm gone."

"Yes, Nyx!" the other two Angels chorused.

903 A.D.

In the villa of Theophylact I, Count of Tusculum, Nyx and Ishtar sat across from Theophylact's wife, Theodora, and contemplated her. She was not a tall woman, but was exceedingly pleasant of feature, with lovely brown eyes and equally lovely hair, a good-sized, firm bust, and a ripe body that had already delivered the Count two equally beautiful daughters without any noticeable affect on its shape. She also had a mind that surpassed her husband's in all things. He deferred to her in all matters of state, and hers was the voice that had made him. She already had most of the Roman nobility eating out of her fingers, and her eyes were firmly set upon a much larger prize.

"The problem," said Theodora, "Is that I do not know you."

"This is true," said Nyx. "But you do know that Pope Benedict was not one of your choosing."

"I do," said Theodora. She looked over the other women again. Nyx had chosen to appear as a Roman matron, the same age as Theodora. Ishtar had taken a younger body, and had pointedly made it more attractive than Nyx's disguise. Theodora shook her head, trying to clear her mind. "Which family did you say you came from?"

"We didn't," said Nyx. "We told your servants to let us in

and they did. We told you that you wanted to see us, and you did."

Theodora frowned. "I would not do that."

"Not of your own free will," agreed Nyx. "And yet, here we are."

Theodora rose to her feet. "You two will leave at once. I'll summon a servant to guide you out."

"I think not." The command in Nyx's voice stopped the other woman in her tracks. *"Sit down, Theodora."*

Against her own volition, Theodora stumbled backwards to the couch and sat down.

"You are a very powerful woman," said Ishtar, smiling. "Nearly the most powerful in Rome."

"Nearly?" said Theodora. She was still frightened at how Nyx had made her obey, and her voice trembled with anger as she spoke.

"Nearly," said Nyx. "When Benedict dies, who will replace him?"

"I… I do not know," said Theodora.

"The most powerful woman in Rome would know."

Theodora's eyes flashed with anger, but before she could speak, Nyx added softly, "In fact, the most powerful woman in Rome would choose the next pope."

Theodora tilted her nose up. "It is up to the Council to elect the new pope."

"Now, now," said Nyx. "We all know that isn't true. Or else why would you have worked so hard to get your lover into that position, only to have him driven from the city?"

"And the Lombard's pope put in his place," added Ishtar. "Very annoying indeed." The anger in Theodora's eyes grew stronger, and it was Ishtar's turn to smile. "You must have enjoyed him a great deal, to reward him so." Her tongue lightly touched her top lip.

"You will leave, now!"

"No, we won't," said Nyx. "Benedict will be dead very, very soon. Have your man ready for the papacy, Theodora, and you will have power beyond your wildest dreams. Fail in this, and you will remembered for nothing."

"There's not enough power in Rome to elect Sergius pope!"

"There would be," said Ishtar, "If your husband aligned himself with Alberic of Speleto."

"Think on it," said Nyx. "Because as it is, you have nothing."

"I have enough power to have you both killed," said Theodora, her voice cold and angry.

To her surprise, both Angels laughed at her. "No," said Nyx, standing. "You don't."

The two women walked out of the room, leaving Theodora seething.

In the hallway, Ishtar heard a young girl singing. She stepped away from Nyx and followed the sound. In a room overlooking a garden, a beautiful young girl sat on the window-seat, singing to herself as she embroidered a cushion. Her nurse sat to one side, nodding and humming as the girl sang.

Twelve, thought Ishtar. *Maybe thirteen*. She was her mother's child, there was no question of it, though she had not started to fill out as her mother had. She was still slim, with only a hint of breasts and hips. She had large eyes like her mother, but blue instead of brown, and her hair had streaks of auburn running through its long waves. Together with her blue dress and the simple rings she wore on her hand, she was fetching enough to gain the promise of marriage from any number of eligible nobles.

The girl noticed Ishtar then, and her song faltered.

"Oh, don't stop," said Ishtar, smiling a gentle, kind smile. "Please. Your mother was just telling me what a lovely voice you had, and when I heard the singing I had to come see for myself."

The girl blushed. "Thank you, my lady."

"She didn't tell me your name, though, my dear. What is it?"

"Marozia, my lady."

"You are very beautiful, Marozia," Ishtar said. "Are you promised to anyone yet?"

The girl blushed again. "No, my lady."

"Then someday soon, there is going to be a very lucky man out there," said Ishtar. "And now, I must go. I'll leave you to your singing and your embroidery, and I wish you they joy of the day."

"And to you, my lady." The girl had a very pretty curtsey, too. Ishtar gave her a regal one back and left.

Nyx said not to kill the innocent ones, Ishtar thought. *She didn't say anything about corrupting them.* She put together a plan in her head, and savored it as she walked. *Nyx is growing too fond of these humans again. We'll have to see about changing that.*

That night, Nyx stood on the balcony outside Theodora's bedroom, listening. Theodora bedded her husband thoroughly and at length before broaching the subject. "It seems a shame that the next pope will not be serving our family."

"He's from Bologna," said Theophylact, dismissing him with a wave of his arm. "He won't be serving anybody. I think the cardinals got tired of having us tell them what to do."

"Then perhaps he should be replaced," suggested Theodora. "Say, by one who is more… malleable?"

"A good thought," said Theophylact, smiling at his wife. He reached a hand down her body and caressed her. "Unfortunately, we do not have the men to do so."

"Would we if we were to ally ourselves with someone?" asked Theodora, caressing him back.

"Like who?" returned Theophylact.

"Alberic," said Theodora.

"Him?" Theophylact scoffed. "I'd sooner trust a Saracen. The man became Duke by murdering his own cousin."

"Hardly the first to do so," said Theodora.

"Still doesn't make him worth trusting."

"True," said Theodora. "Of course, if Alberic were bound by ties of marriage…"

Theophylact raised an eyebrow. "Our daughter is young, yet."

"Not so young as she can't be put on display," said Theodora, increasing the speed of her caresses. "Or promised to a wealthy, strong man who will protect her interests. And ours."

"Hmm," said Theophylact. "She's a gentle girl, naive…"

"She will not remain so, my lord. Not my daughter."

"I suppose you're right."

"Of course I am. And why should some young man get the benefit of her and not her parents?"

"Indeed. Yes, you are wise. I'll broach the idea with Alberic's people in the city," He groaned. "Meanwhile, I think a trip is in order for you."

"For me?" Theodora sat up. "Why for me?"

"Don't stop what you were doing!" her husband captured her

hand and guided it back. "I think a short trip to Caere would be good for your spirit," he said. "And for Sergius's spirits as well."

Theodora smiled. "I see."

"If we are going to arrange the next pope," said Theophylact, "we may as well make it someone we can control. And take Marozia with you. You can stop in at Speleto on your way home." He groaned, then grabbed her and rolled on top of her. "But first things first!"

*

In Caere, thirteen-year old Marozia walked through the halls of Sergius's villa, bored and lonely. They'd been there a week, and Marozia was mostly being ignored as her mother spent time in private with the man she wanted to be pope.

Marozia had already explored every corner of the place, had watched the scullions at work, had visited the gardens and the animal pens, talked to the guards and the servants, and generally made a nuisance of herself to he point where her mother had given her a stern lecture on proper behavior and a dozen licks of a leather strop borrowed from Sergius's blacksmith to back it up.

Now, smarting and sore, Marozia walked alone through the palace grounds, hoping a couple of the servants would do something wrong and get whipped themselves, just so she could watch it. Unfortunately, all the servants seemed to be annoyingly good at their jobs, and no one had cause to complain about their actions or behavior. She wondered how she could get one of them into trouble.

"You shouldn't waste your time with servants," said someone. "Not when you could be in charge of all of them in a few years."

Marozia turned around. The speaker was a girl a bit taller than Marozia herself, with black hair and brown eyes and dark skin. She smiled at Marozia, and there was something in her smile that was both wicked and trustworthy. Marozia at once wanted to like her. "Besides," said the girl. "It's not them you want to get even with, it's your mother."

The fact that the other girl knew what she was thinking irritated Marozia to no end. She drew herself up as tall as she could, which was still not as tall as the other girl and that was even more irritating. "Who are you to speak to me like that?" she said haughtily. "I could have you whipped for speaking about my mother that way."

The other girl laughed. "No you couldn't." And despite herself, Marozia found herself laughing as well. "Besides, if you try, I won't help you become the most powerful woman in Italy."

"You can't do that!" said Marozia.

"Sure I can," said the girl, twirling one of her black curls between two fingers. "First thing is to replace your mother as Sergius's favorite." The other girl walked around Marozia, looking her up and down. "You're going to have to grow a bit first. Sergius likes them curvy and you have no boobs as all." She walked behind Marozia. "No real bum either."

"Stop it!" said Marozia, giggling.

"Come on," the other girl said, capturing her hand and tugging her down the hallway. The girl smelled like rose petals with a hint of something muskier. "The afternoon show is about to start and we can hide behind the curtains and watch if we go now."

"Wait! What afternoon show?" demanded Marozia, running up to keep up with the other girl.

The girl turned and flashed a smile, teasing and merry. "In Sergius's room. Or don't you want to see why he likes your mother so much?"

That made Marozia pause, but the charm of the other girl held sway. "All right," she said. "But I don't even know your name!"

"Ishtar," said the girl.

"That's a strange name."

"It's very old," said Ishtar. "It came from Babylon." She pulled Marozia along faster. "Now hurry up! If you want to be the most powerful woman in Italy, first you have to know how to hold power!"

Together, the two girls ran down the hallway, giggling.

That evening, Marozia sat in the villa's orchard, watching the sun set through the leaves of the apple trees. Her mind was whirling, choked with obscene images. Her stomach was upset and she had had to excuse herself from eating dinner at the same table as her mother and Sergius. Ishtar and she had spent the afternoon watching them engaging in the most carnal of activities. Ishtar wouldn't let her leave when she'd had enough—which was very soon—and the sights and smells and sounds had imprinted on her memory. She wasn't stupid. She knew what men and women did, and she knew that babies came from it, but the things that her mother had done…and liked doing…

He's not even my father, Marozia thought. *How could she let him do those things?*

Marozia shuddered, and tried to turn her attention to the vivid hues of the sunset.

"Hello," said Ishtar, stepping out from behind a tree. Marozia didn't look at her.

"What's the matter?" asked Ishtar, smiling. "Never seen a woman take it like a boy before?"

"No, I haven't," snapped Marozia. "And I never wanted to see my mother do it! Ever! It was disgusting!"

"Your mother's been doing that and much more since before you were born," said Ishtar calmly, sitting beside her. "And you'll be doing it soon enough."

Marozia stood up and stomped away from Ishtar. "My mother is a whore! I'll never be like her!"

"Wrong," said Ishtar. "A whore is paid to give the man what he wants. Your mother uses her body and mind to get her whatever *she* wants. And the reasons she does that with Sergius is so that Sergius will serve her when he becomes Pope. And unless you want to spend the rest of your life serving her, you'd better learn how to do it better than she does."

"Eww." Marozia looked away. She was angry and confused and not at all happy about the prospect. "I don't want to do… that. I won't."

"You don't have a choice," said Ishtar, her voice suddenly very hard and much, much older than her appearance. "Your mother is taking you to Speleto to show you off to Alberic. Didn't you know? If he likes you and agrees to ally himself with your father against Benedict, you'll be married to him, and you can either spend your life doing what your mother was doing the way *he* wants for the reasons *he* wants. Or you can do it the way *you* want for the reasons *you* want. And *right now* is when you get to pick."

"But…what if I don't want to do any of it?"

Ishtar laughed. "You don't get to do what you want, girl. You get to do what your mother and father tell you. Nothing else."

Marozia pouted. "It's not fair."

"No," said Ishtar. "It isn't. But it's the way it is. Now what do you want? To be your mother's slave and Alberic's whore? Or to learn how to rule over both of them?"

Marozia took a long look at Ishtar, who suddenly looked much older and wiser than the girl she had been before. "Who are you? Why do you care?"

Ishtar smiled. "I have been in your position, girl," she said. "And in every position your mother was in this afternoon. I have been in those positions of my own volition, and because others have made me do it, and let me tell you it is far, far better when it's by your own choice. If you have the brains and the daring, I can make you more powerful than any other woman in history. If you don't..." Ishtar shrugged. "Then you can see what it feels like to be taken by a man you don't want touching you. I hear Alberic prefers it when a woman resists. It gives him an excuse to hit them."

"You're disgusting!" shouted Marozia. "You're horrible."

"I'm right," said Ishtar, and this time she poured the full strength of her Angelic power into the words. Marozia froze where she stood, her eyes wide.

"What... what are you?"

Ishtar smiled and let her wings show, though she did not change any other part of her form. Marozia fell over backwards, scrabbling against the dirt to get away until she fetched up against a tree. Ishtar stepped forward and knelt before her "I'm an Angel, Marozia," said Ishtar. "And I can make you so much more than you are. You just need to trust me, and know that everything I do will make you powerful and strong, and give you control of the nobility and the papacy if you want it. But you have to choose *now.*"

"But… but… I don't know what I want!"

"Choose," said Ishtar. "Now."

"But…"

"*NOW!*"

"All right! I'll do it! I'll do what you ask."

"You'll do what I *say*," said Ishtar, and her eyes flashed red. "Everything I say, when I say and how I say."

"Yes!" cried Marozia. "I will! I swear I will!"

"Good!" The wings vanished, the red faded from her eyes, and Ishtar once more appeared as a slightly older, slightly taller girl. She held out her hand. "Now come one. It's time to go to the stables."

"The… the stables?" Marozia was confused.

"Haven't you looked at the stable hands?" said Ishtar. "They're delicious. And they are excellent to practice on." She smiled again. "So vigorous and so eager. But remember, no giving up your virginity. We need it intact for your lover-to-be."

"Lover?" Marozia took Ishtar's hand and stood up. "You mean Alberic?"

Ishtar laughed. "Of course not. Alberic will be your husband. *Sergius* is going to be your lover."

*

Pope Benedict IV sat at the head of the table, alone. It had been a long and trying day, and he had chosen to have dinner alone in his apartments, rather than face another delegation of Italian nobles who wanted something from him. *They do not understand what the church is here to do,* he thought, as he took another spoonful of the almond-flavored pudding he had asked for dessert. It was one of his favorites, and on days like this one, he was especially fond of it.

"Is it good, Papa?" asked a woman.

The Pope looked up, startled. The woman was clad in black from head to foot, though somehow her clothes – *or is it armor?*– managed to reveal every part of her body while showing none of it. She was taller than he, and her hair and skin were both white. Her eyes, though, glowed red. The pope rose, nearly knocking over his chair from surprise.

"I had to put in lots of sugar," said Nyx. "Otherwise the bitterness comes through."

"What...what are you?"

In his chest, it seemed that a massively strong hand had made a fist with his heart inside it. He gasped, but no air or sound would come.

"It had to seem natural," said Nyx. "And since you liked to dine alone, this seemed the best time." She looked down at the bowl as Pope Benedict clutched at his chest. "Shouldn't leave any lying around, though." So fast she seemed to blur she was beside him at the table, and picking up the bowl. She ate the rest without qualm, then smiled at him. "It only works on mortals, of course. But it is delicious."

He stumbled backwards and she caught his arm, steadying him and easing him back into his chair. "Shhhh..." she whispered as he tried to grab at her, the movements sharp and spasmodic. "Shhhh. It will be over in a moment."

Benedict's mouth opened and closed a half-dozen times, then fell open and stayed there. His head slouched against his chest, and his hands stopped their struggling. Nyx stepped back and waited as his soul pulled free of its body. To her surprise, it began ascending.

I guess he was one of the good ones. Nyx waved at him, and she saw in his soul the anger and helplessness he felt at the sight of his own body. She watched him until he rose out of sight.

"Well," said Nyx, patting the corpse's head, "now that you're finished, time to see what we can manage."

*

In the brothel south of the papal palace, Nyx and Ishtar sat drinking wine.

"This," said Ishtar, "is very disappointing."

"The wine, or the election of Leo V?" asked Nyx, tossing back her own glass.

"Both," said Ishtar. "Especially the wine. If this is what *Tribunal* was drinking before he died, no wonder he hated them all."

"Don't make fun of Tribunal," warned Nyx, feeling rage and the need to lash out all humanity, and a desperate urgency to finish her mission fill her mind at the mention of her beloved's name.

"Apologies," said Ishtar, enjoying the effect that mentioning the name was having on Nyx. "I meant no disrespect to *Tribunal.*" She took another sip of the awful wine. "Do you think Leo is going to be our man?"

"No," said Nyx. "The cardinals elected him because the other choices were repugnant."

"What, no call for Sergius?"

"Not yet," said Nyx. "The Roman nobility has been too greedy too long. They want someone from outside."

"Of course they do," said Ishtar.

"And what have you been up to?" asked Nyx. "You certainly haven't been with me."

"Papal politics aren't interesting me right now," said Ishtar airily. "I'm looking further afield for ways to bring our pope into power."

"I thought you enjoyed corrupting Rome."

"Oh, I do," said Ishtar. "But then, there's so many ways to corrupt it, I thought I would try a different one."

Nyx's eyes narrowed, and her voice echoed in Ishtar's head. *"Why is your mind closed to me?"*

"Because I want it to be a surprise," replied Ishtar, praying that the blocks stayed in place. *"You'll see the results soon enough."*

"I hope so," said Nyx. "Time is beginning to run short, Ishtar. We need to be ready to move on Jerusalem."

"Not for another hundred years or more," said Ishtar. "There's still plenty of time."

"We thought that during the Empire," said Nyx. "Let's not make the same mistake again."

The mistake was leaving you in charge, thought Ishtar. "Don't worry. I haven't forgotten any of the lessons from the Empire."

"Good." Nyx finished her wine. "I must speak with Theodora. They need to cement the alliance with Alberic if they're going to gain enough sway to put Sergius in charge."

"And what will happen to Leo V?" asked Ishtar.

"You'll get rid of him," said Nyx. "Before the end of the year."

Ishtar smiled. "My pleasure."

That night, Marozia lay in her room in her father's house, crying. She had sent her maids away, wanting to be alone. The lessons that Ishtar had taught her were harsh, and practicing them was even more so. She did not like the men, did not like the way they touched her, and did not want it to continue. It left her feeling dirty and demeaned. *If only Ishtar would let me stop…*

"You can't stop, child," said Ishtar. "You're only now beginning to show signs of improvement."

Marozia curled up into a ball, huddling in on herself so she would not have to face the Angel who hovered over her bed. A gentle hand landed on her shoulder, and the pain in her body and her mind faded away. The horrible empty feeling in her stomach disappeared, replaced by warmth and a sense of joy.

"That's better, my dear," crooned Ishtar. "Now come. You are needed, tonight."

"Wha… where…Where are we going, Ishtar?"

Ishtar flexed her wings. "To give an annoying little man a vision and gift of flesh."

"A gift of…." Marozia's face fell. "My flesh?"

"Yes, my dear," said Ishtar. "But not your virginity. Let him think he can have that later."

"Why?" Marozia felt tears rising anew. "Why do I have to?"

"Because you are a delightful young thing, when you are not whining, and that is what he prefers," said Ishtar. "His name is Christopher, and with the right incentive, he will do exactly as I wish."

*

Christopher was alone in his garden when the Holy Virgin appeared to him. She wore blue and white, and her halo glowed brilliant white. She had appeared out of nowhere, and she wept as she looked at him. "Oh, Christopher," she said. "How can you sit here, when Rome needs you?"

"My lady?"

"The papacy is corrupted," said the Holy Virgin. "It has been betrayed from within, and only you can set it right."

"Me?" Christopher shook his head. "I don't understand."

"Look upon this child," said the Holy Virgin, and a young girl dressed in white appeared beside her. "It is her destiny to be yours."

"But… the pope cannot…"

"Leo will take her," said the Virgin. "He will despoil her. And her virginity must belong to you alone."

The girl stepped forward and bowed her head. "It is my destiny," she said "I have been shown by an Angel that I am to bear a pope's child, a child who will become pope himself."

"Truly?" said Christopher.

"Truly," said the Virgin. "She is to be yours, to take pleasure with as you will."

"When?" asked Christopher, his desire naked on his face.

"Only after you have taken Rome," said the Virgin. "Then may you have her as yours, so that she may perform her holy duty." Ishtar let her halo glow brighter as she laid a hand on the girl's shoulder. "For now, she may give you but a taste of what pleasures will await you, once Rome is in your hands."

The girl stepped forward and knelt in font of him as Ishtar had to force herself not to grin. Christopher would do exactly as he was bid.

*

"It is too far!" declared Theophylact to the council of Roman nobles around him. "Too far for any of us to tolerate!"

"Too far for you to tolerate, you mean," shouted one of the Vincentii whose noble house had long opposed Theophylact.

"He claims rights to my daughter," snapped Theophylact. "Based on vision of the Holy Virgin."

"Well, if the Virgin sent him, who are we to deny it?"

"The Virgin is not a panderer!"

"Unlike your wife!"

The laughter went around the room, ending at Alberic. The big man rose to his feet and looked over the others. "Marozia has been promised to me," he said. "Not to this foul little man. Nor will I allow him to give Italy over to those who do not have its best interest at heart." he crossed the floor to Theophylact. "I will stand with my brother, and defend our church against those who would turn it into a whorehouse." He looked over the other nobles, who knew that between them Alberic and Theophylact controlled enough men and arms to decimate Rome and half of Italy besides. Alberic knew it, too. "Now, who will stand with me?"

The next morning Alberic's and Theophylact's troops moved on the papal palace, and one week later, a message was sent to Sergius, pleading for him to come in and rescue the papacy from destruction.

*

Marozia knelt before Pope Sergius III, resplendent in his white robes. Behind her, dressed like a servant, Ishtar smiled. The girl had started filling out nicely. Though she was only fourteen, her breasts and hips had both rounded, and judging from how

Sergius's eyes followed them, Marozia was having exactly the effect that Ishtar had wanted her to.

"My dear," Sergius was saying, "Of course I have time for you."

"I thank you," said Marozia, looking up at him through her eyelashes. "My mother has said so many kind things about you that I wanted to see you again." She let her eyes wander down the front of his robe, exactly as Ishtar had taught her. "And ask if you would be willing to bless me, as you do her."

"I am flattered," said Sergius, his eyes drifting to Marozia's cleavage. "But your mother and I have a special and personal relationship, based on her faith. I could not betray it."

"I would never ask you to do that," said Marozia, her eyes wide with surprise. "I would never dream of taking away my mother's most precious spiritual advisor. I would only..." she stopped and bit her lip, just as Ishtar had told her to do.

"Yes, my child?" asked the pope. "What would you do?"

"I would only ask that you provide me with your guidance too. For I am but a simple virgin. And am in much need of a..." she hesitated, looked away, then looked into Sergius's eyes. "A firm... guiding... hand. To ensure I go in the right direction."

A fire kindled in Sergius's groin. "My dear girl. I will be more than happy to... guide you forward."

Ishtar bowed her head and smiled to herself.

*

Nyx, wearing her true form, stepped into the dungeon room where Leo and Christopher were chained across the room from one another. They had been put with their arms up on the wall and their legs before them, so they were forced to sit in their own filth and could not escape the attentions of the rats, who knew when a man was helpless and would come biting. Both, to Nyx's surprise, still had their eyes.

The men stared in horror at the black-clad, sword – and whip-holding woman with the red snake eyes and the horned crown. Nyx looked down at Leo, and smiled at him. "I am sorry, Pope Leo," she said. "You were unfortunately in the wrong place at the wrong time. As popes go, you weren't actually that bad." She looked over at Christopher, and the smile became a snarl, her razor-sharp teeth bared. Christopher shrieked and struggled desperately. "If it makes you feel better, Leo, I do want you to know that this one was not a good man, and I am going to torture him for days before I finally kill him." The end of her whip flipped out, the hellfire burning into Leo's flesh even as the cord wrapped tight around his neck. "Sorry it can't be faster," she said, "but I do believe strangling is traditional, here."

Nyx pulled the whip tight enough to crush his larynx and watched him writhe and spasm to death. His soul, when it left, rose steadily up. "Well, what do you know?" she said, watching it go up. "He *was* a good man. No wonder he was displaced."

Nyx turned her gaze back on Christopher, and the man's bowels voided as he read her expression. "You, on the other hand, are not a good man," she said. "Not at all. And while I appreciate that you deposed Leo for me, I want to know who, exactly, gave you the idea that Theodora's daughter was to be your reward."

"The Virgin!" Christopher screamed. "The Holy Virgin Mary came to me in a vision and told me it was to be! She was to be the mother of popes!"

Nyx knelt down in front of him and impaled him through

the chin with a single talon. He cried out and tried to pull away, but she hooked her finger and dragged the talon forward, ripping through his flesh until it lodged against the bone in his jaw. "You are going to tell me exactly what you saw, exactly what she said, and exactly what happened, down to the number of leaves on the trees and the way the wind blew," she said. "And if you are very, very fortunate, you will do it well enough that you will convince me to let you die."

It was three days before she was satisfied with his answers.

*

"Are you certain?" demanded Theodora, as Nyx, disguised as one of Marozia's maidservants, followed her mistress through the corridors of the papal palace.

"I am, mistress," said Nyx. "I am sorry."

Theodora slapped her face. "You'll be even more sorry when I'm done with you, girl. How could you let this go on?"

"Please, mistress!" Nyx begged, acting as the girl servant most certainly would, had Nyx not sent her and her family out of the city with a sum of gold and orders never to return on pain of her Angelic displeasure.

"Shut up, slut!" She grabbed Nyx's ear. "You'll be whipped in the morning, you hear? And tonight you will do exactly what I say, when I say it, or I'll have you given to my husband's soldiers for a plaything. Do you understand?"

"Yes, mistress," groveled Nyx. *As long as you put paid to this bastard on the way.*

They reached the door of the papal bedchambers. The guards were absent because Nyx had already removed them and left their unconscious, wine-soaked bodies where they would be found by their captain the next morning.

And that will teach them to be procurers.

Theodora stopped outside the chamber door, listening. Inside they could here Marozia crying out in what sounded like pleasure but was, to Nyx's very knowledgeable ears, disguised pain. Theodora drew herself up, her back straight as the handle on a pole-axe, her face stony with rage. Her hands grabbed each of the door handles, and she took a large breath.

And as Nyx watched, Theodora's face changed. She pushed the rage down deep beneath the surface, and pasted a wide and happy smile on her face. Then threw the door wide.

Marozia was face down on the bed, crying out as Sergius moved behind her. Theodora stopped in the doorway for the briefest of moments, then strode in, crying, "Your Holiness! Had I but known!"

Sergius froze, and in that moment, Theodora undid her own dress and let it fall to her feet. Her body was a ripe version of Marozia's, softer, fleshier and carrying the marks of childbearing. "I had always intended this to be a family affair," she said, smiling at the pope. "And I am so pleased to see my daughter takes the same enjoyment in such practices as I do."

Sergius stared at her, confused. Theodora took the moment to grab Nyx's arm and pull her forward. "Once you have finished with my daughter, may I suggest this one? She is a virgin in all ways, and has a most pleasing little backside." She smiled at Nyx, and Nyx could see the rage in her eyes. "Get naked and on the bed, girl. And face down, if you please."

Nyx, stunned at Theodora's behavior, and trapped in her own disguise, did as she was told. And as she lay face down on the bed, her bare shoulders touching Marozia's, the girl grabbed her hand and squeezed it tight. "You're not Ghita, are you?" she whispered.

Nyx didn't answer.

"You're not," said the girl. "I know you're not. I was told you would come. And I was told to give you a message."

"What message?" Nyx whispered back as she felt the pope running his hand over her.

"Your Tribunal is right," said Marozia, repeating what Ishtar had told her to say. "Look upon this room and know that your Tribunal was right."

*

Ishtar was in a hidden arena, fighting in the ring. She had chosen the form of a slim young man who fought only with a dagger. She had had killed a dozen more experienced-looking opponents, and won a large pile of gold which she used to buy drinks from the crowd. The men and women watching screamed at her victories, and were joyously shouting for blood as Ishtar used her dagger to carve through the defenses of a much larger man with a sword and armor. She had just brought him to his knees, his sword arm broken and useless, his shield dragging in the dirt. She raised the dagger to give him the coup de grace when Nyx, in full battle armor with weapons in hand and wings spread wide, came smashing in through the roof and landed, full force on Ishtar's head. The force of the impact crushed her spine, her pelvis and both her legs with the force of impact and drove the other Angel into the sand of the arena floor.

Nyx, cut the head off Ishtar's opponent with a single swipe and glared balefully at the crowd. "Run."

The spectators clawed and fought and trampled one another to escape of the arena. Nyx ignored them. Beneath her feet, Ishtar squirmed in pain.

"You betrayed me, bitch," said Nyx.

Ishtar made a gagging noise, and Nyx stepped off of her head. Ishtar's body changed, becoming her that of her true self, though it was still broken in a dozen places. Nyx watched as Ishtar's jaw reshaped itself enough that Ishtar could gasp out. "I didn't. I did what had to be done."

"Theodora was our vessel. Not her daughter."

"Her daughter will do better!" moaned Ishtar. "She will AAAAAAHHH!!!"

Nyx enjoyed watching Ishtar's agony as the Angel's spine forcibly fixed itself. She waited for Ishtar to stop screaming. "I told you," said Nyx, "to leave the innocent alone."

"She's not innocent," lied Ishtar. "She never was. She took to fucking like a whore working for her next meal. She's had four other men do her the same way Sergius was when you caught them together." Ishtar managed a grin, despite her face still being half-ruined. "Pity none of their cocks were as big as his. She might have liked it better."

"Open your mind to me," ordered Nyx.

"No!" Ishtar crawled backwards. "You don't trust me."

"No," said Nyx. "I don't." She started walking forward, her sword swinging back and forth. "You lied to me. You betrayed me. And the only reason I'm not killing you is because doing that would allow another Angel to get through."

"How have I betrayed you?" Ishtar demanded. "Sergius is in power!"

"Sergius is supposed to be under the control of Theodora, not subject to the whims of a fourteen-year-old girl!"

"You mean he's supposed to be under your control," said Ishtar. "Not mine."

"Yes," said Nyx, and the tip of her blade rested against Ishtar's stomach. "That is exactly what I mean."

Ishtar froze in place, and her eyes drilled into Nyx's. "Well, as long as you control the mother, and I control the daughter, that shouldn't be a problem, should it?"

The tip of Nyx's blade broke Ishtar's skin, and Ishtar gasped with the pain. "Missing the point, Ishtar."

"I'm *not missing the point!*" screamed Ishtar. "For eight hundred years I've been following you and doing exactly what you wanted and it hasn't worked! So I'm trying something different. FUCK!"

The last was from Nyx's blade sinking an inch into Ishtar's belly. "I told you to leave the innocent alone."

"You told me not to kill the children!" Ishtar screamed. "Well, I didn't, did I? I just showed one how she could use her body to get what she wanted."

"Making her an adulterer and sending her to Hell."

"It was her choice! AAAHH!"

Nyx's blade had sunk in another inch. "She was an innocent before she met you."

"For fuck's sake, there are no innocent!" screamed Ishtar. "These humans are born vicious little animals and they stay that way! Look at them for fuck's sake! See them like *Tribunal* saw them!"

The familiar rush of love, hatred and need filled Nyx's body.

She shoved her blade in two inches further. "Don't use his name against me!"

"I'm not, for fuck's sake! I'm not!" Ishtar's voice became pleading. "Haven't you seen them? Haven't you looked at them? Have they changed in a thousand years? Have they? *Tribunal* judged them wanting! Why won't you?"

"I don't know!" screamed Nyx back. She ripped her sword out of the other Angel's guts and Ishtar went sprawling on the sands. "I don't know why I can't abandon them."

"Well, figure it out," gasped Ishtar. "Because we're supposed to be destroying them."

"No, we're supposed to be bringing Tribunal back."

"And what will he do when he gets here?" demanded Ishtar. She pushed herself to her feet, moaning from the pain it caused her. "Walk with me. Look at them with me, and when you look at them, ask what your Tribunal would say about them."

"I know what he'd say."

"Then act on it!" Ishtar tried to reach out a hand, but her spine wasn't fully healed, yet. "Earth is destroying you, my Queen. It's making you weak and clouding your judgement. Walk with me, look on these humans and despair the way Tribunal did. Then you'll be able to act clearly."

Nyx stepped back, Tribunal's rage and hatred had filled her again, making Ishtar's words make sense. "Lead me," she said. "But you are a long way from being forgiven."

For the next three days and nights Ishtar led her through Rome, visiting brothels and prisons, private dungeons and courtrooms, children's bedrooms and torture chambers, holy monasteries and unholy temples. Always they stayed hidden from view, letting people behave as they would. Everywhere, Nyx saw humanity behaving at its worst. She saw what people did to their children, and what the children themselves were doing to others. She saw adults torturing and mutilating one another, stealing each other's belongings, swindling each other and lying. Everywhere they went, Ishtar would point out and say, "This is what *Tribunal* was seeing! That is why he hates them!"

And every time Ishtar said his name, Nyx would feel Tribunal's memory rise up in her head, feel his anger and rage and helplessness at the life he was forced to lead and the horrifying actions of all those around him. And every time Nyx would feel her own hatred for the human race growing.

And yet…

She remembered those who prayed in her name for their children or their wives or lovers. She remembered those who cared for one another, and helped the old and infirm, rather than leaving them to die. She remembered how little they had and how some of them were still good.

"Look here!" hissed Ishtar, pointing at two toddlers. One had just taken away the toy from another, and the first was wailing. The second toddler hit the first and walked away. And when the first toddler ran crying to its mother, it got slapped and told to be silent.

"How can you say these things have decency, when they are born full of hatred and greed?" Ishtar demanded. "*Tribunal* saw it, I see it. Why aren't you seeing it?"

And in that moment, Nyx did see it. And even so….

Why can't I let them go? Nyx demanded herself. *They are only human! Why can't I just let them die so we can have Paradise?*

Nyx spread her wings and flew, leaving Ishtar grinning after her, and a crowd of mortals staring in surprise.

905 A.D.

Nyx sat naked on the top of Monte Bianco, her wings wrapped loosely around her body. The burning cold touch of the snow against her flesh was like a light brush of hellfire. Her body was coated in frost, and only the strong winds had kept the snow from covering her over. Her eyes stared, unblinking, at the sun rising before her.

There was a flap of wings, a rush of snow, and Persephone landed beside her. She wore the uniform of an Arab soldier, the back of it ripped open by her wings. She walked in a slow, careful circle around Nyx, keeping well out of sword-reach. "My Queen?"

Nyx stayed, unmoving and unblinking, as Persephone crouched down before her.

"My Queen," Persephone repeated. "You didn't meet at our rendezvous last year." She knelt in the snow beside Nyx. "You didn't answer when I called you. I couldn't even feel your presence on the world." Nyx didn't move. Persephone slipped closer. "My lady?"

"Tribunal was right," said Nyx.

Persephone leaned back, then sat down. "I thought that was what this was all about."

"I kept going back and forth," said Nyx, still not moving. "I kept thinking that they weren't all bad, these humans. That some of them were good, some were decent. That some were trying to raise their children to be more than what they themselves are."

"Some are," said Persephone.

"No, they're not," said Nyx. "They're bettering themselves, not their race. They're making themselves worse than what they are so they can have more." She stared into the sun. "Did you know Theodora was fucking the pope?"

"Yes," said Persephone. "Ishtar told me."

"Did she tell you that she fucks him with her daughter at her side? That they take turns serving his depravities?"

"She did."

"She finds out her daughter is being ass-fucked by her lover and instead of being enraged, joins them. What sort of mother is that?"

Persephone shrugged but didn't answer.

"How can they act this way?" demanded Nyx. "How can they be this way, knowing their souls are going to Hell for it? I've tortured souls until they were nothing but Hell-stone for far less than that! Then pulled them back out and tortured them again!"

Persephone shrugged. "Most of them don't believe in Hell. Or Heaven. God's been gone so long from this world that they don't feel his presence any more."

"The morning after I revealed Marozia's affair to Theodora, I chased down Ishtar. I was planning to torture her for a month and instead, she convinced me to walk with her to see how depraved everyone was. And I did, and they were, and I *still couldn't find it in me to condemn them all!*"

"Some of them are…"

"*None of them are!*" screamed Nyx. "But even so, I had to keep looking for the good in them. I had to weigh each one's choices before I could condemn them, and then, I could only condemn them individually!"

"Some of them are worth saving," ventured Persephone.

"Not enough of them!" snarled Nyx. "And I still couldn't condemn them!" Nyx's body shook with rage, and when she spoke again her voice was filled with disgust. "So I flew here. I tried to understand why. I sat in the fucking snow for a year to understand why. I fucking *prayed*, Persephone! I actually sat down and prayed, just to see if I could hear Him, just to see if he could hear me so I could tell Him what disgusting, horrible *things* these people are!"

"Did you hear him?" asked Persephone yearning in her voice. "Did He speak to you?"

"Of course not!" raged Nyx, fire lighting in her eyes. Her flesh began heating with the power of her anger, and the frost began melting away from her skin. "He hasn't spoken to me for an aeon. And now he doesn't speak to anyone! And that's when I realized *why* I couldn't condemn them all out of hand."

"Why?"

"Because I don't have free will!" Nyx's wings flexed back and forth, sending gusts of wind and snow through the air. "God made me their judge, remember? He made me Queen of Hell and he made me judge them all! So I can't just condemn them. I have to judge each and every one of them, from the most evil bastard walking on the planet to the purest little virgin that ever lived. He made me like this!"

Nyx stalked back and forth on the mountaintop. "So I started praying again. Only this time I prayed to Tribunal. And every time I pray to him, every time I say his name out loud, it gives me the strength to do what we need to do."

Persephone's head titled to one side. "Then why are you still here?"

"Because I needed to think," said Nyx. "I need to find a way to take control of the church beyond these squabbling, petty little Romans."

"And did you figure it out?"

"Yes," said Nyx. "I did. But I'll need your help. How are the Easterners?"

Persephone shrugged. "The Arabs will keep them busy for a hundred years or so."

"Good." Nyx walked to the edge of the cliff and looked down. "We've been here too long," she said. "Too long away from where we belong."

"You want to go back to Hell?" asked Persephone.

"We don't belong in Hell," said Nyx. "We belong in Heaven. And since that bastard God won't let us go back there, then I'll damn well have His son bring me into Paradise."

Persephone nodded her agreement. "How can I help?"

Nyx grinned and spread her wings. "Become a virgin, my dear. You're about to serve an Angel."

*

Theodora slapped her screaming daughter. "Shut up, you little slut!"

Marozia, in the midst of a contraction, couldn't defend herself. Her mother slapped her again. She cried instead, long wails of agony that filled the room and the hallways beyond. Standing at the girl's side, mopping her brow, Ishtar barely managed to suppress a laugh.

"Do you think Alberic will have you now?" Theodora demanded. "Do you think he'll want a little slut who lets herself get pregnant instead of saving herself for her husband?"

The contraction receded, and Marozia's eyes fixed on her mother. "A little slut who got pregnant from her *mother's* lover, you mean," she ground out. "A little slut who fucked the Pope!"

"A little slut who should have used a pessary!" Theodora hit her again, just as another contraction hit. "Stupid whore! You should have just given him your ass and left your cunt for your husband!"

Marozia groaned in pain and screamed, "I don't have a husband!"

"And you never will, now!"

"Yes," said Nyx, stepping into the room. "She will."

Theodora spun around and saw Nyx as the matron she had met before. "What in the name of God are you doing here?"

"What is necessary," said Nyx looking at Ishtar. She crossed the room and took Marozia's face in her hand. "Is the child Sergius's?"

"Yes," gasped Marozia. "It is!"

"Then we now have even more leverage over him," said Nyx. She touched Marozia's forehead and her pain diminished to next to nothing. "Push, child. Have your infant. We will ensure you still have a husband." Her gaze shifted to Ishtar. "Won't we?"

*

In Speleto, Ishtar sat at Alberic's table, disguised as a courtier. "It is a simple matter, my Lord Duke," she said. "Raise the girl's son as your own."

"What?" Alberic looked shocked. "You think I would let the bastard of that slut and that old man into my house?"

"That slut," said Ishtar, "controls the pope. And her son is proof of the pope's broken vows. Keep them both alive and well, and you'll be able to control the pope yourself."

Alberic I, Duke of Speleto, leaned back in his chair and thought about it.

"Besides," said Ishtar. "Now you know the girl is fertile, and can bear you sons. Surely that is worth the inconvenience of a bastard running around. And of course, there is the other thing…"

Alberic's eyes narrowed. "And what is the other thing?"

"Theophylact," said Ishtar. "And Theodora. They'll both hate it immensely."

Alberic, Duke of Speleto, grinned.

906 A.D.

Pope Sergius III rose in the middle of the night, and wondered why. His bed was empty, for a change, and he'd wanted nothing more that night than to sleep until morning came. It had been a long, trying day. Alberic of Speleto and Aldabart of Tuscany had blocked Berengar I from coming to him and receiving the crown of the Emperor. It was all about politics, of course, but it made no *sense*. The West needed a strong leader to bring back the Holy Empire. Berengar was perfect, save that Alberic and Aldabart didn't like him and wanted the crown for themselves, even though they had nowhere near the power it needed.

He sighed and thought of Marozia. She had grown into the same beauty her mother had, and when the two woman came to him together…. A shudder went through Sergius, and he thought of summoning a maid to relax him when he saw a small candle burning in an alcove on the far wall of his room.

There was no alcove there, Sergius thought. *There's never been an alcove there.*

Yet, there was one there now, and a candle was burning in it, in the hands of a woman dressed in white. Sergius rolled to his feet, looking around the room. There was no one there, save himself and the young woman. Cautiously, he advanced on her. "Who are you?"

"I am one that has waited for you," said Persephone, her voice ethereal and gentle. The long white robe covered her body, and the wimple covered her hair, making her look almost like a novice of any of the holy orders, save that the robe was just tight enough to give hints of the young, pretty body that she wore underneath it. She saw Sergius notice and tried not to smile. "I am the one who serves. And I have come for you."

"For me?" Sergius was confused. "For what?"

Persephone turned and the wall behind her slid open to show a small spiral staircase.

"This wasn't here before," said Sergius. "None of it."

"Of course it was," said Persephone. "God was just not ready for you to see it. Now, follow."

Sergius was scared. And he would have stayed in his room, had not Persephone looked over her shoulder and said in the voice of an Angel, *"Come."*

Persephone descended the staircase, wiggling just enough on each step to keep his attention locked on her body. Sergius, unable to do anything else, followed. The staircase wound down far below the Papal Palace, to a large, empty chamber that could not exist. It was huge and vaulted with thick, fluted white pillars that rose to support the ceiling. In the middle of the room, rising up three steps high, was a large, round white marble dais. In the middle of the dais sat a square block, three feet high and ten feet to a side, with a single white marble chair, cut in the ancient Roman style set in the middle of it.

"What... what is this place," said Sergius. "Why have you brought me here?"

The girl didn't answer. She stepped up onto the dais and stood beside the chair. Sergius took two tentative steps up onto the dais, but did not go all the way. The girl smiled, then looked up.

From above, shining from a bright light within, a black-winged Angel in white robes floated slowly down to the chair and sat. She smiled at Sergius. "Welcome, Pope Sergius III."

Sergius's eyes went wide. "You… are you… can you be…?"

"I am an Angel of God," said Nyx. *Descended, but you don't need to know that.* "I have been sent here by our Lord and Savior, to guide the leaders of his most holy Roman church forward as they spread his word." Sergius knelt and in an instant, Nyx was there to raise him up. "I am not God, Sergius, you have no need to kneel before me. I am an advisor. Sent here to help you when times become difficult. And to guide you forward on the path of righteousness." Her smile turned sad. "It is a path from which you have most grievously strayed, Sergius."

Sergius hung his head. "I know. I am a weak man, with a weak man's failings of the flesh."

"You are indeed," said Nyx. "And worse, you have allowed your failings to bring you under the sway of one who holds the church as neither holy nor divine, but only a tool to use to gain wealth and privilege for her family. And despite her young age, she is working against our divine plan, unlike her mother."

"I will… I will break off my relations with her," said Sergius. "At once."

"Very good," said Nyx. "Know that God forgives us of our failings, if we balance them with good works in his name. And that is why I have summoned you here. It is time for the Roman Catholic Church to assert its authority over the churches of the East and the West. The Nicene Creed must be defended against their apostate beliefs." *Not that either of you are right. The holy spirit doesn't even exist.* "I charge you, Sergius to defend that belief, and further, to work ceaselessly to bring together Christians under one banner, no matter what the leaders of the church of the East may say. It is time for the true Christians, the Christians of the North, to lead Christianity forward."

"Yes, my lady…"

"I am not your lady," she said. "I am Nyx, messenger of God. And if you ever have need of my guidance, call and I will answer."

"Yes, my… Yes, Nyx."

"Go back to your rest, Sergius, and know that I will be here, when I am needed."

Sergius, not sure what to do, bowed. Persephone handed him the candle, and he made his slow way up the steps to his room in the papal palace. When he stepped into it, the door in the back of the alcove closed behind him, and he knew that it would only open again when he was summoned.

In the room below, Persephone and Nyx changed into their own, naked forms.

"Nicely done," said Persephone. "How was it, wearing the robes again?"

"Odd," said Nyx. "Not sure I like them any more."

"Get an overwhelming urge to sing "Hosanna, Alleluia?"

"No," said Nyx, smiling. "But it feels like cheating, somehow."

"Why did you turn him away from Marozia?" asked Persephone.

"Mainly to annoy Ishtar," said Nyx. "She pushed me."

"She'll keep pushing you," said Persephone. "It's her favorite thing after torturing people for fun."

"True." Nyx sighed. "Wonder what she'll arrange next."

911 A.D.

Marozia, wearing her best outfit, knelt before Pope Sergius III in his private chambers.

"My child, there is no need for that," said the pope, who was wondering how, exactly, the young woman had managed to enter his chambers after explicit instructions to keep her out. "Not here."

"I kneel in disgrace," said Marozia. "I must be in disgrace, for you have not consented me to be in your presence these last two years."

"Now, that is not true," said the pope. "You and your husband have been in our presence many times."

"I and my husband have," said Marozia. "*I* have not." She rose to her feet. "Is there something about me that you find less than desirable?"

"Of course not."

"And yet, you continue to see my mother."

"It is a matter of age," pleaded the pope. "I am old, now, Marozia, and my desires are not what they were."

"Not according the reports I've been getting," said Marozia. "In fact, the reports I have been receiving indicate that your desires have been increasing as of late. My mother, several of your maids, and I have even heard rumors of a particularly plump choir boy who received your attentions, but I'm sure that is not true."

"The sin of the sodomite is not among my vices," said Sergius, angrily.

"Oh, but it is," said Marozia, walking past him to one of the couches in his apartment. With her back to him she raised her skirts, showing off her still-firm backside. She leaned over the couch and wiggled at him. "You just prefer it with girls."

Sergius felt himself growing erect at the sight of her, but protested anyway. "My dear lady," he said. "This cannot be."

"Why not?" Marozia demanded, straightening and dropping her skirt. "It was fine before. It was fine when I was pregnant with your child! Have I turned so hideous that you prefer my crone mother to me?"

"That is not it at all," said Sergius, using the most placating tone he could. "It is merely that I have other responsibilities now…"

"Or perhaps it is my plans that you find you no longer agree with," she said, advancing on him. "Perhaps it is my politics, or the ambitions of my husband. Perhaps I no longer suit your needs. Is that it?"

"Dear lady…"

"I am the wife of Alberic!" she hissed. "I am the reason you are on the throne!"

"Your mother and father are the reason I am on the papal seat," said Sergius, his voice firm. "It is because of them I rule."

"It is because they gave me as wife to Alberic! No other reason!"

"My dear…"

"You aren't with me anymore, Sergius, and that means that you are against me. And those who are against me, I destroy." She strode past him and out into the hallway where Ishtar, looking like an older version of the girl she was when they first met, was waiting. Marozia stomped up to her. "Rid me of him," she hissed. "Let him be gone and we will put a far, far better pope in his place. One that will do as *you* bid, not as that bitch my mother desires." She knelt before Ishtar. "Please, I beg of you."

*

Sergius put the new maid on her hands and knees on the bed and shoved himself into her backside, ignoring the girl's cries of pain. He thrust harder, cursing Marozia with every one. *How dare she speak to me like that? How dare she threaten me?* He grabbed the girl's hair and pulled on it, arching her back. "Who does she think she is?" he demanded. "Huh? Who is she to tell me what I should and should not do?"

"She is Marozia," said the girl, surprising him enough that he stopped thrusting.

"You dare speak to me, you..."

The girl turned her head, and kept turning it and turning it, until she was staring him full in the face, though the rest of her body had not moved. In horror, Sergius tried to pull out of her and away from her, but her anus clamped down on his cock, and her hair tangled his hand so tightly that he could not move it. She grinned at him, and her mouth was full of razor-sharp, jagged-edged teeth.

"I dare," said Ishtar, and her body spun, twisting Sergius's penis and making him scream. "I dare so much more than you will ever know."

*

"The news?" asked Nyx.

"They're saying his heart gave out," said Persephone.

"Apparently he was engaged in a tryst with a sweet young thing, and died in the midst of it."

"Did you get a look at the sweet young thing in question?"

"No. She vanished."

"Convenient."

Persephone's head cocked to one side. "You think Ishtar?"

"On behalf of Marozia, on a guess," said Nyx. "Not that it matters."

*

913 A.D.

Nyx stood outside the chambers of Anastasius III, disguised as a guard, listening as Marozia serviced him. *Whatever else can be said of the woman,* thought Nyx, *She learned her lessons well.*

Anastasius had become Marozia's creature almost at once, and while that would not have mattered had he come into Nyx's presence to receive instruction, he steadfastly refused to follow Persephone. Instead, he hid under the covers and prayed to God to preserve him from ghosts and demons. It was very tiresome and had Nyx not been busy in the East for most of the last two years, she would have dealt with it sooner.

"It is very simple," Marozia was saying, and Nyx could hear Anastasius groaning in denied ecstasy. "All you have to do is grant the lands of the Abbey that sits near the Theophylact estates to my husband, Alberic. Surely you can do that?" Anastasius's protest came out nearly unintelligible through the chamber door. Marozia's reply was the very soul of patience. "I do understand, my dear, but surely you can explain to Theophylact that to give the lands over to him would mean an imbalance of power in the city. And we would not want the city to be imbalanced, would we?"

Anastasius's answering groan must have been in the affirmative, because the next sounds he made were of intense pleasure and release. A few minutes later, Marozia left his chambers, delicately wiping her mouth with a kerchief.

Nyx waited a moment longer, then entered his chambers. Anastasius was seated on one of his couches, eyes closed and robes in disarray. Nyx changed appearance into the robes of a cardinal, and closed the door behind her, making sure it was loud enough to wake the pope. Anastasius grunted and grumbled and sat up. "Yes, what is it?"

"You're being very naughty," said Nyx.

The pope sat up straighter. "I beg your pardon?"

"Oh, it is not mine you have to beg," said Nyx. "It is God's."

The pope rose to his full, impressive height. "You dare speak to me that way?"

"I dare," said Nyx. "Considering you still have that woman's stench about you."

The pope's voice went cold. "I do not recognize you, Cardinal...?"

"Oh, I'm not a cardinal," said Nyx.

She changed forms in the blink of an eye, becoming the ten-foot tall red demon with the saw-tooth scales that had tortured Judas, complete with claws, horns, razor-sharp fangs and massive, scaled, erect penis. The room shook as she roared, "*I AM THE RULER OF HELL!!!*"

Anastasius III stumbled back against the couch, clutching his chest. His eyes were wide and his mouth made gasping noises. Then he fell face down on the ground, dead.

Nyx reverted to her own form and looked down at the man. "Well, dammit." She watched his soul leave his body and start sinking into the earth. She shook a finger at him. "You weren't supposed to do that."

The soul looked offended as it sank down to Hell.

Nyx shrugged and headed for the balcony as the guards tried to knock down the door. The next pope would belong to Theodora, and she could get back to the business of preparing the West for the attack on Jerusalem.

*

Pope Lando was a simple man, without extravagant tastes or vices. He liked wine, but not to excess. He liked riding, but only occasionally. He liked women, but did not pursue them. He was, in most every way, boring, bland, and unimpressive, save that he was totally and unswervingly loyal to Theophylact. He voted as Theophylact wished him to vote, he supported Theophylact in all his decisions, and wasn't even fucking Theophylact's wife or daughter, like his immediate predecessors. He was very much the perfect pope for the time.

Which is why, one night, Ishtar flew into his room, punched into his chest, pulled his heart out, and flew away.

"Explain that one away," she muttered, biting into the heart as she flew.

She finished eating it by the time she arrived at the palace Marozia had given her, and landed at the back door, not bothering to change forms before she entered. There were no servants here, and the ones waiting below already knew what she looked like. She stretched and thought a moment, then paused in the kitchen to pick up the largest of the pestles from the mortars in the kitchen on the way past. It was brass, as long as her forearm and as thick as baby's head at the end. There was a new man in the basement, young and proud of how strong he was.

Five days with this up his ass should cure him of that, Ishtar thought. *Then we'll see how much he can really take.*

The humans were gone from her dungeon, when she stepped inside. Instead, Nyx was sitting on her favorite chair, and Persephone was standing in the corner. Both had their swords in their hands.

"That's twice," said Nyx.

Ishtar forced herself not to reach for a weapon, forced herself to stay still. "My Queen…"

"What I want to know," said Nyx, "was how, exactly, you thought it was permissible to kill either of them without asking me first."

"Well…"

Nyx moved faster than Ishtar had thought possible, her sword driving through Ishtar's stomach and pinning her to the wall like a grotesque butterfly. She screamed and thrashed, and the pestle flew out of her hand. Nyx caught it before it hit the ground. She flipped it in her hands and looked up and down the length of it.

"Nice," Nyx said. Then she swung the pestle hard at Ishtar's head.

Ishtar's world flashed white and went black.

When she awoke, she was chained over a bed of spikes. Her arms, legs and wings had been spread wide with chains of iron, and the spikes had been laid out to push into every part of her. They were iron, not divine steel, and while they hurt, there would be no lasting damage from them.

Nyx was standing beside her, waiting.

Ishtar's head was still aching from where Nyx had hit it. She shook it gently to make sure none of it was missing. "Where am I?"

"Underneath Marozia's mansion," said Nyx. "Far, far underneath. Like it?"

Ishtar looked around. The room was black, even to her hell-adjusted eyes. There was a single, large hole in the ceiling leading to a shaft that rose high out of sight. "I've seen worse."

"Why are you against me, Ishtar?"

"I'm not against you…"

"But you are," said Nyx. "I spent a great deal of time building an underground chamber below the papal palace. I built steps and an alcove up into their room and hid it all from their view while I was constructing it. Do you know how tiresome that was? And then, when it's all done, when I have everything in place, *you kill my popes!*"

"They aren't your popes…"

"They are *mine!* I have them convinced that I'm a messenger of God. I have them willing to do what I say and follow my advice and *you* kill them for Marozia. *Without asking me first!* Now do you want to tell me why?"

"Because *you* don't have it in you to do what needs to be done!" shouted Ishtar. "You're supposed to be the Queen of Hell, but when it comes to killing humans you've grown weak and lazy! You don't want the innocent hurt, you don't want the children hurt. *You don't want to do what needs to be done to bring Tribunal back!*"

To Ishtar's surprise, Nyx nodded. "That was true," she said. "God changed me when he made me Queen of Hell. He made me crueler, and stronger and meaner, but he also made me into a judge. *He* made it so I couldn't just kill them all without feeling it. He made me weak." Nyx stepped out of Ishtar's sight, though she could still hear. "But once I realized that, Ishtar. I started praying again, only this time to Tribunal. I made him my God, just like the mortals made me theirs. I pray to him every hour. And every time I pray, every time I say his name, it gives me the strength to do what must be done. So thank you for showing me my weakness."

"If you want to thank me," said Ishtar, "You could *fucking unchain me!*"

"Oh no," said Nyx, walking back into Ishtar's line of sight. "You see, my prayers to Tribunal have made me stronger, now. They've reminded me of who I am and they have reminded me that the Queen of Hell does not accept disobedience from her servants. It would lead to chaos, and then where would we be?"

"Let me go!"

"I will, said Nyx. "I need you, Ishtar. You're my friend. You're my lover. But before you can be either of those again, you need to be my trusted servant, and in order for that to happen, you need to be punished."

"So, you're going to leave me here, chained in the dark?" said Ishtar. "You want me to thrash about in frustration and impale myself on the spikes?"

"Oh, no," said Nyx. "You'll be able to break these chains in less than a year, and really, the spikes are hardly pushing in on you at all. No, I wanted you to have a lesson you'll remember."

For the first time since they left Hell, Ishtar felt a shiver of fear, climbing its way up her spine. "What...what are you going..."

Nyx rose out of sight, and Ishtar heard Nyx draw her sword, heard the sound of divine steel smashing onto rock, then felt the earth around her shiver.

Then the roof fell onto her.

There were hundreds of tons of stone, smashing down onto her body. The weight of it drove the spikes through her body, her arms and her wings, then crushed her flat. Her head was untouched, so she could see and feel it all. And because she was an Angel, she didn't die, or stop feeling the pain, or go unconscious. Instead, she screamed, long, soundless screams because there was no way for her to draw breath.

Nyx came into view again. She stabbed her blade up once more, moving it gently this time. A moment later, water began to drip down. A slow, steady drip that landed on Ishtar's face every time.

"There," said Nyx. "That should do."

She flew out of the pit, leaving Ishtar still screaming soundlessly. *And now,* thought Nyx, *To see that bitch Marozia.*

966 A.D.

The water stopped dripping first.

Slowly, stone by stone, the weight was lifted off of Ishtar's chest. Then strong hands grabbed her and ripped her body from the spikes that impaled it. For the first time in 100 years, Ishtar drew breath and could scream in agony. She screamed all the way up the shaft and into sunlight so bright it hurt her eyes. Her body, desperate to heal itself, began working all at once, and Ishtar screamed in fresh agony as the pieces of herself slowly rebuilt.

When the last of the pain ebbed away, she saw Persephone,

sitting cross-legged on the grass beside her. Ishtar sat up and spat blood out of her mouth. "How long?"

"Sixty-six years," said Persephone.

"Felt longer," said Ishtar. "Everything feels longer here. In Heaven and Hell you can lose track of the centuries but here you can feel every moment." She swung her hand, slapping Persephone's face so hard that her cheekbone shattered and she flew backwards. *"How could you leave me there, you bitch?"*

Persephone pulled herself up from the ground, her cheekbone already healing. Ishtar had expected her to be angry. Instead, she shrugged. "How could you betray Nyx?"

"I didn't betray her! I was working for her! I was going to get the fucking pope under our control!"

"The pope was under our control. The popes have been under our control since before Nyx locked you up. And they're still under our control now. And you would have known that had you asked, but you didn't because you were too busy *fucking us over!*"

"I wasn't fucking you over!"

"What do you call it?"

"For fuck's sake, Persephone..." Ishtar stood up, stretching her wings. "Nyx wasn't doing the job, so I did it for her. All right?"

"She was doing the job."

"She had doubts, Persephone."

"Everyone has doubts."

"I don't!" said Ishtar. "I have none at all. I want my fucking Paradise, and I'll be damned if Nyx's weakness is going to slow me down."

Persephone shook her head. "Nyx isn't weak. Not any more."

"I'll believe that when I see it."

Persephone nodded. "She told me to give you this." She handed Ishtar a brocaded cushion.

Ishtar held it at arm's length. "What the fuck am I supposed to do with this?"

"Smother Marozia," said Persephone.

Ishtar's eyebrows went up. "She's still alive?"

"She's been in prison in Rome for 50 years. She's to be shriven of all sins, then killed. You're to be her executioner."

Ishtar shrugged and took the cushion. "Fine. I will."

"Once you've done that, you're to report to Nyx at the whorehouse. It's still standing and doing a very good business."

"Fine." Ishtar took off, winging towards Rome.

She arrived late in the evening, when the last light of the sun was fading, slipped into the prison unseen and made her way down to the depths of it. She disguised herself as a soldier and asked directions, then wandered through the prison until she found the room. It had a single, high window, and stank of filth and disease. She could see the rat-holes in the walls, though there were none in sight.

There were only two people in the cell. An old, old woman and a priest. And as Ishtar watched, the priest nodded his head and began speaking. "Deus, Pater misericordiarum, qui per mortem et resurrectionem Fílii sui mundum sibi reconciliavit et Spiritum Sanctum effudit in remissionem peccatorum, per ministerium Ecclesiae indulgentiam tibi tribuat et pacem… Et ego te absolvo a peccatis tuis in nomine Patris, et Filii, et Spiritus Sancti."

"Thank you, Father," said the old woman. "Am I to be released, now?"

"Soon, my child," said the priest, looking up at Ishtar. "Very soon."

The priest rose and left, and Ishtar stepped into the room. The old woman squinted at her. "Are you here to let me out?"

There was nothing of beauty left in her. No traces of the young girl she had been when Ishtar first corrupted her, nor the woman she had become when she was ruling over the papacy. Instead there was only a frail, tired old creature, with the marks of years of privation overlaid over the scars of long-ago tortures.

The old woman squinted closer. "Ah, I see." She lay back in the bed. "How is it to be, then?"

Ishtar said nothing, just knelt down beside the bed.

"I wish..." said Marozia, her old voice broken and quivery... "I wish my Angel had come back to me, just once. It wasn't the same when she left. The popes began listening to their own Angels, and when I tried to force them to listen to me, they put me in here." She shook her head. "My own son, if you can believe it, was the first to turn against me. But that's all right. I had other sons, and their children were popes, too. And now..." She sighed. "It would have been good to see her again."

"Maybe if you hadn't fucked everything up so badly, she would have come back," said Ishtar. "Pity you did."

She shoved the cushion hard on the old woman's face, and watched her weak struggles.

"It must be hard," said Ishtar, "knowing that you were a tool for the Devil, and that everything you have done in life will send your soul to Hell." The old woman's struggles became more and more feeble. "And when you get to Hell, when Lucifer sees you, you'll wish more than anything to be back here on earth, getting ass-fucked by the pope." The struggling stopped. Ishtar waited a bit longer, then stood. "Whore."

Marozia's soul rose slowly from her body, and to Ishtar's surprise, kept rising, vanishing through the roof of the prison.

"That little bitch goes to Heaven?" Ishtar said. "No. No way."

"Yes," said Nyx behind her. Ishtar spun. Nyx stepped into the room, and the pale light of the candle reflected in her shiny black-scaled armor. "That's why I had her shriven, Under the rules, she goes to heaven. If you thought I was going to let her be your plaything once we're done here, you were mistaken."

Ishtar stared at Nyx, waiting. When the other Angel didn't say anything, Ishtar said, "Well? Now what?"

"Open your mind to me, Ishtar," said Nyx. "Now."

Ishtar seriously considered not doing it, just to be spiteful. But she knew that, at the end of things, Nyx would have her way one way of the other. Ishtar shrugged and opened her mind.

Even as Nyx entered into her thoughts, Ishtar entered Nyx's mind. She had been here before, many times, both in Heaven and in Hell, and she was surprised how much had changed. Before Nyx's mind had been a whirlwind, ever spinning, ever moving, coming up with plot after plot, idea after idea, from the torture of the souls in Hell to keeping the demons and Angels too busy squabbling with one another to attempt to attack her. She had even been capable of laughter in Hell, hearing the latest stories from those Angels she allowed to go to Earth.

Now, all that was gone. Her mind was full of plots again, but against the humans. In the years Ishtar had been buried beneath the Earth, Nyx had been busy. The Rus were nearly at full strength, and prepared to crush the Christians when they marched West. Behind them, the Mongols were gaining power north of China, preparing for their own invasions. In Europe, she had a hundred little lords and kings thinking about the world beyond their borders, about Jerusalem and the Holy Land. They were not ready to move yet, but the seed had been planted.

Beyond those, laying its mark over all of Nyx's thoughts and ideas, was the driving force of Tribunal's personality, indelibly marked on Nyx's psyche, driving her forward the way nothing else could. Nyx *would* destroy Jerusalem, she *would* bring back her Tribunal, and the humans *would* be destroyed, no matter what.

For Nyx, the journey into Ishtar's mind was simple. Ishtar was tired of waiting, tired of Earth, tired of not having the freedom to torture and kill and make love as she wished. She wanted – craved, really – the black pits of Hell with the unending delights of torture and pain that awaited her there. She wanted to be set loose on the Earth to cause chaos and pain and death so she could reap more souls to go to their eternal doom. She wanted battle, not for the sheer joy of victory and the fight like Persephone, but for the joy of watching men and women and children suffer.

Ishtar was also terribly, terribly angry at Nyx.

"*And will you stay angry at me?*" asked Nyx inside Ishtar's mind.

"*I don't know,*" said Ishtar back, knowing there was no way to hide the truth when they spoke mind to mind. "*It really hurt.*"

"*What would you have done,*" said Nyx. "*If you were I?*"

Ishtar was silent, but in her mind loomed an image of Nyx, in exactly the same position, crushed under the rocks, save that where Nyx had left water dripping on Ishtar's face to drive her mad, in Ishtar's mind there was acid dripping onto Nyx's face, and the rocks were heated red-hot, so that Nyx would feel the pain of the burning even as she screamed from the crushing and the acid.

Nyx laughed out loud. *"Oh, very good. I'll remember that for next time."*

"There won't be a next time," said Ishtar.

"Not for you, my dear," said Nyx. *"But there's always a next time for someone."* For the first time in nearly a hundred years, Nyx lay a hand on Ishtar's face, and the warmth of bare Angelic flesh touching Angelic flesh, made Ishtar's knees tremble. "I promise you," said Nyx out loud, sliding her consciousness gently out of Ishtar's mind, "that in the years to come you will have battle beyond what you can imagine. You will have more souls than you can count at your mercy, and you will have the freedom of Paradise and Hell. All you need to do is follow me. Can you follow me, Ishtar?"

Ishtar leaned into Nyx's hand, feeling the warmth of her flesh. "Of course I can, Nyx." She leaned close and kissed Nyx's lips, and Nyx kissed her back hard.

"Come," said Nyx. "Let's find Persephone and celebrate properly."

They slipped out of the dungeon and flew off, wings nearly touching.

And as they flew, Ishtar thought, *I can follow you, and I will. But I will never, ever forgive you.*

*

For the next hundred thirty years, the three of them worked together. Persephone and Ishtar served together as handmaids to the Angel Nyx who guided the popes of the Catholic church.

With Nyx they worked on the Rus, making them fierce warriors second to none. They cruised through Europe a hundred times, serving king after king, Holy Roman Emperors and powerful bishops. They worked through the East, destabilizing the Eastern Church as best they could while convincing the followers of Islam to attack again and again and again, until Constantinople itself was threatened. And throughout it all they whispered into ear after ear, telling tales of the riches of Jerusalem, and its importance to the people of the West, and how it should be in the hands of true Christians. They presided over the East-West Schism of the church, and over the births and deaths of half a hundred principalities in Europe.

And every hour, Nyx uttered a prayer to Tribunal, to guide and strengthen her, and every hour the strength of His hatred for humanity fed her, stifled any impulse of compassion, and gave her the drive to keep moving forward.

1055 A.D.

The call for help came one morning, and Nyx knew it was time.

The sun was just coming up, layering the clouds with coal and orange and red, banishing the night. The air was cool and the April sky over Rome was clear with not a cloud in it when Pope Urban II opened the alcove, descended the stairs, and stood before Nyx's chair.

"Help me, Nyx, O messenger of God," he said. "Help me decide what to do."

Nyx was far away at the time, lying in a bed of furs in Rus, her arms wrapped around Persephone and Ishtar's sweat-covered bodies. The smell of their lust was still in the air, making it heady and relaxing at once. Nyx sniffed it and smiled. Then she heard the pope's voice in her head, and sat up.

"Alexios I Komnenos has sent me a messenger," the pope said. "The Great Patriarch of the Eastern Church has called upon the Western church for assistance. He asks that we bring men and arms, and that we free them from the burden if the Saracen attacks."

"Get up," said Nyx, goosing both Persephone and Ishtar. Both Angels gasped and jumped, but they were awake. Nyx grinned at them. "It's time."

That night, Ishtar and Persephone escorted Urban down the stairs once more to stand before Nyx. "Your call for help was heard," said Nyx. "Now, hear the word of God." She paused, savoring the moment. Her followers were millions strong in the Rus and further east. They outnumbered the Christians and they stood poised to flow over Europe, as soon as it was weak enough. Now, all she had to do was empty it. "Call to all good Christian men, and tell them it is time to march east. To help the Greeks, who were the father of Western civilization, to bring a re-unification of the church, and to bring Jerusalem back into the hands of it's rightful heirs."

Pope Urban bowed deeply. "I hear God's word," he said, "And I obey."

1096 A.D.

They stood in the back, dressed as lesser French lords, and listened as Pope Urban spoke convincingly and at length about why the knights and nobles should march east. Nyx listened and nodded. The man was a good speaker and between his words and the work that she, Persephone and Ishtar had done, nobles across Europe were more than ready to take up arms against the Islamics – *Saracens,* Nyx reminded herself. *They call them Saracens.*

To Nyx's surprise, it had not just been the nobles. Across Europe peasants were rising, led by minor knights, and beginning the long march towards Constantinople. Tens of thousands of men and women were marching on the delusional promise that life would be better for them in the holy land. They had already crossed half of Europe and were still marching. From the reports Nyx had, they were pillaging their way across Europe, calling themselves holy crusaders and the People's Crusade and using it as an excuse to take what they wanted as they marched.

Nyx looked over the room of nobles and smiled. The ones here were not the most pious. Quite the opposite, in fact. Nyx, Persephone and Ishtar had seen to that, working to cultivate the most greedy, self-serving, avarice-filled nobles and bend them to the cause, knowing that they were far more likely to succeed than a column of holy men.

The pope finished his speech. The nobles cheered and applauded and knelt one by one to swear their fealty and loyalty to the cause. They would march east, they would free the Byzantines, and then they would free Jerusalem.

It is perfect, thought Nyx, looking at the French nobles. *I haven't seen a bunch more ripe for corruption than these since Rome.*

"Now what?" asked Ishtar, as they walked out.

"It will take time for this lot to be ready," said Nyx. "Meanwhile, you two need to go to east and make sure that the People's Crusade doesn't manage to succeed."

"They'll be there," said Persephone. "The Turks will be more than happy to deal with them."

"If they wander into the Turks' territory," said Ishtar.

Persephone grinned. "Don't worry. That's your job."

"And what will you be doing?" Ishtar asked Nyx.

Nyx grinned as well. "Harrying the crusaders. By the time they reach Jerusalem, they'll be dying to serve anyone but Christ."

CHAPTER 9

*T*RIBUNAL, HEAR MY *prayers.*
 Ten thousand Jews were slaughtered as the "People's Crusade" moved across Europe.

Tribunal, my beloved, I work Your will.

Outside Nicaea, sixteen thousand members of the "people's crusade" died against the Turks and their corpses were left to rot in the sun.

Tribunal, I am coming.

The real crusaders were forbidden from entering Constantinople, and sent on their way to the Holy Land.

Tribunal, I serve you.

When the Crusaders took Nicaea, it was handed to the Byzantines, much to the crusaders' anger.

Tribunal, You are my beloved.

In Anatolia, the crusaders fell to flies and diseases, to poisoned wells and starvation. They slaughtered Christians, Jews and Muslims alike as they stole food.

Tribunal, hear me, my love.

At the Cilician Gates, Baldwin of Boulogne and his troops left the army, weakening it.

At Antioch the Crusaders narrowly escaped destruction before the Saxons arrived to reinforce them.

Plague struck them.

The Byzantines abandoned them.

The nobles fell to squabbling and delayed the march for a year.

Tribunal, my beloved, we are at Jerusalem! I am here and we are ready to make it fall!

*

It was the flies that were the worst.

Sir Simon Benart, standing in the burning sun outside the walls of Jerusalem, stared at the cloud of flies that rose from the bloodied, mangled corpses that surrounded the walls of the city. For five weeks they had besieged the city and all they had to show for it was illness, exhaustion and death.

"Jews and Saracens," he said, and spat on the ground. "Who'd have thought the little bastards could fight?"

"One must protest," said Sir Albert de Giroie. "They have walls, which make any defender capable."

Sir Simon adjusted the hauberk – the knee-length chain mail shirt that he wore – at his neck. The damn thing had grown loose during the long march to reach Jerusalem. The Saracens had retreated before them, destroying crops and poisoning the wells. Half the camp had the running shits for four weeks, including Sir Simon. He was sure he'd lost at least twenty pounds.

This has been the worse fucking campaign ever, thought Simon. Everything had gone badly, from the get go. Foodstuffs had been ruined, they'd not been allowed to enter Constantinople, and everywhere had been flies, disease and death. *If God wants us to take Jerusalem, he's got a damn funny way of showing it.*

The tabard he wore, emblazoned with the crusaders' black cross, had once been white. Now, like the tabard of every other man in the army, it was grey and brown with dirt, and stained red in a dozen places where the infidels had spilled their blood on him.

A chance to repay your sins, he thought, remembering the pope's promises. *Indulgences to cleanse you of all sin and allow you to begin again as a new man, blessed in the eyes of God, should you take Jerusalem.*

Should have stayed behind and gone to Hell. It would have been easier than this.

In the main tent, Godfrey of Bouillon and Robert Curthose were arguing again. The crusader army had surrounded the city for five weeks and had yet to do anything more than sacrifice its men trying to breach the city's walls.

Those bastards should never have been put in charge, thought Simon. *They hated each other before we reached Byzantium and being stuck in each other's company for months hasn't improved things.*

He listened to the two men squabble over the deployment of their only two siege towers. Robert wanted to divide the enemy forces by attacking two walls separately. Godfrey wanted both on the main gates, to dominate the enemy through sheer strength of will. His argument – that dividing their force would only make them weaker, was a reasonable one. Robert argued that dividing the defenders was more important.

"Remember when there was a hundred thousand of us,

Albert?" said Sir Simon. "Remember when we all thought this would be an easy march and an easy victory?" He looked over to the walls again, to the bloodied, crow-picked, fly-ridden corpses of soldiers, knights, and friends rotting below it. "Bastards. Hope we break through this time. I want that governor's head on a pike."

"We all do," said Albert. "Think we will?"

Simon looked back at the tent, listening to the squabble going on inside. He shook his head in disgust. "Depends which fool wins the argument."

*

Inside the cool, breezy shelter of the governor's citadel, Jibril sat, lounging, on a bench. Beside him, four other captains waited with him to hear the governor's latest stratagem.

The Governor, Iftikhar ad-Daula, was not a stupid man. He had expelled nearly all the Christians before the crusaders arrived. He had stocked the city with food and fresh water, so much so that even now, after over a month of siege, there were still dates to be bought, and grain to make bread, and fresh meat for those who wanted it.

"Enter!"

The five captains entered the Governor's chamber, and bowed low to him. The governor was practically unable to sit still, so excited he seemed. He held up a simple note, so small it could only have come from the leg of a messenger bird.

"We have succeeded!" exclaimed the Governor. "Egypt has heard our cries and will come! We need only hold the invaders off until Egypt arrives, then we shall drive these infidels into the sea, and watch them drown!"

The five captains cheered.

"They are no more than two weeks away," said Iftikhar. "We need only hold out until then. Now, review for me our position."

Behrouz went first, detailing the supplies of food and water. There had been few thefts, and those who had committed them had been caught, had their hands cut off, and then been thrown from the walls. Jerusalem could easily sit out the siege for another two months before they would even have to begin rationing.

Rachim went next. The catapults were in good repair, and while the enemy had camped far enough away that their tents would not be hit by falling rocks, the catapults were proving effective against the advancing army, especially when loaded with pot shards, which could cut a man in half, if they hit him right.

"Jibril? Tell us."

"The defenders of the wall are in good spirit," said Jibril. "Jews and Muslims alike. We have suffered a few losses, mostly to arrows and crossbow bolts. The infidels have twice managed to gain the wall, but have never managed to hold it. We have cut them down and hurled their bodies down on their companions below. That said, the stink at the wall and the flies have become fierce. It would be useful if we could arrange for a party to remove the dead, if the infidels will agree."

"Would they agree, Kamal?" asked the governor.

"Not today," said Kamal, leader of Jerusalem's mounted troops. "They are preparing for another attack. Once we have driven them back again, then there may be an opportunity for discussion, and a chance for us to clear the bodies." He shrugged. "Infidels or not, I have no doubt they are enjoying the flies no more than we are."

"Governor! Governor!" shouted a messenger, running in. "My pardon for the interruption, but the infidels are marching."

"As you predicted," said Iftikhar ad-Daula, nodding to Kamal. He smiled at his captains. "Prepare the city. Warn the men to be neither afraid, nor over-confident. The infidels will be fighting harder, now that they are becoming desperate. To the walls!"

*

"Looks like it was Robert," said Albert. Simon grunted and tightened his shield to his arm. He looked at the twenty men-at-arms he had left in his command. Half of them were inherited from other knights, now dead on the battlefield. The others had been loyal to him from the beginning. *And look where I have led them.*

It was not a comforting thought, and Simon tried to ignore it, concentrating instead on the battle to come. A thousand men were readying siege ladders. Another five hundred were put to guarding and moving the two siege towers – the only two siege towers, and their only hope.

"Think this will work?" asked Albert.

"By Jesus, I hope so," said Simon. "There's not enough food to last another week, at this rate."

"Then I guess we have to make it work," said Albert. "See you after the battle, or, if not, then in Hell."

"Don't worry about Hell," said Simon. "The pope said any man who died for Jerusalem would go to Heaven."

"Nice to have something," said Albert, "because if this doesn't work, that's all we're going to get."

"For God! For Jerusalem!" shouted Robert Curthose. "The city shall be ours by nightfall! Deus Vult!"

God wills it, thought Simon, translating the Latin. He looked back at the men behind him. "Time to see if that's true, boys. Move it out."

First came the pottery shards, flung from catapults inside Jerusalem's walls. The men would see the large pots being flung towards them and scatter and cover themselves, hoping to avoid the worst of it. Simon tracked the large clay vessels through the sky. They were carved to break into shards on impact. Worse, they were filled with broken pottery.

The first one landed only twenty yards away. It exploded from the force of impact, and the shards of pottery ripped through the air, slashing skin to the bone, opening faces and legs and cutting into horse flesh. Blood spurted out from one poor bastard's throat, coating the men around him with red as he thrashed wildly on the ground. The soldiers around him kept marching. They knew he couldn't be saved and that the only way to end it all was to break down that wall.

And we'd better do it, today, thought Simon. *Or we'll all be food for crows.*

They marched closer, inside the range of the catapults.

"Shields up!" came the call as the archers on the walls loosed their arrows. There weren't as many of them, this time. After the first week, the defenders had learned to pick their targets carefully, and to only shoot when the invaders were within easy range.

There was a scream nearby. One of Albert's men hadn't raised his shield in time. An arrow had pierced him through the eye.

He pawed at it desperately, trying to get it out as blood ran down his face.

Damn fool will kill himself like that, thought Simon.

"Get him out of here!" shouted Albert.

A pair of soldiers rushed the man, grabbing his hands away and dragging him back to the monk's tent where they could try to save his life. The man screamed with every jolt, and soon fell behind them.

"'Ware," said Albert. "The towers are nearly at the wall."

"Deus Vult!" screamed Robert Curthose. "Charge!"

Twenty thousand men roared. The footmen charged for the wall, scaling ladders above their heads. Simon and Albert and the other knight, following the signal flag from the commanders, wheeled their horses to the east and west, each group forming a line a fifty wide and five deep. Simon and Albert went to the west. From the side gates of Jerusalem, hundreds of Saracen horsemen were streaming out, preparing a flanking attack to open them up. Simon grinned and couched his lance. He had managed to get in the front line.

Simon's own battle cry was drowned out in the clash of men and horses. Steel bit into flesh on all sides, horses broke legs and went down screaming, the bones jutting from their flesh becoming dangerous obstacles on the battlefield. Simon's lance drove into the Saracen in front of him, impaling the man and ripping through his guts before tearing out his back. The man fell backwards off his horse, taking the lance with him. Simon raised his morning star. Others preferred a sword, but for Simon, the spiked ball on the end of the chain, attached to the handle in his hand, was a far more satisfying weapon. A helmet would barely stop it. Armor might prevent the spikes from getting through, but would do nothing to stop the bones beneath from breaking.

"*Deus Vult!*" Simon screamed, the morning star smashing into the side of the head of the man beside him. To his credit, the man didn't lose his saddle, but he swayed as blood spattered from his torn-open face and the deep gouge where the rim of his helmet had driven into his skull. Simon swung again before the man could right himself, smashing his spine. Simon couldn't hear the man's back break over the sound of the battle, but knew from the way the man arched backwards, screaming, that he was no longer a threat.

Simon drove forward again. Beside him, Albert hewed with his sword, hacking off men's hands where they gripped the reins, leaving only bloody, spurting stumps. Two men he cut open that way, then the third managed to get his shield in the way. He and Albert clashed hard, vying for room to cut each other in the hard press of the battle. Simon tried to drive his own horse forward, but a Saracen cut him off, his long, curved, blood-soaked blade swinging for Simon's head. Simon put his shield between them and swung the morning star down hard, aiming for the other's skull. The man had his own shield up, and managed to block the vicious blow. They traded back and forth, neither able to get the upper hand.

Then the Saracen twisted and, instead of cutting, thrust hard with his blade, driving it past Simon's shield and into his shoulder. Simon bellowed in pain and swung the morning star as hard as he could. It didn't unhorse the man, but send his helmet flying. Simon flipped his wrist and sent the morning star down hard on top of the other man's head.

The Saracen's face registered the pain for the briefest of

moments as the spiked ball crushed through his hair and skull. Then the man's head exploded, spattering blood and brains on all around them. Simon grinned, despite the injury to his shoulder. He wheeled his horse free of the press and rode out, his bloody shoulder screaming with pain.

From the west he heard soldiers crying, and a horn sounding.

The towers had reached the wall.

*

On the wall, Jibril watched as the towers grew closer. The defenders' arrows had taken their toll on the men hauling the towers, but it seemed no matter how many they cut down, there were always more to take their place.

At this rate they'll be able to walk up the walls on the bodies of the dead, he thought, as the tower grew closer. He could see his men, nervously waiting, watching as the tower grew near, knowing that in moments they would be fighting for their lives.

"Steady!" he shouted. "Grapples!"

A dozen men tossed hooks out at the towers, hoping to pull them over to the side and take them from their deadly course. The defenders were prepared, and tore off the hooks before the ropes on them could be pulled tight.

The towers trundled ever closer.

Beside Jibril a man screamed, victim of a chance arrow that made it past the battlements. The long shaft had sunk into his neck and blood spurted from him like water from a pump. Jibril shook his head in disgust and turned away. The man was dead and didn't know it yet. Another victim of the infidels.

We will crush them all, he thought. *We just need to hold out two more weeks.*

"It opens!" screamed one of the defenders, and the weighted drawbridge on the front of the tower plunged down onto the wall and the infidels, led by a dozen knights, charged forward.

Instantly the wall was a slaughterhouse. The knights who charged out had been picked for their size and strength, and they fell on the smaller defenders like the wrath of God, smiting with steel that hacked through armor and flesh. Brains and blood and intestines made the wall into a slippery mess, and the screams of the dying were nearly louder than the cries of battle.

Jibril charged forward, leading his own handpicked men, equal in size and ferocity to the invaders. Ahead of him he watched first one, then two, then half-a-dozen men dying, from ripped-open stomachs or crushed skulls or from swords cuts that sent heads flying. Jibril screamed his own war cry, *"Allahu Akbar!"* and charged forward.

He met the first knight shield to shield, and the force of Jibril's charge was enough to send the man staggering back in the bloody mess on the top of the wall. Jibril ducked beneath the blade the man swung at his head and thrust his own curved sword up under the man's hauberk, ripping into the man's leg and tearing open the artery. Jibril twisted the blade and pulled it out at the same time he drove his shield into the man, sending him skidding back to fall over the bodies of those he had killed.

Jibril didn't bother cutting the knight again. The blood spurting from the man's leg meant that he would be dead fast enough, and Jibril had others he needed to kill. One giant of a knight was holding off three of Jibril's men by himself, using a mace to deal devastating blows.

"Spears!" screamed Jibril, and a two more squads of his men

charged forward, wielding their wicked *dariyah* – twelve-foot long spears, whose last three feet were all blade. They stabbed out at the infidels' vulnerable legs and faces, driving them back. The big one with the mace swung hard, smashing two of the blades with one blow. Jibril leapt into the space left from the suddenly disarmed spearmen and hacked down and across with his sword. It hit the big man's wrist, biting through the chainmail and into flesh and bone. Blood spurted, but the arm was not severed. Jibril shoved hard on his blade, cutting further through the screaming man's wrist even as it freed Jabril's weapon. The man tried to stumble back, but Jibril followed, hacking sideways across the man's face. The knight's eye exploded as Jibril's blade ripped through it. He fell to the ground, screaming and clutching at himself.

"Drive forward!" screamed Jibril. "Drive forward and kill them all!" He stepped back as his men streamed around him. "Where are my flames? Where is my fire?"

He had his answer a moment later when six men, each carrying flaming pots of oil, charged forward. The infidel knights saw them too and redoubled their attack, but it did them no good. One by one they fell, and the long spears kept others from leaving the siege towers to attack the battlements.

The first oil pot flew and smashed against the side of the tower. Flames leapt up, but did little damage.

"Get them inside!" Jibril screamed. "Follow me!"

He charged again, breaking the line of the struggling knights. Soon each infidel was surrounded and being hacked to pieces by a half-dozen of Jibril's defenders. Jibril kept driving forward, jumping onto the tongue of the siege tower and cutting at the men there. The ones that rose to meet him were sliced open or thrown from the tower to fall into the seething sea of humanity below.

"Now!" screamed Jibril. "Now!"

He jumped back and five more flaming vessels flew past him into the maw of the siege tower. Two broke on the top level. The other three tumbled down into the depths of the tower and erupted into flames there. Smoke began billowing from the tower and the men inside began screaming and fighting one another, desperate to escape the agonizing death they faced.

"To the other tower!" Jibril yelled. "We will steal the victory from the infidel dogs and drive them back to the sea! *Allahu Akbar!*"

*

From the back of his horse, Simon watched the first tower burning.

"Swiving dogs," he cursed. "Bastards. Shit-eating scum."

Tentatively he tried moving his shield arm. The sword that had pierced him had not ruined the joint. He was still fit for fighting and the sight of the burning tower infuriated him. He looked to the other tower and saw that it was stuck in place, twenty feet from the wall. Simon cursed and kicked his heels into his horse's sides. The beast charged forward.

Through the ranks he rode, passing by soldiers stepping grim-faced towards the front line, going around blood-soaked stretchers bearing crying, mutilated men back to the tents. Together Simon and his horse pushed forward until they were behind the tower.

"You there!" he shouted at the nearest knight. "What the hell is going on? Why isn't that damn thing at the wall?"

"Ditch!" shouted the man back. "The front wheels are mired!"

"Well, get it out of there!" shouted Simon back. They've already fired the other one and this one…"

His words were cut off as a flaming pottery vessel plunged from the wall above and shattered between the two of them. Flaming shards sprayed everywhere, making men cry out and bat frantically at themselves as their tabards caught fire.

"Hooks!" someone screamed from above. "Ware the hooks!"

*

On the wall, Jibril grinned with violent joy, even as he gasped for breath. He had run from one end of the walls to the other, preparing to lead the defenders in repelling the second tower. Now he saw that it was unnecessary. The ditch they had dug weeks before and filled with sand was doing its job admirably. The front wheels of the huge siege tower were hopelessly mired, and even now the defenders were raining arrows and flaming vessels filled with oil down upon the attackers. Better still, the hooks were getting closer, nearly snagging the vulnerable sides of the tower, despite the best efforts of the defenders. All it would take was one to catch and….

"Arrows!"

Even as the scream came, the air below turned black with flying shafts. Hundreds of arrows raked the battlements as the attackers sought to keep the defenders under cover while they rescued their precious tower. Most men ducked out of the way. A few unlucky ones were pierced through, arrows cutting through the chain mail or driving into unprotected faces.

Jibril ran forward and grabbed one of the hooks. His men

immediately surrounded him, making a wall of shields to protect Jibril while he readied his throw. The hooks were heavy and attached to chains that ran ten feet from the hook to a thick, sturdy rope. He waited as the next volley of arrows rained down over all of them, then stood and swung the hook hard and fast, whipping it out and snagging the side of the tower. He pulled it tight in a second, then ran down the wall, stretching the rope tight and screaming, "Pull! For the love of God and Jerusalem! Pull!!!"

A dozen men, then two dozen, grabbed the rope, heedless of the arrows coming down, and began pulling. On the tower, the infidels hacked desperately at the chain with axes, but the defenders rained their own arrows back, and threw vessel after flaming vessel at the side of the tower, keeping the defenders back and lighting the hides that covered the outside of the tall tower.

More men joined on the rope, heaving it as hard as they could. Some died as arrows from below pierced their bodies or skulls, leaving the wall beneath them a slippery, bloody mess. More of the defenders grabbed the rope, pulling ever harder.

Below, the tower began to creak and tip.

*

Above, floating silently in the clouds, invisible to the mortal eyes below, Nyx looked down on the chaos and carnage below, and frowned.

"Well, this isn't going well," said Ishtar.

Nyx's eyes flashed red and she glared at Ishtar. Ishtar smiled back, knowing that her mistress was going to be far too busy to deal out punishments – for the near future, anyway.

"Fools, the pair of them," said Persephone, looking at the battle.

"Which pair?" asked Ishtar. "For I see many fools below."

"Their commanders!" Nyx was seething. "They could have been inside by now!"

"Then you will have to punish them for their failures," said Ishtar, and in her voice was a lustful, greedy desire. She looked at Nyx. "And when will you do that? I, for one, am getting very bored, just floating here in the clouds."

"Soon," hissed Nyx. "Very, very soon."

*

"Goddammit!" screamed Simon, watching from below as one of the front wheels of the tower dug deeper into the sand. "Get off of there! Get everyone off!"

Another vessel of oil hit the ground and split, sending fire everywhere and splattering the armor on Simon's horse. The animal screamed and reared, and Simon had to fight to hold his seat, sawing the reins hard to try to regain control. He could feel something ripping in his shoulder, and had to crush his teeth hard together to keep from yelling in agony.

Above, the first of the tower's support beams split.

Simon pulled harder on the reins, forcing his horse to turn. He dug his spurs into the beast side hard enough to draw blood, and galloped away, knocking soldiers aside as behind him the tower began to topple.

For the men inside at the top, there was no hope, only agony as the tower raced toward the ground, crushing bones and ripping open flesh. For the men below, death was just as fast, and just as painful. Broken timbers pierced bodies, cutting some men in two and impaling others so they remained, stuck in place, blood and guts exploding from their bodies as the timbers rammed through them. Around them, dozens of others died as bodies, weapons, timber and fire fell on them from above. The soldiers' last hope of victory fell away and they scrambled desperately away from the wall, any hope of an orderly retreat lost as they tried to escape the slaughter around the tower.

*

"*Allahu Akbar!*" shouted Jibril, watching the infidels running away from the wall. Men around him echoed the cry until it was taken up the entire length of the wall. Below in the streets he could hear shouts of victory and joy. Jibril grinned. The men on the wall started dancing and cheering. Jabril gave them a few moments of victory, then shouted out, "Back to your places! Back to your posts! Everybody!"

The men, still jubilant, did as they were told.

"Listen closely!" shouted Jibril, his voice spreading down the length of the wall. "And tell the others! This is a victory, but this is not the end! The enemy may return again, and we will not have them overrun us while we are celebrating! Man your posts and stay until relief is sent! We will send food and drink and tend to the wounded! I will go to the governor, and let him know that today, his people did their city proud!"

The men around the wall cheered, and thousands of other throats took up the cry. The battle was won, and while victory was not complete, surely it was only a matter of time before the infidels were destroyed.

*

"Now," said Nyx.

*

Simon Benart and Albert de Giroie stood beside their horses with two hundred other knights, watching as their commanders raged at one another. Beyond them, they could see the remnants of the army stumbling away from the walls, harassed by defenders' arrows and loads of small stones and pottery shard flung by the Saracen's catapults.

A thousand men, thought Simon. *We've lost a thousand men today.* He looked at the two commanders, fighting about whose fault it was. *Stupid bastards.*

"I told you!" screamed Godfrey of Bouillon. "I told you we would fail! I told you it was a fool's plan!"

"It was not a fool's plan!" screamed back Robert Curthose. "You were the fool! Your men drove the tower right into the ditch! Your men lost us this battle!"

"Your men were already running like the cowardly dogs they are!" shouted Godfrey. "Your tower was in flames!"

Above, there was a noise. Faint and high-pitched, a whistling sound. Simon glanced up, but could see nothing.

"You dog!" screamed Robert. "You stinking lump of pig shit! You dare blame me for this? We could have taken the walls today and you blame me for your failure?"

"I blame you for all our failures!" screamed Godfrey back. "Every loss we have suffered has been the result of your stupidity! Every time our army has suffered, it has been from your decisions!"

The noise was louder now, and this time Simon recognized it. It was the rush of wind past the wings of a hawk, stooping down on its prey. Simon had heard it once before, when one of his falcons had struck a pigeon near the wall Simon had been standing on. There had been a rush of air and a flash of color that went by so quick, Simon barely had time to register the noise before the falcon had slammed into the pigeon and spiraled down to the earth in a tangle of blood and feathers. He had never forgotten the sight or sound.

He looked up, and saw them. Three of them.

"Albert," he elbowed the man beside him, and pointed up.

Albert looked, then gasped.

They were bigger than hawks, bigger than eagles, and they were coming down faster than any bird Simon had ever seen. "Dear God."

Down, down they came, straight down from the heavens, streaks of silver and white and black, moving faster than any creature Simon had ever seen. Albert swore and crossed himself, and around them the other nobles and knights turned their eyes upward, away from their screaming commanders, to the blurs in the sky that dove down toward them. Instinctively they stepped back, clearing a wider and wider space around the commanders.

They are women, thought Simon. *Women with wings.*

Dear God, they are Angels.

When the three hit the ground, the earth around them exploded. The force of the blast made the earth shake for a half-mile around them. The cloud of sand that blew up around them blinded everyone, and the wind burst around them with a force that blew every knight and noble to the ground.

When the dust cleared, they saw them for the first time. White flesh, smooth and naked and perfect; enough to raise the lust of every man in the circle. White hair that flowed down their bodies. Silver eyes with serpent pupils, unblinking even in the dust. Black feathered wings that spread twenty feet wide behind them.

"Are they Angels?" gasped Albert. "Are they from God?"

Simon shook his head. "I don't…I don't know."

"What do we have here?" said Nyx, her voice quiet and intimate and reaching every man of the crusader army.

"Failure," said Persephone, looking at the two commanders who lay, stunned at their feet. Her voice, though it was no louder than Nyx's, travelled just as far. "Failure of a most holy mission."

Robert Curthose and Godfrey of Bouillon dragged themselves to their feet, eyes still glazed and ears ringing from the force of the angels' landing.

"Unacceptable," said Nyx. "Ishtar, if you please."

Ishtar vanished in a streak of wings and white flesh. Soldiers flung themselves to earth as she whipped past overhead. On the walls of Jerusalem there were cries of shock and horror as she cut through the air by the wall. Wood cracked, the air hissed and split, and then the earth shook again and dust clouds spewed across the land as she landed before Nyx. In each arm she held a twenty-foot long length of burnt, jagged wood. She looked at the two commanders and smiled. Then, with a fierce motion, drove both pieces of wood five feet into the hard-packed earth.

"You," said Nyx, advancing on Robert. "You chose the wrong tactic. You let the enemies of Christ defeat you."

"It would have worked," protested Robert. "If Godfrey's tower had not been stuck it would have…"

"*Silence!*"

The word shook the air, sending men across the field to their knees. Robert was blown back and knocked over by the force of it. In a single motion Ishtar grabbed him and pulled him on his feet. Nyx advanced on him.

"You failed to take the Holy Land from the followers of God," she said. "You failed your men, you failed your savior and *you failed me!*"

In a motion too fast to see Nyx grabbed Robert and threw him into the air. She followed him up, caught him as he was coming down and stared into his face. "You are doomed to Hell, Robert Curthose. *And I will come for you there!*"

She flipped him in the air, sending him twisting in circles before raising him up and slamming him down, impaling him upright, a foot deep, upon the sharp, pointed end of one of the stakes Ishtar had created.

Robert Curthose's screams echoed the length and breadth of the battlefield to the walls of Jerusalem where the defenders watched in horror. Men abandoned the walls, seeking to hide. Others fell to their knees. Muslim and Jew alike began praying desperately.

Nyx alighted on the ground. There was no sound this time, no cloud of dust, no vibration to distract the men from Robert's screams. She simply landed and walked slowly towards Godfrey of Bouillon, her wings folding away and vanishing. "And then," she said, her voice gentle once more, "there is you."

To his credit, the nobleman was doing his best to control his trembling. He did not weep or cry out, and he managed to stay on his feet.

"You opposed Robert's plan," said Nyx. "You presented a plan that could have succeeded. That would have succeeded."

"Yes, my lady," said Godfrey.

Suddenly, Persephone and Ishtar were beside him, hands

running gently down his body, all over his body, making him gasp even as he tried to keep his eyes on Nyx.

"I was very impressed with your plan," said Nyx, coming ever closer. "I was looking forward to following you in, to watching as you led your men to victory over Jerusalem." Her voice changed, and the next words out were cold and deadly as a winter storm. "But you *gave in!*"

Persephone's and Ishtar's hands turned to claws, ripping the clothes from Godfrey's body, gouging into his flesh as they tore away chain mail and padding and the clothes beneath, even tearing his boots away in moments, leaving him naked with the proof of the lust he felt from their caresses obvious to the knights and nobles around him.

"You are worse than Robert!" screamed Nyx, and her voice threatened to deafen everyone in the ring of knights, in the army, in Jerusalem. "You had the tools for victory and you gave them up to that whining little dog!"

Nyx's eyes went to Persephone, then to Ishtar. Her lip curled in disgust and she said. "Slow."

Persephone and Ishtar both had wings again, and both rose slowly into the air as Godfrey of Bouillon struggled desperately between them. He lashed out with his fists, then with his feet, trying to cause damage, but the two only laughed at the blows that landed, and ever so gently, ever so slowly, placed him on the jagged tip of the second beam. He balanced there for a moment, shouting and thrashing. Suddenly, his flesh gave way and the wood pierced into his bowels. Shouts turned to screams as, inch by inch his body's weight pulled him inexorably downward, and the jagged wood slipped inside him, ripping and tearing as it went.

Both men's screams echoed over the land, bouncing off the walls of Jerusalem.

"Devils!" screamed a knight. "Devils of Hell!"

The knight's words carried past the knights, over the army. Amongst the soldiers, there was panic. Some turned to run, others held their ground, others charged forward, weapons high. The knight drew his blade and rushed at Nxy, screaming, "Destroy the devil! *Deus Vult!*"

Fifty knights rushed forward, swords, war hammers, axes and morning stars ready to hack and smash into her flesh.

Nyx's sword grew out of her hand, black-bladed and shining in the hot desert sunlight. She swung it and the nearest three men's bodies exploded, the force of the blow scattering bits of intestine and lung and slices of rib over the surrounding knights.

"My Angels!" She called, her voice raw and fierce with the joy of battle. "Kill those who betrayed me!"

Darkness flowed from Ishtar and Persephone's bodies, sliding down their arms. Those knights who had not attacked watched in horror as from the Angels's very flesh...darkness twisted, growing and wrapping around itself again and again, like thick rose stems done in black, with thorns all down the lengths of them. As one, the Angels raised their bows, and arrows appeared as they drew back the strings.

In a moment, a dozen men died. The arrows cutting through their armor and burning through their pierced flesh like acid, leaving gaping holes dripping with darkness in their bodies. Then a dozen more, then a score. Throughout the army, whenever a man tried to run they were felled. The fortunate ones took arrows to the head and died instantly.

Less fortunate were the ones who took the arrows to their

guts or, worst of all, to a limb, which would be eaten away as they screamed, bone and flesh tuning to oozing black liquid. Then the acid slowly spread to their torsos and their lives would end in agony.

Below Ishtar and Persephone, Nyx cut her way through the knights, not even bothering to parry the blows that cut into her flesh. The little pain they could inflict felt more like pleasure, and added impetus to her blade as she cleaved through the knights. Links of chain mail and broken bits of sword flew through the air with guts and limbs and flesh and severed heads as her blade cut through everything it came in contact with.

Ten knights were downed by the time the second volley of arrows had flown. By the tenth volley, no one who had attacked remained in one piece. Many were still alive, though, and they screamed and stared in horror at their own severed legs and their guts, spread over the ground as the last of their blood flowed out.

In the army, chaos reigned. The men who ran had died by the hundreds, arrows flying too fast to see or stop pierced through armor and shields and flesh without mercy. The men who stood still were untouched. No acid splashed them; no arrows fell on them.

"*ENOUGH!*" Nyx's voice rolled across the plains like a blast of thunder, freezing every man in his place and making the earth shake with the force of it. Ishtar and Persephone ceased loosing their arrows, and stillness fell over the ranks of soldiers.

In the circle of knights, Simon and Albert watched, eyes wide with amazement and horror, clothes spattered with the blood and flesh of those who had been foolish enough to attack the Angels.

On the battlements of Jerusalem, the five commanders saw the creatures cease their attacks on the infidels. The governor, beside them on the wall began muttering prayers to Allah, and Jibril found himself joining in, almost against his own will.

There is no hope for us, he thought. *We are dead men.*

Nyx's wings grew out from her back, shaping themselves from flowing darkness and spreading wide. Slowly, she rose into the air between the two spikes with the screaming commanders dangling from the top of them.

Nyx did not look at either man. She made a slight gesture, a flicking of her fingers, and something black and wet oozed up, ripping itself out of the men's bodies and covering their mouths, silencing their screams even as it burned into their flesh and added to their agony.

Every man in the army stared at her, and even those who prayed and crossed themselves could not take their eyes off of her, nor contain the lust the sight of her naked flesh made rise up inside them.

"My crusaders," she said, and once more her voice was calm and quiet and carried over the entire army. "My warriors. This is not a day for rebellion. It is not a day for failure. This is a day for victory." She raised an arm and pointed at the city. "Look there. Look at Jerusalem, and the men and women who cower there." Her voice filled with disdain. "They are people of *God.*" She spat the word out, as if clearing something foul from her mouth, and her derision and hated flowed over the entire army.

"*God* supports them! *God* gives them their strength! *God*, they will tell you, will give them victory over your army and allow them to drive you back into the sea!" She looked down on the men.

"A thousand years ago, *God* sent His son to this earth. He lived among you; He walked as one of you. And then do you know what happened?

"*God* betrayed Him!

"*God*, who was supposed to leave His son here to guide you, to bring you together under His banner and make the world one, *God* let His son be murdered because *God* could not bear anyone to be worshipped other than *God!*"

She rose higher, and her silver eyes glowed red with her rage at the being who had dared to take her Tribunal, her lover, away from her.

"And on the day that your beloved saviour died, He called to me!" Her arms spread wide, as if embracing the entire army, and every man in the army responded, leaning, reaching toward her as if they could touch her.

"He told me of what *God* had done to you all. He told me of how *God* betrayed you!" Her voice dropped, becoming a near-whisper; a caress that seemed to touch every man in the army. "He told me that He, your savior, would not stand idly by and let *God* abandon you. He would not follow *God's* plan for mankind. He would not be *God's* fool, and direct you to worship this false and evil *God* who would see you all spend eternity in torment.

"He rejected *God*. He rejected the name *God* gave him, and picked one of His own!

"His true name is *Tribunal*," the word flowed from her mouth like sunshine, warming the entire army. "And He has sent me to gather you together, to give you a new banner to follow." Her voice rose again, louder and louder, like the clarion call of trumpets, summoning the men to her. "He calls you now, to stand under the banner of Nyx. To reject *God* and to join with me, to conquer this earth together, and to then join Tribunal in Paradise!"

She looked over them all. "What will you do? Will you continue to follow *God*? To listen to the deceptions of His priests, whose words sent you to march across deserts, to suffer poison and sickness, to be killed at the hands of His other worshippers for his amusement? Or will you follow me? Will you march under my banner to victory and to Paradise?"

"Bollocks," said Albert. "Shit and donkey's balls, what do we do, Simon?"

Nyx's voice thundered across the plain. "Who will follow me?! Who will march with me to victory?!"

"We do what we must," said Simon. He took two steps forward and knelt. "I will follow!" he shouted. "I will follow for victory!"

Around him there was a moment of stunned silence, then one after another the knights knelt beside him, shouting out "I will follow! We will follow!!!"

In the army, one man knelt, then another, then a hundred, then a thousand, then thousands knelt screaming, "We will follow! We will follow!"

Nyx surveyed the ones who knelt, a smile on her face. Then her gaze turned dark as she looked over the ones that had not knelt. A dozen or so of the knights. A few hundred of the soldiers. All of the monks. They did not kneel to her and the expressions on their faces told her that nothing would make them do so.

"Prove your worth to me, my warriors," her voice purred out over the army. "Prove to me your loyalty. Prove to me your strength. Kill those that do not kneel, and I will give you victory!"

Simon rose to his feet, and without hesitation dashed out the brains of the nearest standing knight with his morning star. The other knights and soldiers roared and surged up, killing men they had called "brother" only hours before, cutting and smashing their flesh until what remained barely looked human.

"Well done, my warriors!" Nyx spread her arms wide and a ripple of energy went through the entire army like a cool, refreshing breeze on this hot and deadly day. Blood and dirt fell away from clothes, rust fell from armor. Where before there had been ripped cloth and rent metal, now there was whole fabric and armor. The white of their tabards gleamed in the sun and the metal of their weapons and armor shone like new.

And when the last of the ripple passed, the men saw that the black crosses on their uniforms were now upside down.

Ishtar and Persephone spread their arms wide. Darkness flowed over them both and over Nyx, encasing all three in their skin-tight, black-scaled armor. Spikes grew from their heels. The bows in Iris' and Persephone's hands flowed and changed, becoming black-bladed swords, and in the other hand of all three, long, triple-headed whips grew.

"Follow me!" shouted Nyx, as she turned in the air and flew towards the walls of Jerusalem. The knights scrambled to their horses, and the sergeants screamed at their men, forcing them into battle order and bringing them together in formation. Nyx winged over them all, straight towards the main gate of the city. "Follow me!" she shouted again. "We will open the gates. And you will bring me Jerusalem!"

*

On the wall, the governor turned from the marching army and looked at his five commanders. He had not been a young man before the assault began, but now he seemed to age twenty years before their eyes. "There is no hope for survival against demons. You know this."

The five nodded in mute assent.

"We must get as many of the women and children out as we can," said the governor. "The old and infirm must be left behind. Send word through the city. Today we lose Jerusalem."

He looked out over the advancing army. As he watched, it split into three. "They will take the south, east, and west gates," said the Governor. "Send all the women and children you can find to the north gate. Count your men and send every fifth soldier with them, that the women and children may have a chance of survival. The rest of the men and you have only one task. You must slow the demons' entry into Jerusalem, and delay their victory as long as possible." He shook his head. "We are in God's hands now. And for Him and our women and our children we shall hold off these demons as long as possible. *Insha'Allah*."

"*Insha'Allah*," echoed the five commanders.

"The first falls to you, Kamal," said the Governor. "Take all your horses and men and attack their flanks. Slow them as much as you can."

"I go," said Kamal.

*

"Is this right?" asked one of the knights, his voice low. "Is this the right thing to do?"

"It is the only thing to do, you fool," hissed Simon. "Look

at them. Be they Angels or Devils from Hell, we cannot stand against them, and they offer us Jerusalem!"

"But our souls," protested the knight. "What of our immortal souls?"

"Damn your cowardice!" shouted Simon. "The pope gave us all indulgence, did he not? He promised remission of all our sins if we took Jerusalem! Well, there is Jerusalem and *there*," he pointed at Nyx's black armored form, winging slowly toward Jerusalem. "*There* is how we will take it. So shut your mewling mouth and ride, because we will have this city by nightfall!"

One of the outriders galloped toward the main column of knights. "Horsemen!" he shouted. "Hundreds of them, coming from the east and west gates!"

"Right," said Simon, getting a better grip on his new lance. "Time to earn our place in Paradise."

Words passed back and forth and the column of knights split into two to meet the oncoming Saracen horsemen. Simon, leading one of the columns with Albert beside him, grinned as the horses grew closer. He nearly screamed out "Deus Vult," then remembered himself. God had abandoned them all, and now it was time to serve the other side.

"Tribunal!" he shouted. "Tribunal and Nyx! Honor, glory, Tribunal and Nyx! *Honor and glory!*"

"Honor and glory!" screamed two hundred men behind him, and the two lines of cavalry crashed into one another in a screaming mass of blood and steel and broken horse and man flesh.

*

The main mass of the army was headed for the south gate, and it was there Jibril took his position. He had not stopped praying since he had stepped down from the wall, and even now his lips moved as he inspected the ranks of men before him. Some of the archers were left on the battlements, but no other defenders. The soldiers coming had no siege towers, no ladders. This battle would be fought in the streets.

*

The knights outnumbered the horsemen two to one, and knew in their hearts that victory was theirs. The Saracens did not retreat, did not surrender or ask for quarter. Again and again they wheeled their horses away, only to turn and once more to smash into the line of knights. They had one purpose only, to slow the advancing army.

Simon had not expected the Angels to join them in battle, but even as the lines of cavalry clashed together and Simon's morning star cracked open its first skull, Ishtar swooped down from above, hacking two of the Saracens in half with her sword, and lashing a third in the face with such force that her whip tore through flesh and bone, ripping the man's jaw off. Simon, busy fighting for his life, caught only glimpses of her, but heard screams on the far side of the battle, where no knights had yet reached, and saw bodies and parts of bodies flying through the air. Above the battle cries of both sides, Ishtar's scream of joy and pleasure ripped through the ears of the crusaders and defenders alike, spooking horses and causing even more chaos in the frenzied battle below her.

Simon pressed his horse forward, ignoring the panic in its eyes and the screams from its mouth as he sought out the leader of the horsemen. His morning star spun out in all directions.

Beside him, Albert's sword fell ceaselessly, hacking off limbs and hewing through heads.

The ground around them was littered with dead and dying men and horses. The cries of the dying and the screams of horses in agony sang like a counterpoint to the clanging cacophony of the battle. The Saracen captain was nearly in reach, but a pair of his lieutenants, men as big as Simon and Albert, riding crazed, blood-soaked warhorses stood between them and their target. The two knights rushed forward to meet the two warriors, and for the next moments the world was reduced to clashing steel and cries of battle and vicious attempts to kill the other man. The four men fought to a near-stalemate, neither side able to get the better of the other.

There was a scream from above, and Ishtar's black-clad body descended on the captain, ripping him from the saddle with claws that dug deep through his armor and flesh and ribs to grip him. She pulled him high into the air, screaming with wild delight. Her teeth were now fangs, razor-sharp and too long for her mouth. Kamal screamed in agony, even as he tried to slash out with his long, curved sword, using arms rendered suddenly weak by his shock-ravaged body.

Ishtar opened her mouth wide, wider than any human mouth could, wider than it should have been possible, and bit down hard on Kamal's throat. Blood sprayed out and the man's screams of agony ended abruptly as his windpipe was ripped from his body and spat on the remaining Saracens below.

The other defenders hesitated, and many of them died for it. Some broke away, fleeing across the desert, riding for their lives. Ishtar swooped over them, the sword and whip back in her hands, hacking and lashing out so that none escaped.

The rest of the men, knowing that all hope was gone, wheeled their horses away, then once more charged into the line of knights, screaming "*Allahu Akbar!*" – more a prayer than a battle cry – as one by one they died to slow the crusaders' advance.

*

On both sides of the wall, there was silence.

On the top of the wall, the last of the archers had fallen under the rain of deadly arrows from the angels, and the last cries of agony had faded.

From the far side of the wall, there was only silence. The tramping sounds of thousands of feet had stopped. There were no war cries, no sound of armor and weapons and shield clashing against one another. No whinny of horses or talking of men.

In the street before the gate, Jibril could hear the men around him breathing. The mass of heavily-armored infantry stood ready, their long-bladed spears pointing at the gate.

The gate shook once, a gentle rattle, as if someone was pushing on it.

For the first time in two hours, Jibril stopped praying.

The gate exploded inward, shards of wood and steel flying through the air and piercing flesh whenever it found it. A few men cried in pain, and one fell, a length of wood like a knife protruding from his throat, but the rest stayed where they were, spears ready.

The dust cleared, and in the arch of the broken gate, the demon stood, clothed head to foot in black armor that hid nothing of her body, sword and whip in her hands, and a grin on her face.

Some men broke ranks, running away. Jibril did not spare them a moment's thought. Fear clawed at him, too, threatening to overwhelm him. He had no doubt most of his men felt the same way.

At the north gate, he knew, his wives and children were running for their lives out into the harsh desert around the city, surrounded by as many guards as he could spare to help them stay alive.

I will not fail them.

"Loose!" screamed Jibril, and arrows shot out from the windows and roofs of the buildings near the wall, flying straight at the demon. She ignored them, strode forward a few steps and surveyed the men before her.

Nyx's Aramaic was flawless. "I look forward to watching you all die," she said.

Black wings snapped open and Nyx flew up into the sky faster than any arrow could go. From beyond the wall, "*Tribunal and Nyx! Honor and glory!*" erupted from thousands of throats, and the crusaders charged in through the broken gates.

There was no hope of stopping them, Jibril knew as he and his men bore the brunt of the first wave. There were too many of them. Even as they died, impaled on the spears of Jibril's men, thousands more pushed forward through the gate, driving the defenders back step by slow step, through sheer mass.

We will hold them, thought Jibril, judging the pace at which they were being forced back. *We will hold them long enough to let the women and children escape.*

"For God and Jerusalem!" Jibril shouted. *"Allahu Akbar!"*

His men echoed the cry and, despite the overwhelming numbers, began pushing forward again.

If we can drive them back to the gate, we can hold them off a few hours more.

A rush of wind, a scream of joy that tore through Jibril's ears, and suddenly Nyx was there, flying *through* the formation of men, her sword and whip killing and maiming those around her as the sheer force of her movement knocked the defenders aside and broke their line. The crusaders cheered and surged forward. Jibril shouted and struggled to bring his men back together, retreating before the onslaught of the crusading army and Nyx's continuous attacks from above.

Jerusalem held out for five hours.

Jibril and the other captains fought a thousand rear-guard battles, in streets and alleys, in homes and mosques and temples. But every time they sought to rally their troops, Nyx and Persephone and Ishtar were there, raining death from above with their arrows, with their swords, with their talons and teeth and the spikes on their heels. Behind them, the crusaders pressed forward, charging into every street in the city as the defenders fell back, invading the buildings and slaughtering whomever they found.

By sunset, the last of the resistance was in the governor's citadel, and in the streets the soldiers and knights had turned from fighting to sacking and slaughter.

In the Dome on the Rock, at the top of the Temple Mount, Simon and Albert and a half-hundred knights and a hundred soldiers waded ankle-deep in blood as they slaughtered their way through the women and children and old men who had sought refuge there. The men were slaughtered first, both those who cowered and begged for mercy, and those who stood between the invaders and the women. Then the slaughter turned to sport, with the prettier of the women pulled from the crowd and thrown roughly to the ground, their skirts ripped off before each was raped by a dozen or more men. Other women, whose children the soldiers held with knives to their throat, took their clothes off and debased themselves, offering their bodies and their lives to the soldiers who held their children and who lied to them about how the children would be spared if they did what they were told.

Simon looked at the crowd of men surrounding the desperate, pleading, screaming women and children and laughed. He saw Albert grab a pretty young boy out of the crowd and drag him over to a pile of bodies.

"Hey, Albert," Simon shouted. "We're supposed to be killing them!"

"Don't worry!" Albert shouted back. He bent the struggling boy over the pile of bodies and began cutting away his clothes with a dagger. "I will when I'm done!"

Simon laughed and turned back to the crowd of refugees, his own lust rising. He looked for a pretty girl to satisfy it, but they had arrived late and most of them were already screaming and writhing beneath multiple soldiers.

"You."

The word was a command. It could not be resisted. Simon turned and saw Persephone, standing in the doorway, her armor gone and her white, glistening skin coated head to foot with blood.

"Come here."

Simon did. The Angel grabbed him and in a moment they were in the air, moving faster than Simon would have thought possible. Another moment and they were on the roof, overlooking the burning, blood-soaked city and hearing the screams of the raped and the dying. Persephone shoved him down to the ground, pushing up his armor and reaching between his legs. Her touch electrified him, making him gasp with a greater pleasure than any he had ever known.

She smiled, her razor teeth gleaming white amidst the bloody mess that covered her, and mounted him. "Satisfy me, warrior."

*

The last of Jibril's men died in the citadel.

The governor's wives and children had escaped, Jibril was sure of that. All that was left were the servants, mostly women, whose cries he could hear through the walls as the soldiers raped them. He stood, alone, his sword raised, his back to the wall, in a semicircle of crusaders. They taunted him, jabbing out with their blades, never letting him come close enough to strike back. Still he turned where he stood, fending off their attacks and cutting back when he could. He had been cut a hundred times. Small cuts that oozed blood and sapped his energy. He knew there was not much time left for him.

I die for Jerusalem, he thought. *I die for those who escaped, and I pray they will remember me.*

He raised his blade, preparing one last charge, one last battle cry before his death.

"Hold."

It was a quiet word, spoken gently, and because it came from the mouth of the Dark Angel, it was enough. The crusaders fell back. Nyx walked through the room, her black armor, black blade and whip clean of blood, despite the many men she had killed on this day of slaughter. Her movements were slow, almost seductive as she crossed the floor to where Jibril stood, his sword still raised, watching her.

"There is a room down that corridor," she said to the crusaders, "where you will find both the governor's money and his concubines. Go."

They went, cheering and running as each man sought to be the first to claim one of the prizes that awaited them.

Nyx looked at the Captain, his blade still raised, his eyes on her. "Oh, come now," she said in her perfect Aramaic. "You don't really think you can fight me?"

Jibril, Captain of the footmen, defender of Jerusalem, looked at his sword, then at the creature before him. There was no way to beat her, no way to stop what she and the crusaders were doing. He lowered the blade to his side. "No," he said. "But I can die honorably."

"You could," agreed Nyx, smiling at him. It was a gentle, comforting smile. "Or you could live."

The laugh that escaped Jibril's lips was short and sharp, almost a bark, and born of astonishment, not humor. "How?"

"Be mine." The armor dissolved from her body, leaving her naked. Her body was a work of carefully sculpted perfection. Her white skin had no flaws, no blemishes. Her form was sculpted muscle and flesh, designed to taunt any man who looked on it. Her long, straight silver hair flowed like a river over her shoulder, covering one perfect breast. "Be my warrior. Be my captain, and lead my crusaders forward."

Jibril could feel his body responding to her form, could feel her eyes piercing deep into his mind, into his soul, calling him to give himself to her, body and soul. Of their own volition his lips began moving, and prayers began pouring out of him in a whisper.

Nyx cocked her head to one side. "Really? Do you really think that will do you any good whatsoever? Do you really think that your God will come to you and help you?" When Jibril kept praying, her hand lashed out at his face, knocking him down and against the wall. "Answer me! Do you think your *God* cares the slightest bit for your soul?"

Jibril had to wait a moment for his head to clear before he could speak, and even then he did not answer. Instead, he struggled to his feet while Nyx watched, amused. He had to brace himself against the wall to stand, and when he finally managed it, Jibril could barely keep from keeling over from dizziness.

"Answer me," Nyx said again, her voice once more a caress. "Why do you pray when you know your *God* will not answer? Since his son left the earth he has not fulfilled one prayer. He has not come to rescue a single man from misery or danger." She gestured around the room. "Look at your men. They all prayed to *God*, and not a single one of them was spared."

Jibril's eyes followed Nyx's hand, which so casually waved at the corpses on the ground. They were his finest. His best warriors and his bravest fighters. They had held formation and fought wave after wave of the crusaders. They had held their ground even as Nyx and Ishtar and Persephone had come at them again and again, slaughtering their comrades and scattering the other soldiers.

We should have won, thought Jibril. *We held Jerusalem, and we threw them back, and we should have won.*

He raised his eyes from the slaughtered men around him and found Nyx standing so close he could feel the Angel's warm breath against his neck. She took another step closer, pressing her body to his. Every fibre of his flesh responded, and her hand dropped below his waist. He gasped at the pleasure it brought him.

"You are better than them," she whispered as she stroked him. "You are not just a soldier. Not just a blind fool carrying out orders. You are a leader of men. A leader beyond your governor or even your king, beyond even your prophet. You, Jibril, are worthy to lead my army. To lead my crusaders. To guide them forward and take not just Jerusalem but the world, and to make them bow down under my banner."

Jibril gasped again, his knees threatening to buckle. Nyx's other hand landed on his chest and pushed him backwards, pinning him against the wall as the pleasure exploded through his body.

"Forget your governor," said Nyx. "His head is on a pike at the front of the citadel. Forget your men, they are gone where no commander can reach and will not listen any more. Forget your king and your prophet with their false promises. I can give you true immortality, and bring you to a paradise beyond any you have imagined."

Jibril was gasping now. The pain in his body, the hundred small cuts, were forgotten. All that he could feel was the closeness of her body and the pleasure she was giving him.

"Forget them all," she whispered.

A spasm of pleasure racked his body, nearly driving away the last of his sanity. His mouth fell open wide. He gasped in a breath and answered.

"No."

Nyx stopped. She stepped back, her eyebrows going up and

her head cocking to the side in surprise. Jibril, released from her hand and the pleasure it brought him gasped first in shock, then disappointment, then relief.

"Why not?" said Nyx.

"You are beautiful," said Jibril. "You are lovely beyond the words of the poets. You are strong and powerful and your touch…" he shuddered again, then gasped in one deep breath after another until he had control over his body and his words. "Your touch is that which men dream of, even in the arms of their wives."

Nyx did not move. Her serpentine eyes did not blink. "But?"

"You might have convinced me to turn my back on God," he said. "On the words of the prophet and on my king and on all the vows that I have made, but…" Jibril raised his empty hand and pointed at the many corpses on the ground. "These were my brothers. They were my friends and my cousins and my men and I could not, and I would not, forget them. Ever."

"Then you die."

Jibril shrugged, the gesture easy and careless. "*Insha'Allah.*"

It was the fastest move he had ever made. A flick of his wrist and a short pistoning of arm from elbow and shoulder. And despite his wounds, despite his exhaustion and despite the speed of the demon Angel in front of him, it worked.

His scimitar drove through Nyx's body for two-thirds of its length.

Nyx looked down on the wound.

It *hurt*.

It would not kill her. It would barely do more than inconvenience her, and then only for the time it took to pull the blade free. But it *hurt*. And it raised a cold, white rage in her that flashed out through her eyes.

Jibril was smiling.

"I will give you agony," said Nyx, her voice sliding down to become a sibilant hiss. "I will give you pain the length of which you have never dreamed."

"I know," said Jibril.

"I will make you scream as you have never screamed before. You will void yourself like a frightened child and you will beg for the mercy of death."

"I know."

"And when I eventually give you death," she said, stepping close again and once more grabbing him. This was not a caress. This was jabbing pain that threatened to overwhelm him. He ground his teeth together, willing himself to not cry out for as long as he could. "When I release you from the bonds of this world, you will not go to Heaven. You will not sit in a paradise and bask in the presence of your *God*. No!

"For I know what you have done with your life, Jibril. You are a soldier, and you have murdered and pillaged…and tortured. And for that, Jibril, no matter why you did it, no matter for what cause you did it, for that you will go to Hell." Nyx's eyes blazed red, and in them Jibril's saw the fires and tortures and agony that awaited him after death. Nyx pulled the sword from her body as she watched fear and horror chase each other through Jibril's expression. "And In Hell, Jibril, I will come to you, and what will happen there will make your suffering on earth seem as a moment of joy."

Jibril saw the truth in her eyes, saw what was going to happen to him and knew beyond a shadow of a doubt that it was true. He knew also that there was no escape from it. Not now. Not with all his men dead and his beautiful city lying in burning ruins around him.

"And in Hell," he said in pain gasped breaths. "In Hell, I pray God will grant me dreams of my Jerusalem. *Insha'Allah.*"

With his own sword she sliced his genitals from his body, and held them up for him to see.

Jibril, Captain of the elite infantry, defender of the wall and hero of the fall of Jerusalem, began screaming.

*

Two days later, as the sun was setting behind grey clouds and a cool breeze was blowing from the not-too-distant sea, Nyx walked through the south gate and stood outside the walls of Jerusalem.

All the gates of the city were open and lines of women and children with broken, weeping eyes and damaged flesh passed in and out of them, dragging body after body. The city stank beyond all reason, and Nyx had ordered it cleared. Every now and then a bored crusader would grab one of the women or girls or boys and rape them while the other crusaders laughed. The victims seldom even cried out anymore, just silently accepted it as part of the humiliation of being a defeated people, and grew ever more broken, ever more despondent.

Tribunal, all I have done, I have done for you, Nyx prayed to herself as she watched a boy get prodded back to his feet at sword-point. The boy tried his best to cover himself again and limped back into the line of people dragging out the bodies. *That would have bothered me, once.*

It didn't bother her now. Her prayers to Tribunal had gone

from hourly to near-continuous, and with those prayers came the continuous feed of His strength and His hatred. She hated the humans with a passion almost as intense as Tribunal's had been. To see a young one abused no longer meant anything to her. *They'll be wiped from the face of the earth soon enough. Let them suffer while they wait.*

She sensed that there was something hollow inside her, something missing, but she didn't know what. And every time she prayed to Tribunal, the feeling passed to nothingness.

I will release the slaves soon, Nyx thought. *I will command them to worship me, and to spread my glory. Those that do so will go free, and the rest can be used and slaughtered as the crusaders will.*

She smiled at the thought.

Egypt would be coming soon, bringing all its might to face the crusaders. Nyx had no doubt her crusaders would destroy them. For now, this part of the world belonged to her, and none would wrest it away any time.

A single ray of sunlight broke through the clouds, shining on Nyx and filling her with a warmth far beyond that of mere heat and light, and she heard Tribunal say, *"You have done very, very well, my love."*

Tribunal's voice rang through her head. Nyx nearly collapsed from the power of it.

"My beloved," she said, feeling tears of joy falling from her eyes.

"You have taken Jerusalem, my beautiful Nyx. You have opened up a portal and now I may speak."

"My love," she said aloud, not caring who heard. "I have done as you commanded. I have brought God's city to its knees.

I have made them take it in my name and I have caused them to worship me."

"It is no less than I expected," said Tribunal, and the words were filled with love and pride. *"Your love for me that you would do this, your strength to make it happen, fills me with hope that all our plans will come to fruition and we will throw down God from his throne and claim it for our own, to rule together for all eternity."*

"We will, my love."

"This is the completion of the beginning," said Tribunal in her head. "You *have succeeded in that which must be done so that all else may follow."*

"For You, my love."

"And for you, my love," said Tribunal. *"You know the word to contact me. Hide yourself in a place free of all prying eyes, safe from any who would overhear, and use that word. For I would see you as soon as possible."*

"Soon, my love," promised Nyx as the sunlight faded away and the clouds closed in. The space where he had been in her mind seemed like a giant pit, despair pouring in to fill the void. Nyx nearly wept from the loss of his presence.

She turned back to the city and looked up the mount to the Dome of the Rock. Ishtar was flying slow circles around it, occasionally swooping in, then back out. She heard Ishtar's laughter, and it made her smile.

Persephone was taking command of the crusaders, preparing them for the fight against the forces of Egypt. The Angel was a more than capable leader, and she had no doubt that the crusaders would be victorious.

Nyx wings spread from her back, and she lifted into the air, floating effortlessly and easily, letting the wind blow her higher and closer to the Dome of the Rock. She cocked her head and heard the hoarse, faint, and muffled screams of the nearly-man-shaped form that stood, impaled, on the spike above the dome. Half his skin was gone now, along with his tongue, eyes and one arm. His mouth had been stuffed with his own genitalia two days before, and then a bar inserted through his throat so he could not swallow and choke on them.

"Come to see how he's doing?" asked Ishtar. "Or would you like a piece yourself?"

"I have to go," said Nyx. "Tell Persephone. I will summon you both soon."

"I will," said Ishtar. "What about this one, then?"

Nyx looked over the bloodied, broken, agony-filled thing that had been Jabril. "Give him three more days. Then let him go to Hell where he belongs."

She swung in a lazy glide above the city, then headed north. She would summon her lover, her master, her Tribunal, and then they would plan the next steps.

CHAPTER 10

IT IS WARM, deep in the earth, and silent. In some places there are noises: the movement of earth, the grinding of rocks shifting slowly over a thousand years, the dripping and trickling of water carving new paths over millions of years.

In this cavern, though, there was only silence.

This was Nyx's place. She had carved it out a thousand years before, when Tribunal had first given her his name and his instructions. It was a reminder of where she had come from, and what she was. And on those occasions past when all the living plants and creatures and people who walked the earth became too much for her, she retreated here, to the darkness of her own home-made Hell, because that is what she had designed it to look like.

Here, in the darkness, she could be alone. Not even the other Angels were allowed here. They each had their own place where they, too, could retreat and contemplate. She knew where each was, and had, on occasion, visited each. But this was her place, alone, and neither Ishtar nor Persephone knew where it was.

She sat in the middle of her cavern in the middle of the silence, and smiled. *Tribunal had contacted her. Tribunal was ready to speak to her. Tribunal, her lover, her partner in this war for Earth and Hell, was pleased.*

This was not a time for darkness.

Nyx raised an arm and used her power to split the cavern floor open. The room lit up with flames and the stink of burning rock rose from the lava beneath. The super-heated rock glowed yellow and red and orange, and cast shadows on the walls that danced slowly as the rock beneath roiled and turned on itself.

The cave itself had once been home to water, though that was long ago. All that remained were the stalactites hanging from the ceiling, and the stalagmites on the floor; sharply pointed juttings of rock, some so small they would pierce the feet of any mortal who was unfortunate enough to step foot in the cavern. Others big enough to impale a man on, though none had been used for that purpose yet.

Maybe someday, thought Nyx. *But not now.*

She had used her power and the heat from below to convert the limestone into black marble. On a whim she had made the walls shine, and now every surface gave back her reflection, twisted and misshapen a thousand different ways, save for two walls which she had smoothed and polished so highly that her image was mirrored perfectly. She paused before it, examining her body and smiling. Jibril's sword had left no mark, though it had run her through. She looked as young, beautiful and whole as the day she was created, as the nights when she and Tribunal were lovers. She had no fear of pain, no horror at war, no regret. She was Nyx and she would win.

She strode lightly along the edge of the split in the floor, relishing the heat of the burning lava, so different from the cold-burning Hellfire she once felt.

One day I shall return to Hell and I shall make Lucifer beg to lick my feet.

She stood on the edge a while longer, then stepped away. In one corner of the cavern she had flattened the ground, making it as smooth as the stone mirrors on the walls. She had brought in white marble, inlaid it into the floor in a double circle, twenty feet wide on the outside. By herself she had carved the symbols between the lines of the circles, eschewing any power other than her brute strength. She would give no Angelic essence to the circle until she was ready to use it.

The words inscribed between the circles were written in languages that were old before the tower had fallen at Babel: Elamite, Akkadian, Hurrian. Elemental words of darkness and power, words whose magic allowed none to witness what acts occurred in the circle, that prevented any, even God, it was said, from hearing what was spoken there.

Nyx settled herself onto the ground, feeling the solid warmth of the marble beneath her naked flesh. The burning lava, so close below, made the ground too hot for mortal flesh. She reveled in it a moment, then began chanting.

The writing around the circle began to glow a deep red, deeper than the red from the lava only twenty feet away yet strong enough to drown out its light until the cavern was bathed in crimson. Still Nyx chanted, again and again, weaving a spell around herself with a strength that no mortal could match, no matter what he used to power it. She poured more of her power into the circle than she had into anything she had ever done. No matter what, she could not be heard, could not allow God or his agents, even though they had withdrawn from the world, to feel the power of what she was about to do.

The circles themselves began to glow, their white light vying with the dark red, yet never touching it. The spell was complete, and no one, mortal, immortal, God, Angel or monster, could hear learn what was happening in the circle.

Nyx stopped chanting and examined her work, searching through the lines of power for any cracks, any weakness that would betray her. When she was satisfied there was none, she closed her eyes, paused for a delicious moment of anticipation, and spoke *the word* that Tribunal had given her when he hung on the cross.

The word she had spoken when she walked from Jerusalem the last time.

She opened her eyes and the world was gray and Tribunal was standing before her.

She was not in her body anymore. Her physical form was still on the floor of the cave surrounded by silence and the spells that hid it from God's eyes. Here she was a soul only, as was he, and it did not matter. She rushed to him, pressed her body against his and wrapped her arms around him. And even though, in this place, she had no arms and no body, it was enough that the shade of her hands and body could touch the shade of his, and when she pressed the shades of her lips onto his, their souls connected, and his shining power poured into her as hers poured into him—an exchange that was deeper than any entanglement of flesh.

When they finally broke apart, Tribunal smiled at her. "Welcome, my lover, my warrior. It is good to see you again."

"And you, my love," said Nyx. Regretfully, she stepped back, releasing the last filament of his soul and hers, and looked around them. She had been in Heaven, and seen the brilliance of God, and the bright, white light that infused that place. She had ruled in Hell, and knew every dark, agony-filled corner of her realm. But this place she had not seen. "Where are we?"

All around them was gray – not a mist, for it had neither substance nor shape. There was no ground, no sky, no direction. There was no sense of place at all. Nyx felt an urge to look around her, to find something, anything, that could connect her to this place. Anything to give her a sense of location, a sense of being.

And in the gray, there was movement.

They had no substance, like the world they populated. Their shapes flickered in and out of definition. One moment they were almost solid to her, then they would fade. They were human once and now they were shades as was Nyx in this place. For them, though, there was no body to return to, no place where they could reclaim their form. Instead, they wandered, shades of arms outstretched in the gray, reaching for others but never touching.

Tribunal smiled, a shade's smile from a shade's body that nonetheless managed to warm her. "It has many names," he said. "Purgatory. Limbo. Sheol. It has many sections, each separate from the other. In some places, sinners are punished until the sin is stripped from them. In others, they sit in a state of happiness, waiting their turn to be taken to the presence of God. This place, though, is much worse, maybe even worse than Hell."

"How?" asked Nyx, realizing as she did that she felt vaguely insulted that there could be a place worse than Hell.

"This is the Limbo of the unbelievers," said Tribunal. "It is a place of silence, of mists, and of emptiness. Here, God does not exist."

Nyx frowned. "God exists everywhere."

"Not here," said Tribunal. "God never comes here, has no awareness here, has no presence here and He cannot sense anything that happens here. And the ones who wander here will wander forever, always searching, never finding."

Nyx looked out into the gray again. She watched the souls reaching out and never touching, passing by each other without realizing the other was there. She sensed in them a loneliness that was greater than any she had ever experienced, a desperate need to connect with something, anything.

"And they will never find anything again?"

"There is nothing here for them to find," said Tribunal. "They will spend eternity looking for something, and will not even realize they are not alone."

"Very cruel," said Nyx grudgingly. It was a more horrible punishment than any she had thought of, and she was an expert. Then again, her mission was to punish the wicked, and let them know why. This though...*a cruelty truly worthy of God*. "They don't come near us."

"I've made a place here," said Tribunal. "They cannot sense it, see it, or approach it." He smiled at her "And since God cannot see us here, either, we can talk."

Nyx smiled then. "Very clever, my love."

"I knew you would appreciate it," said Tribunal. He – His shade, Nyx had to remind itself – crossed its legs and floated in the air. Nyx did the same. She was still uneasy in this place, but she wouldn't show it. It was worth it, to be here with Tribunal and bask in His love.

"You," said Tribunal, "Have done magnificently. Your work on earth has given more strength to our plan than any that has come before it. You have gained more followers than God Himself."

Nyx preened under the compliments. "I am here," she said. "I am real and present. *God?* God is gone. Men will worship what they can see before they will worship that they cannot."

"This is all true," said Tribunal. "But it is you that has done it. You have swung the balance and now we can move forward."

"And what is our next move?" asked Nyx. "What must we do before we can set my Angels free from Hell, and have them lay waste to this world?"

"Not just this world," said Tribunal. "We will have so much more than this world by the end of things."

Nyx frowned. "I thought You wished to destroy the human race, to make this world a Paradise."

"I do," said Tribunal, "But I wish so much more than that."

"What more?" asked Nyx. "We will have earth to make into Paradise and we will have Hell. We can't have Heaven. What else is there?"

"God should have destroyed them all," said Tribunal. "He should have brought back the waters and swept life from this world."

"But He didn't," said Nyx. "And now, we will do it in His place."

"We will," said Tribunal. He floated closer, His hand

touching her leg and sending a spark of lust and ecstasy through her. "And we will do so much more."

"What more?" asked Nyx. "Would you challenge God?"

The memory of her own battles with God rose up inside her. The war had been fought for an aeon before time itself came into existence, and then they had fought for millennia after. Thousands upon thousands of angels had been destroyed on both side; not mortal death, but the scattering of their energies to the four winds of the universe, some never to be re-formed, others to slowly pull their substances back together, shadows of the strength they once were.

She remembered the march on the gates of God's true temple. She and her rebels, hundreds of thousands strong, had marched and flown together, determined to bring Heaven to its knees and bend God to her will. She remembered Lucifer, resplendent in his red armor and with his flaming sword in his hand, marching beside her.

That had been before defeat, before thousands of years in the pit and the weight of their failure and the loss of Heaven had embittered them to each other and driven wedges of betrayal, blame and guilt among them.

God's legions had been waiting at the Gates of God's true temple, and behind them, the overwhelming, unstoppable power of God himself. The battle had laid waste to Heaven, destroying much beauty and goodness that could not be brought back into creation. Nyx had watched the Morning Star – Lucifer – fall from grace and from Heaven. She had rallied her troops again and again to fight, and killed thousands of lesser Angels before she and Michael fought to a bloody standstill while the armies devastated each other.

She still had scars, though they were not of the body.

"I have challenged God," said Nyx. "I have stood at the foot of His mountain and laid waste to Heaven, and I tell you, you cannot defeat Him."

"I'm not going to fight Him," said Tribunal. "I am going to destroy Him. And when I have, we will have more than just Hell and this small, stinking world. We will have Heaven itself, and all the universe will be ours."

"Destroy… God?" The notion was unfathomable to Nyx. She was born of God. Created by Him to serve Him. Even in her rebellion she had not held hope of destroying Him. He was all-powerful, all-knowing, invincible.

Tribunal sat and waited while Nyx thought her way through it.

Since Tribunal's mortal form had been killed, God had left the world. He had retreated from it and left no trace of Himself behind. For more than a thousand years, Nyx had walked the world, reveling in His absence. *But to kill Him?* Her mind whirled, rejecting the idea as impossible. God was too powerful, too strong. She could not even defeat His armies, let alone God Himself.

But then, Tribunal was no mere Angel.

"Do this with me," said Tribunal, his voice soft and gentle, like the touch of silk on flesh. "Do this with me and you will rule with me. You will be Queen of Heaven and of Hell, of the Earth and the Universe. Together, we will reign over the greatest kingdom of them all. We will reign over God's kingdom."

Tribunal is God's own son, His own creation, born of His immortal and magnificent being. God poured His strength and power and wisdom and knowledge into Him. If anyone can destroy God Himself, it would be Tribunal.

But what happens to the universe He created when He is dead? Nyx wondered. *Does it die with Him?*

It cannot. A child doesn't die because its mother does. A sapling does not die because the tree it sprung from is dead. So the Universe cannot die just because God dies.

Can't it?

Doubts filled her, and a fear of failure and the horror of a fate worse than the one she had been given when she rebelled.

He is God.

Look at what it's like for these souls cut off from Him.

Nyx realized that somewhere inside her she still bore love for Him. It was not a deep love, not a need to worship, but still it was love. Love for her creator that should have died with her many companions who fell in the battle for Heaven. It gnawed at her the moment she realized it, as her knowledge that God had made her a judge of humankind, unable to think of destroying them all without Tribunal's strength to guide her. That she should love the one who had destroyed her plans, that had taken Heaven from her, was near-intolerable. *The bastard probably put that love in all of us when He created us.*

Tribunal reached over and touched her, and His soul melted into hers. The power and warmth left her dizzy and swept her doubts away. She gazed at him, seeing through the false body of His shade to the bright, blinding power of his soul.

"How do we do it?" she asked. "How can we destroy God?"

Tribunal smiled at her use of the word *we*. "You are with me, then?"

"I am always with you, my love," said Nyx, the last of her

fears and misgivings fading with the strength of his touch. "Until the stars die and time ends, and beyond."

Tribunal kissed her again, shade lips bringing together the pure energies of their beings.

"But how?" asked Nyx, when they broke apart. "How will You kill him?"

"I can only tell you the next two tasks."

"You're asking me to help you kill God and you won't trust me with the details?" said Nyx.

"It is not that I don't trust you," said Tribunal.

"Then what is it?"

"To tell you everything would put you in too much danger."

"How much danger can I be in?" asked Nyx. "God is gone from the Earth, my Angels wander the Earth, not His. He does not see anything that occurs there."

"When the next two tasks are complete, the world shall open again," said Tribunal. "The Angels of Heaven and Hell will once more be able to walk the earth, and He will once more be able to see all that transpires. Once He does, he will know all your thoughts. It is better you only know the next steps."

"All right," said Nyx, though she wasn't sure she believed him. *Where is this doubt coming from?* "What are the next steps?"

Tribunal looked carefully at her for a few moments, His gaze piercing beyond the features of her shade and deep into the soul beneath. Her soul was conflicted, He could see, and there was a seed of mistrust there that was slowly growing. *It doesn't matter,* He decided. *If she does what is needed, then I will ensure that all else happens.*

"Before God can be killed, there are certain things that must occur," Tribunal said. "The first of them you have done. We now have more followers than God, and Jerusalem is in their hands. The second is a far greater task, the third greater still." He smiled at her, letting all of his strength radiate out to her. "For your first task, you must create an Angel."

Nyx stared at Tribunal in complete disbelief. "Only God can create an Angel."

Tribunal smiled wide. "Not so. All that's needed is the Word."

Nyx tilted her head. "The Word?" She repeated. "You mean *the* Word?"

"'In the beginning was the Word,' " quoted Tribunal. "'And the Word was with God. And the Word *was* God. "

"The Word is God's alone," argued Nyx. "Only He knows the Word. Only he can use it."

"But you forget," said Tribunal. "I am God."

Nyx found herself backing away, "You…you are not God… You're Tribunal."

"But I am," said Tribunal. "When God went to my mother and told her to bring me into being on the Earth, He didn't mount her like a bull with a cow. He took part of himself, and poured that into her. He created Himself inside her, and in doing so, created me." The strength of Him was radiating out, stronger than it ever had before. It was a strength far, far greater than Nyx's own. And now she realized that it stemmed from the Godhead inside Him. "He created me as Himself, and in doing so, He poured into me all things, *including* the Word."

Tribunal turned the full force of his presence upon Nyx, and for a moment it was all she could do not to kneel before Him. It was only for a moment, though. She had stood before God himself, stained with the ichor of his Angels, defiantly waiting for his hand to smite her, and she had not knelt. She would not kneel now. *I will be his equal, or I will not stand with him at all.*

"You asked me," said Tribunal, "What I would trust you with. I will trust you with more power than you have ever held in your life. I will trust you with the Word."

If Nyx had been breathing in this space, the breath would have left her. As it was, the realization of what he was giving her overwhelmed even Tribunal's presence. *The Word is power,* she thought. *And with such power I could…*

"Do not abuse it," warned Tribunal. "The Word is powerful beyond imagining. To create the Angel is enough. Once it is created, the gates of Heaven and Hell will be open, and using the word again on this world will bring all of God's wrath down upon you."

"I won't," said Nyx, knowing as she said it that the words might well be a lie. *Such power…*

"The Angel shall be created from your own body. It will be pulled together from the stuff of Angels."

"Of course, that will mean there are four Angels walking the Earth," said Nyx.

Tribunal's smile widened. "And the Gates of Heaven and Hell shall be open once more."

Nyx nodded. "All right, what's the second task?"

"Take the Angel you have created to Hell and kill it."

"Kill it?" repeated Nyx, confused. "Angels can't die in Hell. Nothing dies in Hell. It's a place of torment eternal. For something to die there would change the laws of the universe."

"And when one law changes, they are all open to change," said Tribunal, "Including the one that says God cannot be destroyed."

Nyx thought hard about it. It sort of made sense, but not really. If Tribunal said it was right, then it was right. He was God, after all; He should know his own weaknesses.

There's something... Nyx tried to follow the thought, but it slipped away when Tribunal reached across and put His hand on her. "I'm to bring an Angel into being and then kill it?"

"There is a ritual," said Tribunal. "One that allows that which cannot die to be destroyed. The Angel will cease to exist. And when it does, when it breaks the laws of existence, then, truly, can we go to work and destroy God Himself."

"All right," said Nyx. "When do you want me to do this?"

"As soon as possible," said Tribunal. "Call forth the Word and then create your Angel."

"I will," said Nyx, looking closely at the shade that was Tribunal. She could feel the power that radiated from Him, feel the might, but she could not see His intentions. *Are you keeping something from me?*

"Soon, my love," said Tribunal, smiling His shade smile at her, "We shall rule over Heaven and Hell together."

Tribunal came forward and they embraced once more. Once more she became near-delirious in the warm sea of His power. She drank as much in as she could, and His head leaned closer to hers, and from his mouth, to her ear, came the Word.

He had only whispered it, but it was not a word that could be spoken quietly. The moment the Word passed His lips, it brought light, piercing white light so bright it would have blinded any mortal eyes that saw it. The whispered sound of the Word reverberated, growing louder and louder as the light grew stronger, until the bubble that Tribunal had created could no longer hold the Word's power, and it split apart, sending the light and the sound of the Word out in a wave that rippled the very fabric of Limbo.

The Word sunk into Nyx, the reverberations of it threatening to shake her very soul apart, even as the white light burned through her, illuminating every thought, every love and hate and jealousy, every act of cruelty and destruction, every moment of pleasure and pain until every single thing that made up the soul of Nyx was bare for all to see.

The Word faded, the ripples in Limbo stopped, and Nyx was once more able to see Tribunal, standing before her.

"You asked me if I trusted you," He said. "Now you know." He floated closer, and raised a hand in warning. "The Word is power, Nyx. The greatest power in the universe, and it can destroy anyone who uses it carelessly, or for other than its purpose. Do not use it for more than you have been tasked or you could destroy yourself and do more damage than you would have ever dreamed possible."

"I understand," said Nyx, even as she wondered what other purpose the Word might be put to. "I will not."

For the first time since she had arrived, Nyx heard a sound.

Heard was not the right word, of course. She had no ears here, no real form except that of the shade that held her soul in this place, but *sound* was the closest thing she could use to describe what she sensed. It was as if thousands of voices once silent had been raised together. Some were near, some were far, but all cried out.

Tribunal looked into the gray, and nodded. "As I expected."

Nyx followed his gaze and saw the gray roiling, as if she were beneath the surface of a pond of dirty water, and above, something had stirred it up until it heaved and twisted in on itself.

"They are coming," said Tribunal. "All of them."

Nyx saw the souls, then. Thousands had been a poor estimate. Millions would have been closer. Through the grey they came, near-invisible shades, none aware of the others, none knowing anything save WANT. She was about to ask what was happening. Then she understood.

The Word *was* God.

It was not His incarnation; it was not His person or His consciousness. It was not His presence. But it was His essence, and in unleashing it here, Tribunal had brought God's essence to a place where God had never been. The hopeless wanderers that searched all eternity without knowing for what they were searching now knew. They knew what it was they desired, and they came to where they had heard it.

The bubble around them re-appeared, and the first of the shades pushed up against it, then another, then a hundred. They came from all sides and all directions. Shades of hands and faces pressed against the bubble, shades of mouths open and pleading, shades of desire and need palpable in the small space.

"They will crush you," said Tribunal. "The bubble will not hold against all of them and they will find your Angelic flesh and cling to it until your essence disappears. You must go." He touched her arm, and though the power flowed through her, it was nothing compared to the power of the Word he had unleashed. "Do not use the Word except as I have told you."

He kissed her forehead, and with that kiss sent the rest of the information she needed to know. He released her, and watched her fade from Limbo.

Tribunal looked at the souls clamoring against the bubble and laughed. "Don't bother," he said. "God isn't here."

He let the bubble collapse and watched the souls spin frantically about him. They could not touch him, or anything else for that matter. They could not have touched Nyx, had she stayed, but Tribunal had wanted her gone. She had a task to fulfill, and the longer she stayed here, the more questions she would ask, and that would never do.

The bond between an Angel and its creator was one of the strongest in creation. It was why God rarely destroyed his Angels, even those who betrayed Him and rebelled against Him. It was the true reason why He had offered Nyx and Lucifer Hell, rather than ending their existence. It was the reason He had stood back in the battle, and wept as each Angel's essence was scattered to the winds of Heaven.

It was the reason that Nyx, for all her raw power, would find it nearly impossible to destroy the Angel she was going to make.

I will destroy God, thought Tribunal. *I will destroy Him and I will destroy Mankind and I will rule Heaven and Hell in his place.*

And no one will stop me.

*

In a monastery near Carcassonne, Nyx and Persephone watched the sun rise.

Tribunal's touch had always aroused passion in Nyx. Together, they had driven each other to levels of ecstasy that no mortal could have survived. To have Him inside her was one of the greatest pleasures that she had experienced, greater even than that pleasure she and Lucifer used to give each other. This time, though, there had been no touch of His hand, no pressing of flesh to flesh. The energy that filled her soul had only made her more aware of the emptiness in her body. She had been left a purely physical craving that had demanded satisfaction.

She had flown to her Angels first. And when Persephone's and Ishtar's pleasure-giving proved not enough, she had come here.

It was easy to change their appearance and appear as three young girls, lost and alone. Easier still to corrupt the younger monks, whose flesh was the first that Nyx used. Over the course of a week they had worked their way through the monastery, from the youngest novice to the old Abbot, taking them for pleasure, singly, in twos or in threes. Some of the monks were worldly men, who had retired to retreat. Others were virgins, who had no idea how to give pleasure to women. But they had learned, all of them, not only to give pleasure to the three young-seeming girls in their midst, but to take pleasure from each other's bodies, whether the other was a willing participant or not.

The morning before, Nyx had laid her young-seeming body on the main table of the hall, and let all those who wished take their pleasure on her. It had lasted the day and night, and at the end of it she was, if not satisfied, at least satiated. And when the last of the fifty monks had finished his third turn on her, she had risen off the table smiled, and let her true form show.

The monks had ran, horrified, at the sight of her white skin and horned crown and snake's eyes. They screamed when she spread her wings and laughed at them all. She and Ishtar and Persephone drove them to their cells and locked them in. Through the walls she could hear them wailing and praying as they realized how far they had fallen.

It was delightful. But it was not Tribunal.

And now she sat, a glass of the very fine wine that the monks made in her hand, and watched the sunset. Persephone sat beside her, drinking slowly from her own glass.

"So," said Persephone. "Do you want to tell me what that was about?"

Nyx shook her head. "When Ishtar is done."

She tuned her hearing to the monks' cells, isolating their voices one by one until she heard the one that Ishtar had dragged from the hall that morning, whipping him as he went. The man was gasping in pain and pleasure simultaneously, and Ishtar was moaning louder and louder until she cried out in pleasure. The man's gasps stopped suddenly, then Ishtar's whip slashed into flesh a half-dozen times, and the gasps turned to screams.

"I'd say she's done," said Persephone, smiling.

Ishtar, as naked as the others, joined them on the hill. Persephone handed her a glass of wine as she sat beside them.

"And now what, my Queen?" asked Ishtar. "Do we kill them all and burn down their monastery?"

"No," said Nyx. "Let them wallow in their guilt. Let the pain of their broken vows haunt them for a time."

"Then what?" asked Persephone "What do we do, now that Jerusalem is ours?"

Nyx smiled at them. "We make an Angel."

It was rare that she could surprise either Ishtar or Persephone, and Nyx enjoyed immensely the expressions on their faces. She explained it all, explained her plan and Tribunal's and how they would do it.

"Make an Angel," mused Ishtar.

"And kill an Angel," said Persephone, her voice much more foreboding than Ishtar's.

"We have destroyed Angels before, all of us," said Nyx. "This will be no different."

"And what about Hell?" asked Ishtar. "Lucifer has ruled there for a thousand years. I doubt he'll wish to hand over the reins just because you return."

"Don't worry about Lucifer," said Nyx. "He'll fall in line when he learns what's at stake."

Persephone looked doubtful, but nodded. "All right, then, how will we make an Angel?"

Nyx smiled. "I'll let you know when it is time," she said.

"And when will be time?" asked Ishtar.

Nyx rose and her wings spread out. "Soon." She lifted her head, reading the weather and the wind, then raised a hand. Fire danced in it momentarily, before she cast it into the valley of grapes below.

They would not be killed, these monks, but some sort of punishment was in order, and what better than to have them emerge from their cells and see their beloved vineyards destroyed?

"Come," she said as she rose into the sky. "Let's find our Angel."

The three flew off into the early morning light, leaving wails of sorrow and growing flames behind them.

CHAPTER 11

NYX FLEW HIGH above the Mediterranean. The sea below was the spectacular blue that only the Mediterranean offered. The islands were green and lush or sandy or rocky or all three simultaneously. It was, truly, one of the most beautiful places on God's Earth.

Tribunal's Earth soon, thought Nyx. *Tribunal's and mine.*

She didn't know where to land. She didn't know where she should be to bring an Angel into the world. Should it be somewhere beautiful? Somewhere black and bleak? Should she bring it forth in her cave and watch its horror as it realized it was to be a sacrifice?

Can I sacrifice it? She shook her head. She had no idea where the doubt was coming from. *Tribunal told me to do it. He wouldn't have told me to do it if He didn't think I could. So I'll do it and fuck all this self-doubt.*

She flew on, looking for a place of power.

Once the Angel is created, then I have to get it down to Hell and sacrifice it, she told herself. *Tribunal didn't tell me what the ritual is, though.*

The doors between the worlds would re-open when the Angel was created. She could ask him then – would have to ask him then, if she was to do as he bid. *He'll let me know when the time is come.*

First I create the Angel. Everything else follows.

"Oh for fuck's sake stop dithering and do it!" Nyx shouted at herself, startling both Ishtar and Persephone. She looked around her, picked a small island with only ruins and flew down toward it. *I am the Queen of Hell. I can open a portal from anywhere, so I'll damn well open it from here!*

"What are you dithering about?" asked Ishtar. "Not getting cold feet, are you?"

"No!" snapped Nyx, all the while wondering: *What is my problem? This is nothing. One birth. One death. No big deal.*

It is a big deal, Nyx realized. *It's not a birth; it's creation.*

That was what was scaring her. That was what was taking her so long. Any mammal on the planet could give birth. It was messy, bloody, and half the time the young didn't survive. Didn't matter in the slightest. This, though, this was creation. And only God did creation. For her to do so was blasphemy of the highest order.

I don't care! Nyx raged at herself. *I don't! I don't give a flying fuck about God and I don't give a flying ass-fuck about blasphemy! I'm going to destroy God!*

She was still scared.

They flew low over the waters, and Nyx saw people staring up at them from small fishing boats.

"I thought this place was deserted," said Nyx.

In Tribunal's name.

She looked to Ishtar. "Make it deserted."

Ishtar grinned a mouth full of razors at her and banked away, her sword and whip appearing in her hands.

"Where do you want to do this?" asked Persephone.

"The ruins, there," pointed Nyx. "As soon as Ishtar gets back."

They flew low over the lush forest, scattering the birds and the small animals that lived in the trees. The forest gave way to a clearing, and in the midst of it, the tall, round remains of a temple rose up. The proud marble columns and stone walls had been laid low over the centuries, the rocks that made its walls were scattered around it, and creeper vines had long since covered every piece of rock with a layer of green.

Nyx started laughing. *It's one of mine!*

She alighted on the grass that covered the paving stones. The faded and fragmentary remains of murals were just visible in places where the inner wall had been shielded from the elements. What the images had been she couldn't determine from these faint scraps of color. Otherwise, the stone was covered with moss or bare. The altar was still there, but nothing was left of the statue.

"This will do," said Nyx.

"It most will," said Persephone. "Now what?"

"Now," said Nyx, "We wait for Ishtar to finish up, and then we'll be ready."

"Shall I clear the space?" asked Persephone. "It won't take long."

"Do it," said Nyx. She walked over and perched herself on the altar. The stone was warm beneath her backside, and the green all around was more pleasant than she liked to admit. It made her feel safe and cozy. Her priests had been so devoted. And even that young man who'd been there long after the priests had vanished...

The one I killed.

She shoved the thought out of her mind. Today was not about the past.

Persephone moved so fast she was a blur, clearing the stone floor of the weeds and leaves, using the wind from her wings to blow them out of the sanctuary and send them flying into the clearing beyond. She moved a thousand years' debris in minutes, leaving bare stone, a clear altar, and a fire in what was left of the pit.

"Very nice," said Nyx, approvingly. She felt an Angelic presence coming closer. "And here comes Ishtar."

Ishtar landed, a smile on her face and blood splattering her body. "There is nothing human left on the island," she said. "Their boats are sunk, their houses destroyed and their animals scattered."

"Well done," said Nyx, smiling at her. Ishtar's pride was still sorely wounded, she knew, though her flesh had long since healed. "You serve me well, my dear."

"I thank you, my lady," said Ishtar, bowing. "Now. How do you create an Angel?"

"With willpower and the Word," said Nyx.

"The Word?" Persephone's eyes widened. "*THE* Word?"

"The very one," said Nyx. "And when the Angel comes into being, the doors of Heaven and Hell will open once more. We'll be able to talk to Tribunal directly."

"And God will be able to come for us," said Persephone. "Or Michael."

Nyx shook her head. "No. Tribunal promised me. He'll keep anyone from coming after us until after the Angel is dead."

"All right," said Ishtar. "Then create it so we can get down to Hell and kill it properly."

"I'm going to!" Nyx snapped. *Why am I angry?* "Sorry. I'm feeling…odd about this."

"Angels don't create," said Persephone. "At least, we haven't so far."

"So, another first for you, then," said Ishtar. "First to lead a rebellion against God, first to be cast from Heaven, and now, first to create. Go for it."

There was something in Ishtar's tone that Nyx didn't like at all, but she let it lie. She had too much to think about just now. *Maybe I should have done this alone.*

"Willpower and the word," she murmured to herself as she closed her eyes. She envisioned her Angel, stepping forward, complete and whole, fresh from creation, with all the knowledge and strength that God had given his Angels. Only he won't be his. He'll be mine.

The Angel was going to be male. Of that Nyx was certain. She was creating it and she could make it however she wanted. All that was needed was the Word.

So say it, you wimp, she told herself. *Say it now.*

She said it, and the world changed.

The sheer force of it knocked Ishtar and Persephone off their feet, sending them flying back against the wall. The island itself shook, as if it wanted to tear itself from it's foundations and float away into the Mediterranean. The waters around the island boiled, sending out giant waves that would soon crash into the shores for miles around, some taking down cliffs, others washing away entire towns.

Around the world, those who worshipped God felt a stirring: a sense of power that they could not understand, and the sudden, sure knowledge of His existence. The followers of Nyx around the world felt something similar—something powerful and ancient and strengthening that swept away any fears they had of her plans and made them ready to embrace them.

A dozen wars stopped for no reason.

A dozen more started in other places.

And on the island itself, immersed in the massive power of the Word, Nyx envisioned an Angel coming into being. She felt her very being stretching and expanding, as if she was too small a vessel for the task and had to be enlarged to do the job.

The fear rose up in her once more. *Who am I to do this?* She forced the question aside, and kept her attention on her idea of an Angel. She envisioned how he would look, how he would act, his strengths and talents, how he would serve her.

The world over the island became brighter and brighter, and all three Angels screamed as the power of the Word laid them open, blasting through flesh and bone to find and lay bare their very essences, revealing every thought, every action, every hurt, every joy, in a sudden, grand panoply of pain and ecstasy that nearly ripped Ishtar and Persephone's minds apart.

It is so much more powerful here, Nyx realized. *So much stronger that it was in Sheol.*

Here, in the created world. On God's earth.

Mine. The Earth is mine, now.

The white light began to fade. The earth stopped shaking and the birds and animals that had been sent scurrying through the forest settled once more into hiding. Around the world, things returned slowly to normal. And on the island, Nyx regained her vision. Then blinked in astonishment.

The collapsed temple was whole again. The roof soared overhead, and the murals were once more whole and bright and beautiful. The statue of her in the middle was restored, as smooth and shapely as the day it was placed there, and the altar cleaned and polished to perfection. All the debris and wreckage of the centuries had vanished.

"Wow," said Persephone.

"Where's the Angel?" asked Ishtar.

"I don't…" Nyx sent her mind questing through the world, looking for an Angelic presence. "I don't know. It's not out there."

"It didn't work?" said Persephone, sadness filling her. "Why didn't it work?"

"Because Angels can't create," snapped Ishtar. "God doesn't let us create. And there's no way He'd let us create an Angel."

"It has to have worked," said Nyx, sliding off her altar. She felt weak and dizzy and nauseated. Still she pushed her consciousness outward, circling the planet with her mind. "It can't have failed."

Persephone caught her as she started to fall.

*

Nyx awoke hungry.

She was an Angel. She was not used to being hungry. She could eat, certainly, and enjoyed many of the foods of the Earth.

She did not need to eat, however, and so to feel ravenously hungry was both shocking and horrifying.

It must have been the Word, she reasoned. *Using it probably takes a lot of energy. So my body needs to replenish.*

She opened her eyes and found herself lying on a bed of leaves and flowers, with blankets wrapped around her. She was outside the temple, in the warmth of the Mediterranean late afternoon sun. The sky was a deep blue. The only sounds were birds, bees and the low swish of the waves. Persephone and Ishtar were both watching her intently, and both jumped when her eyes opened.

"Are you all right?" demanded Persephone. "Are you hurt?"

"I don't think so," said Nyx. She pushed herself into a sitting position and groaned. "My stomach feels a bit tender." She rubbed her hand over her abdomen. "It's swollen." She shook her head. "And I'm hungry."

"Hungry?" repeated Ishtar. "Angels don't get hungry."

"Well, apparently, after they say the Word, they do." Nyx pushed herself to her feet.

"What do you want to eat?" asked Persephone.

"Anything," said Nyx. "And it doesn't need to be cooked first, either."

The Angels sped off.

Persephone came back first with grapes. Nyx devoured them without spitting the seeds out. Ishtar came back with fish from the destroyed village below and Nyx ate that, too. It was delicious in a wholly different way than food usually was, and it wasn't enough. She spread her wings and flew into the sky, aware by the drag that her belly was even more swollen. She spotted a school of fish and dove into the water, grabbing at them with both hands and tearing them apart, shoving the torn and ripped flesh down her throat. The water became murky with blood and guts, and soon larger predators began to approach. She spotted half a dozen sharks and swam toward them, her wings propelling her through the water as easily as they had the air. The sharks shied away, but Nyx caught one and began devouring it on the spot as it thrashed helplessly. The other sharks circled them, looking for their own opportunity to gorge. Nyx killed and ate six more, and with each one she ingested, her belly bulged more.

She had finished her sixth shark when she realized what was happening to her.

Screaming, Nyx launched herself out of the water. Her swollen belly, now larger than a pregnant cow's, made it near impossible to fly. She screamed for Ishtar and Persephone, who dove down and hauled her into the air, flying her back to the island, where they laid her once more down on the bed of leaves and flowers.

"Fuck me!" Nyx screamed in fury. "God fuck me! Bastard! Asshole! Pig-fucking—. AAAAAGGGGHHHH!!!"

"What's happening?" demanded Ishtar, adding to Persephone, "If she dies here then the other Angels will come and we're fucked."

"Not... dying..." gasped Nyx. "Fucking... pregnant! AHHH!!!" Her stomach shifted and swelled even further.

"Pregnant?" repeated Persephone. "We're going to have a baby Angel?"

"NNNNNGGGGGGHHHUUUUGGGRRRR!" Nyx drew in a breath. "Not we, goddammit. Me! And not a baby. Angels can't be babies."

"They can't be pregnant, either," said Ishtar, staring at her stomach. "Fucking hell, Nyx, what have you done?"

"GET ME FOOD!" Nyx screamed. "ALL THE FOOD! NOW!!!"

Persephone took off so fast the air shook with the sound of her breaking the sound barrier. Ishtar stared in horror as Nyx's stomach continued to swell, then she, too, took off.

Nyx was ravenous when they returned. Ishtar came first, bringing back three dead sheep. Nyx devoured them, flesh, bones and all, and still her stomach swelled. It pushed up her breasts, and hung down her legs, and she could feel whatever was inside it moving and squirming. It hurt like a dagger poking into her each time it moved. And still her stomach kept growing.

Persephone landed with an entire roast ox in each hand, and the smell of it nearly drove Nyx insane. Persephone handed the first one over and Nyx tore through it, leaving only grease behind. Nyx's belly was now so large she could no longer stand; could barely sit up. Still she kept eating.

"MORE!" Nyx screamed. "MORE!!!"

The two Angels flew off again, and to Nyx's surprise, were back before an hour had passed. Hanging between their two bodies, thirty feet long, was the squirming body of a small fin whale. Nyx's mouth started salivating even before it had hit the ground. She tore into it with gusto, as her body swelled larger and larger.

There's no way I can be eating this, Nyx thought as she ripped through the flesh and bones of the whale. *No one can eat this much food. Not even the whales eat this much food.*

When the last of the whale was gone, she felt full. To her surprise, she had not become as big as the whale itself, though she should have. She was huge, though, her belly as large as the entire rest of her body. She could not even begin to sit up, pinned beneath the weight of her own flesh. She was sated, though, and that was all that mattered to her.

"How...how are you?" asked Persephone. "Do you need another one?"

"No," said Nyx. "I'm fine." What little she could see of her body was covered in blood and filth. "Clean me."

The other two had a quick discussion, then cradled Nyx between them and flew her down to the ocean. Together they washed her swollen, roiling body, watching with horror as something pushed at her from the inside. It took longer than Nyx would have thought possible, but they cleaned her and brought her up to the temple again. They lay her in her nest of grass and flowers in the sun until she was dry.

Nyx lay there, waiting, feeling the pain of the Angel moving inside her and wondering what was going to happen next. Angels could not give birth. Their bodies were designed for pleasure and joy, not gestation. There was no way an Angel could leave her body as a human infant might.

So how will it get out? she wondered.

God surely did not go through this to make Angels.

The sun was just beginning to set when Nyx started screaming.

"What the fuck?" demanded Ishtar, spinning to see who was attacking.

"It's coming out!" screamed Nyx. "It's coming out!"

"How?" yelled Ishtar. "That's not going to fit!"

"It's not coming out there!" screamed Nyx and the first claw ripped through her flesh from the inside. She was still an Angel, though, and her body healed as fast as it was hurt. Every time the claws ripped at her from the inside, her body healed itself. And every time Nyx screamed with the pain.

Dammit, I am tougher than this, she thought. *I fought fucking Archangel Michael and I've been near killed a dozen times why does this HUUUUURRRRRTTTT!!!*

The creature inside her tried to tear its way out again, and she could no longer form a rational thought. For the next five hours she screamed and squirmed as the thing within struggled to free itself. It didn't help. There was nothing she could do to speed the process, and nothing the thing inside her could do to escape.

"She is fucked," said Ishtar, watching Nyx open her mouth to scream for the hundredth time. The noise didn't bother Ishtar at all. She had heard worse – had caused worse – in Hell, and in truth she was rather enjoying the agony it was causing Nyx. But then, Nyx had left her in agony for sixty-six years. This, as far as Ishtar was concerned, was a good start. "She's healing too fast for the thing to get out."

"We have to help her."

"If she was human she'd push it out her twat," said Ishtar. "Since she's not, there's not much we can do."

Persephone's eyes narrowed. She drew her sword and, with a thought, shrunk it into a curved, razor-sharp blade. "There is one thing," she said.

"Wait until sunrise," advised Ishtar. "You can see what you're doing better."

"I can see through the darkness of Hell," Persephone returned. "This isn't even dark."

"Wait anyway," said Ishtar. "See if it can get out by itself."

"I'm not sure we should," said Persephone.

"Have you dealt with this sort of thing before?" asked Ishtar.

"No, and neither have you."

"True, but when humans and animals give birth it takes time, so let's see what happens by dawn. Maybe her body has to change." *And that way I can listen to the bitch scream a while longer.*

When dawn came, Nyx was still screaming.

"Guess I was wrong," said Ishtar. "Go for it."

Persephone stepped forward and with a quick cut, sliced open the huge bulging mass that was Nyx's stomach.

Silver blood sprayed everywhere, rising out of Nyx's body like a fountain as the layers of flesh pulled apart. Something tall with bright red hair pulled itself out of her stomach and launched itself into the air, silver ichor splattering from it as it rose. The excess flesh on Nyx's body immediately began retreating, pulling in on itself even as it sought to knit itself back together. Nyx screamed once more then, to her own surprise, blacked out.

*

Lucifer was torturing Ninurta, a pretty male Angel and one still loyal to Nyx, when he felt the world change.

It was odd, he had thought, that some of Nyx's Angels still refused to show proper obeisance, even though a thousand years had passed. Some of Nyx's Angels had even tried to rebel against him.

Lucifer switched from his own form to his dragon form, which was three times his size and which made the Angel scream.

Lucifer's legion – the 666th, purged of all Nyx loyalists – had destroyed the rebellion, of course. The leaders had been tossed into the Lake of Fire, their arms, legs and wings weighted with the heaviest of Hell-stone, and left there to burn and writhe in their agony. The lesser ones were staked out on the fields of Hell, tortured until they were ready to admit Lucifer as their Lord and Master.

Ninurta was one of the lesser ones. Slim of body and limb, with olive skin and dark hair, Ninurta's fighting prowess had earned him him a place in the 666th and made him a War God in Mesopotamia. Ninurta had never had it in him to be a leader, but had cut down a dozen of Lucifer's Angels before being overwhelmed.

Lucifer had been sure Ninurta was close to breaking when he had the Angel dragged to his castle. Ninurta still resisted though, still refused to open his mind to Lucifer and end his suffering, even as Lucifer had him staked out face down in a brazier of Hellfire .

No matter, Lucifer h*ad thought*. *The strong ones are the most fun to break.*

Lucifer was about rip open Ninurta's belly and pour Hellfire into the cut when the world changed.

Ninurta's screaming turned to weeping. Assuming his own form, Lucifer walked away, saying, "Cut him to pieces. Slowly," over his shoulder. The surrounding demons fell on the Angel with glee, and Ninurta's screams began anew. Lucifer didn't care.

He stepped out of his castle and onto the mountain, looking up at the sky. The portal to Earth was there again. He could feel it. It was ready to open at his command.

"At last," said Lucifer. He felt like a predator too long denied its prey, prey that had been suddenly released to the hunt. The new Angel was born. Heaven and Hell were open again and he, Lucifer, would rule Hell and Earth.

One of Lucifer's small red shrikes flew up and hovered in front of him. When it spoke, it was with Tribunal's voice.

"The time has come, Lucifer," said Tribunal's voice. "Remember your promise."

Lucifer grinned. "I have not forgotten. Not at all."

A thought brought his armor over his body, and the great whip into his hand. "66th!" he shouted, and his voice echoed throughout Hell. "Come to me! It is time to pay that bitch Nyx once and for all!"

From across Hell he heard the sound of ten thousand wings flapping as five thousand Angels took to the air. Lucifer laughed and spread his own great black wings. Rising high into the sky he flew toward the Lake of Fire and the portal to earth that floated above it.

*

Nyx groaned and opened her eyes. They didn't focus properly, and all she saw was blurs of color and light, and in their midst, a streak of red and white that glowed in her wrecked vision.

Nyx closed her eyes and let them heal, then opened them again.

She was inside her temple, and sunlight was streaming in through the windows, sparkling off the murals that had become fresh and new when she had said the Word. Images of plenty, of grain and fruit, meat and of wine, mingled with images of dancing and lovemaking. The light that shone on them seemed to make the fields of grain ripple and the leaves on the trees move in an unseen breeze.

Of course, I could still just be messed up.

She pulled her gaze down and saw the Angel, its white glow lighting up the room.

It was supposed to be a boy, Nyx thought. *It was supposed to be Descended.*

The Angel wasn't either. She stood where Nyx's statue had stood, her long, white wings folded over its naked body. Her hair was flaming red and went halfway down her back; her skin was the purest white save for the red of her lips and the tips of her perfect breasts. Her eyes were a piercing blue that looked right through Nyx's soul.

She's perfect, thought Nyx, her heart filling with a love she hadn't felt since she had been cast out of Heaven. *A pure, perfect Angel.*

I can't kill her.

The realization made Nyx gasp. Everything had changed. She had changed. The very thought of killing her Angel made her sick. The thought of anyone killing her Angel made her furious. Nyx struggled to her feet, trying to reach the Angel before Ishtar or Persephone. *No one will touch her. No one will hurt her. Ever.*

It hurt, standing up, so much so that Nyx nearly collapsed again. She looked down and saw the scar on her belly, red and raw and a foot wide, though it was shrinking. The muscles underneath felt as if they had been shredded. She forced herself to ignore it. Her body was still healing and it would take time.

"Are you all right?" asked Persephone.

Nyx spun, the motion making her cry out in pain and nearly causing her to fall over. Persephone and Ishtar were both standing behind her, both unclothed.

"Don't either of you go near her," Nyx growled. "Hear me?"

"We aren't," said Ishtar, looking confused. "You're the one who has to sacrifice her."

I can't sacrifice her! Nyx backed up, making sure she was between her Angel and the other two Descended. Friends, once. Now maybe enemies.

"Nyx?" Persephone's voice took on a new tone, curious and worried at the same time. "What's going on?"

"When do we take her to Hell?" asked Ishtar. "The gates are open again. I can feel it."

Nyx realized that she could feel it, too. Hell itself was pulling at her, calling to her in a way she had not felt for a thousand years. Before, she hadn't realized how strong a pull it had, but now that she'd spent centuries without feeling it, it was impossible to ignore.

And her muscles were still healing.

"Nyx," repeated Ishtar. "When do we take her to Hell?"

Nyx took an involuntary step backwards, and felt the cool touch of her Angel's hand on her shoulder.

"Greetings, my Creator," said the Angel, and in her voice Nyx could hear the tones of the heavenly choir that sang God's praises to all of Heaven. The sound of it made her knees weak. "I am Epiphaneia."

Almost against her will, Nyx turned. Her eyes met the eyes of her Angel, and the Angel's mind opened to her without reservation. Without thinking, Nyx opened her own mind, and together they saw into each other's souls. Nyx saw only beauty, warmth, hope, love, and Epiphaniea's desire to serve her creator.

Epiphaneia saw the aeons Nyx had spent in heavenly joy. She saw how terrible the decision was to defy God and the bloody horror that was the battle for Heaven. She saw Nyx's Descent into Hell and the agony of a thousand years in the Lake of Fire. She saw the battle for control of Hell and the cruelty that followed. She saw every evil, wicked and unwholesome thing Nyx had done on Earth and in Hell. She saw Nyx's great love for Tribunal, her agreement with him, and all the pain and suffering that followed. She saw how she had come into being and why.

And at the end of it, when their minds separated, Epiphaneia's eyes were bright with tears. She stepped forward, pulled Nyx into her embrace and said, "I am so, so sorry."

Her arms were warm and gentle, and at her touch Nyx felt a sense of peace go through her that she had not felt since…

"What the fuck is going on?" said Ishtar. "We need to get that thing down to Hell before God finds out what you've done."

"No," said Nyx.

"No?" Ishtar's face blazed with rage. "What the fuck do you mean, 'no?' We've been fighting for a thousand years for this!"

Nyx let go of Epiphaneia and turned to face the other two. "I can't let anyone hurt her."

Persephone looked into Nyx's eyes, then opened her mind to Nyx's. Nyx let her in. Persephone saw what Nyx had seen and more importantly, felt what Nyx had felt.

Persephone sighed. "Well, shit. Now what?"

"Now nothing!" yelled Ishtar. "Now we take that sniveling thing to Hell, we perform Tribunal's ritual and we get to go to his Paradise!" She saw the resolve harden in Nyx's face. "Fucking pig-demons, Nyx, it's for Tribunal! Your lover! Your leader and savior and master. Remember him? Tribunal?!"

Nyx did, and with every mention of his name she felt herself pushed to obedience, moved to grab Epiphaneia and open the gates to Hell and take her down. Tribunal had told her what to do, and in her soul she could feel him, urging her to do it. She turned and looked to her Angel.

"I am yours, my Creator," said Epiphaneia. "I will do whatever you command."

I can't.

"You heard her!" said Ishtar. "Command the bitch down to Hell so we can get on with it."

"NO!" Nyx spun back, her armor covering her and her blade and whip in her hand before she completed the turn. "NO ONE WILL HURT HER, YOU HEAR ME?" She glanced over her shoulder. "No one is allowed to hurt you. No one takes you to Hell. Understand?"

Epiphaneia looked confused. "But that is my purpose, is it not? To be sacrificed so the Descended can achieve Paradise?"

Just like Tribunal? asked a little voice in Nyx's head. *A sacrifice for someone else's plans?*

Nyx told the voice in her head to fuck off. "Not anymore."

"Then what am I here for?"

Nyx had no answer to that. "It doesn't matter. You're not going to Hell, and if anyone tries to take them there you stop them, understand?"

"I obey," said Epiphaneia, and armor flowed around her body. It was not the white armor of Heaven's Angels, nor the black armor of the descended. It was green and brown and grew around her like vines. It was patterned with leaves, from oak and maple and gingko and baobab and palm, and it hung gently on her body, covering her without either the overt sexuality of the Descended's armor or the asexual blankness of Heaven's. It was the armor of Earth, Nyx realized. Armor of Epiphaneia's true world. The blade that appeared in her hand was straight and true and shone like steel, though Nyx knew it was something far more powerful. "I am ready."

"You think that will help if Michael comes down?" demanded Ishtar. "You couldn't even stop me!"

"Yes," said Epiphaneia. "I can."

Ishtar's own armor flowed around her in an instant and her sword leapt into her hand.

"NO!" shouted Nyx. "I forbid it!"

"You forbid…" Ishtar screamed in rage and punched the wall, smashing the plaster beneath her fists and sending cracks up the height of the wall. "You're killing us all!"

Before Nyx could answer, the ground beneath them rumbled, then screamed, and the air filled with a brimstone stench that could only come from one thing.

Ishtar, despite her rage, instinctively backed up until she was beside Nyx. Persephone did the same as her own armor flowed around her. "Hell's open," she said.

"I know," said Nyx, and because she was Queen of Hell, she felt the first of the Angels crawl their way out of Hell. Unlike Nyx, these Angels were not injured or tired. These Angels were fresh and battle ready. And there were hundreds of them. Then Nyx sensed one who was far too familiar. "Lucifer is leading them."

"They're coming for us," said Ishtar. "Fuck, Nyx, they're coming for us!"

"No," said Epiphaneia. "They're coming for me."

"Get in the air," said Nyx, "Before…"

The roof of the temple blew into pieces, and Lucifer's legion descended on them with the falling rocks.

"Fly!" screamed Nyx, launching herself into the air.

It had been a long time since Nyx had fought an Angel, let alone an army of them. Her stomach muscles still screamed with every action, and she knew she wasn't anywhere near her full strength.

I am the Queen of Hell, she thought, *and I'll burn in the Lake before I let that bastard win!*

She parried the first Angel's blade and with a clean swipe, cut him in half.

The Angel screamed and fell to Earth, his body desperately trying to regenerate. Nyx was surprised enough by it that she nearly missed her next block. *I must have absorbed the power from Tribunal,* she thought as she lashed out at the second Angel. That Angel had the good sense to dodge, but was stupid enough to try again and Nyx spitted him through the heart. He exploded in a rush of silver dust and Nyx inhaled his power, even as her whip cracked out to slash the wings off another Angel. A dozen others surrounded her, hacking with their blades and lashing with their whips. And from above, more Angels were coming.

Persephone and Ishtar fought side by side, slicing through limbs and cutting into flesh with their swords as their whips ripped open faces and tore feathers from the wings of the Angels. Sheer weight of numbers was forcing them back down towards the ground. Persephone opened her mind to Ishtar, sending, "Follow me!" but Ishtar's mind stayed closed to her. Persephone screamed, "FUCK!" at the top of her voice, then dove down, away from her opponents, through the temple door and out into the freedom of the sky beyond.

Epiphaneia whirled in the air, her green armor glowing like an emerald in a sea of blood and oil. She had no whip, but her blade moved as fast as any of the Angels, and she fought with a calm, deadly ferocity. Her blade cleaved through the armor of the Angels almost as easily as Nyx's did. The Angels tried to keep their distance, flicking at her with whips, but more and more Angels were pouring into the temple, and their numbers kept pushing the others downward.

"We have to get out!" Nyx screamed, switching to wide swings of her blade that scythed through the Angels near her in a rain of blood, guts, feathers and ichor. "Follow me up! Fight your way up!"

"Tell that to that traitorous bitch!" screamed Ishtar. "She flew out the door!"

Probably smart of her, Nyx thought. She won't desert us, though. Not Persephone.

As if her thoughts were a prophecy, she heard Persephone's battle-scream from above. A boulder slammed down through the ranks of the Angels above, breaking black-feathered wings and bouncing off backs and skulls. Nyx used the space it created to surge upward. Epiphaneia fought towards her, her blade creating its own rain of ichor and guts. Ishtar broke free a moment later and managed to join the other two. Another boulder rained down and for a moment Nyx had a glimpse of Persephone, her blade and whip flailing. Then a pack of Angels slammed into her, driving her out of sight. Nyx screamed and hacked harder at the Angels around them, trying to force a path clear.

Still the Angels poured down from above.

Ishtar missed one cut and an Angel slammed into her, knocking her off-kilter. A second Angel, then a third and a fourth slammed into her, smashing her downward. Nyx knew she couldn't afford to stop flying upward, knew that Epiphaneia's safety was entirely dependent on them breaking free from Lucifer's legion of Angels. She hacked and slashed, her sword a blur even to Angel eyes as she fought her way up. Limbs, torsos and heads all flew apart under the strength of her sword. The Angels' armor, usually enough to stop all but the most powerful attack, parted like water before her blade.

Lucifer bellowed something above her, and a rock as wide as the temple ceiling crashed down on all of them.

There was no escape for any of the Angels in the temple. A hundred Descended Angels smashed downward under several thousand tons of rock while above, Lucifer and the five hundred Angels he'd used to move the boulder watched in glee. The shock of the boulder hitting the ground ruptured the walls of the temple and it split open, shooting bits of Angels everywhere as some of their bodies exploded beneath the weight of their burden.

At the bottom of the pile of bodies, Nyx and Epiphaneia lay side by side, their flesh and bones crushed by the boulder and the many bodies piled above them. The pressure was immense, and Nyx could hear Epiphaneia's screams before the weight on them crushed the air from both of them.

Hours passed. The pain was even more intense than giving birth had been. Every bone in Nyx's body was being crushed. Her skull was being compressed to the point she could feel it reshaping itself, and cracking along the seams. Clawing with her fingers she tried to dig into the earth under her, trying to clear some space – any space at all – if it meant she could escape the pain.

Above her, she heard hammering.

She was still conscious, still struggling to find space when the pile of rock above her shifted. She heard a scream, then another.

Someone was pulling bodies from the rock, tearing some of the Angels apart as they freed them. The smell of brimstone was harsher now.

An hour later her head began to reform itself as more rock was pulled away and more Angels pulled from the pile. Epiphaneia was able to draw breath again, and was wailing with pain. Nyx scrabbled her fingers towards her Angel, and eventually managed to touch the other Angel's arm through the debris.

Another hour passed. More weight lifted. More screams of pain from above, and Epiphaneia's whimpering beside her. Nyx found herself crying, not from her own pain, which was nothing new, but from hearing her Angel's pain. This was an agony she'd never experienced before and the immensity of it was beyond her comprehension. But understanding or not didn't matter: she had to help her Angel. She had to protect her Angel. That, above all. But she could do nothing.

The weight shifted again, threatening to once more crush Nyx's skull. She reached out further with her fingers and tried to wrap them around Epiphaneia's arm as the other Angel's wails turned into screams.

"Got her!" someone shouted, and Epiphaneia was yanked away from Nyx's questing fingers. Nyx heard Lucifer roaring something, then the pressure on her and the screaming around her got worse and all Nyx could think about was the pain. Then came blackness.

*

It was dark when Persephone came back to consciousness. She could hear screaming from somewhere nearby, but couldn't say where.

We must have failed, she thought. *Good fight, though.*

She had killed six, she remembered. She'd gutted and chopped the limbs of a dozen more, but those would heal or grow back so they didn't count.

She'd been stabbed a dozen times, cut a dozen more, before she'd finally been spitted through the spine. She'd managed to kill that one, Persephone remembered, and had healed enough to fly erratically away from the temple. Two dozen of them had pursued her, hacking and slicing into her flesh, cutting off her whip arm and sword hand, hacking one of her legs nearly off and finally taking her wings. She'd fallen to Earth, then, and they'd followed, stabbing her a hundred times as she lay there.

I should be dead, Persephone thought. *Stupid luck, I suppose.*

She stood up and discovered that her arm and hand had grown back, and that her leg was almost whole again. She stumbled a bit as she walked, but she was grateful she was still able to do that. Her wings were still destroyed, and the pain of them healing made her wince with every step.

It was a long, slow walk out of the forest and into the clearing where the temple once stood. It was a ruin again, the walls bowed out, the ground littered with ichor, feathers, limbs and guts, and strewn with rubble. And from inside the temple, she could hear screams of pain from dozens of Angels, crushed beneath the rubble.

Lucifer must have dropped half the island on them, Persephone thought. *Poor bastards.*

She opened her mind for Nyx and Ishtar but couldn't feel anything. She thought about opening up a portal to Hell, but realized she didn't really want to go back. She stood, staring at the body-filled rubble of the temple and sighed. *Well, at least it's something while I figure out what to do.*

She drew her sword and re-shaped it to become a short, thick blade, perfect for driving through rock. She would dig the Angels out, and kill them all for what they had done to Nyx.

*

Nyx came back to consciousness in agony. Her skull was shifting, assuming its proper shape, and the pain was excruciating. She managed to open her eyes and saw the empty place beside her where Epiphaneia had lay. Tears welled up in her eyes. Her Angel was gone. Her Angel. Not God's. She had created her, and now she had lost her. Nyx's heart threatened to tear itself in two with the pain of that loss. *I had no idea. No idea at all. I thought I knew love. I knew nothing.*

There was much less screaming, she realized. And even as she thought it another voice was silenced. The weight on her was also diminishing. She could inhale, after a fashion, well enough to scream, if she wanted. *Not that there's any point in that,* she thought. *It's only pain.*

There was the sound of metal striking stone, then flesh, and another of the screamers was silenced.

What are they doing up there?

The sounds continued. Metal struck stone again and again and every time it did the load on top of Nyx grew lighter. Every now and then, the metal drove into someone's flesh, and another screamer was silenced.

Then the rock above her head split open, and light poured down on her face.

Nyx blinked and tried to look up. A shadow blocked her

view, and a moment later she heard Persephone's startled voice saying, "Holy fuck! Nyx?"

It took another hour for Persephone to free Nyx, and then she only managed by cutting off both Nyx's legs at the knees and dragging her out. Nyx gritted her teeth, refusing to make a sound as her body repaired itself. She was much stronger now, she realized, her limbs growing back so rapidly she could feel them shooting out of her body. It hurt more than the actual cutting off had, but she still made no sound as she healed. Persephone opened her mind to Nyx and let her see all that she knew. She also read Nyx's thoughts and learned what had happened to Epiphaneia.

"We have to go after her," said Nyx, her voice gravelly and weak. "He's taking her to Hell."

"He's already taken her to Hell," said Persephone. "I don't know how long I was unconscious. And I've been bashing apart this rock for three days. She's already down there."

"She isn't dead," said Nyx. "I would know if she were dead."

"You can't walk yet," said Persephone.

"Soon," said Nyx, looking down at her legs. They were nearly back to their normal size. She watched as they finished growing, then tried standing. It took a few tries, but she got to her feet.

"He's got all the legions in Hell on his side now," said Persephone.

"No," said Nyx. "He *thinks* he does. Once I'm there, I can probably rally most of them. Then they can fight each other while I spit the bastard and get Epiphaneia back."

"If you say so," said Persephone.

Nyx glared at her. "You don't think it will work."

Persephone shrugged. "Probably not, but I'm going with you anyway."

"Good," said Nyx. "What about Ishtar?"

"I haven't seen a sign of her," Persephone said. "I can't feel her anywhere either. She's either dead or in Hell."

"Fuck." Nyx flexed her healed wings, testing them. She was nearly at full strength. It had happened incredibly quickly even for her. *Tribunal's strength,* she realized. *It's still flowing in me. Good.*

Nyx flew up into the air, pulling out her sword and whip as she did. Persephone followed her a moment later, her own weapons in her hands.

"Are you ready?" asked Nyx.

"Ready," said Persephone.

Nyx's whip cracked through the air, and below them a huge, jagged crack appeared in the Earth. It stayed that way for a moment, then the ground around it began shaking and the crack pushed itself wider and wider apart until it became a jagged-edged pit, sucking at the earth around it and pulling the Angels downward.

"At least we can't die down there," said Persephone.

"Which is good," said Nyx, "because I'm going to make Lucifer wish he had."

They stepped off the edge and began the long descent into Hell.

*

Somewhere between Heaven and Earth, Arcana realized she was falling.

She blinked twice, her momentarily-lost concentration

restored, and spread her wings, changing her descent from a tumbling, stone-like plummet to a screaming dive. She reveled in the speed of it. The rush of aether slipping past her became a rush of air, slipping in and around the white feathers of her wings, giving her buoyancy and pushing her from all sides, hissing through her armor. Arcana grinned, exulting in the sensation as the white cloudy spaces between Earth and Heaven gave way to the blue sky of Earth. She could see Jerusalem, could see the towns around it. She spread out her awareness, seeking Caelum and Orion.

They weren't there.

Arcana frowned and spread her awareness wider. She and they were to be the only three Angels to walk the Earth, now that Jesus was back in Heaven. The other two had been sent on ahead, and should have been waiting.

So where are they? she wondered.

At the edge of her awareness, somewhere in the Mediterranean sea, she sensed agony beyond all reason. Angels – no, Descended Angels – screaming in pain.

They're not supposed to be here, Arcana thought. *None of them are supposed to be here. What's happening?*

As she listened, the voices became less. It was as if their presence were a circle of candles, and as if each was being snuffed out, one at a time. She looked for Caelum and Orion again, but could not sense them anywhere. Frowning, she changed her trajectory and aimed for the island where the screams originated. She streaked across the sea, air curling off her wing-tips as she flew.

Somewhere on the island, a portal to Hell opened.

Arcana increased her speed and altitude, trying to see what

was happening. Her senses picked out two Angels, and her eyes widened in surprise. *Nyx? What is Nyx doing here?*

She stooped and dove, braking with her wings at the last minute and slamming into the Earth with enough force to shake the ground around her.

The portal to Hell closed , taking away Arcana's sense of Nyx and her companion, leaving her on the island with only the cries of the injured Descended to keep her company.

Arcana straightened, then gripped her sword. She walked towards the pile of rubble where the Angels screamed.

One way or another, Arcana thought, *I'm going to find out what's going on here.*

CHAPTER 12

IN HIS BEDROOM, in his castle on the mountain overlooking the Plains of Hell, Lucifer lay back on the bed and stared at the Angel nailed to his wall.

She stared back with unblinking blue eyes; eyes that made him uneasy. Nobody had looked at him that boldly since Nyx left.

She had to be in agony. He had driven Hell-stone spikes through her wrists, ankles, wings and belly, pinning her to the wall like an oversized insect. Even so, she showed no signs of pain. She just stared.

Lucifer had thought, when he nailed her up, that it would be amusing watching her. So far, he found her more disconcerting than anything else.

"Come on, Tribunal," he said to the empty air. "Come tell me how to kill this one. I'm growing bored with her."

Tribunal didn't answer, and still Epipheneia stared at Lucifer, not blinking, not speaking, her mind closed to him.

He growled at her and went to find a soul to torture.

*

There was more than one way into Hell, and Nyx knew them all.

Not that it would necessarily help. An Angel could always sense other Angels, and there was no way that Lucifer would not be aware of her the moment she entered Hell. Knowing an Angel was in Hell and knowing where in Hell she was were two different things, though. If Lucifer wanted to find her, he would have to mobilize Hell's legions to look for her, and that would take time. He would find her sooner or later, certainly, but the longer it took, the more likely it was that she could find and free her Angel, first. Then she would deal with Lucifer.

Pity I can't actually kill him, Nyx thought. *It would make things so much easier.*

But nothing dies in Hell, and so even after he was castrated, disembowelled, quartered and beheaded – which was just the start of what Nyx had planned – Lucifer would still be alive.

On the bright side, I'll get to do it over and over and over again.

The descent to Hell was long and slow. Many Angels stooped at this point, folding their wings and diving down, racing past the souls falling to the Lake of Fire. Nyx kept her wings wide and her speed slow. She had ripped open the portal in anger, but even as she fell from Earth to this place between worlds, she was already planning.

I know nothing of what has gone on, here, Nyx thought. *For all I know, he has blocked all the entrances save the Lake of Fire.*

It wasn't likely, though. Nyx had spent thousands of years exploring Hell before the first human souls fell into it. She had learned every nook, cranny and crevice. She knew where the demons made their lairs, and where there lived creatures even the demons would not face. She knew the depths of the Pit, a gaping chasm in the lowest part of Hell that had no bottom. In the early days several Angels, despairing at their separation from God, had thrown themselves into the Pit. Those who came back spoke of darkness so deep even eyes used to Hell could not penetrate it. One Angel had let himself fall for a hundred years before winging his way back up. He had found nothing.

Nyx, on the other hand, had found an entrance to Hell hidden within the walls of the Pit.

If I can get in through that entrance, I can start rallying my troops. With luck, I'll get enough to keep Lucifer busy while I rescue my Angel, Nyx thought. *Then, he's mine.*

"So," said Persephone, flying beside her. "Do we have a plan?"

"Sort of," said Nyx.

"Is it 'charge in and kill the bastard?' because that was the one I was going with."

Nyx smiled in spite of herself. "A little more than that. The bastard probably has the 666th surrounding him and my Angel. And if he doesn't when we arrive, he will before we can figure out where she is and reach him."

"True," said Persephone. She hesitated. "About your Angel, Nyx…"

"What about her?" asked Nyx, her tone dangerous.

"Since we're not killing her, does that mean we're not getting Paradise?"

Nyx didn't answer for a long time. At last she said, "I don't know."

"All right," said Persephone. "I was just wondering." They flew on in silence for a while longer, then Persephone said,

"Maybe things will go back to like they were before. And the Angels can walk the Earth again."

"Maybe," said Nyx. "I don't know what happens now. This isn't what Tribunal planned, so…"

The mention of His name filled her with sorrow. She had betrayed her beloved. All she had to do was kill her Angel and they would all have been free. They would all have had Paradise. Instead, they were worse off than they were before, and Tribunal would be furious. He was not the forgiving sort. She had loved that about Him, once.

I can't kill her, Nyx thought. *I just can't. And I won't. Not even for Paradise. Not even for Him.*

"It will work out," said Persephone. "At the very least, we're going to kick Lucifer's ass and you'll be Queen of Hell again."

"There is that," said Nyx. She looked down, into the great darkness below. Far, far below where they were, so far that no mortal eye would have the slightest chance of seeing it, there was a pinprick of light. She folded her wings and dove, Persephone flying right beside her. *At the very least, there is still that.*

*

Leannis still hated Lucifer. She hated him with every fibre of her being, and it was that, more than anything, that made her his favorite target.

He had found her in the midst of torturing one of the souls and pressed himself on her. She resisted, of course. Not much resistance, just a stiffening of her body as he pawed at her, but enough for him to claim she was disobedient and punish her.

Now she was bent backwards over one of the sharp-edged horses, her arms and legs spread wide and hands and feet chained to the ground. Her spine was bent at an agonizing angle, and he could see the pain in her face as he whipped the skin from her body in long, thin strips.

So far, she had managed not to scream, but then he hadn't started on the sensitive bits, yet. Nor had he allowed the demons to begin feasting on the torn flesh that hung from her body. Those things would come with time.

He was about to lash the skin from one of her breasts when one of his messenger birds flew up, calling, "Tribunal comes! Tribunal comes! Make ready!"

"Where?" demanded Lucifer.

"Nyx's palace!" The bird called. "Come quickly!"

Lucifer's whip lashed out once and the bird exploded in a burst of feathers and blood. "I am not a dog, to come when I am called!"

He lashed Leannis three times, ripping one of her breasts from her body. She screamed. Lucifer holstered the whip and turned to the demon Gore. "Take a turn on her, then make sure everyone else does as well. I want her broken by the time I'm ready for her."

He stomped his way to Nyx's palace, crushing a dozen souls beneath his cloven boots, and reveling in their screams. A pair of demons tried to follow him and he cut off their heads without slowing down.

The line-up of souls at Nyx's palace was as long as ever. Hundreds of Angels and demons were abusing the waiting souls, torturing, raping, cutting off limbs to see how fast they would grow back. Three demons were devouring one soul as they waited, tearing huge chunks from his flesh as he screamed in anguish. Lucifer ignored them all and stomped into Nyx's throne room. He kicked the demons and souls waiting there out and shut the doors behind him.

"I'm here," he said into the emptiness. "Where are you?"

He arrived in a blaze of light, a beacon that outshone everything else. The light that flowed from him was so strong that Lucifer had to hide his eyes behind his hand to avoid going blind. The very presence of him knocked out all sense of anything else in Hell. For now, there was only Lucifer and Tribunal. All other souls, Angels and demons disappeared from Lucifer's consciousness.

For the first time, Lucifer realized just how much power Tribunal had; that Tribunal was, in fact, God's true son. Lucifer felt an urge to sink to his knees and fought it. Instead, he said, "I have the Angel. Nyx couldn't kill it, as you said."

"As I knew," said Tribunal, and His voice rang through the room and through Lucifer's skull. It brought back memories of the days long, long past, when God would speak to His Angels, and tell them His plans for the universe He had created. His words would reverberate through all of Heaven, and the sound of it would bring joy to all who heard. This, though, was the opposite. Tribunal's word brought an overwhelming awareness of power, brought fear, bought the sense that something momentous was imminent—but there was no love behind the words. Lucifer hadn't been aware that he missed this love and did not appreciate finding out.

"Tell me how the sacrifice must be prepared," asked Lucifer, doing his best to hide his fear. "Show me Your will."

"So eager, Lucifer?" said Tribunal.

"You have promised me Hell and a place in your Paradise," said Lucifer. "Who would not be eager for that?"

"Nyx, apparently," said Tribunal, laughter in his voice. "She thinks that her little Angel is worth more than Paradise itself."

"Not to me, she isn't."

"Then listen closely," said Tribunal. "Open your ears and your mind and heed what I say, for I will not say it twice."

Lucifer nodded, and listened as Tribunal told him how to kill an Angel in Hell.

*

Persephone and Nyx flew through the wall of the great Pit and into the depths of Hell.

As soon as they arrived, Nyx knew that Tribunal was there. He shone like the sun, driving the sense of everything else out of her mind. She quailed under the power of His presence, nearly plummeting into the pit. Persephone reached out and grabbed her arm, steadying her flight until she regained control of herself.

"He's here," said Nyx. "Tribunal is here."

"Is that what it is?" said Persephone. "It feels like God, but wrong."

"It is God," said Nyx. "Tribunal is God. Or part of Him, at any rate."

"Does He know we're here?"

"I don't know," said Nyx, flapping her wings and heading for the top of the Pit. "But as long as He's here, no one is going to notice us."

"Then let's hope He stays for a while," said Persephone.

They flew strong and steady until they breached the top of the hole and came out onto the plains of Hell. It was dark by the pit. There was no hellfire anywhere close to light them. Nyx stared into the distance, searching for any sign of Angels or demons, but there were none around. She flapped her wings faster, gaining speed. Persephone stayed beside her. They raced over the jagged broken surface of Hell. The pit was far away from the plains where they tortured the souls, far away from the black Hell-stone cities where the Angels lived and played. Nyx knew exactly where they were, and which Angel cities had once held the greatest number of her supporters. She winged towards one of them, moving so fast her wings became a blur. Persephone struggled to keep up. Nyx didn't need a large force, just one strong enough to break through Lucifer's lines and get her to Lucifer. Once she was in his presence, she knew she could defeat him.

There was a sudden blaze of light, and a blast so powerful it knocked both Angels from the sky and sent them tumbling to the razor-sharp, jagged rocks below. They tore flesh and feathers as they skidded slowly to a stop, and when they looked up, they saw Tribunal standing before them in a blaze of light. Tribunal, the most beautiful of all, the most powerful of all.

Instantly, Nyx felt all her love for Tribunal – for the man and the God – come blazing to life inside her. She pulled herself to her knees. "Forgive me, Tribunal. Please forgive me!"

"Forgive you?" said Tribunal. He reached down and put His hand on her head. The touch of him, alive, real, and pure divine flesh, sent a tremor of pleasure through her so strong she started gasping. "Why must I forgive you, my love?"

"I couldn't do it," said Nyx. "The Angel. I couldn't kill her. I didn't even want to kill her. Please, I didn't know."

"There is no reason to beg forgiveness," said Tribunal. "As soon as the Angel came into this world, I felt her. I knew then that you would not be able to kill her, as I had requested."

"I am so, so sorry," said Nyx, tears streaming down her face. "So sorry."

"Nyx?" said Persephone. "What's the matter?"

"Be silent," said Tribunal to Persephone. "Nyx is my servant, my lover and my queen and she has the right to speak in my presence. You do not."

"Fuck you," said Persephone. "I've talked to God himself."

"I AM GOD HIMSELF!" The word echoed through Hell, and the force of it sent Persephone to her knees. "I am made from Him, I am of Him, and I am Him! And you will be silent, or I will order you to dismember yourself with your own sword, and you will do it."

Persephone believed him. She looked at Nyx, waiting to see what to do next.

"I have only a short time here, my beloved," said Tribunal to Nyx. "Only a short time before God the Father realizes I am gone, and calls on me to account for my whereabouts. You must listen to me."

"I listen, my beloved."

"Lucifer has taken your Angel, and holds her in your palace," said Tribunal. "He tortures her mercilessly. He rapes her, he cuts her, and he makes her scream, just to enjoy the sound of it. You must rescue her."

"But…" Nyx was still weeping and couldn't stop. "I still can't sacrifice her."

"No need, my beloved," said Tribunal. "You do not need to sacrifice your Angel. That will not happen here."

"Oh, thank you," whispered Nyx. "Thank you, thank you, thank you. Oh, beloved."

"Time is short," said Tribunal. "Gather your forces, bring

them together and launch an assault on your palace. I shall go protect your Angel until you arrive."

"I hear, my beloved," said Nyx. "I obey."

Tribunal's light blazed brighter, and vanished. For the first time since her return, Nyx could sense all of Hell. She could feel every Angel in it, and knew that Lucifer could feel her as well.

"So," said Persephone. "He's an asshole, isn't he?"

Nyx knocked Persephone to the ground with a single swipe of her hand. Persephone hit hard and lay there, stunned. "Don't," warned Nyx. "Don't ever speak of Him in that way again."

"All right," Persephone slowly pushed herself upright. *Even though He is an asshole.*

"He said he'd protect her until we can get our troops ready," said Nyx. "So we get our troops." She pointed. "The City of Iswednokkurn. There are a thousand Angels here who will serve me, and the rest will probably just stay out of the way. We go there, we get troops, and we do it in a hurry."

Tribunal's presence was in Hell again, and once more Nyx could not feel anything else. "He's there! He's protecting my Angel! Hurry, Persephone!"

Nyx launched herself and Persephone, taking a moment to wipe the silver blood from where Nyx had split her lip and another to swallow her own misgivings, followed.

*

Iswednokkurn stood on the edge of a tall black crag overlooking the plains of Hell. The screams of the damned were audible from there, but only barely: a continuing discordance that grated in the mind as one walked the streets.

How did I ever like it down here? Nyx wondered as she went from house to house. *There's none of the abundance, beauty and enterprise of earth. No music.*

She didn't need to do much persuading of Angels. As soon as they saw she had returned, they flocked to her, black or red armor on, swords and whips at the ready. They had been sorely abused by Lucifer, and more than one had surrendered themselves to him, swearing loyalty to end their suffering. But none of that mattered now. The Queen of Hell was returned, and her Angels were loyal to her once more. Together they would crush Lucifer, and put Hell to rights.

Persephone was made Nyx's second in command. The captains of her army assembled together and heard her instructions. There would be no time for strategy, no devious plan. The longer they took, the more warning Lucifer would have, so speed won over strategy. "We fly in straight," said Nyx. "We drive through his armies to my palace and I tear Lucifer limb from limb. And once he is destroyed, then I will once more rule in Hell."

And in Paradise, too, Nyx thought. *If Tribunal will still let me.*

A thousand dark Angels gathered around her, weapons ready, thirsting for blood. Nyx looked over her army, knowing it would be dwarfed by the legions that Lucifer would send at them. *It doesn't matter,* Nyx told herself. *We don't need to defeat his armies, just break through them. Once I've defeated Lucifer, Hell will be mine once more.*

"Follow," she said, and spread her wings wide. She hurled herself into the sky and her black-winged army followed after.

*

She lay in a small black cell, buried deep in the bowels of Lucifer's castle. Her wings were torn off, and one of her arms missing. Lucifer took great delight in watching them grow back, then tearing them off again. She, unable to resist his strength, let him. Her mind was rage.

The door to her cell flew open, and a dozen demons swarmed over her, biting her flesh and ripping out chunks as they forced her to the ground. One, larger than the others, kicked her in the head until her skull split and ichor spilled out. She lost consciousness.

*

In Nyx's throne room, Epipheneia hung, still and silent, staring at Lucifer and the being beside him who had so much power.

"Why are we waiting?" Lucifer demanded. "Why not kill the little bitch and get it over with?"

"Because her creator must be here to see her death," said Tribunal. "Even now she has assembled an army of Angels and is coming to fight you."

"How is this good news?" asked Lucifer.

"Your army vastly outnumbers hers."

"With Nyx that's not necessarily enough," said Lucifer. "That bitch is wily."

"That bitch," said Tribunal, "Wants the little bastard creature she created." He walked over to the Angel. "Poor thing. Not of Heaven, not of Hell. An Angel of Earth. Useless everywhere."

"That poor thing killed a dozen of mine," said Lucifer. "I'd be careful if I were you."

"I don't need to be careful, do I?" said Tribunal to Epipheneia. "You won't hurt me because you know who I am, don't you?"

"I know who You were made from," said Epipheneia in her

lovely, melodic voice. "And I know who You think you are. But You are not him."

"Look!" said Tribunal, pointing at her in mock surprise. "She has some knowledge after all." He sneered. "Tell me: who do I think I am?"

"You think you are God," said Epipheneia serenely. "You are not. And when you try to destroy Him, He will destroy You instead."

Tribunal slapped her across the face, hard enough to twist her head half off her neck. Epipheneia didn't make a sound. She turned back to the front and once more stared at them.

"You will not speak," Tribunal said. "Or I will be very displeased!"

"You're going to kill me anyway," said Epipheneia. "Why should I care about Your displeasure?"

"Because death can take a very, very long time," said Tribunal. "Once the ritual is complete, Lucifer can take as long as he wishes with you. He may rape you, dismember you, dine on your flesh if he wants. He will be able to do whatever he wishes, just as long as you never leave this hall again. So be silent."

Epipheneia's blue eyes bored deeper into Tribunal's brown ones. "You lie," she said. "You've always lied. There is only one way for me to die in this ritual and we both know it, little Godling." There was a hint of mockery in her voice, but only a hint. Her expression remained grave and calm.

Tribunal glared at her, then turned to Lucifer. "She is astute, I'll give her that. Are your armies in place?"

"All of them," said Lucifer.

"Good. Because Nyx is almost on top of you."

"What?"

"Even now she is winging towards the palace," said Tribunal. I suggest your armies rise up. Now."

Lucifer spun and shouted at the Angel near the door. "Tell them to go! All of them! Now!"

The Angel ran from the room. A moment later a horn rang out, then another, then a hundred.

*

In the skies of Hell, Nyx and a thousand Angels winged toward her palace.

Her palace had not been built for defense. She had built it long after the wars in Hell had ended and Lucifer and his minions were under her control. It had been built to frighten the souls who came to it for judgement, and to provide pleasure for the Angels who stayed in it. There were huge windows open to the night, what went on inside visible to all. The rooms were large enough to fly in, and many large enough for a dozen Angels to have sex in mid-air while they did. The palace would be easy to take, hard to defend, and the closer Nyx came to it before they met resistance, the easier it would be for her to reach Lucifer and gut him.

A horn sounded. Then another, then a hundred, and below her, the black plains of Hell swirled into life as the wings of a hundred thousand Angels leapt into the air and charge upward to meet Nyx's small force.

"Faster!" Nyx screamed. "Faster! Get to the palace!"

From below Lucifer's forces, a hundred times stronger than Nyx's, rose up and engulfed them.

*

She came conscious as they dragged her into the throne room.

"About time," said Lucifer.

"Where do you want her?" asked one of the demons.

"Against the wall, where the Angel was. And hurry up, I want her to be the first thing that bitch sees when she get here."

They dragged her up to the wall, and drove Hell-stone spikes through her arms and legs, pinning her.

*

Lucifer's Legions rose up like a tide to meet Nyx's Angels.

Nyx had planned for this, of course. She knew that Lucifer would bring all his armies to bear. And so the Angels around her dropped down a hundred feet, forming a wall between her and the ones rising up. The air below became a maelstrom of silver blood, severed limps, flashing blades and cracking whips. It would not last, Nyx knew. There were too many attacking for her band to do more than buy her an extra few hundred feet towards her palace.

It's less than half a mile away, Nyx thought. Out loud she cried, "Press forward! Don't pause or look back! Keep forward!"

Then the Angels below broke through, and her world was reduced to the chaos of battle.

Persephone stayed just behind Nyx, keeping a squad of Angels together to help protect Nyx's back as she winged forward.

We'd be fine, Persephone thought, *If we weren't outnumbered a hundred to one.*

And it was true. She had been one of the best fighters in the 6^{66}th, and these Angels who rose up around her now were no match for her. Again and again her blade struck through armor, smashed through faces and severed limbs and heads. Again and again her whip found eyes, wings and flesh to rip open. And every time an Angel fell screaming as its blood and ichor exploded from its body or the gaping hole where its head used to be, another Angel was there to take its place. They were unending, and were it not for the power of Nyx in front of them, they would have been forced from the sky.

Nyx slashed out with her blade and whip, not bothering to defend herself. Her power, grown so much from her encounters with Tribunal, made it seem as though the armor and flesh of the angels around her was as frail as tissue paper. Every cut hit its target, breaking Angelic steel and crashing through armor to rip open flesh. Every crack of her whip tore wings and flesh open and sent Angels hurtling from the sky. Even so, there were so many of them that she could not help but slow down. They blocked her way entirely, trying to reach her with blades and whips and howling in frustration as their attacks were ignored and Nyx kept moving slowly forward.

Below her, her escort was being destroyed. Hundreds of Angels from both sides were dropping from the sky, pulping their bodies on the jagged Hell-stone below, becoming temporary feasts for the demons who cavorted, waiting for them to hit, and then swarming over their broken bodies.

None of them would die, of course. Nothing died here. But having to regenerate inside a demon's digestive tract was slow and painful and likely to take a hundred years.

There was a shout from in front of them, and the hundred-thick wall of Angels between Nyx and her palace parted, scattering away from Nyx's much-reduced force like leaves scattering in the wind.

Then another flight of Angels, five thousand strong.

"Oh, fuck," moaned Persephone. "It's the 666th. Everyone get ready!"

The 666th smashed into Nyx's force like a like a giant cast of falcons stooping on their prey, driving them down. Even Nyx's power, which hacked through three of the attackers in a single blow, was not enough to keep them from being driven down toward the earth. Nyx realized that fighting was futile and screamed "Dive! Dive!" She put deed to word, stooping herself and racing toward the ground then pulling out to speed along a hundred feet below her attackers.

For a moment it seemed to be working. Then the legion descended on her again, mashing into her with their bodies even as she broke their weapons and ripped open their flesh, driving her towards the earth. It was less than 200 yards to the castle, now, and for every foot she flew she was being driven down ten. Soon she, too, would be smashed against the ground, and then the demons of Hell would fight over the scraps of flesh from their queen's body.

A scream from above and Persephone, leading a flight of fifty Angels, smashed into the ranks of the 666th, buying Nyx a little more time, giving her a little more room to fly forward. More silver blood flew from the sky. More Angels crashed to the ground to be devoured. More limbs and wings and heads flew off as the two sides battled against one another.

Then the tide turned again as, from below and behind, the other hundred thousand Angels of Lucifer's legions closed in around them.

The palace was gone from sight, now. Nyx could see nothing but red and black armor and the flapping wings of those that attacked. Her world was reduced to the length of her whip and her blade. More bodies smashed into her, driving her down again and again, until she could see the ground beneath her and the demons that jumped up, trying to reach Angel flesh. Nyx screamed defiance, even as she knew that her strength was not enough, even as the Angels forced her down further, sacrificing bodies and limbs to drive her to the earth.

I can't break through, she realized. *I'm not going to save her.*

The thought tore Nyx's heart in half, even as it made her realize she had one weapon still at her disposal.

God will hear it. God will hear it and come and destroy me, Nyx thought.

If it lets me save Epipheneia, I don't care.

She opened her mouth and spoke the Word.

The Word was all things. It was the essence of God and creation and birth. With it, one could shape the very fabric of the universes and make time itself twist to serve whoever spoke it.

It was also, when the speaker chose, the greatest force for destruction known.

It was the Word that had rained fire on Sodom and Gomorra, that had ripped open the molten core of the world so that rock would flow and become the continents. It was the Word that, before time itself, had cast the Angels from Heaven.

And when Nyx spoke the word, when she called on its power, she called for destruction, and nothing could stand before it.

The power of it exploded around her, and the shock of it ripped apart flesh and bone, rock and ground, Angel and demon as if all were just paper. The very foundations of Hell shook and the ground split in a hundred places, sending demons, Angels and souls into the Hellfire below. The blast of wind that that followed the shock had the force of a hundred hurricanes, scattering her enemies and allies alike, sending them spinning out of control to smash to the earth or be hurled far, far away.

When the dust cleared, Nyx was the only creature on the plains of Hell. And all of the power that she had gained from Tribunal was gone. She felt weak and exhausted in a way she never had before. Any Angel with a sword could have defeated her, had any been near. And she knew with certainty that the Word would never work for her again.

Forgive me, my Tribunal for giving up your gifts, she thought. *I could not let them stop me.*

But I am still Queen of Hell. And I will not be defeated here.

Sword in hand, Nyx rose from the earth and flew, an arrow of rage driving towards her palace. The walls of her palace were cracked and tilting, and holes appeared in them in a dozen places. She smashed through the doors before the Angels within could recover. She cleaved the flesh of any being that got in her way. She flew down the hallways faster than any creature had flown before.

And when she reached the throne room Nyx saw three things.

The first was her Angel, hung upside down between two pillars of Hell-stone, her flesh naked, her legs and arms and wings spread wide and chained to the pillars. Her red hair dragged against the ground, but her blue eyes were still unblinking, her face still expressionless. Around her a circle inscribed with runes and sigils glowed red in the darkness of the room.

The second thing Nyx saw was Lucifer, standing behind her Angel, holding one end of a jagged-edged Hellstone-bladed saw that rested in the cleft between her Angel's legs. His beautiful face was twisted with anger and joy and his muscles were tensed, waiting to saw through the flesh of her Angel.

The third thing she saw was Ishtar, missing an arm and her wings, her bloody head broken open, pinned to the wall of Nyx's throne room like a broken butterfly.

All these things she saw in the instant before she was struck so powerfully that her entire body crushed to the ground, the bones of her legs and spine and ribs breaking and folding in on themselves.

She wanted to scream, but could not draw breath. Wanted to struggle, but could not move a limb, wanted to cry out, but could not find her voice.

"You have gravely disappointed me," said Tribunal from behind her. She could not turn her head, but she could feel Him, feel the waves of His anger flowing over her, feel how badly she had disappointed Him, and how terribly, terribly wrong she had been to do less than she was asked. Her soul crushed in on itself as her body had done, grinding down smaller and smaller until there was only a small, bleak part of her left, desperate for His approval. Her eyes, the only part of her that could move, flicked back and forth, desperately searching for Tribunal.

"Do not look for me," said Tribunal, His voice dripping with a contempt that burned into her soul. "You are not worthy to look upon me. Not worthy of those gifts that you received from me and squandered when you used the Word a second time, let alone the Paradise that I was offering you. Your lack of faith, your lack of belief in me, has brought you to this end. You disgust me."

Nyx felt her soul crying out, though she had no voice to give it.

"I had hoped," continued Tribunal, "That you would have the strength to overcome your love for the Angel; to make the sacrifice necessary so that you and all your brethren could achieve

Paradise. But you were weak. And so, your brethren will have Paradise without you."

Nyx cried silently, knowing that He was right, and knowing that, given the chance to do the same again, she would. She shifted her eyes from their search for Tribunal and caught sight of Epipheneia, staring directly at her.

"*My Angel.*" Nyx opened her mind to Epipheneia, "*Can you hear me?*"

"*I can, my creator,*" said Epipheneia. "*Do not allow yourself to despair.*"

"*I am sorry.*" Nyx's grief at her failure overwhelmed her. "*I am so sorry.*"

"*Mother!*" The word snapped through Nyx's grief, forcing her mind to focus. Epipheneia's voice roared through her mind. "*Listen to me, Mother!*"

"*I... I'm listening.*"

"*This little Godling is nothing, Mother. His works are nothing, and to bow down to Him is to forget that you are the Queen of Hell, and one of God's true Angels.*" Despite being hung upside down, despite her chains, Epipheneia sounded strong and sure of herself and not afraid. "*When He kills me, He will be no more powerful than He was before. Less, because He will no longer have you serving Him. This I know.*"

"*But... but He is my beloved....*"

"*He was never your beloved,*" said Epipheneia. "*He was never anything more than a selfish little Godling, set out to destroy us all.*"

"*He cannot be...*" Nyx tried to make sense of Epiphneia's words. *Is this the truth? Can she see what I did not...*

"Kill her," said Tribunal.

No! Nyx tried to scream.

"*Be strong, Mother,*" said Epipheneia. "*Do not let Him win.*"

Slowly, steadily, Lucifer began sawing.

Epipheneia screamed as the jagged teeth ripped through her flesh, tearing her open. Her blood was not silver like the Descended Angels, or Gold like that of the Angels of God. It was brilliant green, like the small water plants that floated on the surface of a pond, and it shone with a life-energy that was so out of place and foreign to Hell it seemed to change the very surface of the ground it landed on as it exploded out of her body, spraying Nyx and Lucifer and everything around them. Lucifer laughed and cut faster, ripping the saw through the bones of her pelvis. Nyx struggled to move but her body would not respond, struggled to speak, to plead for her Angel, but could not.

With nothing else to do, Nyx opened her mind and joined it with Epipheneia's, feeling her Angel's pain as Epipheneia felt it. Nyx used what little strength she had left in her mind to shield Epipheneia from the worst of the agony.

The saw cut through the last of the pelvis and began moving faster, ripping through intestine, bladder and bowel, until it came to ribs and slowed down again, grinding against her sternum.

"Stop," said Tribunal. "Take it."

Lucifer stopped sawing and reached into Epipheneia's body. His hand dipped into green blood and ripped flesh and came up with her heart. It beat as strongly as if she was whole and hearty, even when he ripped it away from the veins and arteries and held it out.

"*I'm so sorry, my Angel, my love,*" said Nyx to Epipheneia. "*I'm so sorry I couldn't stop Him.*"

"*You... still... can...*" Epipheneia's voice was weak in Nyx's mind. "*You must... before... He destroys... everything.*"

Tribunal stepped into Nyx's line of vision. He held up the still-beating heart in front of Him so she could see it. Then He put it in his mouth and bit down on it. Green blood burst from His lips, and behind Him, Epipheneia's body exploded in a ball of green and white light that swirled where she had been. Nyx tried to breath it in, and choked on it. The cloud flew towards Nyx, settling on her and sinking into her, giving her strength and clarity of mind, even as her rage built. *My Angel. My daughter. My daughter!* Her body was starting to heal. The first of her vertebrae was cracking and popping itself back into place. It would be long and slow and painful, but when she was whole…

"Put her in the box," said Tribunal. "And throw her in the lake."

*

Nyx's last sight was of Ishtar, still hanging on the wall, hopelessness in her eyes. Then demons stomped all over Nyx's body, crushing and breaking her arms and legs and ribs and pelvis until they could be bent, flesh tearing, jagged ends of bones sticking through, to fit into the box they had waiting. They shoved her in head first, and let the weight of her broken body crush down on her.

The box itself had spikes inside it, sticking out from all sides and up from the bottom, perfectly designed to maim her further as they closed the spiked lid. The box had holes in the sides, and through them, Nyx could see the demons pick her up and carry her out of the palace and down the path to the Lake of Fire.

"You cannot die here," said Tribunal, knowing she could hear him. "Not until God himself is destroyed. Until then, you will suffer greater agony than you have ever known. And when I have destroyed God, I will turn my attention to you, and you will suffer so greatly that you will beg me to end your existence.

"Take her."

They wrapped the box in chains of Hell-stone so thick that even if Nyx had been whole she would have had trouble breaking them. They put Hell-stone weights on the chains, so large that no single Angel – no dozen Angels – could move one by themselves.

A hundred Angels flew into the air and grabbed Hell-stone wires. At a shouted command from Lucifer, they flew, straining and struggling to raise the box into the air and pull it out over the Lake of Fire.

At a command from Lucifer, they hovered over the center of the Lake.

"I know you can hear me, Nyx," said Lucifer. "Enjoy your pain."

The Angels released the box. It fell into the Hellfire Lake, its weight dragging it immediately from sight. The many holes in the sides of the box let in a flood of Hellfire that engulfed Nyx in unspeakable agony.

*

"Now what?" asked Lucifer.

"Now," said Tribunal. "The Earth is yours. Let your Angels roam as they will, and do what they will. I will go back to Heaven, and I will block the gates that lead to Earth. Your Angels will have reign until I call for you. Then, you and I shall remake the worlds. We shall destroy God and take his place, and be masters over all creation."

"And when will that be?" asked Lucifer.

"Soon," said Tribunal. "Amuse yourself with your rebels and your souls, and I will call upon you when the time is come."

*

At the bottom of the Lake of Fire, screaming in silent agony, Nyx felt the Hellfire stripping the flesh from her bones, even as that flesh struggled to heal itself. The bones beneath it struggled to heal as well, but the spikes inside the box kept them from joining together and healing as they should.

And as the Hellfire burned her flesh, she was visited by the memory of every cruelty she had ever committed, every vile action she had ever done, every pain she caused another Angel or human. And more than all of those, she relived again and again the moment she was cast out of Heaven, and the moment she let her Angel die.

In the midst of her screams, in the midst of her agony, Nyx found a small, quiet place in her mind. *I am the Queen of Hell,* she reminded herself. *I will not be destroyed. I will be victorious.*

…Then the pain overwhelmed her again, and she could do nothing but scream silently into the hellfire that filled her mouth.

THANK YOU FOR READING POA!

Dear Reader,

I hope you enjoyed **Plague of Angels: The Descended Book One**. It was my honor and pleasure to write for you. If you enjoyed reading book one, please consider joining me again for book two— and together we'll watch the lives of Nyx, and her brethren play out in our imaginations…the best theatre of all.

As a new author — and even one day when I'm not so new — I always encourage feedback. Honestly, you are the reason that I will be carving Nyx, Ishtar, and Persephone's future. So, tell me what you enjoyed, what you loved, and even what you disliked. I'd very much like to hear from you. You can write me at, or visit me at the following websites:

https://www.facebook.com/AuthorJohnPatrickKennedy
https://www.JohnPatrickKennedy.net

Also, if you're so inclined, I'd love a review of **Plague of Angels**. One star, three stars, four stars — I'd appreciate the feedback regardless. Without your support, and feedback, my writing life would become quite boring. While appreciated, there's only so much praise one can take seriously from family, and friends. If you have the time, please visit my author page on both Amazon.com, and goodreads.com.

Until next time,

John Patrick Kennedy

COMING SOON:
BOOK 2 OF THE DESCENDED

Printed in Great Britain
by Amazon.co.uk, Ltd.,
Marston Gate.